**Cathy Williams** can remember reading Mills & Boon books as a teenager, and now that she is writing them she remains an avid fan. For her, there is nothing like creating romantic stories and engaging plots, and each and every book is a new adventure. Cathy lives in London. Her three daughters—Charlotte, Olivia and Emma—have always been, and continue to be, the greatest inspirations in her life.

*USA TODAY* bestseller **Lucy Monroe** lives and writes in the gorgeous Pacific Northwest. While she loves her home, she delights in experiencing different cultures and places in her travels, which she happily shares with her readers through her books. A lifelong devotee of the romance genre, Lucy can't imagine a more fulfilling career than writing the stories in her head for her readers to enjoy.

D1152183

# THE TYCOON'S ULTIMATE CONQUEST

CATHY WILLIAMS

# THE SPANIARD'S PLEASURABLE VENGEANCE

LUCY MONROE

**MILLS & BOON**

First Published in Great Britain 2018
by Mills & Boon, an imprint of HarperCollins*Publishers*
1 London Bridge Street, London, SE1 9GF

The Tycoon's Ultimate Conquest © 2018 by Cathy Williams

The Spaniard's Pleasurable Vengeance © 2018 by Lucy Monroe

ISBN: 978-0-263-93552-3

Printed and bound in Spain
by CPI, Barcelona

# THE TYCOON'S ULTIMATE CONQUEST

## CATHY WILLIAMS

# CHAPTER ONE

'THERE'S A PROBLEM,' the middle-aged man sitting in the chair in front of Arturo da Costa stated without preamble.

Art sat back, linked his fingers on his stomach and looked at Harold Simpson, a man who was normally calm, measured and so good at his job that Art couldn't think of a time when *anything* had been a problem for him. He ran the vast legal department of Art's sprawling empire with impeccable efficiency.

So at the word *problem* Art frowned, already mentally rescheduling the meeting he was due to attend in half an hour as he anticipated a conversation he wasn't going to enjoy, about a situation he would not have foreseen and which would be tricky to resolve.

'Talk to me,' he said, his deep voice sharp, knowing Harold was a rare breed of man who wasn't intimidated by his clever and unashamedly arrogant and unpredictable boss.

'It's the development in Gloucester.'

'Why is there a problem? I've got all the necessary planning permission. Money's changed hands. Signatures have been put on dotted lines.'

'If only it were that simple.'

'I don't see what could possibly be complex about this, Harold.'

'I suppose *complex* wouldn't quite be the right word, Art. *Annoying* might be the description that better fits the bill.'

'Not following you.' Art leaned forward, frowning. 'Don't I pay you to take care of annoying problems?'

Harold deflected the direct hit with a reprimanding look and Art grinned.

'You've never come to me with an annoying problem before,' he drawled. 'Perhaps I was rash in assuming that you dealt with them before they could hit my desk.'

'It's a sit-in.'

'Come again?'

Instead of answering, Harold opened up his laptop and swivelled it so that it was facing his boss, then leaned away as if waiting for the reaction he was expecting, a reaction which would have sent strong men diving for cover.

Fury.

Art looked at the newspaper article staring him in the face. It was from a local paper, circulation circa next to nothing, read by no one who mattered and covering an area where sheep probably outnumbered humans, but he could immediately see the repercussions of what he was reading.

His mouth tightened and he reread the article, taking his time. Then he looked at the grainy black-and-white picture accompanying the article. A sit-in. Protestors. Placards. Lots of moral high ground about the wicked, cruel developers who planned to rape and pillage the countryside. *Him*, in other words.

'Has this only now come to your attention?' He sat back and stared off into the distance with a thoughtful frown, his sharp mind already seeking ways of diverting the headache staring him in the face and coming up with roadblocks.

'It's been simmering,' Harold said as he shut the lid of his computer, 'but I thought I could contain the situation. Unfortunately, the lawyer working on behalf of the protesters has got the bit between her teeth, so to speak, and is determined to put as many obstacles in the way of your development as she can. Trouble is, in a small community like that, even if she loses the case and of course she will because, as you say, all the crosses have been made in the right boxes, the fallout could still be…unfortunate.'

'I admire your use of understatement, Harold.'

'She can rally the community behind her and the luxury development that should, in normal circumstances, sell in a heartbeat with the new train link due to open a handful of miles away, could find itself sticking on the open market. She's anti building on green fields and she's going to fight her corner, win or lose and come what may. Expensive people moving into expensive houses like to fancy themselves as mucking in with the locals and eventually becoming pillars of the community. They wouldn't like the prospect of the locals going quiet every time they walk into the village pub and pelting eggs against their walls in the dead of night.'

'I had no idea you had such impressive flights of fancy, Harold.' Art was amused but there was enough truth in what his lawyer had said to make him think. 'When you say *she*…?'

'Rose Tremain.'

'Miss… Mrs…or Ms?'

'Very definitely *Ms*.'

'I'm getting the picture loud and clear. And on the subject of pictures, do you have one of her? Is she floating around somewhere on the World Wide Web?'

'She disapproves of social media insofar as it personally pertains to *her*,' Harold said with a trace of admiration in his voice that made Art's eyebrows shoot up. 'No social media accounts…nothing of the sort. I know because I got one of my people to try to find out how we could follow her, try to get a broader picture of her, but no luck. There's the bones of past cases but no personal information to speak of at all. It would appear that she's old-fashioned like that.'

'There's another word for it,' Art drawled drily.

'I've only had dealings with her over the phone so far, and of course by email. I could give you my personal impressions…'

'I'm all ears.'

'Can't be bought off,' Harold said bluntly, instantly killing Art's first line of attack.

'Everyone has a price,' he murmured without skipping a beat. 'Have you any pictures of her at all?'

'Just something in one of the articles printed last week about the development.'

'Let's have a look.' Art waited, thinking, as Harold

expertly paged through documents in his pile of folders before eventually showing him an unsatisfactory picture of the woman in question.

Art stared. She *looked* like a *Ms*. The sort of feminist hippy whose mission might be to save the world from itself. The newspaper article showed him a picture of the sit-in, protesters on his land with placards and enough paraphernalia to convince him that they weren't going anywhere any time soon. All that was missing was a post office and a corner shop, but then summer was the perfect time for an impromptu camping expedition. He doubted they would have been quite as determined if those fields had been knee-deep in snow and the branches of the trees bending at ninety-degree angles in high winds.

Whatever the dark-haired harridan had said to them to stoke up public outrage at his development, she had succeeded because the untidy lot in the picture looked as self-righteous as she did.

The picture he was now staring at, of *Ms Rose Tremain*, showed a woman jabbing her finger at someone out of sight, some poor sod unfortunate enough to be asking her to answer a few questions she didn't like. Her unruly hair was scraped back into *something*, leaving flyaway strands around her face. Her clothes beggared belief. Art was accustomed to dating women who graced catwalks, women who were best friends with cutting-edge designers and spent whatever time they had away from their modelling jobs in exclusive salons beautifying themselves.

He squinted at the picture in front of him and tried to

get his head around the image of someone who looked as though she had bulk-bought her outfit from a charity shop and hadn't been near a hairdresser in decades.

No. Money wasn't going to get her off his back. One look at that jabbing finger and fierce scowl was enough to convince him of the rashness of going down that road.

But there were many ways to skin a cat…

'So, she can't be bought,' Art murmured, half to himself. 'Well, I will have to find another way to convince her to drop her case against me and get those protestors off my land. Every day lost is costing me money.' With his dark eyes still on the picture in front of him, Art connected to his PA and told her to reschedule his calendar for the next fortnight.

'What are you going to do?' Harold asked, sounding alarmed, as if he couldn't make sense of his workaholic boss taking two weeks off.

'I'm going to take a little holiday,' Art said with a slow smile of intent. 'A busman's holiday. You will be the only one privy to this information, so keep it to yourself, Harold. If *Ms Tremain* can't be persuaded to my way of thinking by a generous contribution to whatever hare-brained "Save the Whale" cause she espouses, then I'm going to have to find another way to persuade her.'

'How? If we're talking about anything illegal here, Art…'

'Oh, please.' Art burst out laughing. 'Illegal?'

'Maybe I don't mean *illegal*. Maybe a better word might be *unethical*.'

'Well, now, my friend. That depends entirely on your definition of unethical…'

* * *

'Someone here to see you, Rose.'

Rose looked up at the spiky-haired young girl standing by the door of the office she shared with her co-worker, Phil. It was little more than a large room on the ground floor of the Victorian house which was also her home but it was an arrangement that worked. The rent she got from Phil and from the occupants of the other two converted rooms—who were variously the local gardening club twice a week, the local bridge group once a week and the local children's playgroup twice a week—covered the extensive running costs of the house she had inherited when her mother had died five years previously. Well, alongside the sizeable loan she had had to take out in order to effect urgent repairs on the place.

She occasionally thought that it would have been nice if she could have separated her work life from her home life but, on the other hand, who could complain about a job where there was no commute involved?

'Who is it, Angie?' Bad time. Middle of the afternoon and she still had a bucketload of work to do. Three cases had cropped up at precisely the same time and each one of them involved complex issues with employment law, in which she specialised, and demanded a lot of attention.

'Someone about the land.'

'Ah. The land.' Rose sat back, stretched and then stood up, only realising how much she'd cramped up when she heard a wayward joint creak.

*The land.*

No one called it anything else.

Between Phil's property law side of the business and her labour law, *the land* had become the middle ground which occupied them both, far more than either had expected when the business of some faceless tycoon buying up their green fields to build yet another housing estate had reared its ugly head.

Phil was a relative newcomer to the area, but she had lived in the village her whole life and she had adopted the cause of the protestors with gusto.

Indeed, she had even allowed them to use her sprawling kitchen as their headquarters.

She was unashamedly partisan and was proud of her stance. There was nothing that stuck in her throat more than big businesses and billionaire businessmen thinking that they could do as they pleased and steamroll over the little people so that they could make yet more money for themselves.

'Want me to handle it?' Phil asked, looking up from his desk, which was as chaotic as hers.

'No.' Rose smiled at him. She could never have hoped for a more reliable business partner than Phil. Thirty-three years old, he had the appearance of a slightly startled owl, with his wire-rimmed specs and his round face, but he was as sharp as a tack and won a breathtaking amount of business for them. 'If they've actually got around to sending one of their senior lawyers then I'm ready for them. It's insulting that so far they've only seen fit to send junior staff. Shows how confident they are of being able to trample us into the ground.'

'I like your faith in our ability to bring a massive corporation to its knees,' Phil said with a wry grin. 'DC Logistics pretty much owns the world.'

'Which,' Rose countered without skipping a beat, 'doesn't mean that they can add this little slice of land to the tally.'

She tucked strands of her unruly hair into the sort of bun she optimistically started each and every day with, only to give up because her hair had a will of its own.

She glanced at the sliver of mirror in between the bookshelves groaning under the weight of legal tomes and absently took in the reflection that stared back at her every morning when she woke up.

No one had ever accused her of being pretty. Rose had long accepted that she just wasn't, that she just didn't fit the mould of *pretty*. She had a strong, intelligent face with a firm jaw and a nose that bordered on sharp. Her large eyes were clear and brown and her best feature as far as she was concerned.

Everything else…well, everything else worked. She was a little too tall, a little too gangly and not nearly busty enough, but you couldn't concern yourself with stuff like that and she didn't. Pretty much.

'Right! Let's go see what they've thrown at us this time!' She winked at Phil and made approving noises when Angie said that she'd stuck their visitor in the kitchen—it would do whoever it was good to see the evidence of their commitment to the cause—and headed out of the office.

She didn't know what to expect.

Overweight, overfed, overpaid and over-confident. Someone at the height of his career, with all the trappings that an expensive top job afforded. Angie had given nothing away and wouldn't have. She was gay and paid not a scrap of attention to what members of the opposite sex looked like.

Rose was only twenty-eight herself but the young people who had been sent to argue the case had seemed so much younger than her.

She pushed open the kitchen door and then stood for a few moments in the doorway.

The man was standing with his back to her, staring out at the garden, which flowed seamlessly into open land, the only boundary between private and public being a strip of trees and a dishevelled hedge of sorts.

He was tall. Very tall. She was five eleven and she guessed that he would be somewhere in the region of six three.

And, from what she was seeing, he was well built. Muscular. Broad shoulders tapering to a narrow waist and legs that moulded perfectly to the faded jeans he was wearing.

What sort of lawyer was *this*?

Confused, Rose cleared her throat to give notice of her presence and the man turned around slowly.

'My secretary didn't tell me your name, Mr...'

'Frank.' The stranger took his time as he walked towards her, which annoyed Rose because this was her house and her kitchen and yet the man seemed to dominate the space and own it in a way she didn't care for.

'Well, Mr Frank. You're here about the land, I gather. If your company thinks that this ploy is going to work, then I hate to disappoint you but it won't.'

Alarmed because he had somehow managed to close the distance between them and was standing just a little too close for comfort, Rose sidestepped him to the kettle, only offering him something to drink seemingly as an afterthought.

'You can sit,' she said crisply. 'Just shove some of the papers out of the way.'

'What ploy?'

Rose watched as he looked at the placards in the making on the kitchen table, head politely inclined. After some consideration, he held up one and examined it in reflective silence before returning it to its original position on the table.

'What ploy?' he repeated.

'The lawyer-in-jeans ploy,' Rose said succinctly. She shot him a look of pure disdain, but only just managed to pull it off because the man was just so…so…crazily good-looking that her nervous system felt as though it had been put through a spin cycle and was all over the place.

He'd sat down but not in a lawyer-like manner, which was also annoying. He'd angled the pine chair, one of ten around the long rectangular table, and was sprawled in it, his long legs stretched right out in front of him, one ankle over the other. He looked effortlessly elegant and incredibly *cool* in his weathered jeans and faded polo shirt. Everything clung in a way that made her think that the entire outfit had been especially designed with him in mind.

She pushed the coffee over to him. He looked just the kind of guy to take his coffee black, no sugar.

'Does your company think that they can send some-one who's dressed down for the day in the hope that we might just soften our stance? Maybe be deluded into thinking that he's not the stuffed shirt lawyer that he actually is?' She narrowed her eyes and tried and failed to imagine him as a stuffed shirt lawyer.

'Ah…' Mr Frank murmured. '*That* ploy.'

'Yes. *That* ploy. Well, it won't work. My team and I are committed to the cause and you can tell your em-ployers that we intend to fight this abhorrent and unnec-essary development with every ounce of breath in us.'

'You overestimate my qualifications,' Mr Frank said smoothly, sipping the coffee. 'Excellent coffee, by the way. I'm no lawyer. But were I to be one, then I would try very hard not to be a stuffed shirt one.'

'Not a lawyer? Then who the heck are you? Angie said that you were here about the land.'

'Angie being the girl with the spiky hair and the nose ring?'

'That's correct. She also happens to be an extremely efficient secretary and a whizz at IT.'

'Well, she was certainly right in one respect. I *am* here about the land. Here to join the noble cause.'

Art's plan had been simple. It had come to him in a blinding flash shortly after Harold had informed him that money wasn't going to make the problem of squat-ters on his land go away.

*If you can't lick 'em, join 'em.*

Naturally he'd known what to expect but somehow,

in the flesh, the woman staring at him through narrowed eyes wasn't *quite* the hippy he had originally imagined.

He couldn't put his finger on what was different and then, in the space of a handful of seconds, decided that it was a case of imagination playing tricks because she was certainly dressed in just the sort of attire he'd expected. Some sort of loose trousers in an assortment of clashing colours. Practical, given the hot weather, but, in all other respects, frankly appalling. A shapeless green vest-like top and a pair of sandals that, like the trousers, were practical but ticked absolutely no other boxes as far as he was concerned.

Her hair seemed to be staging a full-scale revolt against its half-hearted restraints. It was very curly and strands of it waved around her cheeks.

But the woman emanated *presence* and that was something he couldn't deny.

She wasn't beautiful, not in the conventional sense of the word, but she was incredibly arresting and for a few seconds Art found himself in the novel situation of temporarily forgetting why he was sitting here in a kitchen that looked as though a bomb had recently been detonated in it.

And then it all came back. He would join the band of merry protestors. He would get to know the woman. He would convince her from the position of insider that she was fighting a losing battle.

He would bring her round to his way of thinking, which was simply a matter of bringing her round to common sense, because she was never going to win this war.

But strong-arm tactics weren't going to work because, as Harold had made perfectly clear, storming in and bludgeoning the opposition would be catastrophic in a community as tightly knit as this one clearly was.

He was simply going to persuade her into seeing his point of view and the best and only way he could do that would be from the inside, from the position of one of them. From the advantageous position of trust.

Art didn't need opposition. He needed to butter up the unruly mob because he had long-term plans for the land—plans that included sheltered accommodation for his autistic stepbrother, to whom he was deeply attached.

He hadn't gone straight to the site though, choosing instead to make himself known to the woman standing firmly between him and his plans. He was good with women. Women liked him. Quite a few positively adored him. And there weren't many who didn't fall for his charm. Art wasn't vain but he was realistic, so why not use that charm to work its magic on this recalcitrant woman?

If that failed to do the trick then of course he would have to go back to the drawing board, but it was worth a shot.

To this end, he had taken his unprecedented leave of absence. A few days to sort out urgent business that wouldn't happily sit on the back burner and now here he was.

He was sporting the beginnings of a beard, was letting his hair grow, and the sharp handmade suits had ceded to the faded jeans and a black polo shirt.

'Really?' Rose said with a certain amount of cynicism.

'Indeed. Why the suspicion?'

'Because you don't exactly fit the role of the protestors we have here.'

'Don't I? How so?'

'Basically, I have no idea who you are. I don't recognise you.'

'And you know everyone who's protesting?'

'Everyone and, in most cases, their extended families, as well. You're not from around here, are you?'

'Not quite,' Art murmured vaguely, unprepared for such a direct line of attack before he'd even started writing incendiary messages on a placard.

'Well, where *are* you from? Exactly?'

Art shrugged and shifted in his chair. He was beginning to understand why the deputies sent to do this job had failed. Right now, Rose was staring at him as though he was something suspect and possibly contagious that had somehow managed to infiltrate her space.

'Can anyone say *exactly* where they're from?' he threw the question back at her, which only made her look at him with even more suspicion.

'Yes. Everyone on the site, for a start. As for me, I'm from here and always have been, aside from a brief spell at university.'

'I largely live in London.' Which was technically accurate. He *did* largely live in London. In his penthouse in Belgravia. He was also to be found in five-star hotels around the world, several of which he owned, or in one of the many houses he owned, although those occasions were slightly rarer. Who had time to wind down in a villa by the sea?

Strangely, that non-answer seemed to satisfy her because she stopped looking as though she had her finger on the buzzer to call for instant backup. 'So what are you doing here?' she asked with curiosity. 'I mean, why this cause? If you're not from around here, then what does it matter to you whether the land is destroyed or not?'

'*Destroy* is a big word.' Art was outraged but he held onto his temper and looked at her with an expression of bland innocence.

Definitely arresting, he thought. Exotic eyes. Feline. And a sensuous mouth. Wide and expressive. And an air of sharp intelligence which, it had to be said, wasn't one of the foremost qualities he ever sought in a woman, but it certainly worked in this instance because he was finding it hard to keep his eyes off her.

Rose fidgeted. To her horror, she felt the slow crawl of colour stain her cheeks. The man was gazing at her with hooded eyes and that look was doing all sorts of unexpected things to her body.

'It's *exactly* the right word,' she snapped, more sharply than she had intended, a reaction to those dark, sexy eyes.

Never had she felt more self-conscious, more aware of her shortcomings. The comfortable and practical culottes, which were the mainstay of her wardrobe on hot summer days, were suddenly as flattering as a pair of curtains and the loose-fitting vest as attractive as a bin liner.

She reminded herself that she wasn't the star attraction in a fashion parade. Clothes did not the man, or woman, make!

But for the first time in living memory she had the crazy urge to be something other than the determined career lawyer who worked hard on behalf of the underdog. She had the crazy urge to be sexy and compelling and wanted for her body instead of her brain.

'Too many developers over the years have whittled away at the open land around here.' She refocused and brought her runaway mind back on track. 'They've come along and turned the fields, which have been enjoyed for centuries by ramblers and nature lovers, into first a stupid shopping mall and then into office blocks.'

Rose half expected him to jump in here and heatedly side with her but he remained silent and she wondered what was going through that impossibly good-looking head of his.

'And this lot?'

'DC Logistics?' She loosed a sarcastic laugh under her breath. 'The worst of the lot. Certainly the biggest! They want to construct a housing development. But then I don't suppose I'm telling you anything you don't already know. Which brings me back to my question—why the interest in joining our protest?'

'Sometimes—' Art played with the truth like a piece of moulding clay '—big, powerful developers need to understand the importance of working in harmony with nature or else leaving things as they stand and, as you say, DC Logistics is the mother of all big companies.'

He succeeded in not sounding proud of this fact. When he thought of the work that had gone into turning the dregs of what had been left of his father's companies, after five ex-wives had picked them over in outrageous alimony settlements, into the success story of today he was pretty proud of his achievements.

Art had lived through the nightmare of his father's mistakes, the marriages that had fallen apart within seconds of the ink on the marriage certificates being dry. He'd gritted his teeth, helpless, as each ex-wife had drained the coffers and then, after his father had died several years previously, he'd returned to try to save what little remained of the thriving empire Emilio da Costa had carefully built up over time.

Art had been a young man at the time, barely out of university but already determined to take what was left and build it again into the thriving concern it had once been when his mother—Emilio da Costa's first wife and only love—had been alive.

Art might have learned from the chaos of his father's life and the greed of the women he had foolishly married that love was for the birds, but he had also learned the value of compassion in his unexpected affection for his stepbrother, José—not flesh and blood, no, but his brother in every sense of the word, who had been robustly ignored by his avaricious mother. The land was integral to his plan to make a home for José—the reason for Art needing to shut this protest down as quickly and as quietly as possible.

'Yes, it is,' Rose concurred. 'So you're idealistic,' she carried on in an approving tone.

The last time Art had been idealistic had been when he'd believed in Santa Claus and the Tooth Fairy. Witnessing the self-serving venom camouflaged as *true love* that had littered his father's life right up until his death had taken whatever ideals he might have had and entombed them in a place more secure than a bank vault.

'Well, you're in the right place.' Rose gestured to the paraphernalia in the kitchen. 'Obviously I don't devote all of my time to this cause. I couldn't possibly, but I do try to touch base with the people out there on a daily basis.'

'What's your main line of work?'

'Employment law.' Rose smiled and, just like that, Art felt the breath knocked out of his body.

The woman was more than arresting. When she smiled she was...*bloody stunning.* He felt the familiar kick of his libido, but stronger and more urgent than ever. Two months without a woman, he thought, would do that to a red-blooded man with a healthy sex drive. Because this outspoken feminist was certainly, on no level, what he looked for in a woman. He didn't do argumentative and he definitely didn't do the *let's-hold-hands-and-save-the-world* type. He did blondes. Big blonde hair, big blue eyes and personalities that soothed rather than challenged.

Rose Tremain was about as soothing as a pit bull.

And yet... His eyes lingered and his inconvenient erection refused to go away. The blood surging in his veins was hot with a type of dark excitement he hadn't felt in a very long time. If ever.

'Come again?' He realised that she had said something.

'Your line of work? What is it?'

'I dabble.'

'Dabble in what?'

'How much time have you got to spare? Could take a while.'

'Could take a while covering your many talents? Well, you're far from modest, aren't you?' She raised her eyebrows, amused and mocking, and Art smiled back slowly—deliberately slowly.

'I've never been a believer in false modesty. Sign of a hypocritical mind. I prefer to recognise my talents as well as my…er…shortcomings.'

'Well, whatever you do is your business—' she shrugged and stood up '—but if you're good at everything, which seems to be what you're implying, then you're going to be very useful to us.'

'How so?' Art followed suit and stood up, towering over her even though she was tall. 'Useful in what respect?'

'Odd jobs. Nothing major so no need to sound alarmed.' She looked around the kitchen. 'Everyone lends a helping hand when they're here. It's not just a case of people painting slogans on bits of cardboard with felt tip pens. Yes, we're all protesting for the same reason, but this is a small, close community. The guys who come here do all sorts of jobs around the house. They know I'm representing them for free and they're all keen to repay the favour by doing practical things in return. There are a couple of plumbers behind us and an electrician, and without them I have no idea how much money I would have had to spend to get some vital jobs on the house done.'

'So this is your house?' Art thought that it was a bit hypocritical, clamouring about rich businessmen who wanted to destroy the precious space around her so that they could line their evil pockets when she, judging from the size of the house, was no pauper.

Accustomed to storing up information that might prove useful down the line, he sensed that that was a conversation he would have in due course.

'It is, not that that's relevant,' Rose said coolly. 'What *is* relevant is that most of the town is behind us, aside from the local council, who have seen fit to grant planning permission. I've managed to really rally a great deal of people to support our cause and they've all been brilliant. So if you're a jack-of-all-trades then I'm sure I'll be able to find loads of practical ways you can help, aside from joining the sit-in, of course. Now, shall I take you to the scene of the crime…?'

# CHAPTER TWO

'YOU HAVE A nice house,' Art commented neutrally as they exited the cluttered kitchen, out into the main body of the house which was equally cluttered. 'Big. You rent out rooms, I take it?' He detoured to push open the door to one of the huge ground-floor rooms and was confronted with an elderly man holding court with an image of a bunch of flowers behind him on the wall. The image was faded and unsteady because the projector was probably a relic from the last century. Everyone turned to stare at Art and he saluted briskly before gently shutting the door.

'If it's all the same to you, Mr Frank, I'll ask the questions. And please refrain from exploring the house because, yes, other organisations do avail themselves of some of the rooms and I very much doubt they want you poking your head in to say hello. Unless, of course, you have something to impart on the subject of orchid-growing or maybe some pearls of wisdom you could share with one of our Citizens Advice Bureau volunteers?'

'I've never been into gardening,' Art contributed truthfully. He slanted his eyes across to Rose, who was

walking tall next to him, her strides easily matching
his as they headed to the front door. The walls of the
house were awash with rousing, morale-boosting posters. Voices could be heard behind closed doors.

'You're missing out. It's a very restful pastime.'

Art chuckled quietly. He didn't do *restful*.

'Wait a minute.' She looked at him directly, hands
on her hips, her brown eyes narrowed and shrewdly assessing. 'There's one little thing I forgot to mention and
I'd better be upfront before we go any further.'

'What's that?'

'I don't know who you are. You're not from around
here and I'm going to make it clear to you from the start
that we don't welcome rabble-rousers.'

Stunned, Art stared at her in complete silence.

He was Arturo da Costa. A man feared and respected
in the international business community. A man who
could have anything he wanted at the snap of an im-
perious finger. Grown men thought twice before they
said anything they felt might be misconstrued as offensive. When he spoke, people inclined their heads and
listened. When he entered a room, silence fell.

And here he was being accused of being a potential
*rabble-rouser*!

'Rabble-rouser,' he framed in a slow, incredulous voice.

'It's been known.' She spun around on her heel,
headed to the door and then out towards a battered
navy blue Land Rover. 'Idlers who drift from one protest site to another, stirring up trouble for their own
political motives.'

'Idlers…' Art played with the word on his tongue,

shocked and yet helpless to voice his outrage given he was supposed to be someone of no fixed address, there to support the noble cause.

'Granted, not all are idlers.' Rose swung herself into the driver's seat and slammed the door behind her, waiting for him to join her. She switched on the engine but then turned to him, one hand on the gearbox, the other on the steering wheel. 'But a lot of them are career protestors and I can tell you straight away that we don't welcome that lot. We're peaceful. We want our voices to be heard and the message we want to get across is not one that would benefit from thug tactics.'

'I have never been accused of being a rabble-rouser in my life before, far less a thug. Or an *idler*…'

'There's no need to look so shocked.' She smiled and pushed some of her curly hair away from her face. 'These things happen in the big, bad world.'

'Oh, I know all about what happens in the big, bad world,' Mr Frank murmured softly and the hairs on the back of her neck stood on end because his deep, velvety voice was as seductive as the darkest of chocolate.

In the sultry heat of the Land Rover, she could almost breathe him in and it was going to her head like incense.

'And before you launch into another outrageous accusation—' he laughed '—something along the lines that I don't know about the big, bad world because I'm a criminal, I'll tell you straight away that I have never, and will never, operate on the wrong side of the law.'

'I wasn't about to accuse you of being a criminal.' Rose blinked and cleared her throat. 'Although, of course,' she added grudgingly, 'I might have got round to that sooner or later. You can't be too careful. You should roll your window down. It'll be a furnace in here otherwise.'

'No air conditioning?'

'This relic barely goes,' she said affectionately before swinging around to expertly manoeuvre the courtyard which was strewn with cars, all parked, it would seem, with reckless abandon. 'If I tried to stick air conditioning in it would probably collapse from the shock of being dragged into the twentieth century.'

'You could always get a new car.'

'For someone who dabbles in a bit of this and that, you seem to think that money grows on trees,' she said tartly. 'If I ever win the lottery I might consider replacing my car but, until then, I work with the old girl and hope for the best.'

'Lawyers,' he said with a vague wave of his hand. 'Aren't you all made of money?'

Rose laughed and shot him a sideways look. He was slouched against the passenger door, his big body angled so that he could look at her, and she wondered how many women had had those sexy dark eyes focused on them, how many had lost their head drowning in the depths.

She fancied herself as anything but the romantic sort, but there was a little voice playing in her head, warning her that this was a man she should be careful of.

Rose nearly laughed because her last brush with romance had left a nasty taste in her mouth. Jack Shaw had been a fellow lawyer and she had met him on one of her cases, which had taken her to Surrey and the playground of the rich and famous. He had been fighting the corner for the little guy and she had really thought that they were on the same wavelength—and they should have been. He'd ticked all the right boxes! But for the second time in her adult life she had embarked on a relationship that had started off with promise only to end in disappointment. How was it possible for something that made sense to end up with two people not actually having anything left to say to one another after ten months?

Rose knew what worked and what didn't when it came to emotions. She had learned from bitter childhood experience what to avoid. She knew what was unsuitable. And yet her two suitable boyfriends, with their excellent socialist credentials, had crashed and burned.

At this rate, she was ready to give up the whole finding love game and sink her energies into worthwhile causes instead.

'Not all lawyers are rich,' she said without looking at him, busy focusing on the road, which was lined with dense hedges, winding and very narrow. 'I'm not.'

'Why is that?'

'Maybe I chose the wrong branch of law.' She shrugged. 'Employment law generally doesn't do it when it comes to earning vast sums of money. Not that I'm complaining. I get by nicely, especially when you think about all the perfectly smart people who can't find work.'

'There's always work available for perfectly smart people.'

'Is that your experience?' She flashed him a wry

sidelong glance before turning her attention back to the road. 'Are you one of those perfectly smart people who finds it so easy to get work that you're currently drifting out here to join a cause in which you have no personal interest?'

'You're still suspicious of my motives?'

'I'm reserving judgement. Although—' she sighed '—I can, of course, understand how easy it is to get involved if you're a nature-lover. Look around you at the open land. You can really breathe out here. The thought of it being handed over to a developer, so that houses can be put up and the trees chopped down, doesn't bear thinking about.'

Art looked around him. There certainly was a great deal of open land. It stretched all around them, relentless and monotonous, acres upon acres upon acres of never-ending sameness. He'd never been much of a country man. He liked the frenetic buzz of city life, the feeling of being surrounded by activity. He made some appreciative noises under his breath and narrowed his eyes against the glare as the perimeters of his land took shape.

'So you've lived here all your life,' Art murmured as she slowed right down to access the bumpy track that followed the outer reaches of his property. 'I'm taking it that some of the guys protesting are relatives? Brothers? Sisters? Cousins? Maybe your parents?'

'No,' Rose said shortly.

Art pricked up his ears, detecting something behind that abrupt response. It paid to know your quarry and

Harold had been spot on when he'd said that there was next to no personal information circulating out there about the prickly woman next to him. Amazing. Social media was the staple diet of most people under the age of thirty-five and yet this woman had obviously managed to turn her back firmly on the trend.

Since he was similarly private about his life, he had to concede some reluctant admiration for her stance.

'No extended family?'

'Why the Spanish Inquisition?' She glanced across at him. 'What about *you*? Brothers? Sisters? Cousins? Will some of *your* extended family be showing up here to support us?'

'You're very prickly.'

'I…don't mean to be, Mr Frank.'

'I think we should move onto a first name basis. That okay with you? My name's Arturo. Arthur if you prefer the English equivalent.' Which was as close to the truth as it was possible to get, as was the surname, which hadn't been plucked from thin air but which was, in fact, his mother's maiden name.

'Rose.'

'And you were telling me that you weren't prickly…'

'I'm afraid the whole business of an extended family is something of a sore point with me.' She half smiled because her history was no deep, dark secret, at least locally. If Arthur, or Arturo because he looked a lot more like an exotic Arturo than a boring Arthur, ended up here for the long haul, then sooner or later he would hear the gossip. The truth was that her background had made her what she was, for which she was very glad, but it wasn't exactly normal and for some reason explaining herself to this man felt…awkward and a little intimate.

Aside from that, what was with the questioning? Shouldn't he be asking questions about the land instead of about *her*?

On a number of levels he certainly didn't respond in the predicted manner and again Rose felt that shiver, the faintly thrilling feathery sensation of being in slightly unchartered territory.

'You asked about me,' he said smoothly, filling the silence which had descended between them, 'and extended family is a sore point for me, as well. I have none.'

'No?' They had arrived at the protest site but Rose found that she wanted to prolong the conversation.

'Do you feel sorry for me?' Arturo grinned and Rose blinked, disconcerted by the stupendous charm behind that crooked smile. She felt it again, a whoosh that swept through her, making her breath quicken and her stomach swoop.

'Should I? You don't strike me as the sort of guy someone should be feeling sorry for. How is it that you have no extended family?'

'First, I'll take it as a compliment that you think I'm the kind of dominant guy people should fear, respect and admire instead of pity…'

'Did I say that?' But her mouth twitched with amusement.

'And, second, I'll tell you if you tell me. We can hold hands and have a girly evening sharing confidences…join me for dinner later. I'd love to get to know you better.'

Hot, flustered and suddenly out of her depth, Rose gaped at him like a stranded fish, scarcely believing her ears. She reddened, lost for words.

'Is it a promising start that I'm taking your breath away?' Arturo drawled, his voice rich with amusement.

'No... I... You're asking me on *a date*?'

'You sound as though it's something that's never happened to you before.'

'I...no... I'm very sorry, Mr Frank, but I...no. I can't accept. But thank you very much. I'm flattered.'

'Arturo.' He frowned. 'Why not?'

'Because...' Rose smoothed her wayward hair with her hand and stared off into the distance, all the while acutely aware of his dark, sexy eyes on her profile, making a nonsense of her level head and feet-firmly-planted-on-the-ground approach to life. She was no frothy, giggly bit of fluff but he was making her feel a bit like that and anyone would think that she was a giddy virgin in the company of a prince!

'Because...?'

'Well, it's not appropriate.'

'Why not? I may be about to join your cause, but you're not my boss so no conflict of interest there.'

'I...' Rose licked her lips and eventually looked at him, leaning against the open window. 'I...'

'You're not married. You're not wearing a wedding ring.'

'Observant. That's hardly the point, though.'

'Boyfriend?'

'No...not that it's any of your business, Mr Frank.

Arthur. *Arturo*. Do you usually ask women you've only known for five seconds out on a date?'

'How else am I supposed to get to know them for longer than five seconds if I don't? So you're not married, no boyfriend…gay?'

'No!'

Arturo grinned and Rose was certain she was blushing furiously, her reddened cheeks thoroughly letting the side down. 'Then where's the problem?'

'You're very sure of yourself, aren't you?' Rose gathered herself and opened her door. It was very hot. A blazing summer afternoon, with the sun still high in the sky and the clouds little more than cotton wool puffs of white idly floating by. The land looked glorious and untouched. It was a short walk to get to the site where the protestors had set up camp. Yes, she could have driven there, but it was easier to park here and a nice day for walking. Except now she would be walking in a state of nervous tension.

'Is that a crime?' Arturo had followed her out and he looked at her, still grinning.

'I've never been attracted to men who are too sure of themselves.'

'Challenging observation…'

'That's not my intention! You're here to…support us! And I won't be going out with you because… I'm not interested in any sort of relationship at this point in time.'

'Who's talking about a relationship?'

'I don't do casual sex.' Rose was staggered that she was having this conversation, but she had yet to meet a man who was open about what he wanted and surely he couldn't want *her* because, rich or poor, he had the sort of charisma and good looks that would guarantee him a spot in any woman's little black book.

So why her?

But heck, was she flattered? It had been a while since her last disastrous relationship, a while since she had felt like a woman. And, if she was honest, even Jack, earnest and brimming over with admirable integrity, hadn't made her feel like this.

'I thought I just mentioned having dinner,' Arturo murmured, which made Rose feel her cheeks flush what was surely an even deeper shade of red.

'You're playing with me,' she said sharply. 'And I don't like it.'

Their eyes tangled but Rose refused to be the first to back down even though she wanted to.

Art was learning what it felt like to be politely but firmly pushed to the kerb.

'Tell me about the protest,' he encouraged, changing tack, matching her gait with his and releasing her from the stranglehold of her embarrassment as they continued to walk towards the distant horizon. 'How many people are there at the site?'

'Ever been on a protest before?'

'I can honestly say that I haven't.'

'Well, I'm glad that this is of sufficient interest to you to get you motivated into doing more than just sitting on the sidelines and sympathising. So many people have strong views about something and yet they never quite go the distance when it comes to doing something about those views.'

'What made you choose employment law over something better paid?'

'Because money isn't everything! And I'm taking it that you feel the same as I do.'

'Money *can* often be the root of all evil,' Art hedged. 'It's also pretty vital when it comes to putting food on our plates.'

'I like to think that in my job I'm helping other people put food on their plates.'

'And you've always worked for yourself or did you work for a bigger company after you graduated?'

'You ask a lot of questions, don't you?' But she seemed flattered by his interest.

'It's the only way to get to know someone.' Art had the grace to flush. He was here for a purpose though and with him the practical would always take precedence over any unruly conscience. Vast sums of money were at stake and he was only trying to make his point of view known to a group who probably thought that their opinion was the only valid one on the table.

A rich diversity of opinion was a bonus in life. By *subtly* introducing a different viewpoint to theirs, he would effectively be doing her and all of the protestors there a laudable favour.

'Nearly twenty-five,' Rose told him briskly, walking fast, each stride determined and sure-footed.

'Nearly twenty-five what?'

'You asked how many protestors there were on the site. Nearly twenty-five and growing by the day.'

'And what lovely days we've been having…'

'They'd be here come rain or shine,' Rose informed him tartly and he grinned at her.

'And quite right too. Nothing worse than a protestor who packs up his placards and heads for his car the minute the skies open.'

'I can't tell when you're joking,' Rose said, pausing to look at him.

'Oh, I'm very serious about being here indeed. Make no mistake about that,' Art said softly.

'And how long do you plan on staying?' She began walking again and he fell in beside her.

'I reckon at least a few days, maybe longer. Perhaps a week or two.'

'Getting first-hand experience of putting your money where your mouth is.' Rose smiled. 'I commend that. The camp's just up ahead. We've managed to get running water and electricity going. It's been a nightmare but where there's a will there's a way and, like I said, there are a lot of people with a lot of talent who have been keen to help us out.'

Art was looking at a collection of makeshift dwellings. Tents rubbed shoulders with slightly more solid constructions. There was an elaborate portable toilet. People were milling around. Children were playing. It was, he had to concede, a wonderful campsite, dissected by a clear, bubbling stream and surrounded by trees and flowers. It was, however, a campsite on *his* land.

Clearly much loved and admired, the second they were spotted, Rose was surrounded by people, young and old alike. She was part and parcel of the community and Art could see the warmth of the supporters surround her like a blanket, seemingly reaffirming her belief in what they were doing—saving the land for the locals. Several dragged her along to have a look at some new ideas for placards. One old guy involved her in an elaborate discussion about some legal technicality, which she handled with aplomb and a great show of interest, even though he could somehow tell that she was answering his questions automatically.

No one paid the slightest bit of attention to him.

He was introduced, of course, and he, likewise, was shown yet more placards to add to the already healthy supply in evidence.

'Very artistic,' he contributed to one of the middle-aged women who had carted him off to one side. 'I like the…er…'

'Drawings?' She delightedly pointed to the illustration of stick figures holding placards showing stick figures holding placards. 'I'm trying to convey the idea that all of this is a never-ending problem which will just keep recurring until everyone feels as passionately about the countryside as we do.'

'Very imaginative.'

'I guess you'll be helping? Rose says you're interested in what's taking place in this little pocket of the world.'

'Very interested,' Art said with heartfelt honesty, relieved to be dragged away before he could be quizzed further. The woman struck him as the sort who took no prisoners.

Overhead, the sun continued to beat down with ferocity. He felt hot and sweaty and in need of just a handful of those minor luxuries he took for granted. A nice cool shower, for one thing.

He'd brought the minimum of clothes, stuffed into a holdall which he'd left in the Land Rover. They nestled on top of his computer, because there was no way he intended to be completely out of reach. That would have been unthinkable.

'So,' Rose said brightly when she was back at his side, having done the rounds, including squatting on the ground to talk to some of the children, 'I notice that you didn't think to bring a tent.'

'Come again?'

'I'm getting ahead of myself.' She drew him to one side. 'You said that you planned on staying for a few days and you don't have a tent, but I think it might be possible for you to share one. I know Rob over there has a tent that's as big as a house and I'm sure he'd be delighted to share his space with a fellow protestor.'

Art tried not to recoil with horror. 'That,' he all but choked, 'won't do.'

'Why not?'

'Because I have some savings and I will dip into them to stay somewhere…er…locally…'

'But why? Honestly, the site is really very comfortable. Everyone enjoys staying there.'

'And I applaud them, but that's not for me.'

'It's stupid to use your savings to rent somewhere for a week. Or however long you plan on staying. Besides, in case you haven't noticed, this is an extremely touristy part of the country. Dead in winter but the hotels around here are expensive and almost all of them will be fully booked in summer.' She stood back and looked at him narrowly.

'I believe you when you say that you don't have criminal tendencies.' She folded her arms and inclined her head to one side.

'I'm breathing a sigh of relief as I stand here.'

'And I think it's ridiculous for you to waste your money trying to find somewhere around here to rent. You'll be broke by the end of a week. Trust me.' She said nothing for a few minutes, giving him ample time to try to figure out where this was heading.

But she didn't expand, instead choosing to begin walking back to the Land Rover, which was a long-winded exercise because she was stopped by someone every couple of steps. On the way she collected an offering of several files, which she promised to look at later.

'Nothing to do with the land,' she confided to Art when they were finally back in the muddy four-wheel drive and she was swinging away from the land, back out to the open road. 'George is having issues with one of his employees. Wants some advice. Normally it's the other way round for me, but I promised I'd have a look at the file.'

'Generous of you. I can see how popular you are with everyone there.'

Rose laughed, a musical sound of amusement that did the same thing to Art as her smile did, rousing him in ways that were unexpected and surprisingly intense.

He did know that there were pertinent questions he should be asking to further his understanding of how he could win this war without losing the battle but he couldn't seem to get his head in the right place to ask the right questions. Instead, he found himself staring at her from under his lashes, vaguely wondering what it was about her that was so compelling.

'Now that you've turned down my dinner invitation,' he drawled, 'perhaps you could drive me to the nearest, cheapest B&B. I'm touched at your concern for the level of my savings, but I'll manage.'

'There's no reason why you can't stay at my place.'

'Your place?'

Rose laughed, caught his eye sideways and forced a grin out of him. 'It's big and you can pay your way doing things around the house while you're there. Two of the rooms need painting, which is a job I never seem to get round to doing, and there's a stubborn leak in the tap. A constant drip, drip, drip.'

'You want me to fix leaks and paint your house?' DIY and Art had never crossed paths. Paint a room? Fix a leak? He couldn't have flung himself further out of his comfort zone if he'd tried.

'In return for free board and lodging. Oh, how good are you at cooking?'

'It's something I've always tried to avoid.'

'Do we have a deal?'

'Why do you live in such a big house if you can't afford to?'

'Long story.'

'I'm a very good listener. There's nothing I enjoy more than a long story. I guess we can get to that in due course because I would love to accept your generous offer.' He wondered what other skills she thought he possessed. There was a chance they would both end up in Casualty if he tried his hand at cooking, so he disabused her straight away on that count and she laughed and shrugged and laughed again and told him that it had been worth a shot.

'I can cook and when I put my mind to it I actually enjoy it, but I'm so busy all of the time that it always feels like a chore.'

'You might regret asking me to paint a room,' Art said seriously as she bumped along the narrow lanes, driving past clusters of picturesque houses with neat box hedges before the open fields swallowed them up again, only to disgorge them into yet another picturesque village. 'I'm very happy to try my hand at it, but one thing I do insist on doing is paying you for my accommodation.'

'Don't be stupid.'

'If you don't agree to this then you can dump me off right here and I'll sort myself out, whatever the cost.'

Rose clicked her tongue impatiently.

'You obviously need the money,' Art continued almost gently, as the outskirts of the village loomed into view. 'You rent rooms out and the place, from all accounts, is falling apart at the seams...'

'Very well.' She kept her eyes firmly focused on the road ahead. 'In which case, I'll accept your dinner invitation on the proviso that I cook dinner for you.'

'Deal,' Art drawled, relaxing back into the passenger seat. Could he have hoped for a better outcome than this? No.

He was looking forward to this evening. The thorny business of going undercover to talk some sense into his opposition wasn't going to be the annoying uphill trek he had originally foreseen after all…

In fact…hand on heart, Art could honestly say that he was looking forward to this little break in his routine.

# CHAPTER THREE

BY THE TIME they were back at the house the clatter of people had been replaced by the peace of silence. The gardening club crew had departed, as had whoever else was renting one of the downstairs rooms. Phil popped out and Art watched as he and Rose huddled in a brief discussion.

While they talked in low voices, he took the opportunity to look around him.

It was a big house but crying out for attention. The paint was tired, the carpet on the stairs threadbare and the woodwork, in places, cracked or missing altogether.

He made himself at home peering into the now empty rooms and saw that they were sizeable and cluttered with hastily packed away bits and pieces.

It was impossible to get any real idea of what the house might once have looked like in grander times because every nook and cranny had been put to use. Work desks fitted into spaces where once sofas and chaises longues might have resided, and in the office where she worked books lined the walls from floor to ceiling.

'Finished looking around?'

Art turned to find that she had broken off from talking to Phil, who was heading out of the front door, briefcase in hand and a crumpled linen jacket shoved under his arm.

'Which of the rooms needs the paint job?' was his response.

'It's actually upstairs,' Rose said, steering him away from the hall and back towards the kitchen where, he noted, no one had seen fit to tidy the paraphernalia of protest. 'Now—' she stood, arms folded, head tilted to one side '—tell me what you thought of our little band of insurgents.'

'Well organised.' Art strolled towards one of the kitchen chairs and sat down. 'But I'm curious—how long do they intend to stay there and what is the end objective?'

'That's an odd question,' Rose mused thoughtfully. 'Does your contribution to the cause depend on an answer to that?'

'I have a strong streak of practicality.' Art wasn't lying when he said that. 'I'm interested in trying to find out if there's any real chance of you winning with your protests.'

Rose sighed. 'Perhaps not entirely,' she admitted, 'but I really hope we can make some kind of difference, perhaps get the company to rethink the scale of their project. They're eating up a lot of open land and there's no question that the end result will be a massive eyesore on the landscape.'

'Have you seen the plans?' Art asked curiously.

'Of course I have. It's all about houses for wealthy commuters.'

'The rail link, I suppose…'

'You're the only person who has actually taken time out to think this through,' Rose admitted. 'And you're not even from round here. I think everyone somehow hopes that this is a problem that will just go away if we can all just provide a united front. It's a relief to talk to someone who can see the pitfalls. Just strange that you should care so much, considering this has never been your home.'

'I have general concerns about the…er…country-side.' Art had the grace to flush. Yes, all was fair in love and war, and it wasn't as though this little decep-tion was actually harming anyone, but the prick of his conscience was an uneasy reminder that playing fast and loose with the truth was a lie by any other name.

'Does that extend to other concerns?' Rose asked with interest.

'What do you mean?'

'Problems on a larger scale. Climate change. Dam-age to the rainforests. Fracking and the impact on the green belt.'

Art was used to women who were either career-driven—those with whom he came into contact in the course of his working life—or else women he dated. On the one hand, he conversed with his counterparts with absolute detachment, regardless of whether he picked up any vibes from them, any undercurrent of sexual in-terest. And then, when it came to the women he dated… well, that was sex, relaxation and pleasure, and in-depth conversations were not the name of the game. Quite honestly, he thought that the majority of them would have been bored rigid were he ever to sit them down and initiate a conversation about world affairs. If there was a world out there of smart, sassy women who had what it took to turn him on, then he'd passed them by.

Until now…

Because, against all odds, he was finding that this outspoken woman was a turn-on and he didn't know why. She should have been tiresome, but instead she was weirdly compelling.

'Doesn't everyone think about the bigger picture?'

'I like that,' Rose murmured. 'I really get it that you think about the bigger picture. But you surely must have some form of employment that enables you to take off when you want to, be it here or somewhere else…' She turned away and began rustling for something to cook.

'Let me order something in.' Art was uncomfortable with this.

'*Order something in?*' She looked at him incredulously.

'There's no need for you to prepare anything for me.'

'We both have to eat and it won't be fancy. Trust me.'

'Are you usually this welcoming to people who walk off the street into your house?'

'You're a one-off.' She smiled a little shyly. Yes, she had lots of contact with the opposite sex. Yes, there was Phil and a wide assortment of men she met on a daily basis, either because they lived locally and she bumped into them or in the course of her work. But this was different. This was a reminder of what it felt like to be with a man and she was enjoying the sensation.

Of course, she sternly reminded herself, it wasn't as though he was anything more than a nice guy who happened to share the same outlook on life as she did.

A nice guy who just so happened to be drop-dead gorgeous...

'A *one-off*...?' He looked at her with assessing eyes and Rose burst out laughing. He sounded piqued, as though someone had stuck a pin in his ego. In a flash of wonderment because he was simply nothing like any man she had ever met before, she gathered that he was piqued because she wasn't bowled over by him. Or at least because that was the impression she had given. She had turned down his dinner date, had rejected his offer to pay rent and had set him a number of tasks to complete, which was probably a first for a guy like him. He might not have money but he had style and an underlying aggressive sexual magnetism that most women would find irresistible.

Their eyes tangled and Rose felt her nipples pinch in raw sexual awareness, and the suddenness of its potency made her breath catch in her throat.

'That's the problem with living in a small community.' Rose laughed breathlessly, deflecting a moment of madness which had smacked of her being lonely, which she most certainly was not. 'You tend to know everyone. A new face is a rare occurrence.'

'Surely not.'

'Maybe not at this time of year,' she admitted, 'when the place is swarming with tourists, but a new face here for something other than the nice scenery and the quaint village atmosphere…that's a bit more unusual.'

'Why do you stay?' Art asked with what sounded like genuine curiosity. 'And, if that's the case, then surely you must find it a little dull?'

'No, I don't. I'm not just a statistic here, one of a million lawyers sweating to get by. Here, I can actually make a difference. And I don't know why I'm telling you any of this.'

'Because I'm a new face and you don't get to have conversations with people you haven't known since you were a kid?'

Rose flushed and looked at him defiantly. 'Not all of us are born to wander, which reminds me—you never told me how it is that you can afford to take time out to be here. Yes, you've said you do a bit of this and a bit of that but you're obviously not a labourer.'

'What makes you say that?'

'Your hands, for a start. Not calloused enough.'

'I'm not sure that's a compliment,' Art drawled, glancing at his hands. The last time he'd done anything really manual had been as a teenager when he'd had a summer job working on a building site. He recalled that his father had been going through divorce number three right about then.

'Office jobs?'

'You ask a lot of questions.'

'No more than you,' Rose pointed out and Art grinned at her, dark eyes never leaving her face.

He hadn't thought through the details of why he was

here and it hadn't occurred to him that his presence would be met with suspicion. He was having to revise his easy assumption that he could just show up, mumble something vague and get by without any questions.

'I've been known to sit behind a desk now and again. I confess I'm interested in the details of a sit-in, in what motivates people to give up their home comforts for a cause.'

'You're not a reporter, are you?'

'Would you object if I told you that I was?'

'No. The more coverage the better…'

'Well, sorry to disappoint but,' Art drawled with complete honesty, 'I personally can't stand the breed. Nosy and intrusive.'

'But excellent when it comes to getting a message out there to the wider public.'

'They're a fickle lot,' Art countered. 'You think that they're on your side and you usually open yourself up to inevitable disappointment. If you're going to make me dinner and you won't allow me to buy anything in, then the least I can do is help.'

'Okay. You can chop vegetables and tell me why you're interested in what's happening here.' Rose rummaged in the fridge and extracted a random assortment of vegetables, fetched a couple of chopping boards and nodded to Art to take his place alongside her. 'Asking questions is what I do for a living.' She smiled, not looking at him. 'So you'll have to excuse me if I'm asking you a lot of them.'

Art was busy looking at the bundle of onions and tomatoes neatly piled in front of him. He held the knife and began fumbling his way to something that only laughably resembled food preparation. He only realised that she had stopped what she had been doing and was staring at him when she said with amusement, 'You haven't got a clue, have you?'

'These bloody things are making my eyes sting.'

'They have a nasty habit of doing that,' Rose agreed. 'And you're in for a rough ride if you intend to take a couple of hours dicing them. By the way, you need to dice them a whole lot smaller.'

'You're having fun, aren't you?'

'I'm thinking you look like a man who doesn't know his way round a kitchen very well.'

'Like I said, cooking has never appealed.'

'Not even when you're relaxing with someone and just having fun preparing a meal together?'

'I don't go there,' Art said flatly. He gave the onion a jaundiced look and decided to attack the tomatoes, which seemed a safer bet. 'I don't do domestic.'

'You don't *do* domestic? What does that mean?'

'It means that I don't share those cosy moments you've just described.'

'Why not?' she asked lightly.

'I don't do personal questions either.'

Looking into the ancient mirrored tiles that lined the counter, Art noted her pink cheeks. He met her eyes to find her staring at him, her pink cheeks going even pinker. She looked away hurriedly to continue slicing and dicing. Strands of her wildly curly hair fell around her face and she blew some of them out of her eyes, blatantly making sure *not* to look in those mirrored squares in case she caught his eye again.

'You don't do cosy and domestic,' Rose said slowly, swivelling to lean against the counter, arms folded, eyes narrowed, 'and you don't do personal questions. So, if I'm joining the dots correctly, you don't invite women to ask you why you're not prepared to play happy families with them.'

'Something like that.' Art shrugged. He was sharp enough to realise that there was no way he would ever get her onside if he came across as the sort of unliberated dinosaur she would clearly despise.

'No cooking together…no watching telly entwined on a sofa…'

'I definitely do the *entwined* bit,' Art joked. Rose failed to return his smile.

'You don't want to encourage any woman to think you're going to be in it for the long haul because you're a commitment-phobe.'

'I could lie and tell you that you're way off target there,' Art drawled, holding her stare, 'but I won't do you the disservice.'

'I like that,' Rose said slowly, not taking her eyes off him.

'Which bit?'

'The honesty bit. In my line of work, I see a lot of scumbags who are happy to lie through their teeth to get what they want. It's laudable that you're at least honest when it comes to saying what you think.'

'You're giving me more credit than I'm due.' Art stopped what he was doing and let his eyes rove over her. Her skin was satiny smooth and make-up-free. 'I like the way you look,' he murmured. 'I like the fact that you're completely natural. No warpaint. No pressing need to clone yourself on the lines of a certain doll. Really works.'

Rose glanced at him and looked away hurriedly. Those dark eyes, she thought, could open a lot of boxes and kick-start a whole host of chain reactions and she might not know how to deal with them.

Rose wasn't ready for a relationship with anyone and she certainly wasn't up for grabs when it came to any man who was a commitment-phobe. *Thanks, but no thanks.* Enjoying this man's company was a wonderful distraction but anything more than that was not going to be on the table.

She had to shake herself mentally and laugh inwardly at her fanciful thoughts; it wasn't as though she was in danger of any advances from this passing stranger, who had been nothing but open and polite with her!

And even if he *had* made any suggestive remarks then she would, of course, knock him back regardless of whether he was a drop of excitement in her otherwise pleasantly predictable life.

She was careful. When it came to men, she didn't dive head first into the water because you never knew what was lurking under the surface.

With the electrifying feel of those dark eyes broodingly watching her, Rose breathed in deep and remembered all the life lessons from her past. Remembered her mother, who had gone off the rails when Rose's father had died. She'd lost her love and she had worked her way through her grief with catastrophic consequences, flinging herself headlong into a series of doomed relationships. Rose had been a child at the time but she could remember the carousel of inappropriate men and the apprehension she had felt every time that doorbell had sounded.

Then Alison Tremain had fallen in love—head over heels in love—with a rich, louche member of the landed gentry who had promised her everything she'd been desperate to hear. God only knew what she'd been thinking. She'd been hired to clean the exquisite Cotswold cottage owned by his parents, where he and twelve other fast-living friends had been staying for a long weekend. Had her mother really thought that it was love? But he'd swept her off her feet and maybe, Rose had later thought, when she had looked back at events through adult eyes, his heart had been in the right place.

The two had hurtled towards one another for all the wrong reasons. Rose's mother because she'd wanted an anchor in her life. She'd been swimming against the tide and had been on the verge of drowning and he had given her something to hold onto and she hadn't looked further than the wild promises he'd made.

And he…he'd wanted to rebel against restrictive parents and Alison Tremain had been his passport to asserting authority over a life that had been dictated from birth. Their disapproval would underline his independence, would prove that he could choose someone outside the box and damn the consequences. Brimming over with left-wing principles, he would be able to ditch the upper-crust background into which he had been born.

It had been a recipe for disaster from the word *go* and, for Rose, the personal disaster had started when her mother had dumped her with their neighbour: *'Just for a bit...just until I'm sorted...and then I'll come to fetch you, that's a promise.'*

Everyone had rallied around as she had found herself suddenly displaced—the benefit of a small community—but there had been many times when she had entered a room unexpectedly to be greeted by hushed whispers and covert, pitying looks.

Rose knew that things could have been a lot worse. She could have ended up in care. As it was, she spent nearly two years with the neighbours, whose daughter went to the same school as her.

Her mother had written and Rose had waited patiently but by the time a much-chastened Alison had returned to the village Rose had grown into a cautious young girl, conscious of the perils of letting her emotions rule her life.

She'd witnessed her mother going off the rails because of a broken heart and had lived through her disappearing and getting lost in a world, she later learned, of soft drugs and alcohol because Spencer Kurtis had been unable to cope with the daily demands of a life without money on tap. So much for his rebellion. He had eventually crawled back to the family pile and Alison Tremain had returned to village life, where it had taken her a further year to recover before she was properly back to the person she had once been.

Rose knew better than to ever allow her behaviour to be guided by emotion. Sensible choices resulted in a settled life. Her sensible choices when it came to men, all two of them, might not have worked out but that didn't mean that she was going to rethink her ground plan.

She also knew better than to trust any man with money and time had only served to consolidate that opinion.

Her mother had been strung along by a rich man and in the end he hadn't been able to tear himself away from his wealthy background. But, beyond the story of one insignificant person, Rose had seen how, time and again, the wealthy took what they wanted without any thought at all for the people they trampled over.

The community that had rallied around her was, over the years, being invaded because developers couldn't keep their hands away from the temptation to take what was there and turn it into money-making projects. Their little oasis in the Cotswolds was achingly pretty and was also close enough to Oxford to save it from being too unremittingly rural.

In a very real sense, Rose felt that she owed a duty to the small community that had embraced her when her mother had started acting erratically and that included saving it from the whims of rich developers.

She was, for the first time in her life, sorely tempted to explain all of this to the ridiculously good-looking guy who, she noted wryly, had completely abandoned all attempts at vegetable preparation and was now pushing himself away from the counter to hunt down whatever wine was in the fridge.

'I never know what's there,' Rose said, half turning. 'The fridge has ended up being fairly communal property. Once a week someone has a go at tossing out whatever has gone past its sell-by date and everyone more or less tries to replace what's been taken so that we never find ourselves short of essentials like milk.'

'Doesn't that bug you?'

'No. Why should it?'

'Maybe because this is your house and a man's house should be his castle? What's the point of a castle if you let down the ramparts every two seconds to welcome in invaders? Who go through your belongings like gannets? Is this wine common property? Who does it belong to?' He held up a cheap bottle of plonk, which was better than nothing.

'That's mine and on the subject of one's house being one's castle, I can't afford that luxury.' Rose wasn't looking at him as she delivered this observation. In the companionable peace of the kitchen it felt comfortable to chat and she realised that, yes, quite often she longed for the pleasure of having the house to herself. 'I'm just lucky that I have this place. It was given to my mum by…er…by a friend and when she died it was passed onto me…'

Arturo looked at her carefully, but his voice was casual enough when he next spoke.

'Generous gift,' he murmured. 'Boyfriend? Lover? That kind of friend?'

'Something like that.' Rose swivelled, took the wine from him and, having bunged all the vegetables and seasoning into a pan with some sauce, she edged towards the kitchen table, absently sweeping some of the papers away and stacking half-finished cardboard placards into a pile on the ground. 'You're doing it again.'

'Doing what?' Arturo sipped some wine and looked at her over the rim of the glass.

'Prying,' she said drily. 'Is that a habit of yours? No, don't answer that.' She raised her eyebrows and shot him a shrewd assessing look. 'You pry. I gathered that the second you started opening doors to rooms when you first arrived, wanting to find out what was going on where. Must be your nature.'

'Expertly summed up... I like to find things out. How else can anyone have an informed opinion unless they're in possession of all the facts?'

'You're very arrogant, aren't you?' But she laughed, seeing that as commendable in someone who felt passionate about what was happening in the world around him. Too many people were content to sit on the fence rather than take a stand. Digging deep and arriving at an informed opinion was what separated the doer from the thinker. 'I mean that if you don't encourage domesticity and you don't do much talking to women then it's unlikely you ask them many questions about what they think. So why,' she added, 'are you being so inquisitive with me?'

'Maybe because I've never met anyone like you before.'

'Is that a good thing?' Rose detected the breathless note in her voice with a shiver of alarm. She was mesmerised by the lazy smile that lightened the harsh beauty of his face.

'For me, it's…strangely exciting.'

Her eyelids fluttered and her breathing hitched and her whole body suddenly tingled as though she had been caressed.

Arturo looked at her with leisurely, assessing eyes. He was clearly used to having what he wanted when it came to women. She sensed it included immediate gratification.

'I… Look… I didn't ask you to stay here…because… because…' She cleared her throat and subsided into awkward silence.

'Of course not, but I'm not the only one feeling this thing, am I?'

'I don't know what you're talking about.'

'No? We'll run with that for the time being, shall we? Tell me about the house.'

Rose blinked. Somewhere along the line she'd stopped being the feisty lawyer with the social conscience and had morphed into…a gawky adolescent with a teenage crush on the cute new boy in class. The chemistry between them was overwhelming. It slammed into her like a fist and the fact that he felt it as well, felt *something* at any rate, only made the situation worse. She'd spent a lifetime protecting herself from her emotions getting the better of her, had approached men with wariness because she knew the sort of scars that could be inflicted when bad choices went horribly wrong. On no level could this man be described as anything but a bad choice. So why was she perspiring with nerves and frantically trying to shut down the slide show of what could happen if she gave in…?

'The house?' she parroted, a little dazed.

'You were telling me that you inherited the house… that your mother was given it…'

'Right.'

*And how had that come about?* she wondered. *When she was the last person who made a habit of blabbing about her personal life?*

Disoriented at the chaos of her thoughts, she set to finishing the meal—anything to tear her gaze away from his darkly compelling face—but her hand was shaking slightly as she began draining pasta and warming the sauce.

'My mother had a fling with a guy,' she said in a halting voice, breathing more evenly now that she wasn't gawping at him like a rabbit caught in the headlights.

'Happens…'

'Yes, it does.' She swung around to look him squarely in the eyes. 'Especially when you're in mourning for the man you thought you'd be sitting next to in your old age, watching telly and going misty-eyed over the great-grandchildren…'

'What do you mean?'

Rose sighed. 'Nothing.'

'Tell me more.' Art hadn't eaten home-cooked food in any kitchen with any woman for a very, very long time. He dug into the bowl of pasta with gusto, realising that he was a lot hungrier than he'd thought.

He was eating here, just a stranger passing through instead of a billionaire to be feared, feted and courted by everyone with whom he came into contact. This was what normality felt like. He could scarcely remember the feeling. He wondered whether this was why he was intensely curious about her because she, like this whole experience, represented something out of the ordinary. Or maybe, he decided, it just stemmed from the fact that no information he could glean from her would be put to waste, not when he had a job to do. This was all just part of the game and what else was life but an elaborate game? In which there would inevitably be winners and losers and when it came to winning Art was the leader of the pack.

Far more comfortable with that pragmatic explanation, Art shot her an encouraging look.

'It's no big deal.' Rose shrugged and twirled some spaghetti around her fork, not looking at him. 'My father died when I was quite young and for a while my mum went off the rails. Got involved with…well…it was—' she grimaced and blushed '—an interesting time all round. One of the guys she became involved with was a rich young minor aristocrat whose parents owned a massive property about ten miles away from here. It ended in tears but years later, out of the blue, she received this house in his will, much to everyone's surprise. He'd been handed swathes of properties on his twenty-fifth birthday and he left this house to Mum, never thinking he'd die in a motorbike accident when he was still quite young.'

'A tragedy with a fortunate outcome.' Art considered the parallels between their respective parents and felt a tug of admiration that she had clearly successfully navigated a troubled background. He had too, naturally, but he was as cold as ice and just as malleable. He had been an observant, together teenager and a controlled, utterly cool-headed adult. He'd also had the advantage of money, which had always been there whatever the efforts of his father's grasping ex-wives to deprive him of as much of it as they possibly could.

She, it would seem, was cut from the same cloth. When he thought of the sob stories some of his girl-friends had bored him with, he knew he'd somehow ended up summing up the fairer sex as hopeless when it came to dealing with anything that wasn't sunshine and roses.

'Guilty conscience,' Rose responded wryly. 'He really led my mother off the straight and narrow, and then dumped her for reasons that are just too long-winded to go into. Put it this way—' she neatly closed her knife and fork and propped her chin in the palm of her hand '—he introduced her to the wonderful world of drugs and drink and then ditched her because, in the end, he needed the family money a lot more than he needed her. He also loved the family money more than he could ever have loved *her*.'

'Charming,' Art murmured, his keen dark eyes pinned to the stubborn set of her wide mouth.

'Rich.'

'Come again?'

'He was rich so he figured he could do as he pleased and he did, not that it didn't work out just fine in the end. Mum…came home and picked up the pieces and she was a darn sight better off without that guy in her life.'

*'Came home…? Picked up the pieces…?'*

Rose flushed. 'She disappeared for a while,' she muttered, rising to clear the table.

'How long *a while*?'

'What does any of this have to do with the protest?'

'Like I told you, I'm a keen observer of human nature. I enjoy knowing what makes people tick...what makes them who they are.'

'I'm not a specimen on a petri dish,' she said with more of her usual spirit, and Art burst out laughing.

'You're not,' he concurred, 'which doesn't mean that I'm any the less curious. So talk to me. I don't do domestic and I don't do personal conversations but I'm sorely tempted to invite you to be the exception to my rule. My *one-off*, so to speak...'

# CHAPTER FOUR

*TELL ME MORE...*

Art bided his time. Curiosity battled with common sense. For some reason, over the next three days he kept wanting to return to the story of her past. His appetite to hear more had been whetted and it was all he could do to stamp down the urge to corner her and pry.

But that wasn't going to do.

He hadn't pursued the subject three days previously when his curiosity had been piqued because he had known that playing the waiting game was going to be a better bet.

He'd already gleaned one very important piece of information. She needed money. And while she might carry the banner of *money can't buy you happiness* and *the good things in life are free*, Art knew that reality had very sharp teeth.

The house was falling down around her and whilst she did get some money from the tenants, enough to cover the essentials, from what she had told him in dribs and drabs she simply didn't earn enough to keep things going.

And houses in this part of the world weren't cheap. He knew because he'd strolled through the village, taking in all the great little details that made it such a perfect place for an upmarket housing development.

He wondered whether he could offer her something tantalising to call off the protest. He might have to dump the fellow protestor guise and reveal his true identity or he could simply contrive to act as a middleman to broker a deal. At any rate, he played with the idea of contributing something towards the community, something close to her heart that would make her think twice about continuing a line of action that was never going to pay dividends. Harold had been right when he'd painted his doomsday picture of a close-knit, hostile community determined to fend off the rich intruders with their giant four-wheel drive wagons and their sense of entitlement. They'd be wrong but since when did right and wrong enter into the picture when emotions were running high?

And Art needed peace. He needed the community onside. He needed to get past this first stage of development to reach the important second stage. When he thought of the benefits of the equestrian and craft centre he hoped to develop, for his stepbrother and the small intake of similar adults like his stepbrother, he knew just how vital it was for him to win this war with the backing of the people waving the placards. If he barrelled through their protest with marching boots they would turn on him and all his long-term plans would lie in ruins.

He'd met all the people who were protesting and the majority of them had kids who attended the local school.

He could appeal to them directly, imply that the heartless developers might be forced to build a new school.

His role, he had made sure to establish, was a fluid one. He had gone from protestor in situ to keen observer of human nature and general do-gooder who cared about the environment. He'd been vague about his actual background but had somehow managed to imply that he was more than just a drifter out to attach himself to a worthwhile cause. He'd used his imagination and he knew that a lot of the protestors were beginning to turn to him to answer some of their questions.

It irked him that even as he tried to find a solution to the situation and even as he mentally worked out the cost of digging into his pocket to effectively buy them off when there was, technically, no need for him to do so, he was still managing to feel bloody guilty at his charade.

He'd had no idea his conscience was so hyperactive and it got on his nerves.

Although…he had to admit a certain desire to impress the woman he was sharing a house with—fistfuls of cash would mean she could do the improvements she needed. He was cynical enough to suspect that if sufficient hard cash was put on the table she would not be able to resist because she was human and humans were all, without exception, susceptible to the lure of money.

Trouble was, he had to content himself with the painting job she had delegated to him.

'You don't have to,' she had said two days previously, when she had led him to a part of the house that looked as though the cobwebs had set up camp the day after the final brick in the house had been laid. 'You pay rent and, believe me, that's sufficient help.'

But Art had felt obliged to make good on his vague assurances that he was capable of helping out.

Besides, painting the room was proving to be a valuable way of avoiding her because the more contact he had with her, the more interested he became in digging deeper, past the polite conversation they shared, usually in the company of a million other people. After that first night she had shared nothing more about herself. They had had no time alone together. Her house was apparently a magnet for every person in the village who had nothing better to do than drop by for a chat.

The night before, someone she had bumped into several weeks previously had shown up for an informal chat about a problem he was having with his new employer, who had taken over the company and was trying to get rid of all the old retainers by fair means or foul.

To Art's amazement, Rose had been happy to feed the guy and give him free advice. Little wonder she didn't have much money going spare when she failed to charge for most of her services.

Her absolute lack of interest in making money should have been anathema to him but the opposite appeared to be the case. The more she invited the world into her house, the more he wanted her to slam the front door so that he could have her all to himself.

Nothing to do with the reason he was here.

Just because…he wanted to have her all to himself.

He'd managed to find a couple of hours during which he'd touched base with several of his clients and answered a couple of urgent emails and then he'd done some painting.

Now, at a little after six-thirty, he stood back to inspect his efforts and was quietly pleased with what he had managed. The mucus shade of green was slowly being replaced by something off-white and bland. Big improvement.

Still in paint-spattered clothes, Art went downstairs, fully expecting to find a few more waifs and strays in the kitchen, but instead there was just Rose sitting at the kitchen table, poring over a file.

From the doorway, he stood and looked, giving in to the steady pulse of desire rippling through him like a forbidden drumbeat. She was frowning, her slender hands cupping her face as she peered down at the stack of papers in front of her. She reached to absently remove the clasp from her hair and he sucked in a sharp breath as it fell around her shoulders in a tumble of uncontrolled curls. Deep chestnut brown…shades of dark auburn…paler strands of toffee…a riot of vibrant colour that took his breath away.

For once she wasn't wearing something long and shapeless but instead a pair of faded blue jeans and an old grey cropped tee shirt and, from the way she was hunched over the table, he was afforded a tantalising glimpse of her cleavage.

She looked up, caught his eye and sat back.

She stretched and half yawned and the forbidden drumbeat surged into a tidal wave of primal desire.

No bra.

He could see the jut of her nipples against the soft

cotton and the caution he had been meticulously cultivating over the past few days disappeared in a puff of smoke.

His erection was as solid as a shaft of steel and he had to look away to gather himself for a few vital seconds or else risk losing the plot altogether.

'Took the afternoon off.' Rose smiled and stood up. 'Hence the casual gear. Drink? Tea? Coffee? Something stronger? I've actually gone out and bought some wine.'

'The rent I pay doesn't cover food. It's Friday. Allow me to take you out for a meal.'

Rose hesitated. She hadn't been out for a meal with a man for ages. She was twenty-eight years old and the thrills of her social life could be written on the back of a postage stamp.

'Restaurants will be packed out.' She laughed, anticipation bubbling up inside her. 'Tourists…'

'We can venture further afield. Name the place and I'll reserve a table.'

'Don't be silly. You don't have to…'

*'You don't have to…?'* Arturo shot her a wry look from under sooty lashes. 'Anyone who knows me at all would know that those four words would never apply to me because I make it my duty never to feel that I have to do anything I don't want to do. If I didn't want to take you out to dinner I would never have issued the invitation in the first place. Now, name the place.'

God, Rose thought, who would ever think that she would go for a guy who took charge? She was much more into the sensitive kind of guy who consulted and discussed. Arturo Frank couldn't have been less of a consulting and discussing man, and yet a pleasurable shiver rippled through her as she met his deep, dark eyes. 'Name the place? Now, let me think about that. How generous are you feeling tonight…?'

Rose shocked herself because she wasn't flirtatious by nature. Her mother had always been the flirt, which was probably why she had ended up where she had. That was a characteristic Rose had made sure to squash, not that there had ever been any evidence of it being there in the first place.

But she felt like a flirt as their eyes tangled and she half smiled with her head tilted pensively to one side.

'I'm just kidding.' She grinned and ran her fingers through her tangled hair. 'There are a couple of excellent pizza places in the next village along. I can call and reserve a table. So…in answer to your invitation, it's a yes.'

'I'm saying no to the cheap and cheerful pizza place,' Arturo delivered with a dismissive gesture, eyes still glued to her face.

'In that case…'

'Leave it with me. I'll sort it.'

'You will?'

'Expect something slightly more upmarket than a fast-food joint.'

'In which case, I'll naturally share the bill.'

'That won't be happening. When I ask a woman out, she doesn't go near her wallet.'

There she went, tingling all over again! Behaving like the frothy, frilly, girly girl she had never been. He was so macho, so alpha male, so incredibly intelligent, and yet he cared about all the things she cared about. She prided herself on being savvy but she could feel the ground slip beneath her feet and she liked the way it felt, enjoyed the heady sensation of falling.

She wasn't interested in any man who was just passing through, but a little voice asked inside her head… *What if she took a risk?* After all, where had being careful got her?

And an even more treacherous little voice whispered seductively, *What if he delays his plans to move on…? In the end all nomads found their resting ground, didn't they? And there were jobs aplenty for a guy as smart and proactive as he was…*

'Okay.'

'You look a little bemused. What kind of guys have you gone out with in the past? Did they take out their calculator at the end of the meal so that they could split the bill in half? Call me antiquated—' his voice lowered to a murmur '—but I enjoy being generous with the women I take out.'

*So we're going on a date.*

Excitement surged through Rose in a disturbing, all-consuming tidal wave.

Maybe—she brought herself back down to earth—it wasn't a date. As such. Maybe it was simply his way of saying thank you for renting a room in her house and having whatever food and drink he wanted at his disposal. He was paying her a lot more than she'd wanted but it was still a lot less than if he'd been staying in even the cheapest of the local hotels.

But the warmth of his gaze was still turning her head

to mush when, an hour later and with no idea where they would be going, she stood in front of her wardrobe surveying the uninspiring collection of comfortable clothes that comprised her going-out gear.

It bore witness to the alarming fact that when it came to going out she had become decidedly lazy over time. Easy evenings with friends, the occasional movie, casual suppers at the kitchen table, for which she could have shown up in her PJs and no one would really have cared one way or the other.

In fact, working largely from the house as she did, her work clothes were interchangeable with her casual wear. Everything blurred into loose-fitting and shapeless.

*Practical*, she reminded herself, hand brushing past the baggy culottes to linger on the one and only figure-hugging skirt she possessed. Her wardrobe was filled with practical clothes because she was, above all else, practical. Her mother had had the monopoly on impulsive behaviour. She, Rose, was practical.

Yet she didn't feel practical as she wriggled into the clinging jade-green skirt and the only slightly less clinging black top with the little pearl buttons down the front, the top four of which she undid. Then promptly did back up.

There was little she could do with her hair, but she liked the way it hung in a riot of curls over her shoulders, and when she plunged her feet into her one and only pair of high-heeled shoes…well, she would have dwarfed a lot of men but she wasn't going to dwarf the one who would be waiting for her downstairs.

In fact, she would be elevated to his level. Eye to eye…nose to nose.…*mouth to mouth*…

Waiting for her in the kitchen with a glass of wine in his hand, Art was just off the phone from one of the finest restaurants in the area. He wasn't sure how he was going to explain away the extravagance but he was sick of mealtimes being pot luck, along the lines of a bring-and-buy sale in someone's backyard.

He was also sick of conversations with her being halted by someone popping their head around the door. She worked from her house and so seemed accessible to any and everyone. While he had been busy planting questions in the heads of all those protestors squatting on his land in the misguided belief that they were going to halt the march of progress, he hadn't actually got around to planting a single question in Rose's head because he never seemed to find the time to be alone with her for longer than five seconds.

He was also disgruntled and frustrated at the tantalising glimpses of her personal life which he had been unable to explore. He accepted that that was just thwarted curiosity but it was still frustrating. He existed on a diet of being able to get exactly what he wanted, and that included a woman's full and undivided attention.

She had told him something about herself and he had found himself wanting to hear more and had been unable to. When had that ever happened before? Given half a chance, there was no woman he could think of who wouldn't have clawed her way back to that interrupted personal conversation with the tenacity of a tigress.

But no. It was almost as though Rose had more pressing things to do than talk to him.

And yet…there was *something* between them. He felt it and so did she. It was just not big enough for her to actually put herself out to try to cultivate it and that irked him.

All in all, he was looking forward to this meal out more than he could remember looking forward to anything in a long time.

He swirled the wine in his glass, looked down at the golden liquid and then, when he looked up…

There she was.

Art straightened. His mouth fell open. Rooted to the spot, he could feel the throb of sexual awareness flower and bloom into something hot and urgent and pressing.

She was…bloody *stunning*.

That body, long-limbed and rangy under the challenging attire, was spectacular. Lean and toned and effortlessly graceful. She lacked the practised art of the catwalk model, the strutting posture and the moody expression, and she was all the sexier for that.

And she wasn't wearing a bra.

He did his utmost not to stare at the small, rounded pertness of her breasts and the indentation of pebbly nipples pushing against the fine cotton.

He could see Rose's whole body react to that leisurely appraisal and the horrified look on her face which accompanied her involuntary response. It galvanised her into speech and action at the same time, moving into the kitchen whilst simultaneously pinning a bright smile to her face as she quizzed him on where they were going.

Art snapped out of his trance.

'I'll just grab my bag.' She interrupted her nervous chatter to look around her.

'Why?'

'Car keys, for one thing!' she announced gaily.

The kitchen felt too small for both of them to be in it. He was wearing nothing more than a pair of dark trousers and a white shirt, staple components of any wardrobe, and yet he looked jaw-droppingly beautiful. He filled the contours of the shirt to perfection. She could see the ripple of muscle under the fabric and he had rolled the sleeves up so that her eyes were drawn to his forearms, liberally sprinkled with dark, silky hair. The minute her eyes went there they couldn't help but move further along to his long brown fingers and it was then a hop and a skip until she wondered what those fingers would feel like…*on her* and…*in her.*

'What? Sorry?'

*Had he said something?*

'I've ordered a taxi so there's no need for you to drive,' he delivered smoothly, allowing her no time to lodge a protest.

'You're so good at taking over,' Rose murmured, blushing and smiling.

'I can't help it,' Arturo said without apology. 'It's part of my personality.'

He lowered his eyes and offered his arm to her.

'It's been a while since…'

'Since?'

'Since I've been out for a meal.'

'You mean…on a date?'

'Is that what this is?' They were outside and he was opening the car door for her, waiting as she slid into the back seat before joining her. 'I thought…' she turned to him and breathed in the clean, woody smell of him, which made her want to pass out '…that this was just your way of thanking me for putting you up. Not—' she laughed '—that it's been any bother at all!'

'That as well…'

'You needn't have.'

'Again. Those annoying words. It's not a declaration of intent,' he interjected, then his voice lowered. 'It's a… I haven't told you, but you look…remarkable…'

'I know it's not a declaration of intent! You're just passing through and, besides, you're the guy who doesn't do domesticity, home cooking or women asking personal questions. And thank you for the compliment, by the way. I… I haven't worn this old outfit in a long time.'

Her breathing was jerky and she took refuge in gazing through the window at the familiar countryside. She had no idea where they were going, but it wasn't long before she found out because she recognised the impressive drive that led to one of the top hotels in the county, where a famous Michelin-starred chef produced food she could never have afforded in a million years.

She turned to him, her face a picture of bemusement and shock.

'I recently came into some money,' Arturo said smoothly, 'and I can't think of a better way of spending some of it than on bringing you here.'

'I'm not dressed for this place.'

'Do you care what other people think?' He swung out of the car and walked around to open her door.

'Who doesn't?'

'I don't.'

'Maybe it's a legacy from when my mum went away.' Rose was agog as they were shown into the splendid hotel and then escorted like royalty to the most impressive dining room she had ever been in. She was hardly aware of what she was saying. She was way too focused on trying to take in everything around her.

'You were saying…?' he said as soon as they were seated, a corner table with a bird's eye view of the richly ornate interior.

'I was saying that my eyes are popping out.' She swivelled to look at him and her breathing became shallow. What money, she wondered, had he come into? But then, hot on the heels of that thought, came another—her mother had been the recipient of an equally surprising inheritance. Stranger things happened in life. It certainly explained how he was footloose and fancy free…and able to indulge his interest in saving the countryside.

And if he was generous by nature, as he clearly was, then he would probably travel around until the cash ran out before returning to whatever job he had had before. That was a small detail he had never filled her in on.

He'd warned her off reading anything into this dinner invitation but he was crazy if he thought that she wasn't going to be impressed to death by his generosity and by the time and effort he'd put into sourcing this place for them. God only knew how he'd managed to wangle a table but she had seen, in his interactions with the people on the site, that he could charm the birds from the trees.

'And you were telling me why it is that you care about what people think…'

Rose looked at him. He'd shaved but still managed to look darkly dangerous. There was a stillness about him that made her nerves race and brought a fine prickle of perspiration to her skin. Something about the lazy intensity of his eyes when they focused on her.

'And how long did your mother go away for?'

'Two years,' Rose admitted, flattered at his interest.

'Two *years*?'

'I know in the big scheme of things it doesn't seem like a lifetime but, believe me, when you're a kid and you're waiting by the window it *feels* never-ending.'

'In the big scheme of things it bloody *is* never-ending, Rose, and to a kid… How old *were* you?'

'Eight.'

'Eight.' Art was shocked. His father had lost the plot for very similar reasons, which pretty much said everything there was to say on the subject of love, but abandonment had not been an issue. 'Where did you stay… at the age of eight…while your mother vanished on her soul-seeking mission?'

'You shouldn't be too hard on her. She was screwed up at the time. I stayed in the village, of course. Where else? I lived with the neighbours. I'm not sure whether they thought that they'd be hanging onto me for as long as they had to but they were wonderful. That said, I knew there was gossip and that hurt. I was saved from a much harsher fate when my mother started acting up because I happened to live where I did. In a small village that protected its own. I owe them.'

'You owe them…the entire village…a sizeable debt. So…' this half to himself '…*that's* why this fight is so personal to you.'

'Something like that. But you must be bored stiff listening to me rattle on.'

'The opposite.' Art forced himself to relax. All problems had solutions and he was solution-orientated. 'I've wandered through the village,' he said, adroitly changing the subject as he perused the menu without looking at her. 'I'm surprised you haven't thought to use a little bribery and blackmail with the developers who want the land you're occupying…'

'Sorry?' Rose's head shot up and she stared at him with a frown.

'You recall I asked Phil to have a look at the paperwork? Not because I'm any kind of expert, but I wanted to see for myself what the legal position was with the land. Some of the protesters out there have been asking questions…'

'You never mentioned that to me.'

'Should I have? Passing interest. Nothing more.' Art paused. 'The land is sold and there's nothing anyone can do about that.'

'You'd be surprised how public opinion can alter the outcome of something unpleasant.' Rose's lips firmed. She wasn't sure whether to fume at his intrusion or be pleased at his intelligent interest in the situation.

'People might be open to alternative lines of approach,' he implied, shutting his menu and sitting back.

'You're very optimistic if you think that a company the size of DC Logistics would be interested in anything other than steamrollering over us. We're fighting fire with fire and if we lose…then we can make sure that life isn't easy for them as they go ahead with their conscienceless development.'

'Or you could try another tack. Apparently the local school could do with a lot of refurbishment. The sports ground is in dire need of repair. One section of the building that was damaged by fire last year is still out of bounds. Frankly, that's a lawsuit waiting to happen. Ever thought that instead of threatening a company that has deeds to the land, you could always coerce them into doing their bit for the community?'

'You've certainly been digging deep.' Rose sat back and looked at Art. 'Have you been discussing this alternative with my protestors?'

'They're not *your* protestors,' he fielded coolly, meeting her gaze without blinking. 'If you have deeper, more personal reasons for your fight, then they don't necessarily share those reasons. They might be open to other ways of dealing with the situation.'

Wine was being brought to the table. He waited until the waiter had poured them both a glass then he raised his.

'But enough of this. We're not here to talk about the land, are we? That said…it's just something you might want to think about.'

# CHAPTER FIVE

IT WAS THE best meal she had ever had in her life although, as she reluctantly left a morsel of the *crème brulée* in its dish because she physically couldn't manage another mouthful, Rose had to admit that it was much more than the quality of the food that had made the evening quite perfect.

It was the fact that she was here with Arturo.

They had not had an opportunity to talk, to really talk, since he had moved in and for four hours they more than made up for that. He was fascinating. He knew *so much*. He could converse with ease on any topic and he had a wonderful knack of drawing her out of herself, making her open up in a way that revealed to her just how private she had become over the years.

He could be self-deprecating one minute and, almost without pausing to draw breath, ruin the illusion by being astoundingly arrogant—but arrogant in a way that somehow didn't manage to get on her nerves. She couldn't understand how that was in any way, shape or form possible...but it clearly was.

And he'd made her think—about the protest and

other ways that might be found to bring about a positive outcome. He had touched only once more on the subject and the notion of inevitability had been aired—yes, it was inevitable that the land would be developed, but that suggestion he had planted in her head was beginning to look quite promising. She had certain trump cards and there was much that could be done to improve the village.

She was tipsy and happy as they stepped out into the velvety black night.

'I haven't had such a lovely time in ages,' she confided as a taxi pulled to a stop as soon as they were outside. She waited until he was in the back seat with her before turning to him. The darkness turned his face into a mosaic of hard shadows and angles and, just for a few seconds, she felt a tingle of apprehension that warred with the warm, melting feeling making her limbs heavy and pleasantly blurring her thoughts.

She was smiling—grinning like a Cheshire cat—but he was quite serious as he looked at her.

'You look as though you can't wait for the evening to end,' she said lightly, sobering up, smile wavering. 'Don't blame you. You must be accustomed to far more exciting company than me.'

Looking back at her, Art thought that she couldn't have been further from the truth. He hadn't sat and talked with any woman for that length of time for years. In the normal course of events, an expensive meal would have included some light conversation but the evening would have been overlaid with the assumption of sex and the conversation would have been geared towards that.

'What makes you say that?'

'Something about you,' Rose admitted truthfully. 'You're not like anyone I've ever met before and if I can see that, then so can everyone else. You strike me as the sort of guy who's never short of female company. Is that why you steer clear of involvement? Because you don't see the point of settling down when there are so many fish in the sea?'

'I steer clear of involvement because I watched my father ruined by too much of it.'

'Oh.' Rose paused. 'How so?' she asked seriously.

Art had surprised himself by that admission and now he wondered what to say. A series of divorces? A carousel of avaricious blonde bombshells who had been out to feather their own nests? A fortune depleted by the demands of alimony payments? Where to start?

Art had been defined by one disillusionment after another, from the isolation he had had to endure as a child when his father had retreated into himself after his wife's sudden death to the abruptness of having to deal with boarding school, and all played out to the steady drumbeat of his father's failed relationships and the consequent, expensive fallout.

He shifted, stared briefly out of the window then back at her. Her gaze was calm, interested but without fuss and fanfare—curious but not overly so.

'My father had a habit of repeating his mistakes,' Art told her heavily. 'He was always quick to get involved, only to regret his involvement but then, just when he'd managed to free himself from one woman, he would repeat the cycle all over again. Your mother had her way of coping with losing her husband…' His mouth twisted into a crooked smile. 'My father coped in a slightly different way.'

'But in a way that would have equally damaging consequences… We certainly didn't strike jackpot when it came to childhood experiences, did we?' She shot him a rueful smile and reached out, almost impulsively, to rest her hand on his.

The warmth of her hand zapped through him like a powerful electric charge, tightening his groin and sending a heavy, pounding ache between his thighs.

With relief, he recognised that the taxi was pulling up outside her house.

He was in urgent need of a cold shower. Maybe even a cold bath. Blocks of ice would have to play a part. Anything to cool the onset of his ardour.

'All experience,' he said neutrally, pushing open his door and glancing back at her over his shoulder in a gesture that implied an end to the conversation, 'is good experience, in my opinion. But I'm very glad you enjoyed the evening.'

He all but sprinted to the front door. She fumbled with the front door key and he relieved her of it, acutely aware of the brush of her skin against his.

'I don't usually drink as much as I did tonight,' Rose apologised with a little breathy laugh, stepping past him into the hall. 'I'm beginning to think that I should get out more, live a little…'

'All work and no play… You know the saying…'

* * *

For a few moments they both stood in the semi-darkened hallway, staring at one another in taut silence, and the breath caught in her throat because she could see the lick of desire in his eyes, a sexual speculation that set her ablaze with frantic desire because it mirrored her own.

'Right, well…' Rose was the first to break the lengthening silence. 'Thanks again for a brilliant evening…' She began turning away but then felt his hand circle her arm and she stilled, heart racing, pulse racing—*everything* racing.

'Rose…'

With one foot planted firmly in the comfort zone of common sense and the other dangling precariously and recklessly over the edge of a precipice, Rose looked at him, holding herself rigid with tension.

'It would be madness.' Arturo looked away, looked back to her, looked away again, restless and uncomfortable in his own skin and yet powerless to relieve either discomfort.

'What?' Rose whispered.

'You know what. This. Us. Taking this any further.'

For a few seconds she didn't say anything, then eventually she murmured, briefly breaking their electrifying eye contact, 'I agree.'

'You can't even begin to understand the complications…'

'Do I need to?'

'Explain.'

'We're not anticipating a relationship.' She tilted her

chin at a defiant angle. Sex for the sake of sex? She'd never contemplated that. The urgent demands of lust, the taste of a passion that was powerful enough to make a nonsense of her principles…well, those were things that had never blotted her horizon. 'We don't have to think about all the complications or all the reasons why it wouldn't make sense for us to…to…' She reddened and caught his eye.

'Make wild, passionate love until we just can't any longer?'

'You're just passing through…'

'Sure that doesn't bother you? Because I won't be staying. A week, tops, and I'll be gone and that'll be the last you'll ever see of me.'

'You wouldn't be curious to see where the protest you joined will end up?'

'I know where it'll end up.' He clearly didn't want to talk about that. He raised his arm to stroke her cheek with the back of his hand, a light, feathery touch that made her sigh and close her eyes.

'Let's go upstairs,' she breathed unevenly, her eyes fluttering open to gaze at his impossibly handsome face. She stepped back and took his hand. If this was wrong, then why did it feel so *right*? Before hitting the stairs, she kicked her shoes off and then padded up ahead of him, still holding his hand, glancing back over her shoulder twice, wishing that she knew what was going through his head.

She shyly pushed open her bedroom door and stepped in, ignoring the overhead light in favour of the lamp by her bed, which cast an immediate mellow glow through the room.

It was a large square room, with high ceilings and both picture rails and dado rails.

Arturo had not been in it before. He looked around briefly and then grinned. 'I didn't take you for having such a sense of drama…'

Rose laughed, walked towards him and linked her arms around his waist. 'I'm sensible when it comes to pretty much everything but—' she looked at the dreamy four-poster king-sized bed with floaty curtains and dark, soft-as-silk bed linen '—I used to dream of having a four-poster bed when I was a kid.'

'Was that when you were waiting for your mother to reappear?' Art murmured, burying his face into her hair and breathing in the sweet smell of the floral shampoo she used.

'How did you guess?'

'I'm tuned in like that.' A memory came from nowhere to knock him for six—a memory of his mother leaning over him, smiling, with a book in one hand. Had she just read him a story? Was she about to? She was dressed up, going out for the evening.

He clenched his jaw as the vivid image faded. 'Enough talk,' he growled, edging them both towards the bed. Rose giggled as her knees hit the mattress and she toppled backwards, taking him with her, although he niftily deflected the bulk of his weight from landing directly on her. But he remained where he was, flat on his back next to her.

'The canopy has stars,' he commented, amused, and he heard the grin in her voice when she replied.

'That's the hidden romantic in me.'

Art turned his head to look at her and she did likewise.

'You don't have to worry,' she said flatly, before he could jump in with another warning lecture on his nomadic tendencies—warning her off the temptation to look for more involvement than was on the table.

'Worry about what?'

'I may have the occasional romantic lapse, but I'm pretty level-headed when it comes to men, and latching onto a good-looking guy who has an aversion to putting down roots is the last sort of guy who would tick any boxes for me.'

'I tick at least *one* box,' Art murmured, smiling very slowly.

'Well, yes…you tick that one box.' Flustered, she held her breath as their eyes locked.

'Never knock the physical attraction box. It's the biggest one of all.'

'We'll have to agree to differ on that.'

'Think so?' Art grinned, settling on his side and manoeuvring her so that they were now facing one another, clothes still on and that very fact sending the temperature into the sizzling stratosphere. 'Oh, I wouldn't talk too fast if I were you…' He slipped his hand under her top and took his time getting to her breast, waiting until her breathing had become halting, her eyelids fluttering and her nostrils flaring. Then and only then did he touch her, cup her naked breast, feel the tight bud of her nipple. He'd spent the meal in a state of heightened awareness and the feel of her now was electrifying.

While he was busy telling her just how fast he could make her believe in the importance of sexual attraction because nothing was better than good sex, and he was very, *very* adept at giving very, *very* good sex, he was simultaneously on the verge of blowing it by getting turned on too quickly. In his book, speed and good sex rarely went together for a sensational experience.

He kept looking at her, holding her gaze, while he played with her nipple.

He wasn't going to go a step further until he got himself under control.

But, hell, those sexy eyes that were just on the right side of innocent, however sassy she was, were doing a million things to his body.

'You think you can convert me?' Rose breathed, squirming with want.

'No harm in trying.' Art let loose a low, sexy laugh. In one slick movement, he eased himself up to straddle her prone body, caging her in with his thighs. He hooked his fingers under the top and began slowly tugging it up.

'No bra,' he murmured. 'I like that.'

'I...' Rose gulped and wished that she hadn't switched any lights on at all, although would she have sacrificed the joy of looking at him to preserve her modesty? She felt faint as her top rode higher and then the whisper of cool air brought goosebumps to her naked skin. Automatically, she lifted her arms to cross them over her bare chest and, just as fast, Arturo gently pushed them aside and stifled a primal groan of pleasure as his eyes feasted on her.

'Beautiful,' he whispered, circling one straining bud with the tip of his finger.

Rose had never felt quite so exposed. She wasn't ashamed of her body. She simply recognised its limitations. Lights off worked when it came to dealing with those limitations and to have him looking at her like that...

She sneaked a glance at him and felt a surge of thrilling excitement because his eyes were dark with masculine appreciation.

'I'm not exactly the most voluptuous woman on the face of the earth,' Rose apologised, blushing. 'That's why I can go without a bra a lot of the time. Not much there to contain.' She laughed and watched his finger as it continued to circle her nipple, moving onto the other.

'You should never have hang-ups about your body,' Arturo said thickly. 'It's amazing. Your nipples are stunning...dark...*succulent*...'

'Arturo!'

He laughed and shot her a wicked look from under his lashes. 'Is that the sound of you begging me to continue telling you why you should be proud of your body?'

'No!' But she laughed, a little breathless laugh that was unsteady with anticipation.

'I'm going to have fun tasting them,' Arturo told her conversationally. 'Does it turn you on to imagine the feel of my mouth on your nipple?'

'Stop!'

'You're red as a beetroot.' Arturo grinned and gently tilted her averted face so that she was looking at him.

He vaulted off the bed, fumbled to make sure protection was handy and then he began getting undressed.

Rose stared.

She forgot all about her inhibitions because never had she seen anything so glorious in her life before.

He was all muscle and sinew, his broad shoulders tapering to a washboard-flat stomach. He ditched the shirt and raised his eyebrows with amusement at her rapt expression.

'You have no idea,' he murmured, taking a step towards her, at which she promptly hoisted herself onto her elbows, automatically leaning towards him, 'what that expression is doing to my libido.'

'Really?' Riveted, Rose continued to stare at him.

'Really,' Arturo said drily, 'but you'll see for yourself soon enough…' He burst out laughing when her eyes skittered away just as he began unbuttoning his trousers.

He seemed to revel in the intensity of her gaze.

The trousers were off.

The boxers followed suit.

Rose gulped. He was more than impressive. Big, thick, throbbing with *want*. Standing there, he was absolutely lacking in inhibition, carelessly indifferent to the perfection of his nakedness.

Rose sat up, then slid off the bed to stand in front of him. She was half naked and now all she wanted to do was yank down the skirt but, before she could, he stayed her fluttering hand and moved towards her, holding her just for a moment so that she could feel his hardness pressing against her belly.

'Allow me…' he murmured.

Arturo wasn't going to rush anything, even though his body must be clamouring for satisfaction.

He eased the skin-tight skirt off her to reveal plain cotton panties. For a few seconds, Arturo stilled.

He was kneeling and he drew back to look at her. Hands on her bare bottom, Arturo delicately teased the folds of her womanhood with a gentle touch, causing her to gasp and then exhale on a whimper.

When his tongue slid into the slippery crease she gasped again, this time on a guttural moan, and her fingers curled into his hair as she opened her legs wider to receive his attentions.

Rose was melting. Every bone in her body was turning to water as his tongue flicked over her, squirming deeper until he located the pulsing bud of her core.

The pleasure was intense, unbearable almost, nothing that she had ever felt before or could ever have imagined feeling. It was pure sensation and every thought, confused or otherwise, shot straight out of her head.

She realised that she was moving against his mouth in an unconscious rhythm.

She almost squeaked a protest when he drew back and stood up to lift her off her feet so that he could deposit her onto the bed, as though she weighed nothing at all.

Rose was expecting something fast and furious but instead he pinned her hands above her head, ordered her not to move a muscle and then sat back on his haunches to gaze at her with open admiration.

If this was how he was in bed with a woman, she thought in a heated daze, then she was surprised that there wasn't a demanding queue of ex-lovers banging on her front door, braying for him to return to bed with them.

'Just for the moment,' he said huskily, 'indulge me and allow me to take charge.'

With her hands still above her head, burrowed underneath the pillow, Rose half smiled.

'Are you trying to tell me that you don't take charge in everything you do?' she teased, 'because if you are then I don't believe you.'

'It's true. Some people have accused me of occasionally being somewhat…assertive.'

He seemed determined to assert himself right now. Starting with her breasts.

He kissed them, nuzzled their softness, making her writhe and stretch underneath him, her movements feline and sensuous. He licked one nipple with his tongue and then sucked on it, drawing it into his mouth and teasing the sensitive tip with his tongue. As he ministered to her breast, he dipped down to rest his hand between her thighs, lightly covering her mound with the palm of his hand and then pressing down in lazy circular movements.

Bliss.

Rose was dripping wet and she didn't care. She was explosively turned on. Something about the position of her arms heightened the sensitivity of her breasts and each flick of his tongue and caress of his hand made her want to cry out loud.

He trailed a path of kisses along her stomach and she inhaled sharply, wanting more than anything for him to taste her *down there* again, there between her legs where the ache desperately craved his touch.

As he found that place and began, once again, to tease her with his tongue, she arched up, spread her legs wider and bucked against his questing mouth.

Sensation started with an electric ripple that spread outwards with the force of a tsunami until she was lost in a world dictated by her physical response to his mouth. She could no more have strung a coherent thought together than she could have grown wings and taken flight.

When she came against his mouth it was with such force that she cried out, hands clutching the bed linen, her whole body arching, stiffening and then shuddering as everything exploded inside her.

She eventually subsided on a wave of mind-blowing contentment.

'Felt good?' Arturo lay alongside her, then curved her against him, pushing his thigh between her legs.

Rose linked her fingers around his neck and darted some kisses over his face. 'I'm sorry.' She looked at him with such genuine apology that he winced.

'Sorry about what?'

'Just lying there and…um…enjoying myself…'

'You have no idea how much enjoyment I got from pleasuring you.'

Rose smiled and curved against him, taking the initiative this time, adoring the hard, muscled lines of his body as she ran her hands over it. Along his shoulders, over his hard, sinewy chest, taking time to tease his flattened brown nipples.

His erection was thick and pulsing and she lowered herself into a position where she could take him into her mouth and he, manoeuvring her, could take her into his.

An exchange of intense pleasure that brought her right back up to the edge from which she had only recently descended.

Rose had never experienced such a lack of inhibition. She had always approached the opposite sex from a position of caution, a place where mechanisms were in place to prevent her from being too hurt. She'd never let go with anyone, not that her life had been cluttered with an abundance of men, and it astounded her that, of all the people in the world, she should be so free and open with one who wasn't destined to play any kind of permanent role in her life.

It didn't make sense.

But wonderfully open was exactly what she was feeling as she licked and teased and sucked him, as she felt him move between her thighs, tickling her with his tongue, their bodies fused as one.

They both knew when the time was right for the foreplay to end before it cascaded into orgasm.

Arturo eased her off him, groaning as their bodies broke contact. It was a matter of a few fumbling seconds and then, protection in place, he positioned himself over her.

Rose could barely contain her excitement. Her whole

body ached for the ultimate satisfaction of having him inside her and when he drove into her, thrusting hard and firm, she groaned long and low.

He filled her up and with each thrust she came closer and closer to the brink.

Art had never been with anyone as responsive as she was. It was as though he was tuned in to her, sensitive to just how far he could take her before she came, able to time his own orgasm to match hers, and when they came it was mind-blowing.

Deep inside her, embedded to the hilt, he drove hard and felt her shudder and cry out just as he rocked with waves of such intense pleasure that he couldn't contain his own guttural cry of satisfaction.

It was a few moments before they could unglue their bodies from one another. Unusually, Art didn't immediately feel the urge to break the connection by escaping to have a shower.

Instead, he slid off her and held her. What the hell had he done? He'd come here on a mission and this most definitely had *not* been any part of his mission.

But he looked down at her flushed face, her parted mouth, felt the warmth of her beautiful body pressed against his, and all he wanted to do was have her all over again.

Art knew that this was a weakness. In fact, sleeping with her at all had been a weakness. Since when had *any* woman taken precedence over common sense and, more importantly, work?

And what happened now?

Art knew what *should* happen. He should walk away. He should walk away and keep on walking until he hit London and the reality of his life there. He should put an immediate end to this charade and conduct whatever business needed conducting through his lawyers and accountants. The land belonged to him and tiptoeing around that stark fact was a matter of choice rather than necessity.

Okay, so maybe if she got stuck in and took a stand, the community would view his development as a blot on their landscape and react accordingly to the newcomers buying properties, but that wouldn't last. Within six months everything would settle down and life would carry on as normal.

His presence here and his willingness to do his best to ease the process would bear testimony to his capacity for goodwill.

It would also be useful because, in due course, he would be putting in another planning application and a hostile community would make that more difficult.

But in the end he would get what he wanted because he always did.

And, in the meantime, this…was a complication.

'What are you thinking?' Rose asked drowsily, opening her eyes to look directly at him. 'No,' she continued, 'I know what you're thinking.'

'Mind reader, are you?' Art smiled and kissed the tip of her nose. He cupped her naked breast with his hand and marvelled at how nicely it fitted. Not too big, not too small.

'You're thinking that it's time you went back to your

bedroom and you'd be right because it's late and I want to go to sleep.'

'Is that the sound of you kicking me out of your bedroom?' he murmured, moving in to nibble her ear and then licking the side of her neck so that she squirmed and giggled softly.

'It's the sound of a woman who needs her beauty sleep.' She wriggled away from him so that she could head for the bathroom.

'But what,' Art heard himself ask, 'does a red-blooded man do if he wakes in the early hours of the morning and needs his woman by his side?'

Rose stilled but when she answered her voice was still light and teasing. 'He goes downstairs for a glass of milk?'

'Wrong answer.' Art heaved himself into a sitting position and pulled her towards him. 'I never thought I'd hear myself say this, but let's spend the night together...and, by the way... I'd like it if you called me Art. Not Arthur...not Arturo. Art.'

# CHAPTER SIX

ART GAZED AT the vast swathes of empty land around him. Open fields. The very same open fields that had confronted him on day one when he had arrived with a plan and a deadline.

Slight difference now. The plan and the deadline had both taken a battering. He'd slept with Rose over a week and a half ago and even as his head had urged him to turn his back and walk away, his body had argued against that course of action and had won.

They'd shared a bed every night since then. He couldn't see her without wanting her. It was insane but whatever attraction kept pulling him towards her, it was bigger than all the reserves of willpower at his disposal.

And the land…

Art strolled to the very spot where the protesters had set up camp. There were some stragglers but most had left. He'd been busy arguing his corner whilst making sure not to stand on any soapboxes bellowing his opinions. He'd listened to everything that had been said and had quickly sussed that, however fervent they were about the abstract notion of the land being developed, when it came down to basics, the offer of those very same heartless developers doing some good for their community had won the day.

Financial assistance for the primary school; a fund towards the local library, which also served as a meeting place for most of the senior citizens; playing fields to be included on some of his land which, as it happened, suited Art very well indeed, bearing in mind his future plans for the site.

Art had advised them to contact the team of lawyers working for DC Logistics.

'There's always a solution when it comes to sorting problems,' he had asserted, safe in the knowledge that they would find no hindrance to their requests. Not only was he happy to ease the situation but he was positively pleased to be able to do so because he had grown fond of all of them, had seen for himself, first-hand, how strongly they felt about the land.

In London, community spirit of that kind was noticeably absent and he'd been impressed by what he'd seen.

And, crucially, Rose had more or less conceded that it was the best solution because, like it or not, those tractors and cranes would move in sooner or later.

His job here was done and satisfactorily so.

He could be pleased with himself. He could start thinking about step two. He knew in his gut that there would be no obstacles in his way and step two had always been top of the agenda. Art might have been cynical when it came to the romantic notion of love, but familial love, discovered in the most unexpected of places, had settled in his heart and filled the space there.

He'd thought outside the box and it had paid off. Now, as he looked at his land, he realised that thinking outside the box and getting what he'd wanted had come at an unexpected cost.

Rose.

He abruptly turned away, headed for the battered Land Rover which couldn't have been more different from his own fleet of super-charged, high-performance cars.

She'd temporarily loaned him her car.

'I'll be buried in case files for the next week or so.' She had laughed, her arms wound around his neck, her eyes sparkling, her half-clad body pressed against his. 'You'll want to be out and about. Lord knows you've become some kind of mentor to half the protesters...with that promise of yours that the developers are going to meet their extravagant demands! Mind you, I'll be pleased to have my kitchen table back.'

Art would have to come clean. There was no way around it. He couldn't believe that he had been disingenuous enough, when thoughts had entered his head about sleeping with her, to believe that he could have a fling and walk away.

Two adults, he had argued to himself. Two consenting adults who fancied one another. What was the problem? All he had to do was make it clear to her from the very start that he wasn't going to be hanging around and his conscience would be clear.

He'd approached all his relationships with the opposite sex like that. With honesty and no promises. If some of them had become distraught when he'd walked away because they'd been pointlessly looking for more than he had in him to give, then so be it. Not his fault. How could it have been when he'd done nothing but warned them off going down that road?

But the situation with Rose was different and that was something he had failed to factor in.

He'd conveniently whitewashed the whole business of *why* he had turned up, unannounced, on her doorstep into something that wasn't really relevant—he wasn't going to be sticking around so she would never actually discover his true identity. Therefore, why did it matter *who* he was?

Except it did.

And now he would have to pay the price for his not-so-innocent deception.

It was not quite six in the evening. He had spent the day partly in the library, where he had worked in pleasurable peace, and partly in a five-star hotel near Oxford, where a high-level meeting had been arranged with the CEO of a company he intended to buy.

He wondered whether his attack of conscience had been kick-started by that return to the reality of his high-powered city life. Sitting at that table, back in his comfort zone of work, business and making money... had it brought him back down to earth with a bump? Reminded him of the single tenet he had always lived by—work was the only thing upon which a person could rely?

Art didn't know. He just knew that he owed Rose more than a disappearing act.

He made it back to her house within fifteen minutes, to find her still in her office alone, Phil having gone for the day.

Rose looked up and smiled.

He'd told her that he didn't do commitment and he didn't do domesticity and yet they'd cooked together and discussed everything under the sun from world politics to village gossip.

'You're just in time,' she said, standing up and stretching. 'If I read any more of this file I'm going to end up banging my head on the desk in frustration. You wouldn't believe the spurious arguments this company is using to get rid of one of their longest-serving employees just because it would be cheaper for them to get a young person on board.'

'The world of the underdog would be nothing without you...' Art framed that light-hearted rejoinder in a voice that lacked his customary self-assurance.

He clenched his fists, walked towards the double-fronted bay window, sat down on the ledge and stared out for a few silent seconds.

'Are you disappointed in the outcome of the protest?' he asked abruptly, swinging around to look at her but remaining where he was by the window, perched on the broad ledge, his legs loosely crossed.

He had no idea how to begin this conversation and even less idea as to where it was going to end. For once in his life he was freefalling without a safety net and he loathed the sensation.

For a man to whom control was vitally important, this lack of control was his worst nightmare.

Rose tilted her head to one side. The smile with which she had greeted him had faded because she was sensing that something was out of kilter, although she wasn't sure what.

'Not disappointed, no...' She gave his question consideration. 'I always knew it was going to be a token protest because the land had been bought and all the channels had been navigated with planning permission, but I do think it's a result if the developers consent to all the things they've made noises about.'

'They will.'

'You seem very sure about that.' Rose laughed because this sort of assertiveness was just typical of him and it was something she really...

For a few seconds her heart stopped beating and she could feel the prickle of perspiration break out over her body. Something she *really found amusing*. Not something she *loved*, but something she found *amusing*.

'I am.'

'Well, I must say, it would be fantastic for the community as a whole. Naturally, I still stand by my guns when I say that I hate big developers who think they can descend and gobble up whatever slice of land they want, but it's fair to say that not many would go the extra mile to appease disgruntled locals.'

Art didn't say anything. He'd slept with her and done a hundred small things with her that he'd never done with anyone else. That, in itself, was unsettling and he latched onto that sentiment with some relief because it made him realise that he was clearing off in the nick of time. Sharing cosy suppers and painting bedrooms wasn't in his genetic make-up and never would be! He wasn't cut out for anything like that and had he stayed on he knew that the inevitable boredom with her would have set in.

She invigorated him *at this moment in time*, but it wouldn't have lasted.

He would have become restless, got itchy feet. It never failed to happen.

Which was *why*, he thought with conviction, it was imperative he left. Rose, underneath the tough veneer, had risen above the odds dealt to her in her background and turned out to be endearingly romantic. Were he to stay on, there was a chance that she would have fallen for him.

*And then what?* A broken heart when he vanished? A life in need of being rebuilt? Looking at the bigger picture, he was doing her a favour.

'That's because,' Art told her patiently, 'there's always more to people than meets the eye, and that includes billionaire developers.'

'Really? I hadn't noticed. Do you want to tell me what's going on here, Art, or shall I make it easier for you by bringing it out into the open myself?'

'What do you mean?' He frowned.

'I mean you…*this atmosphere*…' She breathed in deeply and exhaled slowly. 'Something's off and I'll spare you the discomfort of spelling it out in words of one syllable, shall I? You're leaving. Your time here is up. You came for a protest that ended up a damp squib. Perhaps you were hoping for more fireworks.'

'The opposite,' Art told her quietly.

'You're…not off?'

'No, that bit you got right. I… It's time for me to pack my bags and leave.'

Rose stared at him, horrified at how painful it was to hear those words. Everywhere hurt. He was going. She'd known he'd be off but, now that he'd confirmed it, it felt as though she'd been hit head-on by a train. Her legs had turned to jelly but she kept standing, holding her ground and hoping with everything inside her that the pain tearing her apart wasn't reflected in her face.

'Of course,' she said politely.

'You always knew I'd be leaving.'

'Because you're a wanderer in search of a cause.'

'Not entirely.'

'What do you mean? What are you talking about?'

'I think this is a conversation better conducted with you sitting down.'

'Why?' Rose wondered whether she would be able to move at all without falling to the ground in an undignified heap. That was what jelly legs did to a person.

'Because…you might find what I'm about to say somewhat surprising.'

Rose looked at him uncertainly, then galvanised her body into action. She wasn't going to sit at her desk. She wasn't conducting an interview! Although the atmosphere felt hardly less formal.

She walked towards the sitting room, which was the only room downstairs, aside from the large cloakroom, that hadn't been converted into something useful that could be modified and used as a source of income.

Like all the other rooms in the house, it was high-ceilinged and gracious in proportions. It was painted in soothing shades of grey and cream and lavender and the furniture was well-made and tasteful.

Rose flopped down onto the sofa and then watched in tense silence as he prowled the room, his beautiful lean body jerky as he darted thoughtful glances in her direction.

'Are you going to spare us both the drama and just say what you have to say? It's not as though you haven't warned me in advance and you needn't worry that I'm going to do anything silly like break down and cry.'

'It might be better if I show you,' Art said slowly. He pulled out his phone, found what he was looking for on the screen and handed it to her. And waited, eyes glued to her expressive face. Every nerve in his body twanged with the sort of tension he had seldom experienced in his life before.

He watched as bewilderment turned to confusion, as confusion turned to disbelief and then, finally, as disbelief morphed into appalled horror.

Long after she should have finished reading the article about him, just one of many to be found online, she kept staring at the phone as though hopeful that it might deliver something that would make sense of what he'd shown her.

His biography. Succinct. Replete with his success stories. Sycophantic in its adoration of the man who had made his first billion before the ripe old age of thirty-five.

She finally looked up with a dazed expression.

'*You're* DC Logistics…?'

Art flushed darkly but he wasn't going to start justifying himself.

'Yes,' he said flatly.

'*You're* the guy we've been fighting…'

'Yes.'

'You came here… You pretended to be… *Why*?' She shot up, trembling, as thousands of implications clearly began sinking in. 'You *bastard*.' She edged away from him, recoiling as though he was contagious, and took up position by the large Victorian fireplace, leaning against it and staring at him with huge round eyes.

'You came here with a plan, didn't you? You came here so that you could infiltrate and get us onside. You didn't like the fact that we were protesting about you putting up a bunch of houses that no one wants!'

Art's jaw hardened but there was nothing he could say to refute her accusations since they were all spot on. 'I owned the land. I was going to build, whether you stood in the way or not. I thought it diplomatic to try to persuade you to see sense before the bulldozers moved in and trying to persuade you within the walls of my London offices wasn't going to work.'

'You *used* me.'

'I…' Art raked his fingers through his hair. 'There was no need for me to come clean. And I did not *use* you. We both enjoyed what happened between us. I could have walked away without saying anything.'

'Are you asking for a medal because you finally decided to tell the truth?'

'There was also no need for me to grant the concessions that I have.'

'No wonder you were so confident that the big, bad developers were going to accept our terms and conditions. Because *you* were the big, bad developer.'

'I played fair.'

'You lied!'

'A small amount of subterfuge.'

'You came here…you…' She turned away because she needed to gather herself. Everything was rushing in on her and she was beginning to feel giddy. She took a few deep breaths and forced herself to look at him. To her fury, he met her gaze squarely, as if he was as pure as the driven snow!

'I let you stay in my house.' Rose laughed bitterly. 'No wonder you insisted on paying rent! You're worth a small fortune. It must have troubled your conscience that you were sponging off someone who couldn't hope to come close to matching you in the financial stakes. Someone with rooms in need of decorating and plumbing on the verge of waving a white flag and giving up! I bet you've never painted anything in your life before or done anything manual *at all*!'

'Going through each and every detail of the ways you feel deceived isn't going to progress this.'

'I slept with you.'

Those four words, delivered without any expression

whatsoever, dropped like stones into a quiet pond and silence settled between them, thick and uncomfortable.

'I'm guessing…' Rose kept her voice level but the blood was rushing through her veins like lava '…that that was all part of the game plan? To get me onside?'

'That's outrageous!'

'Really? Is it? Why? You conned your way into my home!'

'I was more than happy to go stay in a hotel.'

'You accepted my hospitality and you *used it* to get what you wanted out of me! I can't believe I was stupid enough to actually think that you were a man of integrity.'

'Sleeping with you was never part of any plan.' Art shook his head and dropped down on the sofa, legs apart. She walked towards him and stood in front of him with her arms folded. 'You doubt me?' he growled, staring at her, and even in the height of this scorching argument, when she was burning with rage, those fabulous dark eyes still had the power to do things to her body. Rose's lips thinned.

'Do you honestly believe that I could make love with you the way I have if I wasn't seriously attracted to you?'

Hot colour flooded her cheeks. Rose remembered the intensity of their lovemaking, the flaring passion in his eyes. She remembered the way he had touched her, his fingers as they'd explored her body and the urgency of those times when he just couldn't wait to have her.

No, he hadn't been faking *that*. Somehow that was

something she just knew. He'd come here on a mission but going to bed with her had never been part of the plan. Should she feel better for that? Maybe, but then, with a bitter twist, she also remembered the way *she* had felt about *him* and her stupidity in actually thinking that there might have been more to what they had than just a romp in the sack.

It was *always* going to be just a romp in the sack, had she but known, because she had *always* just been an enjoyable add-on to the main reason he was there, a pleasant side dish but never the main meal.

Humiliation roared through her, stiffening her backbone and settling like venom in her veins.

How on earth could she have been so stupid? She, of all people! Always cautious, always watchful…how could she have thrown herself in the path of a speeding train and actually thought that it would be okay?

'You need to leave,' she said coldly.

'I was honest with you.' Art rose to his feet, a towering, dominant presence that made her step back in alarm.

He sucked the oxygen out of the room, left her feeling as though she needed to gasp for air, and the strength of her reaction terrified her because she knew that, mixed in with the rage, the hatred and the bitter disillusionment, was something else…something she didn't want to put her finger on.

'And now that I'm weeping with gratitude at your terrific display of honesty, are you going to renege on all the things you said you'd do for the village?'

'Dammit, Rose!' Art roared. 'I could have just disappeared. Instead, I came clean. Why can't you cut me some slack?' He stepped towards her, ignoring her crab-like shuffle away from him, until he had cornered her without her even realising it was happening.

She collided with the wall and he placed both hands squarely on either side of her so that she had nowhere to run.

'I didn't come here to—' he looked away and clenched his jaw in frustration '—mess you or anyone else around.'

'You came here to get on our good side so that we would get off your case and make things easier for you!'

'Where's the crime in that? I purchased the land going through all the proper channels. Okay, yes, I admit I figured that life would be a lot smoother if I didn't have to steamroller my way through protesters waving placards, but I can't think of many *big, bad wolves* who would have given a damn about the protesters *or* their placards.'

'You could have done the decent thing and been honest from the start!'

'You would have had the sheriff run me out of town before I got the first sentence out.'

'That's not true.'

'Isn't it?'

Rose flushed. She could breathe him in and it was doing all sorts of crazy and unacceptable things to her nervous system.

'I thought,' Art said heavily, 'that this would be fairly straightforward. How hard could it be to talk sense into a group of people who were never going to win the war?

I never banked on really engaging with anyone here and I certainly never entertained the idea that...'

Rose tilted her chin and stared at him in hostile defiance. 'That what? That you'd break that code of yours and start sharing space in a kitchen with a woman?'

*To think that she had actually entertained the idea that having him do all that domesticated stuff might be an indication of feelings that ran deeper and truer than they had both originally predicted.*

'Something like that,' Art muttered, glancing away for a few taut seconds before returning his dark gaze to her face. 'You're hurt and I get that,' he continued in a low, driven voice.

Rose raised her eyebrows. She was keeping it together by a thread, determined not to let him see just how devastated she was, but it was so, so very hard, especially when he was standing so, so very close to her, when, with barely any effort, she could just reach out and touch that body she had come to feel so much for. Too much.

'Thanks. I feel so much better for that,' she said with thick sarcasm.

'I'm no good for you.' He gave her a crooked smile and pushed himself away, although he remained standing in front of her.

'No, you're not,' Rose said shortly.

'You deserve a far better man.'

'I do.' She tossed her hair and for a few seconds her expression changed from anger to on-the-edge-of-tears disappointment. 'I always knew that guys with money were unscrupulous and I proved myself right.'

'I refuse to get into a debate about this. I don't think

your fellow locals will agree when they find themselves the recipients of some spanking-new additions to the village. I don't think they'll be gnashing their teeth and shaking their fists and cursing my generosity.'

'You can wave money around but that doesn't make you an honourable man. It doesn't mean that you've got any sense of...of *spirituality*.'

'I didn't think you were paying too much attention to my fascinating lack of a spiritual side when we were in bed together.'

'How dare you bring that up?' The silence that greeted this was electric. Her nostrils flared and her pupils dilated and every pore in her body burned with humiliation because the warmth between her legs wouldn't let her forget the shameful truth that she still found him unbearably sexy even though she absolutely loathed him for how he had played her.

She breathed deep and closed her eyes and wasn't aware that he was reaching out until he was. Reaching out to lightly stroke the side of her face.

'You still want me,' he murmured and Rose glared at him furiously. 'You still want me and you can't deny it.'

Rose opened her mouth to utter an instant denial of any such thing. How dared he? Her skin burnt from where he had touched her. *How dared he?*

'Are you going to lie?' Art asked in a low, sexy undertone. 'You can't possibly stand there and accuse me of being a monster of deceit only to lie about something that's so obvious.'

'Well, it doesn't matter,' she said on a sharply indrawn breath. 'So what if I'm attracted to you? You're an attractive man. But I will never be tempted to act on that attraction again, not that the situation is ever likely to arise.' She took a deep breath. 'I can't fault you for being honest and telling me from the start that you weren't going to be sticking around. Fair enough. But you hurt me with your deceit, whether that deceit was intended or not. I'll never, ever forgive you for that.'

Art's lips thinned.

'Forgiveness has never been high on the list I've striven for.'

'Can I ask you something before you disappear back to that jet-set life of yours?' Rose folded her arms, proud of the fact that her voice continued to betray nothing of what was going on inside her, the roil of tumultuous emotions tearing her up.

'I'm guessing that's a question you will ask whatever my response.'

'If we'd stood firm, would you have steamrolled us all away? So that you could have your acres and acres of land for the sake of a handful of flash houses?'

'Yes.'

Rose frowned because she had sensed something behind that flat monosyllabic reply. A curious shadow had crossed his face but then she wondered whether she'd imagined it because when he fixed his deep, dark eyes on her they were as remote as hers were. Two people who had shared intimacies she had never dreamed of and now here they were, standing opposite one another with a huge unsurmountable wall between them.

Rose looked away quickly because she could feel the treacherous onset of tears.

She put distance between them and gathered herself.

'I'll get my things,' Art said abruptly. 'I'll be fifteen minutes, tops.'

'I expect you won't need to borrow my battered car to get you to the station? Maybe you could call your personal chauffeur to swing by for you. Or, if that's not efficient enough, I'm sure you could find a corner of your field to land a private jet.'

'My driver is on his way.'

'Of course he is,' Rose said acidly. 'I'll leave you to get on with your packing. You know where the front door is.'

She didn't look back. She headed straight to her office and she made sure to close and lock the door behind her. But she didn't cry. She knew how to contain the tears. She'd learned that trick at a very young age.

# CHAPTER SEVEN

SITTING AT THE head of the conference table, around which twenty people were all looking to him, Art could feel nothing but a certain amount of apathy even though a deal that would harvest several million was on the verge of completion.

With some surprise, he realised that he had doodled Rose's company logo onto his legal pad, a detail he wasn't even aware he had stored in his memory bank.

He'd last seen her three weeks ago and the memory of that final encounter was one that he rehashed on a daily basis.

It was getting on his nerves.

His concentration levels were down. His focus was erratic. He'd made two dates with women. The first he'd managed to stick out for an hour or so before admitting defeat and making up an excuse to leave early. The second he'd simply bailed on before subjecting himself to the possibility of another evening of torturous banalities.

He dreamed of Rose.

Not only did the memory of her haunt his waking

hours, but it didn't have the decency to allow him to get a good night's sleep when he fell into bed in the early hours of the morning.

Art had come around to thinking that she had taken up residence in his head because things had not ended *properly* between them.

He'd left still wanting her and, like an itch that needed to be scratched, that *want* kept clamouring for satisfaction.

It didn't help that he'd also left knowing that *she* still wanted *him*.

It was frustrating because he had never had any area of his life over which he was unable to exercise complete control. In this instance it had gradually dawned on him that he would never get her out of his system unless he took her to bed once again.

Pride dictated that he drop all seditious thoughts along those lines. Common sense warned him away. The litany of complications if they ended up in bed again was too long to catalogue and it beggared belief that she would actually *want* to sleep with him anyway. Yes, she fancied him. She'd admitted that much. But her amazing eyes had been full of scorn even as the admission had been leaving her lips.

When Art thought about that, he felt a spurt of raw frustration that left him confused and at odds with himself. He wondered whether this was what it felt like to be dumped, a situation he had never personally had to endure.

He went through the motions for the remainder of the

morning. The deal was signed. His company's bank account was inflated to even more impossible proportions.

None of that touched him. What *did* affect him was when, two and a half hours later, he dialled Rose's number and sat back in his office chair, waiting to see whether she would ignore his call or pick up. His name would flash on her screen, warning her of his identity. Whatever she did now would dictate the way he responded. He would leave it to fate.

For the first time in weeks, Art felt comfortable. He was doing *something*. Circumstances hadn't simply conspired to yank the rug from under his feet and leave him feeling at odds with himself, restless and unable to concentrate.

The slate had been wiped clean. There were no more half-truths between them. He would see her. He would feel out the situation and then, who knew...?

Life was an unfolding mystery.

He heard her voice and automatically straightened, all senses on full alert, every primitive instinct honing in to what he wanted to do, where he wanted to go with this...

'Been a while,' he drawled, relaxing back in his chair and swivelling it so that he could stretch his legs out.

Rose had debated whether or not to take the call. His name had flashed up on the screen and her insides had immediately turned to mush even though, over the past long three weeks, she had played and replayed in her mind how she would react if he got in touch.

'What can I do for you?' she asked coolly.

'Surprised to hear from me?'

'Are you phoning about anything in particular, Art? Because I'm quite busy at the moment.'

'I'm almost there, finalising the details of my investment in your community.'

'I wouldn't know. I've handed that over to a property lawyer in Oxford, who is a close friend of mine. I'm sure he would be happy to supply details of the ongoing process but I've told him that there's no need to fill me in until everything's sorted.' Images of Art jumped into her head, sickly reminding her of the powerful and dramatic effect he had on her body. Even the sound of his voice was enough to make her breasts tingle and her breath shorten.

'I rather think,' Art drawled, 'that I would like *you* to be personally involved in the closure of all of this.'

'Me? What? *Why?*'

'You started it, in a manner of speaking. It's only fair that you should finish it. Aside from which, if I'm to sink a vast sum of money into the community, it would benefit from someone knowing the place first-hand, knowing where best to divide the cash and how to put it to the best possible use. I may be generous, but I'm not a pushover. I have no intention of seeing my money ineptly spent on whatever takes some councillor's fancy. So handing over the file to someone else to tie up all the loose ends isn't doing it for me.'

'I haven't got time.'

*What would it involve?* She surely wouldn't have to meet him again! She couldn't face it. It was bad enough hearing the deep, dark, sexy timbre of his voice down the end of a phone line. She couldn't get her head around the possibility of actually ever seeing him in the flesh. He'd deceived her and he'd slept with her, knowing all the time that whilst she had been opening up to him, which was a big deal for her, she'd been opening up to a stranger.

'Well, then, you'll have to make time.' Art sliced through that objection swiftly and conclusively. 'You've turned caring for the community into an art form, Rose. It's not asking too much for you to step up to the plate and finish the job. When can you get to London so that we can discuss this?'

*'We?'* Rose queried faintly, as her stomach fell away and her mouth dried.

'Why, me and you, of course,' Art said in a tone of incredulity that she should even have thought to ask such an obvious question. 'I can't very well ask you to finish the job when I don't do likewise, can I? My people have handled all the formalities. We can agree the sign-off. And I think it would be beneficial for you to have a look at the details of the houses I intend to build on the land.'

'But I don't see why.' Rose cleared her throat, anxiously wondering what would happen if she flat-out refused. Would he renege on the deal? No! She knew he wasn't that sort but the possibility still niggled. It would be a disaster because he now had the complete, enthusiastic backing of everyone in the community and if it all collapsed because of her then she would be mortified.

'I don't see the point of another lengthy explanation. Now, when can you get down here? I wouldn't suggest commuting—I think you should plan on having a couple of days in London. There are legalities we can iron out between us and I will need to see some plans for the distribution of my money. In fact, it wouldn't be remiss of me to suggest a week. I can arrange for a makeshift office to be set up at my headquarters in the city if you need to spend some time communicating with clients. Or you could always take a bit of holiday. Enjoy the sights. It's quite different to the countryside.'

'Get down there? London? And yes, Art, I *do* realise that the big city is a little different to a field of cows and a village with a post office, a corner shop and a pub in case anyone wants a nightlife.'

'Not my thoughts and certainly not my words. I have my diary to hand. I could block out some time from the day after tomorrow. It won't be easy but the sooner this business is wrapped up the better, and construction can start on the land. And I won't remind you that any delay to the work beginning is a mere formality and a courtesy to you.'

Rose detected the crispness in his voice and pictured him glancing at his watch, raring to get on with more important business. He was doing what he felt was the right thing, involving her in the final process, and what he said made sense. She had supported the protesters and it was only fair to them and to the community that she take an active part in deciding how the money should be distributed to best benefit everyone.

She was overreacting because of the tumult of emotions that still coursed through her at the thought of him.

It wasn't like that for Art. He had taken a bit of time out with her but he was back where he belonged and she would be no more than a fast-fading memory for him. If she did what she wanted to do, namely launch into a thousand reasons why she had no intention of having anything further to do with a man who had deceived her, he wouldn't understand. He had given her his reasons for having done what he had, he had come clean and frankly, as far as he was concerned, had elevated himself to the position of self-proclaimed saint because he could have just walked away, leaving her none the wiser. What was the big deal now? All water under the bridge.

Playing it as cool as he was, she thought, was the only way to deal with the situation and maybe, just maybe, seeing him again and in a different environment would kill off the effect he continued to have on her, against all reason.

He would be in his natural habitat. He would be surrounded by all those trappings of wealth that she had never had time for in the past. Plus, speed would be of the essence for him. He wanted the whole business sorted fast. A couple of days in his company might be just the thing for clearing her head because ever since he'd disappeared she'd done nothing but think of him and the longing, the anger, the disenchantment and the regret were wreaking havoc with her sleep and distracting her from her work.

Bucked up by this process of reasoning, Rose felt a little calmer when she answered.

'If you hold for a minute, I'll check my schedule…'

\* \* \*

Art held. For a minute, two minutes…when he looked at his watch with some impatience it was to find that she had kept him hanging on for five minutes. Inconceivable. He gritted his teeth and wondered what he would do if she turned him down flat, as she had every right to do. He could waffle on about the importance of both of them jointly putting the finishing touches to the deal that had been brokered to ease acceptance of the construction of his development, but any close inspection would reveal more holes in that argument than a colander.

'Well?' he pressed.

'Okay.'

'Okay?' Art straightened, a slashing smile of intense satisfaction softening his lean face. 'Good. Tell me when, exactly, you will be arriving and I will make sure that suitable accommodation is sorted for you.'

'I can sort my own accommodation,' Rose asserted hurriedly.

'You're not paying for a hotel.'

'No way am I…'

'I believe this is a favour it is within my remit to return,' Art said flatly, cutting her off in mid-protest, 'and, just in case you're thinking of a speech about accepting favours from me, let me assure you that no money will leave my hands.'

'What do you mean?'

'I own the hotel.'

'Of course you do,' Rose snapped. 'I wonder why I'm not surprised at that. I did look you up online but the list of things you owned was so long that I fell asleep before I could get to the end. I didn't get to the hotel.'

'Chain.'

'I beg your pardon?'

'Hotel *chain*. A little sideline I invested in some years ago that has ended up exceeding all expectations.'

'Good for you. I shudder to think what must have gone through your head when you were confronted with a paintbrush, a can of paint and four walls with peeling plaster.'

Art burst out laughing. 'It was an unforeseen challenge. Now, back to business. Do you require somewhere to work? And, before you say no, I'll tell you again that it would be no trouble for me to have someone arrange an office for you.'

'It would be helpful,' Rose said through her no doubt gritted teeth. 'With a bit of juggling, I shall try to arrange a couple of client visits while I'm in London. It would work if I could have somewhere to go with them. And, of course, at some point I'll have to see Anton.'

'Anton?' Art's ears pricked up and he frowned.

'Anton Davies. He's the lawyer who has been handling the formalities in Oxford. If there's going to be a transition of duties then we'll have to get together to discuss that and to work out his fee accordingly. Although…he's not the sort to quibble.'

Art heard the smile in her voice, the softening of her tone, and his hackles rose accordingly.

But, he thought, if she was working under his roof, so to speak, then he could easily find his way to whatever space had been allocated to her and meet the guy.

It was a taste of jealousy rarely experienced and he moved on from that to conclude the conversation.

Less than five minutes later, everything had been sorted. It took one phone call to his PA for the hotel room to be arranged and a work space sorted.

She was going to experience the joy of five-star luxury and the seclusion of an office in one of the most prestigious buildings in the city.

He sat back and luxuriated in a feeling of pure satisfaction that was very far from the cool, forbidding and controlled exterior he showed the world.

Rose had no idea really what to expect of her time in London. She had been all cool logic and common sense ever since she had agreed to Art's proposal but now, standing in front of the daunting glass tower where his headquarters was housed, her heart plummeted faster than a boulder dropped from a great height.

At her side was her pull-along case, neatly packed with essentials. Work clothes. Prim, proper work clothes which were nothing like the relaxed, informal stuff she was accustomed to wearing in her own house. The image she wanted to project was one of inaccessible businesslike efficiency. There was no way she wanted him to think for a passing minute that she was the same woman who had hopped into bed with him, breathless and girly and excited.

To that end, she had actually bought two reasonably priced grey skirts and a jacket, two white blouses and a pair of black pumps. The perfect wardrobe for a woman who was in London for business.

She was wearing a sensible white bra which matched her sensible white knickers and bolstered her self-confidence as she continued to gaze at the aggressively thrusting glass facade with a racing heart.

She had asked for a schedule and a schedule she had duly received. Arrival at ten. She would then be shown to her temporary working quarters and then taken to the hotel, where she would deposit her belongings. At that point she could choose to return to the office to work if she liked. In all events, she wouldn't be seeing Art until early evening in his office, where they would briefly discuss some of the details of the projects that lay ahead for the village.

She had liaised with his personal assistant by email for all of this and, reading between the lines, she had got the message that Arturo da Costa, billionaire and legend in the world of business and finance, was a man who had precious little time to spare so what she was getting would be his leftover free time, a few snatched moments here and there when he happened not to be closing an important deal or entertaining important big shots.

Rose had held her tongue and refrained from pointing out the obvious. Why on earth was he bothering to see her at all if he was *that* busy? But then she remembered that he was the guy who had gone the extra mile to appease the natives and this was just a duty-bound finishing touch to his benevolence.

Anyway, she thought now, taking a deep breath and propelling herself into the glass tower, it was great that he was only going to be around now and again.

That way, she would see enough of him to kill all the foolish, nostalgic, whimsical memories that seemed to have dogged her, against all her better judgement. She would have a world class view of the real man and he wasn't going to be the easy-going, sexy, laid-back guy who had painted a room in her house and stood by her side in the kitchen pretending that he knew what to do when it came to food preparation, joking and teasing and turning her on just by being *him*.

A little disorientated, she found herself in a vast marble-floored foyer, manned by an army of receptionists who would not have looked out of place in *Vogue* magazine and, just in case anyone might think that there was an unfair proportion of female models in front of those silver terminals and where the heck was feminism when you wanted it, then they'd have to think again because there was a fair sprinkling of men alongside them who also looked as though they'd have been quite at home on a catwalk. People were coming and going. There was an air of purpose about the place. This was what the business of vast money-making looked like. It was as far removed from her own workplace as an igloo was from a hut on a tropical beach.

She had no idea who would be meeting her but she was expecting the helpful PA.

She was certainly not expecting Art and, indeed, was unaware of him until she heard his voice behind her, deep and dark and sexy.

'You're here.'

Rose spun around. She'd gone from ice cold to

scorching hot in the space of two seconds. Dazed, she focused on him and the heat pouring through her body almost made her pass out.

'I wasn't sure whether you were going to come or not,' Art remarked, already turned on even though the deliberately uninspiring office outfit should have been enough to snuff out any stirrings of ardour.

It was her face. It had haunted him and one look at her revived every single image that had been floating around in his head and every single lustful thought that had accompanied those images.

He was pleased that he had been proactive. He could have sat around thinking of her. Sooner or later the memories would have vanished into the ether but he wasn't a man to rely on a *sooner or later* scenario.

The interruption to the smooth flow of his work life had been intolerable and the solution he had engineered had been worth the trouble.

Art hadn't known how he was going to play his cards when she arrived. He'd acted on impulse in engineering the situation in the first place, had ceded to the demands of his body.

Now, for the first time in his life, he was taking a chance and venturing into unknown territory. At an age when he should have been having fun, Art had had to grow up fast to deal with his father's unpredictable behaviour and the emotional and financial fallout each relationship had left in its wake. Before he had had a chance to plot his own life, he had already concluded that the only safe course was to hold tight to his emotions and to his money. Lose control and he could end up like his father. Adrift and ripped off.

This was the biggest chance he had ever taken. At least he wasn't going to be ripped off and she would be gone just as soon as he got this *thing* out of his system.

He still wanted her. He accepted that as his body surged into hot arousal. Didn't make sense but there you had it. What they had required a natural conclusion and looking at her now, seeing the way her cheeks reddened and noting the slight tremble in her hands, Art knew that she felt the same.

Even if she didn't know it. Yet.

He dealt her a slow smile of utter charm and Rose's mouth tightened.

'Well, here I am,' she replied neutrally. She wondered whether that remark of his had hinted at a suspicion that she might have tried to avoid meeting him because of the effect he still had on her. Had he thought that she had hesitated because she'd been scared of seeing him again? Or was that just being fanciful?

The way he was looking at her…

She dropped her eyes and resisted the temptation to fidget. 'I was under the impression that your secretary would be meeting me.'

'Change of plan.'

'Why?' She looked at him and it took a lot of will-power not to instantly look away because gazing into those fathomless dark eyes was the equivalent of having a shock delivered to her nervous system.

'Call it respect for the fact that what we had was bigger than the sum total of what I'm going to contribute to your community.'

Rose felt the sting of colour creep into her cheeks. She didn't want the past recalled. She wanted the brief time they'd shared neatly boxed up and shoved somewhere out of sight.

'There was no need,' she said tightly. 'I'm not here to have a stroll down memory lane, Art. It's not appropriate. I'm here to sort whatever details need sorting and then I'm heading back home. The quicker we can deal with what we need to decide the better.'

'In which case,' Art said briskly, 'let's start with your work space…'

It was the same size as the room which she shared with Phil and their assistant and all the various people who came and went at will. Compared with the clutter of the office in her house, the clean white modernist vision she had been allocated made her jaw drop.

She thought of the warm chaos of her own house and the familiar sounds of occupied rooms and felt a pang of longing so great that it took her breath away.

Life pre-Art had been simple. Making ends meet as she'd buried herself in her worthwhile causes had been a walk in the park because, when it came to stress, there was nothing more stressful than dealing with emotions. She had managed to avoid that for her entire life because no one had ever penetrated the protective wall she had built around herself.

'What is it?'

'Nothing,' Rose muttered, looking down at her feet.

'Don't you like the office space?'

He'd moved directly in front of her and Rose only managed to stand her ground through sheer willpower and a driving urge not to feel intimidated.

'It's very…nice.'

'Very *nice*?' Art looked away briefly, then returned his dark searching gaze to her face.

'It's not what I'm used to.' Rose cleared her throat and gathered herself. 'It really makes me see the gaping chasm between us.'

Art flushed darkly. 'We've been over this. Let me take you to the hotel. You can drop your bag and then we'll go for lunch.'

'Art, there's no need to put yourself out for me. I don't expect you to take me to lunch or anywhere else, for that matter. Your PA gave me the impression that I wouldn't actually be seeing a great deal of you.'

'Like I said, plans change. You'll be thrilled to hear that I've cleared my diary for you.'

Rose looked at him wryly, eyebrows raised. 'Do I look thrilled?'

'I've missed your sense of humour. Some men might be turned off because you're not simpering, but not me.' Art held her gaze and raked his fingers through his dark hair, his lean body taut and tense.

Rose stilled. Her whole body froze and for a few seconds she wondered whether she had heard correctly. His fabulous eyes were giving nothing away but there was something there that made her mouth go dry.

'You *missed* me?'

Her body came to life. Her nipples pinched and a

spreading dampness between her legs was a painful reminder of the dramatic effect he still had on her.

She'd hoped that seeing him in his gilded surroundings would kill off what remnants of idiotic sexual attraction lingered inside her, but looking at him now…

She was no expert but that suit looked handmade, to match the shoes which also looked handmade. His smooth, ridiculously sophisticated attire would probably have cost the equivalent of what most normal earthlings earned in a year. It should have got up her nose, been a massive turn-off, and yet she had a sudden urge to swoon.

'Well, I have not missed *you*,' she croaked and he looked at her steadily, eyes pinned to her flustered face. 'And I don't appreciate you…bringing this up. What happened between us…happened and I'm not here to rake up the past. As I've already told you.'

'I know. I'm crashing through all those barriers and voicing what you don't want to hear.'

'Shall I be honest with you?' He dropped the loaded question into the lengthening silence and waited.

'No,' she whispered.

'I still want you, Rose. Just standing here is doing all sorts of things to my body, turning it on in ways you couldn't begin to imagine. You're in my system and, I won't lie, you're screwing up my working life because I can't get you out of my head.'

'Art, don't…' Rose heard the weak tremble in her voice with horror. She glanced at him and her breath hitched in her throat.

'I still want you in my bed,' he continued roughly.

'It's the only way I can think of to get you out of my system. I won't lay a finger on you but…every time you look at me, you should know that I'm thinking about touching you.' He stared away.

'I should never have come here!'

'But you're here now. Do you want to leave?' His smouldering dark eyes fastened on her, pinning her to the spot.

Rose hesitated. As he said, she was here now and she would sort out all the fine detail he had summoned her to London to sort out. She had promised all those loyal protestors that she would return with plans in place for them to start thinking long-term about improvements to the community. She wasn't going to let them down.

'I'll do what I came here to do,' she replied, breathing in deep and not looking away. 'I told everyone I would have details for them to pick over and I have no intention of going back empty-handed. What you think when you look at me is your business.'

# CHAPTER EIGHT

IF ART HAD planned on dropping a bomb in her life then he'd succeeded.

He still wanted her. He still wanted to take her to his bed. He still wanted to do all those things to her that she still wanted to do to him.

When Rose thought about that she felt giddy. She knew that, by being honest, he had deliberately dropped that bomb to wreak havoc with her peace of mind. Honest or selfish? Did he really care if he ended up getting what he wanted? He'd got her to London under false pretences and now he was playing a waiting game.

It had only been forty-eight hours but already her nerves were shredded. She felt like a minnow being slowly circled by a shark and, worse, the minnow was finding it hard to stop fantasising about its predator.

Now, he was taking her out to an elaborate dinner.

'Networking,' he had explained succinctly, having earlier dropped by her office, which had also turned into her sanctuary, where she could find a brief reprieve from his overwhelming personality.

She had looked up and given him a perplexed frown,

which had clearly done nothing to dampen his high spirits.

'I'm not here to network.'

'Granted, but this is a charity event hosted by some fairly prominent members of the international legal community. All those causes you take such an interest in? Well, they'll be represented across the board. Several people you'll have heard of will also be giving speeches and, for the intrepid, I gather there will be an opportunity to go abroad to places where civil liberties are at risk. You may not want to personally vanish to the opposite side of the globe on a crusade to eradicate injustice, but you might be interested in meeting fellow like-minded citizens who are.'

'A charity event?'

'Reasonably smart, I should point out, as these things invariably are. A few degrees off black tie.'

'I haven't brought any smart clothes with me, Art.'

'Nothing but the *hands-off* suits that could have been designed to deter roving eyes and repel curious hands,' he murmured, in his first departure from the perfectly well-behaved gentleman he had been since his warning of intent. 'Why don't you get yourself something? You can charge it to my company account. Elaine, my PA, will sort that out for you.'

'I couldn't…'

He'd shrugged but he'd dropped the bait and she'd taken it.

How could she not?

Rose immediately told herself that it didn't mean anything. She'd been presented with an opportunity to meet people she admired so why shouldn't she grab the chance just because Art had arranged it? She could pat herself on the back for not letting his suffocating presence plunge her into a state of permanent confusion. And since he seemed convinced that she wouldn't take him up on his offer to subsidise an evening dress for the event, then why shouldn't she prove him wrong and do what he least expected?

Rose wasn't stupid. She knew how to sift through the deceit and ferret out the truth. Art had descended on their village with one thing in mind and that had been to persuade her to stop the protests that were slowing up development of the land he'd bought. He could have run roughshod over all of them because he had the law on his side but he was clever enough to know that a diplomatic solution would have been preferable and so that was the road he had decided to go down.

He hadn't banked on her being a nuisance and getting in his way but he'd found her attractive and she knew why. It was because she represented everything he wasn't accustomed to. From the way she dressed to the person that she was, she was a woman far removed from the stereotypes he was used to dating and he had found that appealing.

He went out with catwalk models. Nothing could have been further than a pro bono lawyer whose wardrobe consisted of flowing skirts, baggy tops, faded jeans and waterproof anoraks.

She'd been a trip down novelty lane and that hurt.

When Rose tried to equate that to her own feelings

towards him she drew a blank because she had been drawn to him against all good reason.

It didn't make sense but everything about his personality had appealed to her. She'd been cautious but in the end she hadn't been able to resist the pull of his intelligence, his easy wit, his charm. Was she more like her mother than she realised? It didn't matter whether her mother had been a loyal wife. When her husband had died she had behaved in a way that had had lasting consequences for her daughter. She had been promiscuous and eventually she had ended up with a guy who had been so out of her league that it was a mystery that they had lasted as long as they had. Rose had been careful all her life not to repeat any of the mistakes her mother had made and it frightened her when she thought of where she was now.

She had opened up to Art. Even before he had shown his true colours, she had *known* that he wasn't the kind of man who should have registered on her radar, but she had *still* fallen for him and she had actually fooled herself into thinking that *he* might have had similar feelings for her.

Not so.

For Art, it was all about the sex, hence his openness in telling her straight off the bat that he still wanted her. Had she given off some kind of pheromone that had alerted him to the fact that she still fancied him?

That horrified her but she was honest enough to realise that it had probably been the case because, the second she was in his presence, her head and her body took off in two different directions and she was left rudderless and floundering and he was a guy who could pick up on things like that in a heartbeat.

With her thoughts all over the place and her body threatening to go its own way and let the side down, Rose had gone to town shopping for something to wear to the charity event.

Part of her was determined to show him that she was more than just a country bumpkin lawyer with no dress sense.

Another part was curious to see whether, exposed to the sort of gathering that didn't frequently occur in her life out in the sticks, she would find that there were other interesting men out there. That Art hadn't netted all her attention to the exclusion of everyone else. Had he been as much of a novelty for her as she had been for him? Was she giving him too much credit for having burrowed into the heart of her when, in fact, she had just been vulnerable to a charming man because she'd been out of the dating scene for too long?

To this end, she had gone all out and now, with a mere forty minutes to go before Art's driver called for her, Rose contemplated her reflection in the floor-to-ceiling mirror with satisfaction.

In the background, she absently took in the sumptuous surroundings that had made her gasp the first time she had entered the hotel room. The lush curtains, the blonde wood, the pale marbled bathroom…the decadent chandelier that should have been over the top but wasn't…the handmade desk on which was stacked fine quality personalised stationery and a comprehensive collection of London guidebooks which she had had precious little time to peruse.

She refocused on her reflection.

She had gone for drama and chosen a figure-hugging dress in a striking shade of raspberry. The narrowness of her waist was emphasised by a silver corded belt that lent the outfit a Roman appeal and the dress fell elegantly to mid-calf. In nude heels, her legs looked longer and her body more willowy than she had ever noticed before.

And her hair. It fell in tousled waves along her shoulders and down her back and was as soft as silk because she had managed to squeeze in an appointment with a hairdresser, who had done some wonderful things with highlights and blow-dried it in a way she couldn't possibly have done herself.

She'd also bought a shawl in the same nude shade as the heels and she slung that over her shoulders and smiled, excited.

She felt like an exotic bird of paradise.

For the first time in her life, Rose wasn't being cautious. No, she amended, gathering all her stuff as her cell phone buzzed, alerting her to the arrival of the driver...

She'd already thrown caution to the winds when she'd jumped into bed with Art. She was just carrying on in a similar vein and enjoying herself in the process.

It was sufficient to bring a guilty tinge to her cheeks but she was composed as she slid into the back of the glossy Mercedes and she maintained that composure all the way to the venue and right up to the moment she spied Art, who was waiting for her, as arranged, in the lobby of the hotel.

Stepping out of the car, with the door held open by one of the parking attendants who had sprung into action the second the car had pulled up, made her feel like a movie star.

This was more than just *fancy*. There were journalists snapping pictures of the arriving guests. In a daze, she realised that she recognised faces from the world of movies and television and one or two prominent politicians and their other halves.

But all those faces faded into a blur alongside Art, who had begun moving towards her and, in the process, created a bubble of excitement around him.

He looked magnificent. The whiteness of his dress shirt emphasised his bronzed complexion. The black bow tie looked ridiculously sexy instead of stuffy, as did the very proper black suit.

Rose was barely aware of him moving to politely usher her inside.

'You look,' he breathed without looking at her and only inclining slightly so that he couldn't be overheard, 'sensational. Was that the intention?'

'Thank you. That's very kind.' But her pulse raced and she shivered with wild pleasure at his husky undertone.

Art laughed as they strolled away from the lobby and into the impressive ballroom, which was buzzing with the great and the good. 'Not a description that's been used much about me but I'll take it.'

'I mean it. Look at the women here.' She was holding onto him for dear life, very much aware that they were being stared at. 'I recognise some of them from fashion magazines.'

'And I thought that you never read anything as frivolous as a fashion magazine.'

'But thank you for pretending that I look okay,' Rose said distractedly.

'Where's this sudden attack of modesty sprung from?' They'd left the paparazzi outside; there was still a sea of people but without the gawping of the public and the reporters. Art drew her to the side and looked down at her. 'You're the most self-confident woman I've ever met.'

'When it comes to work…'

'You knock spots off every woman in this place.'

Rose burst out laughing. If he wanted to put her at ease, then he was doing a good job of it. 'I don't. But thanks.'

'You're fishing.'

'Of course I'm not!'

'You know how I feel about you. The only thing I want to do right now is get you out of here and into a bed so that I can make love to you until we're both too exhausted to carry on. I want to peel that dress off your luscious body and touch you in all the places I know you like being touched. So when I tell you that you put every other woman in the shade here, then trust me. I'm not kidding.'

'Stop!' Her blood was boiling and she was so very aware of him that she could barely think. 'You know I don't want you saying things like that…to me.'

'Say that like you mean it.'

'I *do* mean it. I'm just a little…nervous.'

'No need. Look around you. If you were hoping to attract some glances, then you've succeeded.' Art heard the edge in his voice and knew that it was a few degrees off the light, amused tone he had intended. *She* might not have noticed, but *he* had seen the way men had turned to have a second look. Most women were dressed to kill in black. Rose was a splash of exotic colour, a bird of paradise with her long wild hair and her strong intelligent face. She announced to the world that she was *different* and that was a very sexy trait. And not just to him.

Halfway through the evening, he realised that she had disappeared into the crowd. The man who was accustomed to a high level of irritation with women clinging like limpets to him at functions like this found that his irritation level was skyrocketing now and for a different reason.

Where the hell was she *now*? And why was he having to hunt for her?

It got on his nerves. She was a flash of red but, before he could pin her down, she was gone. Nursing a whisky while a blonde tried to get his attention, Art decided that, for Rose's own good, he would take her back to the hotel.

'Got to go.' He interrupted the blonde abruptly. Pushing himself away from the wall, against which he had been leaning, he ignored a couple of MPs who had been trying to gain his attention.

Rose was laughing at something some guy was telling her. Art wasn't born yesterday. He could recognise a man on the make a mile away.

He came to an abrupt towering halt in front of them and Rose blinked and frowned at him.

'Mind if I interrupt?' Art interrupted anyway. 'I've barely seen you all evening...'

'That's because I've been chatting to all the interesting people here,' Rose returned gaily, swiping a glass of wine from a passing waitress. 'For instance, this is Steve and he does some amazing work for the UN.'

Steve reddened and straightened and stuck out his hand, clearly awed by Art, who felt ancient and cynical beyond his years in comparison. He politely asked a couple of interested questions but his attention was focused on Rose and his body language dismissed the young fair-haired man, who duly evaporated into the crowd after boldly exchanging phone numbers with Rose.

Which made Art's teeth snap together with annoyance.

'I think it's time to go,' he said without preamble.

'But I'm not ready to leave yet.'

'Tough. It's been over four hours, which is two hours longer than I usually stay at these things.'

'I'm having fun. There's no need for us to leave together, is there?' Rose squinted at his darkly disapproving expression. 'I know,' she pressed on, 'we came together, in a manner of speaking, but it's not as though we're on a date and there are so many more interesting people I still want to meet.'

'Repeat. Tough. Anyway, don't you think you've had

your fill of interesting people? Or is the entire room interesting after a few glasses of Chablis?'

'Not fair.'

Art shifted uncomfortably, recognising that she had a point. He raked his fingers through his hair and shot her a frowning glance. 'I apologise.' He tugged and undid the bow tie. 'But you've had a few drinks and you're not accustomed to that. I wouldn't feel comfortable leaving you here on your own to get on with the rest of what remains of the evening.'

'Do you think the poor little country girl might end up making a fool of herself? These shoes are killing me, by the way. Are there any chairs around here?'

'I think the poor little country girl might end up finding herself in slightly more hot water than she bargained for. And not many chairs, no. The expectation is for networking, not falling asleep in an armchair.'

'What do you mean about me finding myself in hot water?'

'You're sexy when you get angry.'

Rose blushed and pouted. 'Don't try to change the subject. What do you mean? I'm more than capable of taking care of myself. I've been doing it most of my life.'

'This isn't a quiet, sleepy village in the middle of nowhere.' Art didn't care how this sounded. There was no way he was going to leave her here on her own. The thought of predators circling her, moving in for the kill, made him see red. She was stunning and part of her appeal was the fact that she was so natural, so utterly without pretence, so patently open and honest. Aligned to her intelligence and her dramatic looks...well, it was a recipe for disaster in the big, bad city. If she didn't see that, then it was just as well that she had him around to see it on her behalf.

'I'd noticed, now that you mention it.'

'Have you paid any attention to the number of lechers who have been hanging around you all evening?'

'Have *you*?'

Art flushed. 'You came with me. I can't be blamed for wanting to look out for you.'

Rose's mouth twitched.

Art noted the way her pupils dilated and her eyes widened. He clocked the way her breath hitched and was suddenly turned on in a way that shocked him in its ferocity.

'Should I be grateful?' Rose breathed huskily.

'Don't.'

'Don't what?' The entire roomful of people could have evaporated. There was just the two of them, locked in a bubble in which he was acutely sensitive to every fleeting expression on her face, to the rasping of her breath and the deep, deep longing in her eyes.

'Don't look at me as though you want to touch me. Do that and you're playing with fire.'

'I started playing with fire the minute you came into my life,' Rose said in a tone of complete honesty.

'We should go,' Art told her roughly, leading the way, his hand cupping her elbow.

She was coming on to him. He felt it and, much as he would have liked nothing better than to have followed up on those hot little signals she was giving off, a tipsy Rose wasn't going to do. He wanted her sober and desperate for him, the way he was desperate for her. Nothing else would do.

It was cool and crisp outside and his car was waiting. Art propelled her into it and slid alongside her in the back seat.

'Do you think you have to show me to my door just in case I get waylaid by some of those lecherous men you seem to think are waiting around every corner for a country bumpkin like me?'

'How did you guess?'

'It's the dress. It stands out. When you said that it was going to be smart I had no idea what to buy. I didn't think that everyone would show up in black.'

'I could have warned you. Those functions are usually deadly. Black is an appropriate colour. Anyway, it's not the dress.'

'You don't think so?' Their eyes tangled and she didn't look away. She licked her lips, shivering in the burning intensity of his stare.

'We're here,' Art murmured, relieved.

'So we are. And just when I was beginning to enjoy the car ride.'

'I take it you're enjoying yourself,' he responded once they were out of the car and making their way up to her suite.

'What do you mean?'

'Enjoying playing with me.' Art shot her a wry smile. 'You must know what you're doing to me… I don't play games when it comes to sex…'

'You played a game with me when you slept with me.' She slid the card key into the slot and pushed open the door to her room. When she walked in she didn't push it shut behind her and she didn't tell him that it was fine for him to leave now that he had done the gentlemanly thing and seen her safely to her door. She looked over her shoulder, face serious.

'No game,' Art muttered in a strangled voice. 'The sex was for real. Stop looking at me like that… I'm not going to do anything, Rose. You…you've had a bit to drink. You don't know what you're doing. You don't know what you're playing with.'

'Fire. You've told me that already. I'm playing with fire.' The bed beckoned, oversized, draped in the finest Egyptian cottons and silk.

Rose turned to face him. The lighting in the room was mellow and forgiving. 'I've had a bit to drink,' she admitted without skipping a beat, 'but I'm not the worse for wear. I've been drinking a lot of water in between the wine and I've also eaten for England. Those canapés were to die for.' She walked towards him, kicking off the heels on the way. 'Want me to walk a straight line for you?'

'There's a lot I want you to do for me and walking a straight line doesn't figure.'

'What? What would you like me to do for you? What about this?' She reached down to cup the bulge between his legs and felt his swift intake of breath. Now or never.

Art pressed his hand over hers. He had to because, if he didn't, he wasn't sure what his body was going to do at the pressure she was exerting on his arousal.

'I want you.' Rose maintained eye contact. She'd never seemed more sober. 'When you told me who you really were I felt betrayed and deceived and I never, ever wanted to see you again.' She moved her hand and reached up to link fingers behind his neck. It was as if she'd given herself permission to touch and it was all she wanted to do now. 'I thought that it would be easy to put you behind me. How could I carry on wanting a guy who had used me?'

'Rose...'

'I know you're going to go into a long spiel about why you did what you did but that doesn't matter. What matters is I *couldn't* put you behind me. It didn't matter what you'd done, you'd still managed to get to me in ways...in ways I just never thought possible.'

'You underestimated the power of sex,' Art murmured, resting his hands on her narrow waist.

'I thought that if I saw the real you, the unscrupulous billionaire, then I would be so turned off that this stupid attraction would wither and die.'

Art inclined his head and knew that he had felt something similar, that if he saw her out of her surroundings and in his own terrain then common sense would reassert itself. 'No luck?' He ran his fingers along her back then over her ribcage, leaving them tantalisingly close to her breasts, close enough for her to shiver and half close her eyes.

'It doesn't make sense,' Rose practically wailed.

'Some things don't.' Art hadn't planned on taking her to bed, not tonight. But this wasn't a Rose who was not in control of her faculties. This was a Rose who was so in control that she could vocalise why she was doing what she was doing. This was the Rose he knew—open, honest, forthright and willing to confront a difficult decision head-on.

She couldn't have been a bigger turn-on.

Sex. The power of it. Never more than now was he forced to recognise the strength of body over mind. For someone always in control, this was like being thrown into a raging current without the benefit of a lifebelt. He looked forward to the challenge of battling against that current and emerging the victor.

He hooked his fingers beneath the straps of the sexy red dress and slid them down. She was wearing a silky bra that cupped her breasts like a film of gauze. Art groaned at the sight. The circular discs of her nipples were clearly visible, as was the stiffened bud tipping each pink sphere.

'You gave your phone number to another man,' he said illogically.

'Were you jealous?'

'I wanted to punch him straight into another continent.'

'But you told me I should network...'

'I can't stand the thought of another man touching you.'

'Take me,' she breathed, reaching behind her to unhook the bra, which she shrugged off, stepping back then to unzip the dress at the side and then wriggling out of it so that she was standing in front of him in just her lacy panties.

'Is this the wine talking?' Art was close to the point of no return. She wasn't tripping over her feet but there was no way he was going to get up close and personal with her, only to find himself pushed to one side because she'd fallen asleep on him. He intended to hear groans of pleasure as opposed to the snores of someone who'd had a glass too many.

He smiled at the image because if there was one woman alive who would fall asleep on him it was Rose.

'You're grinning.' Rose began undressing him, clearly trying her best not to rush.

'I'm grinning because I'm busy picturing you falling asleep on me and snoring like a trooper, leaving me with the consolation prize of a cold shower.'

'No chance of that,' Rose said huskily. 'You don't have to worry that I'm under the influence.' She shot him a wicked look from under her lashes. 'Don't tell me that you're so lacking in self-confidence that you think a woman will only sleep with you if she's had one too many.'

'Wench…' But he burst out laughing and propelled her gently back in the direction of the bed, simultaneously completing the job she had begun of getting rid of his clothes. 'Shall I show you how timid and lacking in confidence I am when it comes to pleasuring a woman?'

Rose hit the bed and flopped back onto it, laughing and pulling him down towards her.

'Please,' she breathed, arching up to kiss him. 'Please, please, please… That's exactly what I want…'

# CHAPTER NINE

ROSE HAD FANTASISED about those nights when she and Art had made love. She'd delved deep into her memory banks and closed her eyes and tasted, in the emptiness of her bed after he'd disappeared in a puff of treacherous smoke, the touch of his mouth on hers, the feel of his hands tracing the contours of her body, the heavy weight of him on top of her and the way her legs had parted for him, welcoming him into the very core of her.

Now, touching him again, she realised that no amount of recall could ever have done justice to the reality of him.

Running her hands over his lean, hard body was like tasting nectar after a diet of vinegar.

He felt so good.

She traced the corded muscles of his back and then squirmed so that she was taking charge of proceedings, flattening him against the bed and angling her body in such a way that she could devote all her attention to his vibrant arousal whilst, at the same time, he could pleasure her between her legs.

She'd forgotten how well their bodies meshed, as

though created to fit one against the other. She moved against his questing tongue, her breathing fast and furious, making little guttural noises as she licked and tasted him, feasting on his hardness and playing with his erection while she explored it with her mouth.

Her long hair was everywhere and she flipped it over her shoulder and then arched up, her whole body quivering as ripples of an orgasm began coursing slowly through her.

'Art…' she gasped, not wanting to come.

Not yet.

This time it was Art who took control. With one easy move, he flipped her so that she was now facing him and he edged her up so that there was next to no pause in his ministrations.

She was sitting over him, allowing him the greatest intimacy as he continued to flick his tongue over the stiffened bud of her core. Hands firmly on her waist so that he was keeping her in position, he teased her with his mouth and when her breathing quickened and her body began to stiffen he concentrated on bringing her to a shuddering explosive orgasm.

She spasmed against his mouth and he revelled in the honeyed moistness of her orgasm.

He'd missed this.

He'd missed more than this. It felt so good that he had to reach down and hold his own erection firm because he felt on the very edge of tipping over even though he wasn't inside her, which was where he wanted to be.

Rose subsided, temporarily spent. She lay down next

to him and wrapped her legs over his and, as one, they turned to one another so that their naked bodies were pressed up tight, hot and perspiring.

'Not fair,' she said shakily, but there was a smile in her voice as she wriggled against him, nudging her wetness against his arousal.

'No, it's not,' Art murmured indistinctly. Decidedly unfair that she had this dramatic effect on him, that she was capable of derailing his life the way she had. Just as well that he was putting it back on track. 'Dump the hotel,' he heard himself say, 'and move in with me for the rest of your stay in London.'

'Dump the hotel?'

'It's inconvenient.' He'd never asked any woman to stay in his penthouse apartment but he was comfortable with this decision because a precedent had already been set. He'd shared her space with her so no big deal if she were to share his space with him.

He wanted to be able to reach out and touch her in the middle of the night. He wanted to feel her, warm and aroused, lying next to him. He curved his hand between her thighs and stroked her soft, silky skin, nudging up to feel her wetness graze his knuckles.

He stepped away to fetch a condom from his wallet.

'I guess I could,' Rose murmured as he slipped back into bed to pull her against him. 'I guess it could work…' She parted her legs and sighed as her body began to get excited all over again. 'I mean,' she continued, voice hitched, 'I hadn't banked on any of this happening.'

'That's been the story of my life from the second I saw you,' Art agreed with heartfelt sincerity. 'You may well have converted me to the pleasures of the unforeseen.'

'We both have the same goal.'

Art caressed her breast then levered himself into a position where he could taste it. He flicked his tongue over her nipple and then took it into his mouth so that he could suckle on it while he played with her other nipple, teasing it into tight arousal.

'The same goal...' Her words registered and he slowly kissed his way up to nuzzle against her neck before settling alongside her in a lovely, comfortable position where he could carry on teasing her nipple between his fingers.

'I don't want to want you.' Rose imagined that his next girlfriend might have brains, might have more staying power, might be the woman he let into his life because he had now seen for himself that being in a kitchen together and sharing a meal and then doing the washing-up whilst talking about anything and everything was not something to be feared and reviled. She had done him a favour in pointing him in a different direction and her heart twisted because when he left her behind and walked away it would be into a relationship that might prove to be *the one*.

'And,' she continued, tugging him up because she couldn't focus on anything when he was doing what he'd been doing, 'I know you feel the same.' She paused, a fractional little pause during which he could have jumped in with a denial or said something that might have indicated an interest in more than just *getting her out of his system.* He failed to take the bait. 'So, yes, perhaps if I moved in with you for a couple of days… well, while I'm here, then this thing we have going on… well, we can get it out of our systems faster.'

Art frowned. 'My way of thinking,' he said, on cue.

'There's something about familiarity…'

'You certainly know how to massage a guy's ego. In a minute you'll start comparing me to a virus.'

'Well, it *is* a bit like that.' Rose laughed shakily.

'And what if it doesn't conveniently blow over in a couple of days?'

Rose knew that he was playing devil's advocate. 'It will,' she said firmly. 'We don't have anything in common, Art. We don't have what it takes to have a proper relationship, which is the only thing that would stop this *thing* from blowing over.'

Art frowned. 'Define a *proper* relationship. Is there a checklist for something like that?'

'More or less, if I'm being honest.'

'So now you're saying I tick none of the boxes.'

'There's still one box that gets a very big tick.'

'Glad to hear it.'

'But for me,' Rose said on a sigh, 'a relationship is so much more than just sex.'

'And yet sex, like it or not, is so much a part of any relationship. Too much talking. I get the picture. We're here and this is something we have to do and I can't tell you how much I'm going to enjoy doing it.'

He'd just never mentioned a timeline…

Rose lay in bed, half dozing, drinking him in as he

strolled through the bedroom of his penthouse apartment, completely naked, hunting down his laptop computer because, even though it was still only six in the morning, he was up and ready to work.

She was warm and replete and contented. He'd roused her an hour earlier, nudging her into compliant wakefulness, and they had made love oh, so slowly. Caught in that hazy, half asleep place, Rose had let him take her to places that had left her crying out with pleasure. When, after touching her everywhere, after exploring her soft, warm body, he had finally thrust into her, filling her up, she had felt tears leak down her cheeks and had had to surreptitiously wipe them away because that definitely wasn't part of the deal.

The package deal had kicked off three days previously, when she had fallen into his arms like a starving woman deprived of food who suddenly found herself with a ticket to an all-you-can-eat banquet.

They had made love and then, after a handful of hours' sleep, had made love again and the very next morning she had moved in with him.

They hadn't discussed how long this arrangement was going to last. How did you talk about something like that? How did you work out the length of time it would take for one person to get sick of the other?

How long would it take for him to get bored with her?

Rose knew that that was the way it was going to play out because she wasn't close to getting him out of her system. Indeed, with every passing minute spent together, he became more embedded in her bloodstream.

They'd talked about sex. He did that a lot. When they

made love he would whisper things in her ear that made her whole body burn. He would tell her, in a husky, shaky voice, how much he wanted her and what he wanted to do with her.

He was ruled by lust. He couldn't keep his hands off her and the more he showed that want, the more she needed something more. Something more powerful than *want*.

But that was off the cards and it was always going to be off the cards.

Except…now…looking at him and his careless elegance, Rose felt her heart twist and she knew with an awful sense of despair that she was powerless to initiate the necessary break-up.

She was held in place by something far bigger than lust.

Somehow, against all odds, she had fallen in love with him and she was as powerless now as a speck of flotsam being tossed around this way and that on an unpredictable, fast-flowing current.

She could only make sure he never saw her vulnerability because if he did he would run for the hills.

Love was not on his radar. Not with her. And it never would be. The novelty value that had drawn him to her might not have yet released him from its hold but, now that she was immersed in his life, she knew with dreadful certainty that she was only ever going to be a distraction for him.

He didn't do love. The highs and lows of emotion were things he would seek to avoid. Above everything, he enjoyed the power of control and that included control of his emotional life. He would find someone but she knew in her heart that he would not want someone who was as emotional as she had turned out to be.

Far from being the level-headed woman she'd imagined she was, love had turned her to mush and she wasn't ashamed of it.

Even though she knew that hurt was lurking around the corner, waiting for her.

He produced the laptop from where it had been residing under a bundle of discarded clothes on a chair in his bedroom with a grin of triumph and turned to her. 'First time this hasn't been at my fingertips.'

'You were in a hurry last night.' She forced herself to grin back, keeping it light.

'So I was,' he murmured, dumping the computer and making his way back towards the bed to lean over her, then dropping a kiss on her forehead. 'You do that to me.'

'Make you want to run?' Rose teased, playing with words.

'I can't get to you fast enough.'

Art looked at her for a few serious seconds and Rose had the feeling that there was something he wanted to tell her. A cold chill spread through her but she kept smiling, keeping it light. There could only be one thing he could have wanted to tell her that would have put that serious expression on his face and those words were not ones she wanted to hear. She swallowed down the nasty lump of desperation.

'Stay in bed with me,' she urged. 'Surely work can wait.'

'Not this.' He was still looking at her with that expression on his face.

'Big deal you have to close? I can't imagine there's any deal big enough that you can't ignore it for a few more minutes.'

His expression lightened. 'And to think I've always prided myself on being the kind of guy who can hold out for longer than a couple of minutes…although,' he mused, 'fast and furious does hold a certain appeal, I have to admit.' He sighed, glanced at his cell phone and looked at her again with that pensive expression, thinking thoughts she couldn't begin to fathom. 'Unfortunately, this has nothing to do with work, as such…'

'Why am I getting the feeling that you're speaking in riddles?'

For a few seconds Art remained silent and during those few seconds Rose felt her heart clench tightly, painfully in her chest. Now was the time for her to voice her thoughts and either give him permission to walk away or else pre-empt his departure by announcing hers first.

She was spared any decision because just at that moment his phone buzzed. He looked at the number, then at her.

'Private call,' he said lightly, turning away.

He'd never done that before. Fighting down a wave of nausea, Rose hurriedly leapt out of the bed the second he had left the bedroom, shutting the door quietly behind him. She flew into the bathroom and had a very quick shower. She was dressed and ready for the day and he still had not returned.

Was the call so important that he had to take it at

this ungodly hour, without even taking time out to get dressed?

*Was it another woman?*

She knew that he had conference calls at strange hours from people in a different time zone, but he had always been fully prepped for those. He'd always conducted them in front of his computer, accessing information while talking to whoever might be on the line.

This was…different.

Rose couldn't credit that he might sleep with her whilst having something going on with someone else. He just wasn't that kind of guy, but then maybe, quite by chance, he had met someone in the last day or so. Was that so tough to believe? Hadn't she already come to the conclusion that he was a changed man, even though he might not see it for himself? A man more open to the possibility of letting someone into his life? A suitable woman.

People gave out vibes without even realising it. Had he projected some sort of availability-to-the-right-woman vibe?

Tense with anxiety, she stood back and looked at her reflection in the mirror. She was nothing special, however much he might wax lyrical about her sexiness.

She was tall and rangy and her looks, such as they were, were unconventional.

Was his private call with a woman with more to offer in the looks department? Was he returning to his comfort zone after his brush with a girl from the wrong side of the tracks?

She found him in the kitchen and he was no longer

on the phone. He was also no longer buck naked but had a towel slung around his lean hips. He must have nabbed it from the spare bathroom while he had been strolling to the kitchen.

Coffee was on the go.

He was so drop-dead gorgeous. So sinfully sexy. So horribly addictive. She remembered that she had fallen for him within five minutes of meeting him. So much for her much-prized defence system when it came to the opposite sex!

'What was that about?'

Art stilled. He'd been reaching for a couple of mugs and he paused for a fraction of a second.

'Coffee?'

'You're not going to answer?'

Rose was dismayed at the shrill, demanding tone of her voice. She had aimed for banter mingled with amused curiosity. She had ended up with shrewish nag but she couldn't claw her way back from the question and she wasn't sure she wanted to. If he was going to break it off with her because of some other woman then he should have the decency to come right out and tell her.

She shouldn't have to second-guess.

'I didn't think that sharing my private phone calls was part and parcel of what we had.'

Rose flushed. 'Who was it?' she was horrified to hear herself ask.

'I think this is a conversation best put on hold,' Art said coolly.

'And I happen to think that I deserve an answer. If it was a personal call with another woman, then I deserve to know. I realise this isn't anything serious but I'm not interested in sleeping with anyone who's seeing someone else on the side.'

'Is that what you think?' he asked quietly.

Rose hesitated but, like someone who had crossed a certain line, she was now doomed to carry on walking that road. And besides, she roused herself to a place of self-righteous justification, she *did* deserve to know if he was thinking about ditching her for someone else!

'How do I know what to think if you won't tell me what's going on?' she muttered.

'I'm going to get changed.'

'You're walking away from an uncomfortable conversation,' she challenged but he was already heading back to the bedroom and after a while she tripped along behind him.

Art stopped dead in his tracks and looked at her, eyes flint-hard. 'I don't do this,' he said calmly.

Rose returned that gaze with one that was equally cool. 'Do what, Art?' She folded her arms, determined to brave out what she knew was going to be their final conversation. 'Discuss anything you might find a little awkward? I know this isn't about love and commitment, but it should be about respect and if you respected me you wouldn't baulk at having this conversation.'

Rose hoped that he would read nothing in her eyes that gave the lie to that statement because when it came to love she was drowning under the weight of it. Pride would never allow her to admit that, however. She was going to leave but she would leave without him ever having cause to think that he had had a narrow escape from yet another needy woman who had foolishly disobeyed his *Do Not Trespass* signs and developed unacceptable feelings towards him.

He had let slip in conversation the headaches he had had with a couple of previous girlfriends who had wanted him to meet the parents, who had mentioned the possibility of making plans further ahead than the next couple of hours.

Rose had absorbed those passing comments and was not going to be bracketed in the same category, to become yet another irritating ex to be produced during some future conversation with some future woman.

Art's eyebrows shot up but something made him hesitate before heading back to the bedroom.

'I'm not going to have this conversation,' he said abruptly. 'If you feel that I am the sort of man who disrespects women, who has somehow disrespected *you*, then it's clear that we should not be together.'

'Art...'

'I'll be back but don't wait up.'

'Is that your way of saying that you'd like me to be gone by the time you return? Because if it is then why don't you have the guts to come right out and say so?'

'No one speaks to me like that!'

Rose folded her arms and stared at him mutinously. On the inside she was breaking up into pieces. On the outside she refused to show him just how much she was hurting. 'Then you're right,' she said gruffly. 'It's clear that we shouldn't be together if I'm only allowed to speak to you in a certain way!'

The tense silence between them stretched on and on and on…stretched until she could feel all her wretchedness washing over her in a painful tidal wave.

'Like I said,' Art drawled, 'don't wait up.'

Rose watched in silence as he threw aside the towel to get dressed. She found that she couldn't look at him. Even at the height of this toxic argument, she could still be moved by his sheer animal beauty. She didn't want to be moved.

He left the room without a backward glance and for a while she actually hoped that he would have second thoughts and return.

He didn't.

She had no idea where he'd gone and her feverish imagination provided her with all sorts of unwelcome scenarios. Had he disappeared into the waiting arms of some other woman? Had he somehow manoeuvred a situation in which she would react in a way that would give him an out?

She wasn't going to hang around to find out and there was nothing more to be said.

She gathered her things in record time. She hadn't brought much with her and what little she *had* brought took ten minutes to toss into her case.

She paused to look at the wonderful dress she had worn for the charity event that had been so memorable for so many reasons.

No way was she taking it with her.

It took her half an hour and then she was out of the mansion block and casting one last look behind her from the back of a black cab.

\* \* \*

Art returned to an empty apartment. Of course he knew that she would be gone by the time he got back. He'd disappeared for over four hours. No explanation. What would have possessed her to hang around?

He flipped on the lights and went straight to his computer and switched it on. In his peripheral vision, he could tell that all her belongings had gone with her. There was no need for him to waste his energy hunting for evidence of her departure.

The screen opened up and he stared at it and realised that it really was possible to look at numbers and letters and symbols and see absolutely nothing whatsoever.

She would have caught a taxi to the station and would be heading back to her house by train. He was tempted to look up the possible departure times of the trains and resisted.

He'd done the right thing. That reaction was sufficient to harden his resolve. He had been weak once, had engineered a situation because he had still wanted her and had been unable to resist the demands of his body, but that weakness was something that had to be overcome.

He had seen where emotional weakness could lead. Those lessons had been learned when he had been too young but they were lessons he would never forget.

His indecision had been getting on his nerves and so he'd killed it fast. He hadn't signed up to a querulous woman throwing a hissy fit because he refused to be subjected to a cross-examination.

So what if that phone call had had nothing to do with a woman?

He scowled, mood plummeting faster than the speed of light. Right about now she should be winding her arms around him, warm and naked and distracting.

Right about now he should be forgetting about work and climbing right back into bed with her because he couldn't do anything *but* climb into bed with her whenever they were in this room.

Art envisaged what her reaction would be in a couple of months, when the full extent of that phone call became common knowledge.

He'd deceived her once but she had returned to him and he knew that it had been something she would not have undertaken lightly.

Sex was all well and good but she would have had to square it with her conscience and he'd never met any woman with a more lively conscience. Her conscience practically bounced off the walls.

To discover what she inevitably would, to find out without benefit of any explanation...

He abandoned all attempts to focus on work, sat back and wearily rubbed his eyes with the pads of his thumbs.

He'd never thought himself to have a particularly active or vivid imagination but he was imagining now, in a very vivid fashion indeed, the horror that would engulf her were she to discover, as she would in due course, that there would be more going on that vast acreage of land than a handful of tasteful houses.

It would be the ultimate deception for her because she would know that he would have had countless opportunities to raise the issue. To be deceived once was forgivable. To be deceived twice would be the ultimate sin in her eyes.

He should have broached the subject. That phone call would have provided the perfect opportunity to raise it. Instead, the shutters had slammed shut on her. Habit. He had never been a man to be nagged or cajoled into saying or doing anything he didn't want to say or do. He had reacted with stunning predictability.

And it had been a mistake.

The truth was that she deserved honesty—and that was exactly what he was going to give her.

The slate would then be wiped clean.

Mind made up, Art didn't bother consulting anything as pedestrian as train timetables. Why would he? He had two options. His private helicopter or his driver. Or he could take any one of his fast cars and drive himself.

Which was exactly what he chose to do.

He didn't know whether he would reach her house before her but it didn't matter. What mattered, and mattered with an urgency he couldn't quite put into words, was that they talked.

He'd say what he had to say and then leave.

Traffic was light as he left London. A Ferrari was built to eat up the miles with silent efficiency and it did.

Under normal circumstances, he would have kicked back and enjoyed the dynamic horsepower of a car he rarely got to drive but his mind was too busy projecting the conversation that was going to take place.

He made it to her house in record time and knew, without even having to ring the doorbell, that she wasn't yet there.

With any luck, she was going to show up soon and hadn't decided to do a spot of sightseeing before catching the train back.

Art positioned the powerful car at the perfect angle to see her just as she entered her drive. He wasn't going to let her run away this time.

Rose was spent by the time she made it to the local outpost where trains arrived in their own sweet time. The slow journey would have got on her nerves at any other time but on this occasion she relished the unhurried tempo of the trip. Her head felt as though it was bursting with thoughts, too many thoughts to be contained, just as her heart was bursting with too many feelings.

And at the very centre of all those thoughts and feelings was the dark, throbbing knowledge that she was not going to see Art again. The void that opened up inside her when she thought about that was so big that it threatened to swallow her up like a sinkhole.

At the station she hailed a taxi, which exited the small car park as though urgency was a concept that didn't exist. She knew the taxi driver. She had done some pro bono work for his father two years previously, and she heard herself chatting to him but from a long way away.

She was so tired.

Lapsing into silence, she closed her eyes and wasn't aware that she was approaching her house until the taxi began to slow, until it swerved slowly into the drive, and only then did she open her eyes and stir herself into wakefulness.

Only then did she see the red car in the drive, sleek and elegant and so, *so* sexy.

# CHAPTER TEN

ART WAS OUT of the car before the passenger door of the taxi had opened. He'd been hanging around for over an hour. He'd stretched his legs a couple of times but he still felt cramped and restless.

Watching through narrowed eyes as she emerged, he felt at peace for the first time since he had left London.

No…since she had re-entered his life, if not before.

His thoughts were so clear he felt washed clean.

He could see the wariness in her eyes and he strode towards her before that wariness could persuade her to get back into the taxi and disappear, leaving him stranded on her doorstep.

'What are you doing here?' Rose's voice was curt as she paid the taxi driver, who was watching proceedings with keen interest. 'Thanks, Stephen—' she said to the driver through the window of the car, eyebrows raised '—I won't keep you. I expect Jenny and the kids would like to have you home.'

'That the big-shot she's been banging on about for weeks?'

'No idea, Steve. I don't know how many big-shots

Jenny's met recently...' She slammed shut the door and leaned towards him. 'Give her my love and the thumbs-up that everything's in place for the changes to the library. She can start picking out colours for the new kids' space.'

Rose was playing for time but, with no distraction left, she remained where she was as Steve headed away. Her case was on the ground at her feet.

'I've been waiting here for over an hour.' For the first time in living memory, Art was nervous. He almost failed to recognise the sensation. He couldn't take his eyes off her. He wanted to climb into her head and read what she was thinking but her expression was cool and remote and he wondered...where did he go from here?

Scowling and ill at ease, he walked towards her and was pleased to note that, almost indiscernibly, she flinched. He was having some kind of effect on her and that was good because, going by her expression, he could have been a wind-up toy.

'So sorry to have kept you waiting,' Rose said coolly, tilting her head at a mutinous angle and refusing to back away. 'And you still haven't told me what you're doing here.'

'I...' He shook his head, looked away, raked his fingers through his hair and then returned his dark gaze to her pale, cool face. 'I...shouldn't have...let you leave... with the wrong idea...' was pretty much all he could find to say.

'Not interested,' Rose muttered, looking away. 'You're a free agent and you can do what you want. You're right. You don't owe me any explanations.'

'Are we going to carry on this conversation out here?'

'I didn't think we were having a conversation. You came here to explain whatever it is you feel you should explain and I'm liberating you from that responsibility. So there's no conversation to be had.'

'It was about the land.'

'Sorry?'

'I was on the phone to someone about the land. The land you were protecting from greedy developers like me. I wanted to tell you…' Art looked away but only momentarily.

'The land?' Rose looked at him in confusion because this was the last thing she'd been expecting to hear. 'You weren't on the phone to a woman?'

'I'm monogamous.' His lips quirked in a dry smile but he had no idea how this was going to play out and the smile only lasted a second. His usual panache and easy self-assurance were nowhere in evidence. 'And when would I have had time to think about frolicking with another woman? You've kept me pretty busy…'

'What about the land?'

Lengthening silence greeted this and eventually Rose spun around and began walking towards the house.

'Tell me you haven't been keeping more from me about the land,' she said quietly as soon as the front door was shut behind them. She clearly hadn't wanted to invite him into the house but he'd left her with no choice.

'You don't have the complete picture,' Art said flatly. Cold dread was gripping him and he knew now that full disclosure should have been his approach. But events had moved swiftly and now…

He was going to lose her and if that happened he had

no idea what he was going to do because he couldn't contemplate a life without her in it. He'd screwed up.

'Start small, end up big. Is that the complete picture?' They were in the kitchen. Rose felt as if she could do with a stiff drink but instead she began the business of making herself a cup of coffee—anything to still her nerves, which were running amok as she gradually worked out that he had deceived her once again.

Had he slept with her the second time round so that he could build up to yet more revelations about what he intended to do with the acres of land he had bought?

Had he sweet-talked her into phase one with the intention of sweet-talking her into phase two, except she'd scuppered his plans by overhearing that conversation, jumping to the wrong conclusion and then walking out on him before he could complete what he had set out to do?

She felt sick.

'You didn't want a handful of tasteful mansions with lots of spare land, did you? That wouldn't have made financial sense. What you wanted was to start with a handful of tasteful mansions and then what, Art? A housing estate? Mass housing that would mean more profits for you? As if you aren't rich enough already.'

She managed to make it to the kitchen table, now free from placards and posters and cardboard with rousing slogans, and she sank into one of the chairs.

'Way too rich.' Art drew a chair up close to hers, as if to stop her from somehow fleeing the room. She didn't like his positioning and automatically drew back into herself, freezing him out as her defences came down. When he leaned forward, elbows resting loosely on his thighs, he was practically touching her.

'Too rich to think about whether putting up a hundred houses is going to net me more money than putting up ten.' He sighed heavily, caught her eye and held her gaze. 'But you're right. I haven't been entirely honest with you.'

'I don't want to hear.'

'And normally that would work for me,' Art returned. 'Normally justifying myself in any way, shape or form isn't something I would see the need to do, but in this instance...'

'Am I supposed to think that you have a conscience?' Rose questioned painfully.

'I don't suppose I've given you a lot of reason to trust anything I have to say.'

'Spot on.'

'But...' He shook his head. 'I'll try to start at the beginning. I... You'll have to bear with me. I don't... know how this is done.'

'How what is done?'

'This talking business.'

'This *talking business*? What does that even *mean*?' But there was an air of vulnerability about him that she'd never seen before and it did something to her even though she fought hard to resist the pull and tried to remember that this wasn't going to end up in a good place.

'I... I've never had much time for talking, Rose. Not when it came to women. When it came to women, things were very clear-cut. It was all about mutual pleasure.

Nothing lasted and nothing was meant to. It was the way I liked it. When I met you, I had an agenda, but in no way was sleeping with you part of that agenda, and of course that should have set the alarm bells ringing. The fact that sleeping with you made no sense and yet I had to do it, had to get you into bed. It was as though something bigger and stronger than me had taken charge and was dictating how I behaved when it came to you.'

Rose looked at him with a jaundiced expression and wondered whether she was supposed to melt at that admission. She wished he'd back away a bit. His proximity was suffocating her.

'You need to just tell me what else you've been hiding from me,' she said quietly. 'I don't want to hear about…how much you wanted me…'

Art sat back and half closed his eyes, then he looked at her for a while in silence.

'There was always an agenda for that land. I had to have it. Had to make sure that everything went through and I had to get the residents of the village onside. Yes, for the expensive houses that were going to be built but also, in due course, for more building work that I had planned.'

'I thought as much.' Rose looked away, heart pounding, bile in her mouth.

'You really don't.' He turned her face to his, finger lightly under her chin, compelling them to lock eyes, and Rose gazed helplessly at him.

'I can't bear the thought of being used, Art. All my life, the one thing I've taken away from what happened to my mum is that I would never allow myself to be used by any man. She abandoned me for a man she met and knew for five seconds! Yes, she came back but I'd lost a lot in that time that she'd been away and I'd grown up and learned lessons. Lesson one was that when it came to my heart, common sense was always going to be more valuable than stupid, crazy *lust*.'

'We're singing from the same song sheet,' Art murmured. 'We both had lessons ingrained into us thanks to our backgrounds. Rich or poor, our experiences made us the cautious people we ended up being. I was happy to be ruled by lust. I just resisted anything more than that. Until you. Until you came along.'

'What do you mean?' Rose found that she was holding her breath and she exhaled slowly, hoping that her calm, detached exterior was still in place, making no assumptions even though her heart was beating fast now but with forbidden excitement.

'I told myself that it was a mistake to sleep with you. I didn't want the waters to be muddied. I had come for a specific reason and I naturally assumed that a minor temptation wasn't going to confuse the issue. How wrong I was. I decided where was the harm? There wouldn't be any fallout because I was always, had always been and always would be, in control of my choices. We were both consenting adults and, if anything, getting you into bed would give me an added advantage in persuading you to listen to reason when it came to the protest.' She looked away sharply and Art tilted her stubborn face back to his.

'The truth of the matter was that I couldn't resist you. You did something to me and you carried on doing it even when I left and returned to London. I couldn't get you out of my mind. I kept drifting off into inappropriate fantasies at inappropriate times. In the middle of conversations, in the thick of an important meeting, just as I was about to sink my teeth into the finest food money could buy. And yet I still didn't wake up to what should have been blindingly obvious.'

'Which is what?'

'Somewhere along the line I fell in love with you. Please don't say anything because I need to tell you about the land. After you've heard what I have to say I'll leave, but I felt you needed to know…how I felt.'

'Art…'

*He'd fallen in love with her? Did he really mean that?*

Her heart had migrated to her mouth so when she spoke her voice was muffled and she had to clear her throat. 'Do you mean that?'

'I wasn't looking for love. I've never been looking for love. My father had so many ex-wives that so-called *love* was always in plentiful supply and always, without fail, ended up in the divorce courts, where each and every one would wrangle until they went blue in the face for a slice of his money. I was jaded beyond belief by the time I left my teens behind. Love was for idiots and I was never going to be an idiot. The truth is that I just never fell in love and I never realised that love makes idiots of us all.'

'Why didn't you say something?' Rose whispered.

'How could I,' Art asked wryly, 'when I didn't recognise the symptoms?'

*Symptoms?* Never had that single word held such thrilling promise.

'Please tell me about the land.' Everything should have been perfect. The man of her dreams had just declared his love for her and yet the rest of his story cast a long shadow, even though she couldn't see what could possibly spoil the moment. She just knew that a fly in the ointment could turn out to be a lot more toxic than it might first appear. If she was going to get toxic, then she wanted to get it straight away.

'I targeted that land because I want to build an equestrian centre there,' Art said heavily. 'And not just an equestrian centre, but something of a farming complex. You won't be getting the neat arrangement of polite, high-spec houses you signed up for and there's no other way of putting it but to tell it like it is.' His mouth twisted crookedly. 'In hindsight, if I could have predicted how circumstances would unravel, I would have taken the plunge from the very start but hindsight, as I've discovered to my cost, is a wonderful thing. And, like I've said—' he smiled with self-mockery '—hindsight isn't something I've ever had time for. My predictive talents had never been challenged and when you know what's coming you're not glancing over your shoulder and shaking your head because you took the wrong turning.'

'Sorry? You want to build *a farm*?' Rose was finding it hard to get past that stark announcement.

'Long story, but… I have a stepbrother, José. He's severely autistic and currently in a home in the New

Forest. He's not yet twenty-two but the home, good as it is, really can't deal with the needs of a young adult.'

'You have a brother...'

'Stepbrother. And the only step-sibling I've ever had time for. Ironic, given his mother had very *little* time for him. In fact, my father had no idea he existed at all until after the marriage had ended. Eliza kept her son's existence under wraps, just in case it jeopardised the pot of gold at the end of the rainbow. At the time, José had been shoved in a mixed bag home and practically forgotten. I met him and felt sorry for him. No, more than that. I wanted to protect him and then I grew to love him. He was honest and trusting and incredibly talented in certain areas but he'd been hung out to dry by his scheming mother, who had no time for him. To her credit, she did pop her head into the home now and again but where she left off, I found that I was taking over. Years after she disappeared from my father's life, she was killed in a road accident, at which point I took José under my wing. I was climbing the ladder of success. It became my mission to ensure that he got the best that money could buy. I saved José but, in a strange way, I think José also saved me.'

'Art, my head is spinning.'

'There's no concise way to explain all of this. I just need you to understand that my dilemma was finding a place where I could develop a centre for José and for other kids like him. A handful. He is soothed by horses and enjoys being outdoors. He has a way with them. The farm would be something of a therapeutic centre.

Some arts and crafts could be incorporated. You'd be surprised at how talented some of these kids are.'

'But why on earth didn't you say anything about this?'

'To the council?' His eyebrows shot up. 'People can be strange when it comes to having anyone different as their neighbours. It took a long time to find a suitable location, somewhere commutable for me, a convenient middle ground for other occupants. I wasn't going to risk jeopardising the project by introducing it from the beginning. I thought that by the time the community got accustomed to the notion of the land being developed they would be more open to my future plans for the place.'

'I love you,' Rose said simply, because all of this showed her a side to him that she'd known was there, a caring, thoughtful side lurking underneath the ruthless billionaire exterior.

It was the side that had sucked her in and, even when he'd confessed to his deception, had kept her sucked in because deep down she had known him for the good guy he was. She'd seen the moral integrity underneath the tough *love is for the birds* exterior.

'You're not upset that I lied to you yet again?' Art looked as though his heart was soaring.

'I'd like to meet your stepbrother one day.'

Art reached out but he didn't tug her towards him. Instead, he held her hands in his. It was a chaste gesture that made her smile.

'You will,' he said gruffly. 'But first you have to promise me one thing.'

'What?' She nudged closer to him and played with his fingers. She couldn't help herself. She reached out and stroked the side of his face with the back of her hand, then she traced the contours of his mouth.

She leaned into him and kissed him, a slow, tender, melting kiss and it felt good to have her love out in the open, to be as vulnerable as he was.

'Promise me that you'll marry me,' Art said in a muffled voice. 'Because I can't imagine a life without you in it. I want to go to sleep with you and wake up to you. I don't want to ever let you go.'

'Yes.' Rose smiled. 'A thousand times *yes*.'

They were married just as the finishing touches were being put to the local library.

It had been planned as a quiet wedding but it turned out to be rather larger than either of them had expected. Once one person had been invited others had to be included, and Rose discovered that she had done a lot more for the residents of her quiet community than she had ever dreamed.

Everyone wanted to come.

Everyone knew her story and the wedding was almost as much of a fairy tale for them as for her.

She wore a simple cream dress and little silk buds were woven into her long hair, and the look on Art's face when he turned to look at her as she walked up the aisle of the little country church was something she would take with her for as long as she lived.

And now…

Six months later, life couldn't be better and so much had changed. For starters, the house had no more leaks in need of fixing. It had been renovated to its original splendour but, with all the right planning permission in place, was now a fully functioning office catering for several start-up companies as well as the legal practice which Phil, Rose's partner, had taken over in its entirety.

Rose no longer lived there but whenever she returned she marvelled at its wonderful transformation.

'I don't think,' she confided to Art a few weeks after she had moved out and shortly before their wedding, 'that I ever really saw it as *my* house. Even though, technically, it was. And even though I always, always knew it to be a real blessing. I guess I always somehow associated it with a time in my life that brought back bad memories so, whilst I'm happy it's renovated, I'm pleased I no longer live in it.'

Where she lived now could not have been more wonderful. Not the sprawling modernist vision in London which Art had occupied but, he also admitted, never actually viewed as anything other than a handy space in a useful location, but a country cottage that was the perfect blend of ancient and modern.

It was just outside London, convenient for commuting both back to London by train and to the centre in the Cotswolds where José would be eventually located.

Rose had fallen in love with the cottage at first sight.

With the husband of her dreams and the house to match, she hadn't thought that life could get any better but it had.

She started as she heard the front door open and her heart quickened, as it always did at the arrival of her husband.

She rose to greet him and smiled at the naked love and desire etched on his lean face.

He was so beautiful and he was *hers*. She smiled at the thrill of possession that swelled inside her.

Art smiled back, moving smoothly towards her while undoing the top couple of buttons of his shirt.

'You don't get to look like that without accepting that there'll be consequences.' He pulled her towards him, cupped her rounded bottom and crushed her against him so that she could feel the tell-tale stirring of his desire.

'Look like what?' Rose burst out laughing, drawing back and capturing his face between her hands.

'Oh, you know…pair of jeans, tee shirt, flip-flops…'

'Oh, you mean my *fancy* outfit.'

'You've gone all out on the dinner, I see.' Art peered around her to see the kitchen table, which was candlelit and set in some style. 'What have I forgotten? It's not a birthday and it's definitely not our anniversary, unless it's the anniversary of the first time you decided that I was the best thing that ever happened to you, which would have been, hmm, about five minutes after we met?'

'Time's done nothing to dim that ego of yours, Arturo da Costa, has it?'

Art burst out laughing. 'Don't keep me in suspense. With any other woman, I'd be inclined to think that you're bracing me for some wildly extravagant purchase, but then, my darling, you're not any other woman and I thank my lucky stars for that every day.'

Rose tugged him into the huge open-plan kitchen with its granite countertops and its wonderful state-of-the-art built-in appliances.

'Champagne,' Art murmured, glancing at the counter. 'Now I'm really beginning to get worried.'

'Then don't. I actually would have dressed up for the occasion but I opted for comfortable over glamorous.'

'Don't distract me.'

'The champagne is for you. I'll be sticking to mineral water for the moment and for the next, oh, let's say… nine months or so…'

'Are you telling me what I think you're telling me?'

'I'm pregnant.'

Art wrapped his arms around her and held her tight to him for several long minutes. 'I couldn't have asked for a better end to my day, my darling. I love you so very much.'

'And I love you too. Now and for ever.'

\* \* \* \* \*

# THE SPANIARD'S PLEASURABLE VENGEANCE

## LUCY MONROE

For my readers, because you've stuck with me through the challenges that make writing so hard. Your letters reminded me that my stories touch real people's hearts  and that is why I write, so thank you! I am so grateful to each of you who picks up a book and completes the circle of connection to me, the author, and especially thankful for the readers who have encouraged me through some of the most difficult times in my life. I write for all of you.

# PROLOGUE

"I DON'T NEED a damn appointment! I'm his sister, you cretin." The sharp American accent and strident tone of Gracia's voice reached Basilio through his partially closed office door.

The heavy door opened forcefully, slamming back against the rich paneling of his wall, but surprisingly, his administrative assistant made it into the office a step ahead of Basilio's sister. "Sir, I'm sorry." The distress at not holding her post was clear in his admin's tone. "She refused to even wait for me to ascertain if you were still on your conference call."

Gracia came storming around his admin at the same time as his executive assistant came rushing in from her annex office.

"What is going on in here?" Her hair in a severe chignon, her navy business suit immaculate, his fifty-year-old executive assistant could do freezing aristocratic disapproval better than even Basilio's mother, who was actually the daughter of a count.

His admin immediately began apologizing again as he stood from his desk, giving his sister a look that would have made Basilio's mother proud. Gracia halted in her approach to his desk, her annoyed expression morphing to one of consternation.

She gave the EA a moderately polite look before looking at Basilio with wariness. "It is a family emergency."

Basilio merely waited in silence for more information.

His executive assistant wasn't so patient. "I see, and there

was no time for you to call and apprise us of your imminent arrival so we could clear your brother's schedule on
your drive from the airport?" Camila Lopez asked with
clear censure.

Gracia looked between Basilio and his EA, her cheeks
going pink. "I wasn't thinking of calling. Only getting here."

"And if *Señor* Perez had been away from the office?"
Camila pressed with a single raised, perfectly shaped black
eyebrow.

"I didn't think of that."

As amusing as he found his sister's interaction with his
executive assistant, Basilio did not have time for the entertainment. He did, in fact, have a very busy day.

"Thank you for your assistance and I will need the next
thirty minutes for Gracia," he said to both his admin and
Camila. "See that we are not disturbed."

"Of course, *señor*," Camila said to him with just the
right amount of deference before offering his sister a look
that said clearly, she wasn't worried about someone *else*
interrupting.

Once the other two women had left his office, both doors
through which they'd gone closed firmly behind them, Basilio indicated one of the chairs facing his desk. "Sit down,
Gracia, and tell me what has you forcing your way past
my admin."

Gracia sank into the seat with more grace than her behavior had shown so far. "It really is a family emergency, Baz."

For the family that so rarely remembered he was a member?

"Explain," he demanded as he settled back into his own
chair.

Gracia frowned at his tone. "You remember when that
awful teenager hit little Jamie with her car?"

"I am unlikely to forget." Five years before, his then four-
year-old nephew had spent two weeks in a coma after being
hit by a car while on an outing with his mother.

"Well, apparently, she changed her name and moved away from Southern California."

"Unsurprising." While Basilio had been in Spain at the time, saving his father's company from bankruptcy, he knew that Miranda Weber had been vilified in the broadcast media and even worse on all the social media outlets.

"Yes, well. Some idiotic reporter found out who she is and is resurrecting the story."

And this was the family emergency that she needed Basilio's help with? When usually both Carlos and Gracia were happy to forget they were half siblings most of the time.

Putting aside his own sense of cynicism about their definition of family, Basilio said, "I can see where that would be emotionally difficult for Carlos and Tiffany."

"Yes. It's awful! And this time some fly-by-night morning gossip show wants to interview the girl. She's all set to give them her side of the story."

"She's not a girl any longer, surely." Miranda had been nineteen five years ago.

"Woman, then," Gracia said dismissively. "She'll go on television and lie. About our family!"

"Surely Carlos has PR people who can handle this." Not to mention lawyers. If the woman lied in a public forum, they could bring a civil suit.

"You know he prefers you call him Carl."

Yes, because it was less Spanish, letting him forget he ever had a father named Armand Perez. "That is what you want to discuss now?" Basilio asked, his voice dry.

"No, of course not." Gracia wrung her hands. "It's just you have to do something!"

"What do you imagine I can do that Carl and Tiffany cannot? They are not exactly without resources." Carlos's wife came from an old and wealthy East Coast family.

Basilio's brother ran his stepfather's business, one of respectable enough size to have public relations people on retainer. While Perez Holdings was much bigger and more successful now, that had not always been the case.

"She had a restraining order taken out against both Carl and Tiffany. It includes any representative working for, or on retainer from, them."

"How did she manage that?" Basilio wondered aloud.

"It's insane, I know."

That was not what Basilio had meant. For Miranda Weber to obtain such a thing, serious threats had to have been made. Cursed with a deep-seated sense of entitlement, his brother could be a hothead, as well. Carlos had never had to save a company, or put the hours into shoring up his family's name in the international community as Basilio had done. When their father split with Carlos and Gracia's mother, she'd remarried quickly and both of Basilio's older siblings had embraced their new American family wholeheartedly, taking their stepfather's last name and rejecting their Spanish heritage for their American mother's way of life.

While Basilio was not sure he could blame Carlos, considering the current circumstances, clearly the older man's temper and certainty he could do as he pleased had cost him access to Miranda.

When Basilio didn't say anything right away, Gracia added, "I think it might have been her brother-in-law or something."

"She has a sister?" He didn't remember that. He'd thought the woman who put his nephew into a coma was an only child.

"Apparently. Only a half sister, but still…"

"Yes, still." Basilio knew just how little regard his sister and brother had for the concept of a half sibling.

"Oh, get off it, Baz. I didn't mean you."

"As you say."

Gracia leaned forward. "You need to do something."

"What would you have me do?"

"Well, Carl's company doesn't have quite the sway yours does."

That was an understatement. Basilio had ruthlessly built Perez Holdings into a powerful multibillion-dollar international entity, while his brother's realty group was worth mere millions. "The Madison Realty Group is hardly a global concern" was all Basilio said, though.

"Exactly."

"So?" Basilio prompted.

Gracia's expression turned crafty. "So, maybe you can convince the brother-in-law to withdraw his support."

"Who is this in-law?"

"His name is Andreas Kostas. That's Greek, isn't it? I don't remember the name of his company."

Surprise made Basilio sit up straighter in his chair. "Yes, it is Greek, and I know exactly who he is. My company uses his company's security software, or what used to be his company. I believe he recently merged with Hawk Enterprises."

Andreas Kostas was a shark's shark and he was now in business with one of the biggest sharks swimming in their waters. No wonder Carlos needed help dealing with Miranda's family.

Gracia waved that information away. "Whatever. He didn't respond well when Carl contacted him, hoping to convince him to talk Miranda out of doing the interview."

"If he threatened him, I don't imagine so." Kostas wasn't known for tolerating fools or blowhards. Unfortunately, Carlos had played both on occasion.

"Who said Carl threatened anybody?" Gracia sounded indignant, but her guilty expression didn't jibe with her words.

Basilio just gave his sister a look until she squirmed in her chair.

"Okay, he may have said some things he didn't mean,

but come on." Gracia waved her hands in agitation. "He and Tiffany went through enough five years ago."

"On that we can agree."

"So, you'll do something?"

"I will come to the States and look into the situation." That was all he would promise.

If it came down to it, Basilio wasn't above using his influence and power to push either Andreas Kostas or his sister-in-law into doing what was best for Basilio's family because for him family came first, last and always. However, first he would get some real answers about what was going on.

"You have to hurry. She's slated to do her interview in three weeks. The recent media storm is just starting to die down, and if she does that interview, it's bound to blow everything up again."

"Understood. What name does she go by now?"

"She kept her first name, but changed Weber to Smith."

"Very anonymous."

Gracia's lips twisted in distaste. "Yes."

Well, Weber or Smith, Basilio had every intention of finding the woman who had already cost his family so much. Whatever it took, he would protect the brother and sister-in-law who had suffered enough.

# CHAPTER ONE

LATE FOR DINNER with her newfound sister and recently acquired brother-in-law, Randi rushed out of her even more recently acquired office.

She'd been shocked and delighted when Kayla asked Randi if she was interested in taking over managing responsibilities for Kayla's for Kids, the shelter her sister had founded for at-risk children and youth. The opportunity to do what Randi loved while living near enough to get to know her long-lost sister had been too good to pass up. Besides, she got to use both her degree in business and adjunct degree in social services.

Part of her new job would include launching a second site in the western suburbs of Portland. Apparently, Andreas had donated enough for the expansion as a wedding gift, in addition to designating his new company's charitable contributions all to Kayla's for Kids, making fund-raising efforts a lot less stressful for Randi's team.

It was Randi's dream job and she adored her sister and brother-in-law for making it possible.

Collision with a hard, muscular wall on the sidewalk abruptly halted Randi's headlong flight to her car.

She cried out and then immediately started apologizing, even as she felt her balance waver. "I'm so sorry! I didn't see you."

Big, strong hands on her upper arms stopped her bounce backward that would have landed Randi on her backside. "Is that a common occurrence, running into people you didn't see?" he asked, a foreign accent subtle but unmistakable.

Randi winced. The man could not know the old wound his words bled yet again.

She pulled herself together with a firm mental yank and shrugged. "I'd love to say *no*, but I have a tendency toward klutziness, especially when I'm in a rush."

Why she was admitting that particular failing to this gorgeous man, she did not know. Because man, total hottie alert. Easily as tall as her brother-in-law, who stood at six feet four inches, the black-haired man with sexy stubble on his face towered over Randi's own five feet five inches.

Espresso-brown eyes locked on hers. "I see. Are you in a rush often?"

For whatever reason, she didn't step back from him. "Not really, just sometimes. Though it's usually walls I run into, or doorjambs, or you know, furniture. I hardly ever bump into people."

Even, white teeth flashed in a smile that didn't quite reach his dark brown eyes. "I'm special, then."

"You could take it that way, yes."

He released her arms. Finally, but he did not step out of her personal space. "I believe I will."

"Okay." Heat climbed up her neck and into her cheeks that Randi could do nothing about.

He offered his hand. "Basilio Perez."

"Oh, um, Randi Smith." She laid her palm against his.

Instead of shaking hands, he lifted hers to his lips, brushing a barely there kiss on the backs of her knuckles. "Nice to meet you, Ms. Smith."

Randi finally understood what it meant to be electrified by a man's touch. His lips against her skin sent frissons of sensation throughout her body and she gasped.

"Ms. Smith? Are you all right?" There was something in his too-knowing gaze that said he was perfectly aware of the effect he was having on her.

She tried to speak, then cleared her throat and tried again. "Randi, please."

"Randi is short for?"

"Oh, um, no one ever asks. They just ask stuff like if I enjoy having a boy's name."

"So?" He hadn't let go of her hand and he now brushed his thumb over her knuckles, where his lips had been.

She had no thought of not answering. "Miranda."

"Lovely name."

"You think so?" She'd always found it old-fashioned.

"I do."

"Basilio is pretty neat, too. Spanish?" she guessed.

"You got it in one. My friends call me Baz."

"My friends call me Randi."

"I prefer Miranda."

Did that mean he didn't want to be friends? Only he'd implied she should call him *Baz*. "Are we going to be friends?"

"I would like that."

Good. "Me, too. I mean…" But she wasn't sure what she'd meant to say, the sexual chemistry between them playing havoc with the efficient firing of synapses in her brain.

"I hope you mean just that."

"Yes, okay."

"So, dinner tonight?" he asked, still caressing her hand.

"I have plans with my sister and brother-in-law." And as much as she wanted to spend time with her sister, giving up a date with such a delicious man was hard.

"After-dinner drinks?"

"Really?" Oh, man, why had she asked that? "I mean, that would be great. Fine."

She was just going to sink into the sidewalk right now.

"When and where?"

She thought about the location of the restaurant she was supposed to meet her family at and a likely spot near it. "How about the piano bar at the Heathman?"

It was quiet, with lots of places to sit in an intimate *tête-à-tête*.

"Fine. What time?" Basilio asked.

"Eight o'clock?" She was having an early dinner with Kayla and Andreas.

"Perfect. I will get my own dinner and meet you there."

Taking a risk, Randi asked, "You could join us?"

"You are sure I would not be an unwelcome intrusion?"

She loved the formal cadence of his speech, so different from her own. "Not at all. I'm sure Kayla and Andreas would not mind at all."

But she'd better call and give a heads-up on her way over.

"Then I would be pleased to accept."

"Great. Um, you can meet me there?"

"Naturally. I would not expect you to get into a car with a stranger after such short acquaintance."

And why she wished she could, she wasn't even going to think about. Ever since the trouble five years before, Randi had become very wary of new people and even making friends, much less dating. But no way was this man a grubby reporter, looking for lascivious details from the years-old tragedy.

Not in his five-thousand-dollar suit and shoes that probably cost more than she made in a week.

They made arrangements to meet at the restaurant in twenty minutes. Then Randi was running for her car, even later than she had been.

Basilio pulled into the valet parking for the Heathman.

A walk from the restaurant to the piano bar would be further opportunity to draw out Miranda Smith née Weber. Bumping into her on purpose had made two things very clear. One, the picture in the file he'd had compiled on her did not capture the sweet naïveté she wore like a cloak, nor her unconscious sensuality. Two, seduction might well be his best course of action in achieving the goal his family needed.

While intimidation tactics were not yet off the table,

he had a feeling using the instant attraction between them would be more easily effective.

Walking into the restaurant a few minutes later, he was once again struck by the clarity of her gray eyes as they met his across the roomful of diners in the upscale steak house. Even in the subdued lighting of the restaurant, the gray orbs glowed. Miranda was sitting with Andreas Kostas and another woman with eyes the exact color and vibrancy of Miranda's, declaring her the sister.

Basilio allowed the maître d' to lead him across the restaurant to the linen-clad table for four. Appetizers and bread were already on the table, indicating the Kostases had been there for a while.

Miranda stood up. "You made it."

Basilio nodded, finding her enthusiasm almost charming. There was such an innocence about this woman, he found it hard to believe she had plans to blow his family's peace right out of the water. She did not look or behave like someone who would go on a talk show to spite them, particularly after committing such a heinous act as hitting a small child with her car.

But he had it on good authority that Miranda Smith, for all her airs of innocence, was exactly that kind of woman.

He could not afford to forget that fact.

"This is my sister, Kayla Kostas, and her husband, Andreas." Miranda indicated the other two people with one hand, nearly knocking over a filled water goblet.

Her brother-in-law saved the table from getting doused with a discernible lack of impatience.

Basilio inclined his head to the married couple. "It is a pleasure to meet you."

"Randi said she met you on the street?" Kayla asked as Andreas sat down, clearly wanting more information.

Miranda had dropped back into her chair across the dining table from him. She smiled shyly at him, her cheeks tinged with color. Was she embarrassed she'd allowed him to pick her up?

He winked at her and watched the color darken along her lovely cheekbones, then turned his head to meet Kayla's eyes. "We bumped into each other."

"More like I mowed him down in my rush to be on time."

The twinge he felt that she was taking responsibility for the collision he had orchestrated was odd, and Basilio ignored it. "You were in a rush to get here, I believe."

"I was late."

"I guessed."

She ducked her head. "Yes, well…"

"Do you make a habit of picking up women you bump into on the street?" Andreas asked, his tone cynical.

"Having dinner with a beautiful woman is never a hardship." Basilio met the assessing green gaze steadily.

He'd spent years rebuilding his father's company and the Perez name in business circles. Basilio had learned long ago not to allow anyone else's opinion of him, or his actions, to disconcert him.

Andreas Kostas was not the only dangerous business shark in the room.

"You didn't answer my question." The other man was not easily fobbed off.

Basilio didn't mind. "I did not."

He was going to leave it that way until he noted the uncertainty clouding Miranda's expression. His plans required her trust.

So he spoke to her, not the nosy Greek sitting to Basilio's left. "I have never picked up a woman I met on the street. I did not pick you up like a lost puppy. I asked you for drinks. You suggested dinner and I was pleased to accept."

"If that's not the definition of a pickup, I don't know what is," Kayla inserted.

But Miranda looked happier and that was all that Basilio was worried about. She smiled at him. "I'm glad to hear that."

"Be assured you are not one of many." She was, in fact, the only woman who could give his family what they so desperately needed: peace.

Miranda let out a small gasp, but the sound that came from her brother-in-law was far more cynical.

Basilio gave him a dry look. "How do you like venture capitalism? Different from digital security?"

"You meant to run into Randi!" Kayla exclaimed. "You wanted to meet Andreas. You know who he is."

Miranda's head jerked, and her beautiful gray eyes filled with hurt.

This was getting ridiculous. Basilio frowned at the sister. "While I applaud your concern for Miranda, please stop putting such negative thoughts into her head. I assure you, if I wanted to meet your husband to discuss a business venture, he would take my call."

Andreas narrowed his gaze. "Don't glower at my wife. She's just looking out for Randi."

"As I said, laudable, but unnecessary."

"What does he mean, Andreas? Do you know something about Basilio?" Kayla asked.

Andreas's jaw hardened, like he'd just realized who Basilio was. "Basilio Perez is the president of the worldwide real estate and hotel consortium known as Perez Holdings. He has fingers in more pies than Sebastian Hawk."

"You are?" Miranda asked, looking pale.

"I am. That does not change your desire to dine with me, does it?" he teased, knowing it wouldn't. He'd never met a woman not drawn to his power and position.

She looked like she wasn't sure of her answer, though. "I'm not in your league."

"I'm not looking for a baseball team to dine with, just one quirky, charming woman and her very suspicious relatives." Not that they had nothing to worry about in her regard, but their concerns were in all the wrong directions.

While Basilio dated his fair share of women, he was by no means a womanizer. And he was not looking to use her for her family business connections.

"Oh, that's kind of sweet," Kayla said.

Miranda nodded. "It is."

Andreas was still watching Basilio with suspicion. However, after they ordered their food and the evening progressed, the other man thawed some. Basilio found himself actually enjoying conversation with the somewhat socially awkward Kayla, her very business-savvy husband and the unexpectedly sweet Miranda.

"So, are you here looking at an acquisition?" Andreas asked at one point.

Basilio put down his glass of very good scotch after taking a sip. "That's not something I can discuss."

"Why not?" Miranda asked, pausing with the bite of steak she had been about to eat dangling on her fork.

"If word got out I was looking at a property, the sale price would increase immediately."

"Because you have deep pockets?" Miranda asked, sounding like she was trying to understand.

"Exactly." He was, in fact, looking at a property, a historic hotel that had closed down and would need extensive remodeling and updates before it could be opened again.

But the property was beautiful and the bones of the hotel were strong. He hadn't made a decision about the purchase yet, though.

"So, property acquisition is your thing?" Kayla asked.

"Sometimes." He had too much to do running Perez Holdings for him to be a full-time acquisitions manager. "I enjoy it."

"Then maybe you can help Randi find the property for our expansion house."

"Expansion house?" he asked, like he didn't have all the details in his report on the family back in his hotel suite.

"I run Kayla's for Kids." Miranda smiled, her tone saying how much satisfaction her job gave her. "It's a shelter for children and youth."

"Not their parents?"

Miranda's smile did not dim. "If their parents are around, we have services to help them, but our focus is the kids. The number of homeless teenagers and children in need of a safe place after school is greater than the facilities available to serve them."

"And you want to help these children?" Was she looking for absolution in service after what she'd done five years before?

"I do." Miranda's eyes darkened to molten silver. "Children deserve the best we can give them, but just as important, they are the beginning of change. If we give them hope for now, a chance to learn and grow, there's no way of knowing how much each child will touch and influence the world in their lifetime."

"So it starts with giving them a place to play games after school?"

"And experience art, a place to read a book in peace, a place to be safe." Her passion was damn near addictive.

Could he believe she was that committed to the welfare of children and still be the woman willing to tear his own nephew's life apart with media interest?

"You are adding on another shelter, then?" he asked.

"Yes, where the rate of homeless teens is one of the highest." She named a western suburb of Portland. "But I don't expect you to help me find the building. I'm sure you're way too busy."

"On the contrary, I would be happy to help you." Doing so would give him the excuse he required to spend time with her.

"Really?" she asked, her lovely face covered in delight.

"Yes."

"That's great. I'm supposed to look at properties tomorrow."

"Send me a list of the properties and your requirements for the shelter. I'll vet them and see what else I can find for you."

"Seriously? You'd do that? I've got a Realtor working with me. She's going to donate her commission to the shelter, but doesn't seem to understand the concept of a budget and long-term running costs."

"Send me her name, as well, and I will make sure she understands your requirements, or I will find a Realtor who will."

"Oh, I don't want you intimidating her. Like I said, she's generously donating her commission to the shelter."

"That donated commission could end up costing you quite a bit more in the long run."

"I tried to tell both Kayla and Randi this." Andreas gave both women a speaking look. "But they're convinced that anyone willing to donate their income is as committed to the best interests of the shelter as they are."

"Give me her name and I will make certain."

Miranda bit her lip. "I really don't want you scaring her."

"You think I would?"

"Um, just sitting at dinner with you is a little intimidating. Being under your scrutiny in a business setting?" Miranda gave an exaggerated shiver. "That would be downright frightening."

"And then some," Kayla said with a firm nod.

Andreas looked just a little horrified at his wife's honesty, but Basilio merely laughed, not offended in the least. He filed away the knowledge that Miranda was quite a bit more discerning than he'd given her credit for.

She might even recognize on some subconscious level

that he was a danger to her. Unfortunately for her, she didn't understand just how ruthless he really was.

No man got to where he was in the business world without being an apex predator.

# CHAPTER TWO

RANDI CAUGHT HER breath as Baz put his arm around her waist to walk to the piano bar.

He was so virile and strong. Rich and gorgeous.

An overwhelming example of the male species, and that was no exaggeration.

She was having a hard time understanding what he was doing with her. She wasn't hideous. Or embarrassingly awkward company, but that didn't mean she was the usual sort of date for a man like Basilio Perez.

Randi knew who and what she was. A usually shy, moderately pretty woman, who found the company of children easier to navigate than most single men.

She didn't date a lot, especially after the accident five years ago. Unable to deal with the media frenzy and social media ostracization, the man she'd thought she was going to marry had broken things off. Then Randi had been tricked into dating a reporter who wanted the inside scoop on the woman accused of destroying a family with her carelessness.

Each defection had devastated and demoralized her, the loss of friendships and even her university scholarship only adding to her sense of betrayal. She'd learned not to trust quickly or easily, not with new friends and particularly not with possible boyfriends.

She never allowed strange men to talk her into dinner and drinks.

But Baz wasn't exactly some random stranger. He was the president of a multibillion-dollar conglomerate. No way did he have a hidden agenda. Randi had nothing the man could want.

However, that didn't make this date any less bewildering, not to mention disturbing. The more time she spent with him, the more her attraction to him grew. She'd never felt anything as powerful. She *wanted* him. Seriously, deeply.

His arm around her waist was not helping her sense of self-control, either.

That simple point of contact ratcheting up the unexpected, unfamiliar and yet incredible sensations of desire coursing through her.

"So, um, do you come to Portland often?" She nearly winced at her gauche question. It sounded like she was fishing for the future and she was too smart to think they had one of those.

"This is my first time."

"Really? It's an amazing city that prides itself on being weird." She adored the eccentricity mixed with a good dose of cosmopolitan culture and had grown to love her new home in a very short amount of time.

"So I've been told."

"I just moved here a couple of months ago, but I wouldn't mind showing you some of the sights, if you like." Randi waited with cautious hope for Baz's answer to what was for her a very bold and unprecedented offer.

"I would like that." Dark eyes glinting with something like satisfaction, he smiled down at her. "Getting a feeling for the area is part of how I make decisions about whether or not to buy."

"So you *are* here looking for a property." She knew it.

But she did her best to ignore the tendril of hope unfurling inside her. If he bought a property, he'd come back. Wouldn't he?

"Perhaps" was all he said.

She laughed, finding something about his caginess endearing. "I'm not going to blab. Even if I did, who could

I tell that would impact you?" she teased. "I'm a social worker, not a real estate mogul."

His responding laughter sent shivers of sensation through her. "As you say."

"But you're still not going to tell me, are you?"

"No."

"You're a very cautious man."

"I would not be where I am if I were not."

"Walking down the street with a woman you just met hours ago?" She made no effort to hide the laughter in her voice, because really? If she was acting impulsively, so was he.

He stopped and pulled her around to face him, their bodies inches apart, his attention intent and on her only. "You enjoy your own humor, don't you?"

"Someone should."

He wasn't smiling exactly, but humor gleamed in his espresso-brown gaze. "You are not as shy as you appear at first."

"I feel comfortable with you." Which was really dangerous, but she also found him super-attractive. Could attraction undermine common sense completely? She'd never thought so, but she was adjusting her thinking on that issue fast.

"That is good to know."

"I think so, too." Her words trailed off as his head lowered toward hers. She stared up into his dark gaze; her lips parted of their own accord. "Are you going to kiss me?"

His answer was his mouth pressing to hers.

Sensation exploded inside Randi. Zings of electric current coursed through her body, radiating outward from where their lips touched and sending goose bumps in waves over her skin. Need like she had never known throbbed in her core, making her press her thighs together in instinctive effort to alleviate it. It didn't work, of course.

She ached for way more than a simple kiss.

Though there was nothing *simple* about the way Baz's lips *owned* hers, giving no quarter, demanding response or submission, with no option for backing off.

At least as far as her body's response would allow.

Though his hands were on her upper arms, Baz did not actively hold her in place with anything but the press of his lips. Randi responded on a primal, visceral level that would not allow her to hold back, bringing forth sensations she'd read about, but never actually experienced.

Overwhelming passion. Gut-level desire that burned hotter than the California wildfires in the summer. Her nipples beaded with near-painful intensity; her most intimate flesh pulsed with a need for touch; her lips softened and molded to his with hungry ardency.

Randi reveled in every single unfamiliar sensation, responding to the kiss in a way that a public display on the busy sidewalk did not warrant, her own lack of control acting as an irresistible aphrodisiac.

She could no more help giving him kiss for kiss than she could stop breathing.

Breathing might even be less necessary.

Randi curled her fingers around the lapels of Baz's suit jacket, pulling his body closer to hers. Only then did warm, masculine arms come around her, holding her tight now, his hands pressed tightly to her back and just at the top of her buttocks.

The kiss morphed into something more than possession. It became two people equally intent, equally impassioned, equally lost to their desires.

There could be no doubt, until Baz pulled his head back.

At least his breathing was ragged like hers, his expression pained. "We've got to stop. On a public sidewalk is not the place for this."

Randi didn't care. This was something new for her. Something craved. Something *needed*. Refusing to give up the amazing sensations his kiss caused, she rose on her tiptoes, seeking his mouth again, only realizing as his lips cut them off that the needy little sounds she heard were coming from her.

And she did not care. There could be no embarrassment in this level of yearning.

He groaned, the deep, masculine sound traveling through her body, leaving devastation in its wake. Baz invaded her mouth with his tongue. It was not finessed; the demand of his tongue sliding against hers had no lead in, no buildup to the increased intimacy, and again… Randi *did not care*.

She opened wider for him, melting under the demanding forays. Her tongue tangled with his, taking in his taste, unlike any other taste, pure sex, pure man. Randi kissed him back, letting him feel the unfamiliar and overwhelming passion exploding inside her.

He made a deep sound in his throat, all male want, but then he did the unthinkable. Again.

His hands landing on her shoulders to push her away at the same time as he broke the connection between their mouths for the second time was not only not welcome, it was also torture. Didn't he understand? She needed his lips, his tongue, his arms tight around her.

She could not suppress the sound of keen disappointment, or control her involuntary move back toward him.

But Baz was made of sterner stuff than she was, apparently, because he held her firmly away. "No, Miranda. Not here. We have put on enough of an entertainment for others."

She looked around and saw that they did indeed have an audience, several smiles and thumbs-ups directed her way. Only in Portland.

Blushing to the roots of her hair, Randi allowed herself to be set away from the source of her temptation. "I guess we should go into the piano bar, huh?"

Baz inclined his head. "If that is what you wish."

"I…" What was he saying? Was he ready for the evening to be over?

"Or we could go into the hotel and get a room?" he suggested.

She'd never done that, not once. Randi had not only never had a one-off with a man she'd just met, she'd also never rented a hotel room with a man for the sole purpose of having sex. The illicit nature of the idea was way too alluring.

And that worried her. Where was her deeply ingrained sense of self-preservation?

She asked the only thing her mind could conjure without giving away just how much she wanted to do exactly as he suggested. "Don't you have a room already?"

His shrug was dismissive. "An executive penthouse condo, but getting there would require waiting to have my car brought around by the valet. Besides, I can't travel alone. If I'm in my penthouse, my staff can find me even if I turn off my phone."

She couldn't imagine that kind of pressure, the knowledge that privacy and alone time were little more than an illusion. Even so.

"You're saying you want me so much you want to get a room, right here at the Heathman, so we can…" She couldn't make herself spell it out.

"Pick up where that kiss left off, yes."

"Oh."

"Oh?"

"I mean, yes, I'd like that." *What was she saying?* Was she agreeing to a hookup in a hotel room with a man she'd only met hours ago?

And if she was, why wasn't she more freaked out about the idea?

Randi was barely a nonvirgin, having had sex exactly twice. Neither of which had turned out well for her. She and her almost fiancé had gotten intimate just before the accident and subsequent media storm. The reporter had gotten Randi into bed after a few weeks of dating and pretending to be someone else, only to walk away the next morning with his exclusive.

But Baz was not some jerk with a hidden agenda who would break her heart after using her body. It might only be one night; their mutual passion might be a temporary aberration, but at least she wasn't worried about the aftermath.

Randi was tired of living in the bubble of loneliness that had surrounded her for the past five years.

Whatever happened tomorrow, tonight she got what she just knew was going to be amazing sex, with the most magnetic man she'd ever spoken to, much less kissed.

Baz looked down at her, his dark-chocolate gaze filled with desire. "Well?"

An atavistic chill ran down her spine. This man was a primal alpha and she wanted to meet him passion for passion. "Yes."

"Yes to the hotel room?"

She nodded.

"I need the word, *mi hermosa*. There can be no doubt."

"Yes."

His smile was killer. *"Muy bien. Vente mi, cariña."* He took her hand and set a fast pace for the main entrance to the hotel.

So, he lost his English when he was turned on. Randi liked knowing she could affect him so strongly. And she liked the endearments, too. Even if it was only a one-night stand, what woman didn't want to be called beautiful and darling? Though *beautiful* might be stretching it, she wasn't about to tell him so. Let the man look at her through the filter of lust-filled glasses.

She hadn't been into the main lobby of the Heathman in years, its nearly hundred-year-old beauty as pristine as when it had first been built in the nineteen-twenties. Both luxurious and gorgeous, with its decorative, rich wood walls and pillars, two-story-high ceiling and elegant decor, the cavernous room intended for greeting guests was nothing short of awe-inspiring. Baz, international business mogul, led her to the desk and had no trouble procuring a room, despite his lack of reservations. The fact he was happy to take the Grand Suite for the night probably had something to do with that.

Randi couldn't help gasping when she heard the clerk tell Baz how much one night would be. She could pay the rent on her small apartment for two months with what he was willing to pay to have the convenience of a hotel room right that minute.

With original art on the walls—art rarely seen outside a museum, no less—the suite's full-size living room and dining area decorated in pure modern elegance was separated from the bedroom by a spacious foyer, making the suite bigger than her apartment and way more lavish.

"Stop looking at the furniture. I want your eyes on me," Baz instructed as he pulled her into his arms.

"But this place is incredible," she teased, having no problem following his demands.

Even the opulent suite couldn't hold a candle to the man pulling her close into his body.

Baz's expression turned thoughtful. "You like it? The clerk said it was booked for tomorrow, but I could probably persuade them to accommodate us."

Of course the billionaire thought so, despite the fact it was probably some kind of celebrity coming in to stay.

"No. I… It's just… This place is bigger than my apartment!"

His smile was indulgent. "And would you rather explore it, or me?"

That fast, the desire buzzing along her nerve endings went critical. "You."

"Then let us go to the bedroom."

And without warning, she was suddenly in his arms, being carried like a princess into a bedroom fit for royalty.

He set her down and ripped the extra pillows from the bed, tossing them onto the floor, before flinging back the duvet.

Then he turned to her. "I think we are both overdressed for what is about to happen."

Her mouth gone instantly dry, she nodded.

He slipped off his tailored suit jacket and hung it carelessly on an armchair, before toeing off his shoes so he could slip his trousers off and do the same with them. His legs were pillars of muscle; his olive skin sprinkled with dark, masculine hair. He kicked off his socks without looking away from her, no evidence of even the slightest discomfort in his near nudity.

Paralyzed with want and no small dose of insecurity she'd rather pretend she never felt, Randi just watched the Spanish business shark strip.

"You are not going to join me?" he asked, his tone teasing, no doubt there that she wanted what he so clearly did.

The power tie went next, and then the buttons on his shirt before Baz shrugged it off to lay it over his other clothes on the chair, putting acres of golden olive skin on display.

She sucked in air as his muscular, defined torso and chest came into view. "I think your abs have abs. What do you do, like a million sit-ups a day or something?"

"My exercise routine is what you want to talk about?" he demanded, humor lacing his voice, but oh, his eyes.

They burned with everything she felt.

Truthfully? She didn't want to talk at all. Randi wanted to touch, crossing the few feet of carpet separating them to do just that.

While the tent in his snug, black, silk-knit boxers called to her, she reached up to brush her hands through the black hair on his chest. "So soft."

"You expected something else?"

"I've never been with a man with chest hair before," she admitted.

"I do not want to hear about other men."

His words thrilled her, but she wasn't so far gone she was going to let him see that. "So possessive for a one-night stand."

"You believe I will have all I want of you in a single night?" he asked with disbelief. "Not a chance."

The breath in her lungs whooshed out. "Good to know," she choked out.

His hands were on the hem of her gray knit dress, the smocking over her chest that she'd always considered cute and comfortable, now confining against sensitized flesh and peaked nipples. He pulled the dress up and over her head without another word and she let him, the cuffs on the three-quarter-length sleeves catching for a breathless second on her hands, leaving her blinded by fabric and vulnerable before him.

*"Bella,"* he husked out as the dress finally disappeared, giving her a renewed view of Baz. Heated espresso eyes burned her with their intensity as his gaze ate her up. "You are a surprise."

Again with the beautiful. Randi had reason to be glad she'd learned Spanish in order to communicate with the children whom she assumed would come through her office at social services for which it was their first language.

Only belatedly did she realize what exactly had him surprised, and apparently mesmerized. "My sister likes shopping at the lingerie store."

"And she takes you with her?" he asked as he made no effort to hide his fascination with her breasts covered by a sheer lift bra and the matching panties that allowed him to see the soft brown curls at the apex of her thighs, the fabric a pearlescent gossamer.

Under the perfectly opaque fabric of her dress, she could wear whatever sexy underwear she liked and never considered someone else seeing them. "They remind me I'm a sexual being."

A reminder she had needed very badly before tonight.

"I assure you, no one else could forget."

"Right." She didn't have her sister's generous curves, Randi's own body as subtle in its femininity as she was shy.

"You doubt me?" He indicated the rampant erection barely contained by his boxers. "You think I do this kind of thing with every woman I meet?"

Another blush heated her skin, but desire made her even hotter. "No, I don't doubt you want me. I want you, too."

"Then let's get your boots off and you into bed."

She couldn't feel awkward standing there in her brown, nearly flat-heeled boots that reached her knees, and nothing else besides the diaphanous underwear. Not with the approval glowing in his dark gaze.

"You like this look?" she couldn't help teasing with a cant to her hips.

"Very much, but I believe you will be more comfortable without footwear."

She nodded. Even in her current state, she'd feel all kinds of wrong climbing onto the luxurious bed with her shoes on.

They made quick work of her boots and then she was on her back, on the bed.

Baz pulled off her panties, his gaze fixed firmly on the triangle of curls hiding her most sensitive flesh. "I love the sexy lingerie, but full access is even more exciting."

Feeling embarrassed for the first time, she put her hand over herself. "I used to wax."

"I prefer this. Did you know if I touch you carefully, like so…" He gently pulled her hand away before his fingertips barely brushed over the tips of her private curls. "You will feel it deep inside."

She couldn't help the arch upward, or the gasp of pleasure as his caress made truth out of his words. Really? Her *hair* was an erogenous zone, and quite an effective one. Desire ran rampant through her blood, every nerve ending on high alert for the barest touch from him.

"You are beautiful here." No question, from where he

was looking and the brush of his fingers, what he was talking about.

"That…you…" She wanted to deny the words, deny that he could find her most intimate place *beautiful*. "That's for touching, not looking."

He got off the bed, stripped off his boxers and indicated his very hard, very big—at least in her experience—and very obvious erection. "You do not get turned on seeing my sex?"

Why was he asking her this? "You're awfully blunt." But she couldn't move her gaze away from tumescent flesh and knew deep in her heart that seeing it soft would be no less arousing.

His expression dared her to deny his words.

She wasn't a liar. "Yes, seeing you excites me. A lot." But she hadn't realized it would, hadn't thought of herself as a visual person when it came to sex.

"And looking at you, the very part of yourself you hold most private, inflames me." His accent had thickened, lending a warm Latin lilt to his words.

He rejoined her on the bed, straddling her thighs, his erection pressed against her sensitized mound.

He ran a finger along the bit of exposed breast above the top of her bra. *"Muy guapa."*

"I'm…" More compliments to her body. How was she supposed to take them?

The way Baz was with her, his touches and words, was so outside her experience in the bedroom—what little there was of it.

Randi gasped as he cupped both her breasts with his hands, rubbing expertly against her already hard and tight nipples through the silky fabric. "Glad. I'm glad."

"Good to know." His expression was all approval. "You are so responsive."

"I never have been."

His eyes narrowed as if he was thinking, his head cocked a little. "You aren't very experienced, are you?"

"You told me you didn't want to hear about other men."

"The lack thereof in your past is an unexpected turn-on."

"It is?" she gasped out as his ministrations to her breasts sent sensation zinging straight to the core of her.

"Yes."

"Unexpected?"

"As a rule, I stay away from women lacking in experience."

He wanted lovers who could keep up with him and maybe knew the score. Right? She understood that. And was doing her best to keep that score in mind, no matter how devastating his touch.

A billionaire Spanish businessman wasn't going to keep a social worker from her family background, even if he *did* want more than one night. She did, too, so that was okay. Right?

She wasn't going to fall in love with this sexy man.

She wasn't.

"But not me," she confirmed.

"No. Not you. You, I want."

"I want you, too."

He leaned down and kissed her then, his tongue demanding entrance almost immediately. She gave it to him, reveling in how he took control of her body and the kiss. She'd never wanted to give herself this way, to let a man touch her like she was *his*.

Randi's characteristic cling to independence and self-control, no matter the situation, was conspicuously absent, though.

His hands were all over her body, touching spots she had no idea could be erogenous, but which had her repeatedly arching up off the bed, seeking more. She wanted to touch him, too, but somehow every time she went to caress him, she lost her focus and her hands ended up resting against his chest, kneading like a cat with her short nails.

He seemed to like that, groaning against her lips, moving his body to spread her legs and press his erection firmly against her most tender flesh. Randi went taut with pleasure as he somehow managed to maneuver his erection against her clitoris in mock coupling, thrusting against her and stimulating her so well she cried out with the joy of it.

Randi gasped out her pleasure at the amazing feeling. "Baz! Oh…" It was too good, too much, her body racking with shudders of ecstasy.

"You are so deliciously responsive, Miranda." His voice deep with approval and husky desire, Baz continued to thrust against her, his big hands inciting her pleasure with incredible knowledge of the female body and what would feel good.

She tossed her head on the fluffy pillows, feeling like she needed something more, but unwilling to change what was already giving her so much marvelous sensation. "You're really good at this."

"This?" he teased, gently rolling her nipples between thumb and forefinger.

Oh, wow. That was… It was… Even her inner monologue could not come up with the right adjectives. She'd never before realized the direct line between the turgid peaks and her feminine sex. Sure, it felt good to be touched there, but never like lightning was striking through her body.

"Yes, that and all of it."

"It is easy to give pleasure when it is so well received."

"Are you saying I'm easy?" she gasped out, teasing and not.

She'd never found it so simple to give in, to allow a man so close so fast. This whole conflagration between their bodies was entirely outside her experience.

Sex was not all that.

Only now it was. Now it was everything. Necessary.

"I would never be so crass."

That was not a denial. She met his gaze earnestly. "I'm not, you know."

"Not?"

"Easy. I don't *do* one-night stands."

"Good, but fair warning—I have no intention of stopping at one night with you."

He wasn't offering anything long-term. How could he? He lived in Spain. She lived in Portland. He was a powerful billionaire. A social worker turned shelter manager had no place in his glittery life, but for now? She did.

She fit in this ridiculously expensive bed he'd bought for the night.

Her body fit under his. Her lips fit perfectly against his.

His mouth owned hers and she let it. Knowing this was temporary, but not a single night, gave her the confidence to let go in a way she had not before, and probably wouldn't again, with anyone else.

She responded to his kiss, parting her lips, inviting his tongue inside, letting hers explore his mouth, shivering with feeling as the kiss morphed into something crazy passionate. Her body melted into the bed under him, accommodating his hard planes with every cell.

He lifted up enough to pull her toward him so he could remove that last piece of clothing she was wearing, her bra.

When he let her settle back against the pillows, Randi reached down between them and grasped his erection, the heated, satiny skin warming her palm.

He thrust up into her fist. *"Sí! Que es tan bueno."*

It *was* good. All of it. Randi loved knowing she could elicit such a pleasurable response, that her touch impacted him as surely as his touch made Randi lose her mind.

"I want this inside me." She squeezed the hard column of flesh once…twice, again.

Baz let out a guttural sound that sent response arcing through Randi. He reared back but didn't pull his sex from her hand, though she got the sense that was his initial intent. "Let me get a condom."

"You just carry them around with you?"

"I do, in fact, always have one in my wallet." He shrugged. "I am a man."

"We're going to need more." No way was a single time going to be enough tonight. Not for such a sexually ardent lover.

"I'll take care of that later." His smile was all predatory male.

# CHAPTER THREE

RANDI NODDED, HER words lost for a moment in the pleasure of their bodies together.

Long moments passed in another incendiary kiss, his sex pressing into her hand, her own aching with the need to be filled. When he finally broke the kiss to get up, she made a mewing sound she'd never heard out of her own throat before.

He stood with quick, efficient movements, and moved to the chair on which his trousers lay with a few long, rapid strides. Seconds later he was back beside her, the condom packet in his hand. "Do you want to put it on me?"

In answer, Randi eagerly reached for the foil square. Baz dropped it into her hand and she tore it open, pulling out the small bit of latex. She pressed the circle of latex against the head of his penis, thrilling to the moment of anticipation this particular act elicited. She rolled it down his length, an intentional caress with more enjoyment than experience, hoping to make the act erotic for both of them.

He didn't seem to mind her fumbling attempts at covering him. He was, in fact, moaning and staring at her with clear sexual approval.

Once she got the condom on, he pushed her onto her back, but instead of immediately moving between her thighs, as she expected, he reached down to touch her, his fingers deftly caressing her slick folds.

"Oh, goodness! This is…that is…" Exactly what she needed, making her incoherent with sensation, senseless words of pleasure tumbling from her lips.

He seemed to have no problem deciphering her babbling, touching exactly where she needed. Sliding his fingers over her clitoris, gently circling, pushing gently at intervals, he caressed her with just the right pressure before slipping one, then two inside her, preparing her for what was to come.

She could no more stop her body surging toward his touch than reach out with her own hands, seeking the lodestone of his body. Anything to help her maintain sanity in this maelstrom of emotion and sensation, where by rights no emotion should be.

They did not know each other. It should be pure physicality, but her heart was beating a strange, desperate tattoo of feeling she had no desire to acknowledge.

Baz crooked his fingers inside her and pressed upward. Jolts of intense ecstasy radiated out from that heretofore unexplored cluster of nerves inside her. She'd heard about the G-spot, but thought it was a myth. Oh, glorious elation, it wasn't!

Rapture spiraled inside Randi, drawing her body tight with impending orgasm, but Baz was careful not to take her over the edge.

Darn it!

She tried to move her body, to take herself over that precipice. "Please, Baz. Please!"

"You will come with me inside you," he proclaimed, even as he *finally* shifted between her legs to press his engorged sex against the slick and swollen opening to her body.

"I've never come from that," she warned him, though just the feeling of him so close to penetrating her was setting off all sorts of fireworks inside her. Not that she had loads of experiences to go by anyway, but neither time had made her believe she was one of those women who could.

"Let us see what we can do about that." Challenge gleamed in his espresso-brown eyes.

A shiver of anticipation—or was that trepidation?—

rolled through her. "Just do me," she implored, not caring if she climaxed in that moment.

She was empty. She needed to be filled and Baz Perez with his big, hard sex would succeed where she knew others had failed. Giving her pleasure and a sense of completion, even if she didn't actually come from it.

But Baz, she learned quickly, did not dismiss a challenge. He attacked it with skill, patience and purpose.

He made love to her as no other guy had done, driving the pleasure inside her body higher and higher with each expert thrust, every swivel of his hips that managed to stimulate her clitoris in ways she'd thought impossible during copulation. Finally, he reached down and brushed over that swollen nub with his thumb, at first pressing in and then circling, then pressing in again, then circling, and Randi lost what sense she'd maintained.

The euphoria building inside her detonated, the roman candle of ecstasy exploding with a shower of sparks throughout her body. Her womb contracted, her muscles convulsed and her heart nearly seized from the glorious power of it. She cried out as her vaginal walls tightened around his hard sex in spasms of pure bliss.

"That's right," he praised, his body taut with unfulfilled desire. "You are so beautiful in your excitement."

The words registered only peripherally as her body shuddered with a surfeit of pleasure. "Baz…"

She couldn't say anything more than his name, couldn't form a coherent thought, could only arch against him, prolonging the overwhelming sensation. He resumed movement, his lunges growing more powerful with each surge forward of his pelvis, strong thrusts inside her causing aftershocks of ecstasy nearly as intense as her initial orgasm.

"*Sí, hermosa, sí!* You are so perfect inside. Tight, hot, wet."

Oh, man, did men really talk like that in bed?

"You hold me like a warm, slick fist."

Clearly, they did.

And those words intensified the residual waves of excitement. "Baz, oh, Baz!"

With a final lunge forward, he went rigid above her and then gave a low, guttural shout, filling the condom with his hot spend, his face fixed in a rictus of ultimate pleasure.

Randi reached up with arms like noodles to clasp his shoulders, needing even more connection than the ultimate joining of their bodies. "I...you..."

He kissed her, cutting off whatever she'd been about to say. She kissed him back, reveling in the press of soft lips against soft lips while he was still inside her.

No other moment in her life had been so perfect.

Later, after he'd taken care of the condom and cleaned up in the en suite, Baz ran a bath in the jetted tub.

Randi lounged in the bed, feeling decadent surrounded by luxury linens and the sound of running water. She heard him on the phone, too, but couldn't make out his words.

When he returned to the bedroom, she asked if he had to leave.

He leaned against the doorjamb, gloriously naked, unashamed by what others might consider vulnerability. "Why would you think that?"

"You were on the phone." For men like him and Andreas, a phone call, whatever the time, often precipitated the need for some kind of action on their part.

Billionaires were busy people, or so she'd learned since her sister and Kayla's new husband came into Randi's life.

"I called housekeeping and asked for a box of condoms to be delivered. Then I called room service and ordered champagne and strawberries." Baz let his lips tilt in an enigmatic half smile. "It seemed appropriate."

Who ordered condoms to their room? "Lavish."

"And do you not deserve lavish?" he asked in what should

have been a tease, but something in his gaze probed hers with serious intent.

"It's not my norm, that's for sure." She wasn't the one with a super-rich husband catering to her every need.

That was her sister, and Randi loved the way Andreas took such pains to care for Kayla, but Randi refused to let her brother-in-law subsidize *her* living expenses, so she made do on what she considered a generous salary from the shelter. Though it hardly stretched to the kind of luxury Baz seemed to take for granted.

He shifted away from the door, his big body moving with surprising elegance, despite his lack of clothing. "I will enjoy spoiling you."

And she would probably enjoy being spoiled. Too much. Too easy to get used to the attention, but as long as she never forgot it was temporary, she might actually survive with her heart intact.

"You're not like any other man I know." She sat up. Letting the bedclothes fall away from her body, she reminded herself that he'd already seen everything she might try to hide and had seemed to like it very much.

His gaze ran over her with more heat than she would expect so soon after what they'd just finished. "Men like me are a rare breed."

"You so are."

His smile was lethal as he leaned down to pull her from the bed. "Come on. I have a mind to share a *lavish* bath with you."

"A bath is a bath."

Minutes later as she sat in the steaming, scented bathtub, water made ultra-soft with oils, a plate of chocolate-dipped strawberries within reach, two glasses of champagne perched on the tub's lip, Randi had reason to retract her own statement.

"Okay, this is definitely sumptuous."

"You think?" Baz had donned the complimentary robe

to receive both the delivery from housekeeping and room service.

"I do, yes."

He dropped the robe and stepped toward her, once again magnificently naked. "You look like a nymph in that swirling water."

"Not hardly." Randi had a mirror, and sea nymph, she was not.

"Do not ruin my fantasy with your sense of the prosaic."

"I would not have considered you a fantasy kind of guy."

"We all have dreams."

"I suppose."

"Don't you have dreams, aspirations, desires?"

"I learned five years ago that life doesn't dole out the fulfillment of dreams equally to everybody." After all, she'd been on the cusp of engagement with her boyfriend, enrolled at her top choice university and surrounded by friends and a family who loved her. She'd come to terms with having a wholly narcissistic mom with tendencies toward violence when thwarted, and Randi had been, for a time, really happy.

His attention sharpened, his expression assessing. "What happened five years ago?"

"My world imploded."

"You cannot make such a statement and not explain."

She shook her head. "Some things are too painful for the consumption of strangers."

"Are we still strangers?" His expression turned carnal. "I would say we have enjoyed some very intimate moments."

"We've been intimate with our *bodies*," she emphasized. "Emotions and memories are another thing entirely." A man with his experience couldn't believe anything else, could he?

Baz climbed into the hot water with her, muscular limbs sliding against hers, accentuating the lack of barrier between them. Renewed desire sent a flush over her body, more acute than that brought on by the hot water.

His hand traveled up Randi's leg from her ankle, stopping at the top of her inner thigh. "Let's get a little more physically intimate, then, shall we?"

"Yes." Relief that he was not pushing for answers about something she hadn't meant to mention mixed with sensual delight as his hand moved against her inner thigh.

His fingertips rubbed against her most intimate flesh, making her languid with need.

He tugged her unresisting body closer. "Come here, *mi hermosa*."

She let herself be pulled into him and maneuvered so she was facing away from him, leaning against the bulging muscles of his body. There was something so sexy about being in his arms in the water, her back to him, his hands on her. The message going to her sexual brain was that he was focused on her pleasure. And her pleasure alone.

Maybe she should feel bad, should do something to balance the focus, but she didn't. This whole night, so far, felt too good, too different from anything she'd ever known.

His hands moved up her body, caressing her hips, her torso and finally settling to cup her breasts, touching already sensitized nipples, sending thrills of bliss through her.

Lips brushed behind her ear. "You are addictive, *cariña*."

"The way you make me feel could easily become a necessary habit." And wasn't that terrifying? Because he *wasn't* sticking around.

No way could he.

Not Mr. Spanish Billionaire Businessman.

"Good to hear." He nibbled against her neck, sending shivers throughout her body.

"You think so?" Was he really blind to how bad that could be for her?

"Don't you?" he asked against her skin, before tugging ever so gently on her earlobe with his teeth.

She convulsed with a new set of shivers. "Not so much, no."

His laugh was unexpected, husky and warm. "You are very refreshing, Miranda."

"I guess *that* is a good thing."

He made a noncommittal sound. Maybe he'd miss refreshing. Maybe addictive was just as bad for his long-term peace of mind as hers.

One of his hands left her breast, and seconds later, a chocolate-dipped strawberry pressed against her lips. "Take a bite." The words whispered against her ear, making the prosaic instruction all sensual and sexy.

Randi opened her mouth and let the dark chocolate and strawberry flavors burst on her tongue as she did what he told her to. She ate with decadent delight, taking a sip of her champagne after finishing the strawberry. All the while Baz continued to caress her entire body with tender stimulation, one hand touching her with more effect than should be possible.

She plucked a strawberry from the plate, then reached back to offer it to him. Baz took a bite, letting his tongue flick out to taste her fingers, sending more pleasure jolting through her. As she fed him the rest of the fruit, he continued to lave her fingers, pulling one into his mouth and sucking on the digit with sensual mastery.

"That feels good," she panted, her words coming out on separate little gasps of air. "It shouldn't feel so good."

"You think not?" he asked after releasing her finger from his mouth.

"I… No…it's not something…"

"You are so experienced, then," he gently mocked.

She had no thought to lie. "No, I'm not in your league." Her heart rate sped up as his fingers rubbed over her clitoris in the slippery water. "I think we both know that."

"We've already discussed this."

"And you pretended ignorance to what I meant, but be real. You're a player."

"I am not." He sounded affronted. "In fact, I never have more than one sex partner at a time."

"Serial monogamy." She'd heard the term before, but never known someone it *fit*.

"If you like."

"And right now, I'm it?" she asked with disbelief, even as her body warned her that logical reasoning was going to shut down soon in the face of abject ecstasy.

*"Sí."*

"No woman back in Spain?"

"None."

"I'm not seeing anyone, either."

"That is good to know."

Something in her instincts told her he was the type of man who would have checked before bedding her the first time. Why hadn't he? Had he been as lost to physical sensation as she?

Her thoughts scattered as his touch changed and the orgasm she'd thought was well off was suddenly right *there*. Spasms of pleasure rolled through her as he continued to stimulate her to the point just short of pain.

She grabbed his wrist, holding it tight. "Too much!"

He let his fingers slide away, wrapping her in a tight embrace she realized she needed desperately to keep her connected to reality. She'd never climaxed twice in one night and she had the distinct feeling they weren't done yet.

As her body eventually settled, Randi's breaths returned to normal and her heart scaled back from a beat that felt like it was coming out of her chest, she became aware of the hard length pressing against her back. An erection she had every intention of doing something about.

She turned in his arms, letting herself rub against him before coming to rest with her arms crossed on his sculpted chest. Satiated and lethargic, she still smiled up at him with invitation. "You're still hard."

"I like a little self-denial."

"Why?"

"It makes the eventual climax all the stronger."

She stared at him. "I think I don't even know as much about sex as I thought I did."

"You know what you need to." His return gaze was filled with heat and maybe approval.

Did she? So far she'd been a very passive partner, and that didn't cut it for Randi. She might not be as experienced as he was; she might not have even realized some people did that thing with putting off their pleasure to make it stronger later, but she was not a selfish lover.

"I believe I do," she agreed. "Will you sit on the edge of the tub?"

"Why?"

"Because I want to taste you."

His jaw hardened at her words, the muscles in his neck straining as he swallowed, his gaze going molten with lust.

Right. He liked the idea.

If there'd been any doubts, the swiftness with which he moved to a sitting position, with his legs the only thing in the water, settled them.

Randi pressed his legs apart and moved to kneel between them, her own womb contracting in remembered pleasure at the sight of his tumescent flesh.

Reaching out, she took him in her hand, her fingertips not quite touching. "You're thick," she murmured huskily.

"I'm extremely turned on. Touch me like that and you'll make me come."

"That's the idea." Before he could retort, she dropped her head forward and took the tip of his erection in her mouth.

He muttered an imprecation, which she took as approval.

Licking him, she took in his taste, all male and exactly what she craved, the pearls of pre-ejaculate almost sweet. Randi suckled his tip while running her hand up and down his length, loving the feel of his silky uncircumcised flesh moving over his hard column of flesh. Muttering something in Spanish she did not recognize so assumed was blue language, he settled one of his hands on her head. He did not press for her to take more of his big sex into her mouth, but his hand completed the circle of their connection.

If she didn't watch herself, she'd nuzzle into the hold, exposing more than she wanted.

His hand in her hair excited her, but she wasn't getting sidetracked from her final goal of bringing him the ultimate pleasure. She caressed his balls with the hand not around his penis, very careful not to press too hard on fragile skin, reveling in the spate of Spanish curses that touch elicited.

He gave a hoarse cry. "Yes, keep touching me, *mi hermosa. Que es tan bueno.*"

She didn't need words telling her how good it was, not with his reaction, but she enjoyed the fervent Spanish anyway. She would have smiled if her mouth wasn't full of him, her heart warmed at his approval. Doing her best to take as much as she could of him into her mouth, Randi stretched her lips wide, pressing forward of her own volition, very mindful of her teeth. She'd no desire to cause even the slightest pain to her temporary lover.

She didn't know how long she was lost in pleasuring him, but suddenly he was pulling her head away with the warning, "I'm coming. *Diablo, sí, ya voy.*"

He wrapped his hand around hers, guiding her to take a tighter grip on his column of flesh and increase her pace on the up and downward strokes. There was something really sexy about having his hand wrapped around hers, controlling his pleasure even as *she* gave it to him. Then he was shouting as he climaxed in her hand, barely missing her head with jets of his spend.

"You definitely have all the experience you need." Baz's voice, warm with approval and deep with sexual satisfaction, washed over her after he had regained control of his breathing.

Randi felt utter satisfaction that she'd brought him to this place.

Basilio woke with one arm under the head of his bed partner and the other wrapped snugly around her waist, barely stifling the instinctive curse the situation warranted.

He did not cuddle. Not even with lovers of what was for him long duration. Yet he'd spent the entire night either having sex with the woman in his arms, or holding her. They'd coupled twice more after her inexpert, but mind-shattering, blow job the night before.

He was the one that was supposed to be seducing her, bringing Miranda Smith, née Weber, around to his way of thinking in regard to doing that exposé interview. However, he'd been seduced himself by her innocent sensuality, her sexual candor, her enthusiasm for life and her understated beauty.

There was something about the sweet twenty-four-year-old that got under Basilio's skin.

He didn't give the emotion a sentimental name. It was just another aspect of sex he had not yet experienced. Basilio had promised himself at a tender age, he would never fall into the disastrous morass that romantic love and its companion emotions caused.

He'd seen the effect on his father of following that path, had felt those effects in his own young life as stepmothers changed too frequently for stability.

Nevertheless, he had a difficult time reconciling the woman in whose body he found such satisfying pleasure with the hard-hearted bitch that wanted to tear apart his family's peace.

While that did not change his plans to seduce her into agreeing to cancel the interview, it did have him wondering if there was an aspect to what happened five years ago that Basilio did not understand, or know about.

He needed to get her to talk about the past and why she thought going on television would help her own cause when he could only see heartbreak ahead for her. She'd done something many would find unforgivable. In a moment of inattention, she'd hit a child with her car. And while the consequences could have been worse, they'd been bad enough.

His phone buzzed, interrupting his thoughts, and Basilio carefully eased himself away from Miranda, her sleep so sound, she didn't so much as stir. He tucked the blankets around her, not wanting a draft to disturb her slumber.

She made a soft sound and snuggled into her pillow.

He allowed himself a smile of pure male satisfaction. He'd worn her out and he liked knowing it. Some might call him a throwback for his attitude, but he didn't really care.

He was who he was. And in other circumstances, Miranda Smith would be his ideal bed partner.

He grabbed his phone and swiped just before it went to voice mail. "Wait a moment," he instructed his brother while moving into the living room of the spacious suite.

"Baz?" his brother demanded impatiently, without waiting as Basilio had asked. "It's Carl."

*"Sí."* His phone had already told him as much.

"Have you talked to her yet?"

"I met her. I have not broached the subject of the interview."

"Why not?" his brother demanded, his tone caustic. "We're running out of time."

"There is still more than two weeks until she's scheduled to go on air."

"You need to take care of this now. We can't wait until the last minute." Carl could certainly be strident, but he failed to understand the dynamic of the situation.

"You asked for my help. You will take it as I offer it," Basilio informed his brother.

"Baz, have you forgotten who the younger brother is here?"

"Have you forgotten that you already managed to instigate a restraining order?" If his *older* brother hadn't screwed up, Carl wouldn't need Basilio's help.

"It was a misunderstanding."

"That resulted in legal action. It must have been a rather large misconception."

His brother huffed. "Look, just get her to agree. Tiffany can't take any more from this tragedy."

"Why wasn't there legal action taken at the time? Miranda was guilty of negligence in her driving at the very least."

"I don't know. That was a decision the DA made. Maybe it had something to do with her connections."

That did not ring true, and his brother should know it. "She has only recently discovered she's related to the wife of Andreas Kostas."

"Like I said, I don't know." But something about his brother's words did not have the feel of veracity.

"What about civil action? If you had sued her, she wouldn't be doing this supposed tell-all now, would she?" His brother's lawyers would have made sure part of the restitution would have been no publicity or book deals based on the tragedy Basilio's nephew had suffered.

"We were too distraught at the time. Now it is too late."

Basilio was pretty sure both of those claims were lies. So what was the real reason his brother had refused to take civil action against Miranda Smith?

Perhaps this was something Basilio needed to look further into. He'd never considered that there were extenuating circumstances to his nephew ending up in the hospital in a coma for two weeks, then needing to learn all over again how to speak. Even now he could not imagine what they could be, but one thing was certain.

Carl's attitude was off for the injured party.

Basilio acknowledged his cynicism could have something to do with the fact that he'd never trusted the brother, or sister, for that matter, who dismissed their Spanish roots so completely they'd taken on their stepfather's name and preferred the American versions of their own. The fact they had always treated Basilio like an unwanted distant cousin importuning them for favor, rather than a brother, wasn't in Carl's favor, either.

But family was family and Basilio never let his down. He wasn't about to start now.

His father had drilled family loyalty into Basilio his entire life, but more important, Basilio knew that his father would probably still be married to his first wife had it not been for the fact that Basilio's mother had gotten pregnant with him. Fidelity had never been Armand Perez's thing, but loyalty was. And he'd remained loyal to his wife until he had another child on the way at risk of becoming a bastard.

Basilio carried the weight of his family's dynamic on his shoulders.

Even if he was inclined to let his brother swing in the wind, Basilio would always protect the children of the family with the same commitment his father had shown Basilio. Armand Perez had given up the stability of his marriage, virtually lost all contact with his firstborn son and his precious daughter whom he still adored with a father's unconditional love, having to stand by while they took on another man's name. He'd lost the connections his wife's family offered to him and Perez Holdings, which had harbingered the beginning of the company's decline, and weathered scandal fueled by his wife's fury and desire for revenge.

All for the sake of an unborn son that Armand had never once laid any blame on, no matter what his first wife said in her more caustic moments, or Basilio's own brother and sister had on the few times they visited during his childhood.

While Armand still grieved the loss of his relationship

and parental status with his two older children, he had never made Basilio feel like he was not enough, that his father had ever regretted, even for a minute, that he'd lost so much in order to claim Basilio.

It was a standard of adult commitment to the children of the family Basilio would live up to. Jamie and Grace were entirely innocent and deserving of every bit of Basilio's effort on their behalf.

"How are my nephew and niece?" he asked.

"The entire family is under stress."

"You have kept your children from the media, surely?"

"Jamie is in school. Other children talk."

"Well, keep him home until the furor dies down." Basilio knew his admonishment was too late in coming as the media furor was already on the wane, and Jamie must have already been subjected to it.

Basilio had had his own PR people apprise him of the latest mini-storm of media attention due to the reporter discovering Miranda's connection to a billionaire businessman.

"Don't be ridiculous," Carl said dismissively. "We're not calling him home and disrupting his schedule on account of that woman."

That was right. Jamie attended boarding school. Something Basilio's father had not wanted for his own children, despite his wealth at the time of their childhood and his preoccupation with his paramours. "I would have thought it would be on his own account."

"Don't get sanctimonious with me," Carl barked. "He's my son and I'm doing my best to protect him."

"Are you?" Because from where Basilio sat, it seemed *he* was the one intent on protecting the child.

Carl hung up and Basilio put his own phone down with indifference.

His willingness to help was not reliant on his brother's warm regard.

Basilio was embarked on his current course for the sake

of both his nine-year-old nephew and two-year-old niece. While Grace was unlikely to know what was happening, her home life wouldn't be pleasant if Miranda did the interview, and poor young Jamie would be subject to all sorts of scrutiny and comments at school. Again.

# CHAPTER FOUR

STILL REELING FROM their whirlwind meeting and the amazing, unexpected, explosive, impulsive all-night sex marathon at one of Portland's most luxurious hotel suites, Randi waited impatiently for Basilio to pick her up so they could go look at properties for the second shelter site with his broker.

How had this billionaire, business shark, super-good-looking guy come into her life?

Really, what were the chances she would nearly mow down the guy of her dreams?

The fact he wouldn't make those dreams come true was something she was used to and not about to complain about. Randi practiced living in the moment these days, without too high of expectations for the future. She'd learned her lesson five years ago.

However, his insistence on helping her find a property? That was white-knight stuff she couldn't ignore.

Apparently, the Realtor she had been working with was not up to snuff as far as Baz was concerned and he'd ensured her that his recommended property broker would be happy to donate his commission on the sale, too. Impressed, she ran a mental list of the properties the broker had found already, properties the other Realtor had been convinced were not available at the price Kayla's for Kids could pay.

Her phone buzzed with a text. He was on his way up to her apartment. He could have just told her to come down, but not Basilio Perez. He knew how to treat a woman like she mattered, even if she was a very temporary fixture in his life.

Randi opened the door and looked down the hall toward the elevator just as Baz came through the door from the stairwell. Of course.

No elevators for only a couple of stories up for this man. He was just that guy. Doing everything better, stronger and faster than other mere mortals.

He'd changed into another tailored suit, his shirt now a deep burgundy instead of the traditional white he'd been wearing the day before. His lack of tie and the five o'clock shadow from his dark beard gave him a rakish air not quite fitting with the head of a multinational real estate conglomerate.

But really, what did she know?

Maybe modern-day businessmen were just the new era of pirates?

He slipped the phone he'd been texting on into his suit pocket. "You have a strange expression on your face, *cariña*. What is that about?"

"Um… I was picturing you as a pirate."

He startled, his dark eyes widening in surprise, but then his head went back and he laughed. Long and full, the sound was filled with genuine mirth.

"You don't think you're a pirate?" she asked with her own smile.

He stopped laughing, his expression going more serious than the thought warranted. "I'm sure there are several business rivals, small property holders and employees that would say that is exactly what I am."

An atavistic shiver went down her spine. "That's a lot of people."

He shrugged. "My father had run Perez Holdings into near bankruptcy by the time I was twenty. There was no time for me to get an MBA. My education came in the cut-throat halls of big business."

"And you were determined to win?" This man would never accept anything less.

"For the sake of my family and the Perez name? Oh, yes, I was more than willing to become a pirate."

"You're kind of a ruthless guy, aren't you?" So different from her, and yet not.

Family was important to both of them. The welfare of children mattered to them both. During one of their hiatuses between sexual bouts, he'd told her he admired her career choice and believed children deserved the best the world could offer them.

"There is no *kind of* about it." He reached out and tucked a strand of her hair behind her ear. "There is no room for sentiment in business."

"Wow. I'm not sure I could dismiss people's feelings like that." And honestly, she had a hard time seeing him do it, too.

He reached for her jacket, lying over the back of her sofa, and held it up for her to put on. "You do what you have to when you are backed in a corner."

"I bet you didn't stay cornered for long." She flipped her hair from out of the jacket collar.

"You'd be surprised." Instead of going toward the door, Baz stepped in closer to her. "Bringing Perez Holdings from bankruptcy to the multibillion-dollar international entity that it is today did not happen in a week, a month or even a couple of years."

"So does that ruthlessness translate to your interpersonal relationships?" she asked, breathless from his nearness and doing nothing to hide that fact.

That ship had sailed.

"I can be pitiless both on behalf of and *with* my family when it is necessary." There was no apology in his voice, no sense of regret at what he considered necessary action.

Suddenly realizing just how little she really knew about this man, Randi shivered.

Baz's brows knitted, his espresso eyes filling with concern. "Are you well?" he asked solicitously.

"Yes, of course." She'd just had another wake-up call, which she shouldn't have needed, but apparently did.

His hands landed warmly on her shoulders. "My father has been married many times, but the first time lasted the longest. She turned a blind eye to my father's infidelity and he was utterly loyal to her and my siblings."

"What happened?"

"I did." Baz looked surprised by his own admission. "My mother was my father's mistress, but she got pregnant and suddenly he had to weigh having a child of his grow up without his name and protection, or divorce."

"He chose divorce."

"*Sí.*" And from the look in Baz's dark gaze, he still carried a sense of responsibility for that fact.

"You know you were innocent in the choices your parents made, right?"

"Of course."

"Why don't I believe you?"

"I cannot say." He brushed his thumb up her neck, leaving shivers in the wake of the small caress. "Are you ready to go look at properties?"

"I am." Only didn't they have to step away from each other and, well, *leave the apartment* for that to happen?

"First things first, though." Oh, man, those dark eyes of his.

Who could resist them? Not her.

"Wha—?"

His lips cut off her inquiry, his mouth instantly heated and possessive against hers.

Despite knowing how all this was going to end, with him in Spain, probably with some gorgeous European supermodel, and Randi in Portland, doing what she'd always done, she gave herself to the kiss, allowing Baz to pull her into his arms without hesitation.

He held her close, his hands inside her coat, warm and sure against her back.

After several minutes of blissful loss of self, she made an instinctive protest when Baz stepped away.

He winked. Seriously. Winked. "If we don't leave now, we'll never get to all the properties on our agenda tonight."

The man was too delicious and good at kissing for her to be thinking logically right then. "And that's important."

"Isn't it?" he asked, his tone teasing and arousing at once.

She took a deep breath, let it out and forced her brain to function. "You know it is." She smiled. "And I appreciate your efforts on behalf of Kayla's for Kids a lot."

"While I believe in what your sister wanted to do with these shelters, make no mistake, I've offered my help on your behalf."

Heat suffused her, but she wasn't losing her head again. "I can't believe your broker found such great possibilities."

"Sometimes, in real estate, it is who you know. Not all properties get listed on the MLS immediately. Some never do."

"That doesn't make any sense." It really didn't. "Wouldn't people want to have the biggest pool of potential buyers?"

"Sometimes the only buyer you need is the one who prefers exclusivity."

"But we're not looking for a multimillion-dollar property."

"No. Your budget is not exactly that of a pauper, either, however."

Funny, that wasn't the way her original Realtor had behaved. Her continuous message was that they needed to increase their budget, or lower their expectations.

"Besides," Baz went on, "you're buying on behalf of a nonprofit. If the seller is very wealthy or a corporate entity, they may be in a place where they desire the write-off of offering the property under market value. They save on capital gains as well as increasing their yearly tax shelter."

Okay, that did make sense. And was kind of smart, to boot.

Randi grabbed her backpack purse and slung it on. "Is that how the broker found properties in our price range that fulfilled most, if not all, the items on our wish list?"

They left the apartment, Randi turning off lights just before shutting and locking the door.

Baz answered her question on the way to the elevator. "I would assume so, yes."

"I'm beyond impressed."

"He's a very savvy guy. He wouldn't be working for me otherwise."

"That I believe."

He grinned, looking younger than his thirty years for a brief moment. "My reputation precedes me already."

She shook her head in wonder. "You're really confident, aren't you?"

"Some call me arrogant." And he didn't sound like that bothered him at all.

"That doesn't bother you at all?"

"Not particularly, no."

"You write your own rules to life." That was for sure.

"And you, whose rules do you live by?"

Randi wasn't sure she had an answer to that. She'd spent so much of her adult life, and early childhood, reacting.

"I think I live by the rule of survival."

"So then, we have that in common. The survival of the Perez name, my family's survival, my company's survival, these are paramount to me."

They were on their way to the first property when she asked about the family he kept mentioning as being so important.

Baz cast her a sidelong glance as he pulled the luxury car to a smooth stop at a red light. "My father maintains a nominal position in the company while he negotiates his fifth marriage."

"That's a lot of wives. He must have tons of kids." And pay a lot of alimony.

No wonder the man's company had been doing so poorly.

"Actually, there are only three of us." Baz pulled into traffic again, his olive-toned hands curled loosely around the leather steering wheel.

"Are you close to the others?" Randi asked, thinking how much she wished she'd grown up with Kayla as part of her life.

"Not really. My older brother and sister were content to keep to themselves once our father divorced their mother." There was something subtle in Baz's tone that implied pain at that truth, despite his nonchalant attitude.

"I'm sorry to hear that." She laid her hand on his thigh in what she hoped was comfort. "Finding Kayla is one of the best things that has happened in my life."

"That is a sweet sentiment."

But he didn't do sentiment and maybe she understood his stand on that a little better. A dad who went through wives like disposable commodities, siblings who ignored his existence and a young adulthood spent learning life's lessons in the merciless school of big business, Baz had little opportunity to appreciate the softer emotions.

"What about your mom?"

"She married my father for his money and negotiated their prenup with more acuity than any woman or man I've faced across a conference table, with lawyers lining both sides."

"She knew her marriage had a sell-by date."

"She was smart enough to realize that even though she was only the second wife, she would not be the last."

"What about her relationship with you?"

"I lived with my father after the divorce."

"What? Why?"

"His first wife had taken his children to another country. He insisted on that provision in the prenup. In exchange for a very generous divorce settlement, he got primary custody."

"That must have been heartbreaking for both of you."

"Not so much. She got visitation, and my father, for all his womanizing ways, was a decent parent."

"My mother kept my sister from me. I didn't even know about her until this last year. I'm not sure I'll ever forgive her for that." Not to mention other things her mother had done that kept her firmly out of the running for decent human being, much less Mother of the Year.

"My father did not keep me from my siblings, or from my mother."

But someone had, at least from his siblings. Because she could read between the lines and the message there was that Baz did not feel like he was a part of their family, despite how *he* saw them.

"Your loyalty to your family is surprisingly strong."

"My father may have failed spectacularly at marriage, but his familial loyalty to his own parents, siblings, wives, ex-wives and children was and is absolute. He required no less from me."

Add that to the guilt Baz so obviously carried in regard to his father's first marriage's breakup, that made for some compelling motivation for his sense of loyalty toward people that might not deserve it.

"But not your siblings?" She also had to assume that by familial loyalty, Baz did not mean sexual fidelity. Or there wouldn't have been four ex-wives to this point.

"After taking them back to her own country after the divorce, their mother remarried quickly. They didn't just take on their stepfather's last name. They were raised with a different set of values."

"You're more understanding than I would have thought considering your pirate nature." She used the small tease to lighten the suddenly heavy atmosphere in the car.

"Yes, well, I can be surprising."

"You've shocked my socks off since meeting, that's for sure."

He cast her a heated glance. "It's not merely your socks I'm keen to see you out of."

Randi blushed to the roots of her hair. Darn him. "You didn't get enough of that last night?" Or that morning? They'd been intimate again after breakfast, necessitating a second shower before checking out of the hotel suite.

"I believe I have already told you that one night would not be enough."

"Lucky me."

"I am glad you think so, though I consider myself the one favored by fortune."

She patted his thigh, hard muscles bunching under her fingers, distracting her and forcing her to think about what she was going to say. Oh, that was right. "I wouldn't have taken you for a sweet-talker."

"I am not. I mean what I say." His hand settled over hers, pressing them both more firmly against his leg.

She sucked in air at how quickly she got turned on by that simple move. "And I'm glad to hear that."

They toured two properties, the banter between them never abating, and were now in the third facility.

"It looks like a school," she said uncertainly. On paper this property had all the room the shelter required, but she'd never considered it might be an institutional building.

"It was a boarding school. The remodel necessary for your purposes would be minimal. The entire second floor is already living quarters. The classrooms, offices and public spaces dovetail into your vision for this new Kayla's for Kids."

She loved that he'd paid such close attention to the things she'd told him.

When they got inside, she saw exactly what he meant. The building was in surprisingly good repair and offered everything she could want for the housing of hard-to-place foster care children and homeless teens, and offering after-school activities to even more at-risk youth.

She stared around the dining hall, shocked it was still furnished with tables and chairs. "Is there a note the furnishings are for sale, as well?"

"They are."

"The seller would probably want more than our budget."

Baz referred to something on his phone. "She's a seventy-year-old very wealthy philanthropist. My guess is when she finds out what you want to do with the property, she'll either offer the furnishings for nothing or well under market value."

Randi got the best kind of chills. "You think so?"

"I do. She was instrumental in funding the school as well as providing the facility."

"She sounds like an amazing lady."

"Perhaps we can arrange a personal meeting if you buy this property. It never hurts to have another benefactor for a nonprofit."

Randi stepped closer to Baz, taking his lapels in her fists. "You're always thinking, aren't you?"

"*Sí* is a word I like. *No*, not so much." His sexy grin sent thrills through her.

She huffed out a laugh. "I totally believe it."

An hour later, after a quick text exchange with Kayla that included a ton of pictures, Randi and Baz had worked out an offer for the property with his broker.

"I'm certain this will be accepted, particularly once we apprise the seller of what you are buying the property for." The broker shook first Baz's hand and then Randi's, showing that despite her being the buyer, he knew who buttered the broker's bread.

"Shall we go out to celebrate a successful evening's work?" Baz asked when they reached his silver metallic sports model Mercedes.

"I don't want to jinx it by celebrating too early."

"Surely you are too well educated and intelligent for

such superstitions." The locks snicked and Baz opened the passenger-side door for her.

She slid into her seat, but looked up at him as he leaned against the open door. "No one is too educated or smart to learn life's lessons."

"And you have learned that dreams do not always come true?"

"I told you I have."

"But not why."

Last night she couldn't imagine sharing one of the worst times in her life with this man, a practical stranger. After he'd helped her, shared insights into his own life and, well... made love to her so many times, he didn't feel like a stranger anymore.

She brushed her hand over the leather dash of the Mercedes as Baz climbed into the driver's seat. "I wouldn't have thought you could rent a car like this by the week."

"Money makes many things possible."

The fact that he didn't pressure her further into sharing confidences took away the last of Randi's reservations about doing so.

"Five years ago I was driving back to my dorm at the university after visiting my dad." She was glad they were in the car for privacy, but she wished he was driving. Meeting his eyes right now was hard, but she did it. "The street I was on only had a thirty-mile-an-hour speed limit and I was going under. I was always cautious because as well as businesses, there were houses and apartments along that stretch."

Baz made no move to put his seat belt on or start the car, but stayed facing her, his focus entirely on Randi. "And?"

"And a little boy ran out from between two parked cars. He'd been with his mother at a park two blocks away. She had no idea he was gone until she heard the sirens."

"What?" Baz looked shocked, his olive complexion going pale.

An understandable reaction to where the conversation was obviously going, she thought.

"I couldn't stop fast enough." She paused, taking several shallow breaths. This never got easier to talk about. Randi wasn't even sure she would have told Kayla until the whole fiasco a few weeks ago when a reporter discovered that Randi Smith used to be Randi Weber from Southern California. "There were cars in the oncoming lane and parked cars beside me. I had nowhere to go. Though I tried. I still clipped that tiny body with my car. It was the most horrific moment of my life."

Even worse than the terror and emotional agony she'd felt when her mother had tried to drown her when Randi was six.

"I would imagine." There was a strange quality to Baz's voice.

"Believe me when I say I'd had other terrifying moments, but nothing that compared."

"Was the child okay?"

"Eventually. He was in a coma for weeks and he had to learn how to speak and walk again once he woke up. It was my worst nightmare." It would have been anyone's.

"You say there was nothing you could have done?" The still quality to Baz's voice gave Randi pause.

And made her feel defensive, which surprised her. She shouldn't be, though. His reacting with understanding would have been the true shock, wouldn't it? No one else had. Not until Kayla and Andreas learned about what had happened.

"No, there was nothing."

"So?"

"Do you think knowing I had no options makes me feel better? That I haven't gone over those two seconds in my mind a million times, looking for a different outcome? There wasn't one, but it didn't matter. Not when his parents turned their PR machine on to the task of discrediting me. I guess they didn't want anyone to know it was the mom's fault."

"She did not hit him with her car."

Randi felt those words like a blow and had to look away from him. "No, she didn't, but no child of four should have been on that street unaccompanied." She looked back, her face tight with anger she would no longer hide, not out of misplaced compassion for the Madisons, people who had shown they had absolutely none for her. "The doctors said that if I'd been going the speed limit, he would be dead. His tiny body was no competition for even my eco-friendly subcompact."

"He would not have been, no." There was definitely a dark overtone in both Baz's words and manner.

"The papers, news reports, people all over social media, they all took your attitude."

"My attitude?" he asked.

"They believed it was all my fault. I must have been driving recklessly or not paying attention. The Madisons made sure that was the message being fed to every outlet. Mrs. Madison played the victim very well."

"She was a victim, surely. Her child was in the hospital."

She was going to be sick. She should have been prepared for this, but she wasn't. "And that is why despite the police ruling it an unavoidable accident, despite screen shots and traffic cams that proved she was negligent, I said nothing. I knew she must be going through hell and I wasn't taking her through more. Not even with the truth."

"If she was negligent, she would have been charged."

Unbelievable. Okay, they'd only slept together one night, but didn't she deserve even a tiny bit more consideration than a complete stranger? "By that same argument, then I must have been innocent, right? After all, if I was the monster the Madisons painted me, wouldn't they have taken me to civil court, even if the DA declined to prosecute?"

"That is a point, yes."

Could he have been any more skeptical in his tone?

Randi was definitely regretting telling this piece of painful history to the man with the stony expression. "You still think it was my fault."

"I did not say that." But his attitude and the expression in his espresso eyes did.

"Would you please take me back to my apartment?"

"Does it matter so much what I think?"

"I've had my fill of being judged a monster when there was more than enough blame to go around." She knew better than to open herself for more of the same.

She'd been a fool to think it was safe sharing one of her most painful secrets with a temporary sexual partner, regardless of his help in finding a home for the Kayla's for Kids shelter.

"Are you going to do something about it?" he asked.

"As a matter of fact, I am. I have plans to set the record straight with the media."

"People have already made up their minds, according to you. What difference will a press release make?"

"An interview, on national television, not a press release." Which was overwhelming and scary to think about, not that she would offer that proof of more vulnerability to him. "I'll get to tell my side, the truth."

That was what was important. She had to remember that.

"Why would you put the family through that?"

Seriously? The family angle again? She supposed to a man so steeped in obligation toward family it made sense, but what about her? What about what *her* family had been through when she'd been vilified for behavior she'd never engaged in: reckless driving, inattention, not caring?

"You don't think it's fair?" she demanded skeptically. "After the media crucified me because of the story the Madisons fed them, I lost my almost fiancé, my scholarship and my position at the university. To achieve any measure of peace and anonymity in my life, I had to give up my last name and move away from my father and grandparents. Now the Madisons are trying to do it all over again. I'm not giving up another thing for their sensibilities."

"What do you mean they're trying to do it again? What are they doing?" he asked like the answer really mattered.

She wasn't buying that bridge. Not again. But she didn't mind telling him. It wasn't a state secret. "Their best to keep the truth under wraps, to make me their scapegoat again."

"Trying to find peace after such a tragedy is hardly making you the scapegoat," he scoffed.

Was this really the man she'd shared her body with the night before? The same man who had worked so hard to find the best property for her without anything in it for him? "What would you call threatening to destroy my *new* life?"

"The attempt to protect his family by a desperate man."

"Oh, my gosh, you don't even know these people, but you're their champion?"

He frowned, looking almost guilty. "It is clearly an untenable situation for everyone."

"I guess I should be grateful you include me in that *everyone*."

"It was a terrible time in your life. That accident cost you a great deal. I would have to be blind not to see that."

"You think?"

His lips twisted with frustration. "Yes, I do. However, I do not think bringing it all back up in front of the national media, no less, is going to make your life better. It will certainly hurt a family that has already been through hell, especially their children. The young can be so cruel."

She had firsthand experience with just how cruel *adults* could be. "And the hell I've been through?"

"Won't disappear by opening yourself up to further comment and potential vilification."

"You don't think it matters if the truth comes out?"

"I don't think it will help you, or them." He reached

across the console, cupping her cheek. "Don't stir it all up again."

She jerked her face away from touch that should not be comforting. "I'm not the one doing that."

"Then who?"

"First it was a small article written for one of the on-line news media, nothing that really got a lot of attention, but then somehow Mr. Madison became aware of it, and before I knew what was happening, I was being trolled on the only social page I keep. Other articles started popping up, all with a heavy slant to what *my* supposed carelessness had cost the Madison family. It was five years ago all over again, only this time Mr. Madison came to me personally. He threatened me, threatened to get me fired."

"He didn't realize you work for your sister?" Baz sounded disgusted by such incompetence.

It would have been funny in another situation.

"No. We've never shared the same last name. Only the people closest to us even know we're sisters."

"And you threatened him back," Baz guessed, proving he had no inkling of who Randi really was.

"No. Not at all. I told him to leave, but he wouldn't. He had some goon with him, a big man who wouldn't let me leave, either."

"This goon, did he restrain you?" Now Baz sounded furious.

She couldn't imagine why.

"He and Mr. Madison. I screamed. Carl Madison slapped me. I was terrified. He said he was going to make people believe I had abused the children I worked with. He said what was left of my life wasn't going to be worth living when he was done with me."

"That is not…" His voice trailed off, the expression on Baz's face murderous. "Did you file charges for assault?"

"Not at first. I was so used to feeling guilty, to believing the Madison family needed protecting after what had happened to Jamie, that's the name of the boy, I just broke down. The goon threw me on the floor, and after a few more vicious threats that made me wonder if my life was seriously in danger, they left."

"And then?"

"And then I went home."

"But somehow you got from there to here."

"That was Kayla. I was still shaken up the next day when we had a meeting about Kayla's for Kids. She pried the whole story out of me, and for the first and only time, someone learned about the horrible day without judging me a monster."

"I do not think you are a monster."

She wasn't touching that denial. Randi knew what she'd seen in his eyes. "She and Andreas convinced me to press charges. Not that it did much good. Mr. Madison has a whole bevy of expensive lawyers on his side. He got a plea deal that allowed for a misdemeanor, settled with a fine. Andreas was adamant I take out a restraining order after that."

"So you did."

"Yes. Andreas may be a shark like you, but he cares about people's feelings and he was livid about the way I'd been treated. He's the one who set up the interview on the morning talk show."

"Your hero." There was no mistaking the sardonic tone to Baz's voice.

"Yes, finally I had one."

"Not your own father?"

"Dad is a high school English teacher. He had to change schools after what happened. His principal was one of the people who thought I was a monster and he let Dad know it. No, my dad never doubted me. Neither did my grandparents, but none of them could help me. Not in the face of the Madison wealth and influence."

She swallowed against the tightening in her throat and blinked back tears. "That's not to say they didn't help me at all. Dad made sure I got into another school. They all pitched in to help support me while I made the move to Sacramento. It was my dad's idea to change my last name. I took his mom's maiden name, but couldn't get a job until all the paperwork cleared the courts and I got my new identification."

"And then there was your lost scholarship."

"Yes. My grandparents joined with Dad to keep me in school. I worked, too, but I never would have gotten my degree in social work without them."

"Do you think you chose to help children because you felt guilty about what happened to Jamie?" he asked, for once not sounding judgmental, just curious.

"No. I know exactly why I got into the field I did and it had little to nothing to do with what happened five years ago."

"What, then?"

"You've gotten all the confidences you're going to get out of me."

"Do not be like that. I told you, I do not judge you."

No, he'd said he didn't think she was a monster and Randi hadn't believed him. "Believe it or not, your opinion makes very little difference to me."

"I do not believe, *cariña*."

"Don't call me that."

"Why not? You think because you shared this burden we are now going to go our separate ways like we never met?"

Yep, that was the plan. "You think the sex was good enough to justify having more with a woman you believe responsible for a small boy ending up in the hospital. I don't have to agree with that sentiment."

"What I think is that you are unnecessarily defensive about something that has caused you enough pain. Do not allow the sharing of it to cut off the pleasure we find in one another's company."

That was not what she was doing, was it? No. "You defended them. I'm the woman you slept with, but when I told you, your whole concern was for the Madisons."

"I apologize that is how it seemed. It is not the case. You matter to me, Miranda. Your feelings matter to me and our time together is not over."

"You don't make any sense." But hearing she mattered soothed the rough edges of the wounds he'd inflicted with his attitude.

"I make perfect sense. I told you this was no one-night stand."

"Even after what you just heard?"

"Especially after that. Right now you could use another friend and we are good together. A tragedy in your past does not change that."

Did he really believe that? "You defended people who did everything they could to destroy my life. How is that being my friend?"

"Do not hold my ability to see both sides of this situation against me. Especially when it was your own compassion toward the Madisons that allowed you to remain silent so long."

Okay, maybe he had a point. "You're sure you see *both* sides?"

"Do not doubt it."

She pulled her seat belt across her body and snapped it in the lock. "I'll work on the not doubting thing, but right now could you please take me back to my apartment?"

"If that is what you truly desire."

"It is."

# CHAPTER FIVE

BAZ IGNORED MIRANDA'S obvious hints that he needn't park the car, but could just drop her off in front of the apartment complex.

Instead, he found a spot under a light in the visitor section of the parking lot and turned off the engine.

She unclipped her seat belt, her focus on the dark night out the window. "I'm not really in the mood for more company."

"I will walk you up." He'd work on her desire to get rid of him once he was in her apartment. He'd messed up spectacularly when he'd allowed his natural inclination to defend his family rise to the surface.

It wasn't like him to make a mistake like that, but when he was around Miranda, Basilio found himself showing more of the man who lived inside the corporate shark's body than with anyone else. Even the family with which he was currently damn angry.

With the exception of his nephew and niece. They continued to be the innocent victims in a terrible situation that should never have had the cost to Miranda's life it had, but should definitely not be allowed to destroy theirs, either.

"That's not necessary."

"I think it is."

She rolled her eyes, but didn't argue further. However, for the first time that evening, she did not wait for him to come around and open her car door, but got out of the Mercedes immediately, closing her door with more force than necessary.

She was angry. And he did not blame her. As far as she knew, he *had* defended a complete stranger over the woman who had shared his bed with so much passion the night before.

If her story was true—and despite the fact he'd only known her a short while and his family was, well…his family, he believed her—then she had good reason to despise his brother *and* his sister-in-law. Miranda had taken the high road five years before, protecting people who had been indisputably vile to her when she had shown them nothing but compassion.

Regardless, however, Basilio had not been lying when he told her that doing the interview would not serve her. The media furor was dying down and stirring it up again would do her no favors, no matter what the truth was.

Basilio could easily verify Miranda's accusations against his brother. Police records were not something that could be dismissed with a plausible story by Carlos. Which meant Basilio's older brother had assaulted Miranda and made heinous threats. He had not simply begged her to let things die down and give their family peace, as both Gracia and Carlos claimed.

Basilio was beyond angry at the prospect he'd been lied to by his family, but he was even more furious about what his brother had done to Miranda. He would be calling Carlos later and letting him know just how unacceptable his behavior had been, but right now it was time to mend fences with Miranda.

Because he could not alter his course in trying to convince Miranda to cancel the interview, though. Not for her sake, and not for the sake of Basilio's family. While the adults might not deserve his protection, his innocent niece and nephew did. And while they were called Madisons, the Perez name was at stake, as well.

"You're awfully quiet now." She sounded suspicious.

He could not blame her. He did, in fact, have plans and she was an intelligent woman.

"Am I?" he asked as they exited the elevator on her floor. He preferred the stairs, but she'd made it clear she intended to take the conveyance.

"You had plenty to say earlier."

"Too much if I've offended you so much you no longer want my company." He'd been so shocked by Miranda's claim the accident happened because of Tiffany's apparent neglect to Jamie's welfare, he'd gone into family protection mode immediately.

Shown too much of himself to the woman whom he found it too easy to do that with.

At first, he hadn't even wanted to believe Tiffany had been at fault, but he'd come around fast. Miranda simply was not a dishonest woman, which made her vulnerable to people like Basilio's brother, who did not care if they had to use lies to protect an unpleasant secret.

It made sense of the fact that Basilio never saw Tiffany with the children without the nanny. He'd thought it rather affected that the nanny even accompanied her on visits to her mother's home. Now he wondered if that was because no one trusted her to watch her own children with proper diligence.

And what did that say about the unleashing of the Madison PR machine on the hapless nineteen-year-old Miranda?

Nothing good, that was for damn sure.

Miranda stopped outside her door and turned to face Basilio, but she made no effort to meet his gaze. "I'll say good-night now. Maybe you can call me tomorrow." She didn't sound like she thought there was even a remote chance of that happening.

And she was right, but not for the reasons this beautiful, vulnerable and entirely too compassionate woman thought. "I'll see you inside." He had every hope of being there in the morning.

"I don't think that's a good idea."

"Please, *mi hermosa*. Do not do this." He never pleaded, but right now it was his job to equalize things between them.

And if that required him swallowing a tiny bite of his Spanish pride, so be it.

Finally, her head tilted up, her expressive gray eyes clouded with emotion. "Why?"

"You can ask that after last night?" He paused, letting his words sink in. "And this morning?"

"That's sex. You can get it elsewhere. So can I."

Chance would be a fine thing. As far as Basilio's investigators could tell, the woman had been celibate since her last disastrous relationship five years previous.

"Not that kind of sex. Not the mind-blowing, expectation-smashing joining of two bodies." He moved in on her, pressing her back against her door, watching for denial that never came. "What we experience together is something special."

"For you?" she demanded with clear disbelief.

"*Sí.* Do not doubt it."

Miranda shook her head, her golden-brown hair rubbing against the door. He kissed her before she could say something they would both regret, like that he should leave. Which he would do if she requested.

After her recount of what had happened with Carlos, Basilio refused to do anything that might spark similar fear in her.

But Miranda did not fight the kiss, or even refuse to respond. Her mouth went soft against his with a sound that was very much like surrender. Relief all out of proportion for the situation shot through him.

Basilio reached down to where she held the keys in her hand and gently took them. Without breaking the kiss, he found the proper key for the locks through trial and error, and finally the door swung open behind her.

Miranda stumbled backward and he followed, closing the

door behind them. The way to her room was strewn with discarded clothes as they kissed with a passion so much bigger than what he felt with other women. He hadn't been blowing smoke up her skirt when he said this kind of sex was special for him; it was entirely outside his undeniably sufficient experience.

He'd had enough women in his bed to know that finding one so compatible, so combustible, was extraordinary. So rare, he'd never actually coupled with a woman he was so instantly into, or one whose kiss could have him so close to coming without even a touch to his sex.

By the time they reached the bedroom, Miranda was down to another sexy set of lingerie and he was completely nude.

"As tantalizing as these are, there is no place for any covering between us when we reach that bed." He pointed to the full-size bed stacked high with colorful pillows and covered in a spread that looked like it might have come from India.

She measured him with her gray gaze. "Then maybe you should take them off."

He didn't need a second invitation, reaching out to do exactly as she suggested. In a matter of seconds the final bits of clothing were lying on the floor, and nothing hindered his gaze from consuming her elegant curves, the way her nipples were already taut and flushed with need, the glistening patch of curls at the apex of her thighs.

"You are truly beautiful."

"English tonight?"

"Probably not for long." She made him lose his ability to communicate in anything but the most primitive.

A shadow seemed to lift from her, as if his admission had given her some kind of reassurance. He was glad he had allowed truth to speak in that case.

Her bore her back to the bed, her soft thighs a cradle for his hard muscles, her hands coming up to grip the back of his head.

Their kiss went incendiary and the hours that followed were even better than the night before. What sleep they got, they spent wrapped in each other. There was really no choice, not in the double bed that wasn't really meant for two people.

Especially when one of them was six foot four and broad-shouldered, and showed a heretofore unknown tendency to cuddle.

In the middle of the night, he woke to her touching him and was so damn turned on by her initiating their lovemaking that he didn't even think of the condom until after he'd climaxed in her tight, wet heat.

He didn't actually think of it until she started swearing, which so far he'd never heard her do, and then pounding on his shoulder. "Move. Get off me. We forgot the condom! I can't believe this. It's not happening. *We forgot the condom.*"

Despite the urgency in her tone, he was careful as he withdrew from her body. Basilio rolled to his side, but didn't jump from the bed and held her wrist when it was clear that was what she wanted to do. "Don't have a fit."

She yanked her arm away and sat up, turning on the light. "How can you say that? We just had *unprotected sex.* I've never even asked to see test results from you. I can't believe I didn't. Kayla keeps reminding me I need to be safe, but I never thought it would come up. I wasn't even dating anyone!"

"Calm down, *bella.* You are fine. *We* are fine. I can show you the results of my latest physical." He counted it a win that she'd stayed in the bed.

"How long ago was that? More important, how many women? Did you have sex with *them* without protection?" The questions came fast and furious, her lovely gray eyes wild.

"No. Never before. You have nothing to concern yourself with."

But she was freaking out, her body strung like a bow,

tension emanating off her in stress-filled waves. Her pupils were blown with shock, not pleasure. Unfortunately.

"Of course I'm going to concern myself. I can't believe I never asked to see anything before. What's the matter with me?" she practically shrieked. "I totally fail at this modern woman reveling in her independence thing."

He would have laughed if she hadn't said the last with such a sense of despondency. "You are getting hysterical for no reason."

"I'm not hysterical!" She shot him the glare of death. "How can you say that? I don't get hysterical."

Okay. Sure. "So, I can see."

"Don't patronize me." She smacked the bed for emphasis, the sheet covering her breasts slipping down.

He reached out and readjusted the bedding, tugging it up and tucking it around her. "You must stop this spiraling. Trust me, you have nothing to fear from me."

"What about pregnancy? What about that?"

Alarm coursed through him. "You're not on birth control?" What woman today did not protect herself from unplanned pregnancies?

Maybe a celibate one. He'd read the report; he should have paid attention to what that meant.

"No! I told you, I suck at this!"

"The only kind of sucking you do is very pleasurable and wholly positive."

"This is not a joke!" She was spiraling again.

"Of course not." He reached out, going to touch her again, relieved when she didn't pull away this time. He put his hand against her neck and let it slide down to cup her shoulder. "There is the morning-after pill."

"Yes. Right. Yes. Where do I get that?" She looked around wildly, like she expected to find one lying on the nightstand or dresser.

He bit back another smile. "At the pharmacy, I would imagine."

"Oh, right. Of course." She reached over and grabbed her phone off the bedside table. Soon she was lost to whatever she was reading on the screen. "It says here for the one I don't need a prescription for, I've got three days. That's good, right?"

*"Si, esta bien."*

"But it also says that even the one that is good for up to five days doesn't work if I'm already ovulating. What if I am?"

"Do not assume the worst." He tried to see what she was reading on her phone, but the text was too tiny. "People try for years to get pregnant and don't manage it. There's no reason to think one transgression is going to result in you carrying my child."

The thought of it, though? Was more alluring than alarming.

Ridiculous.

Basilio squashed that train of thought fast. While he knew a great deal more about Miranda than she realized, courtesy of the report he'd had compiled on her, they'd only met the day before. Great sex did not equate to a relationship solid enough to build a family on.

If he'd learned nothing else from his father's serial infidelity, Basilio knew that to be true.

"It says here... Oh, my goodness... I'm right in the middle of when I should be ovulating." She looked at him with stricken eyes. "I'm not ready to be a mom. I don't know if I ever will be."

A woman who dedicated her life to children didn't want any of her own? How was that possible? "Stop borrowing trouble. Please. We will go to the pharmacy as soon as it opens in the morning if that will make you feel better."

"But what good will it do? I've probably already ovulated."

"We'll call the doctor. Maybe he will have a solution."

"My doctor is a woman."

"She, then."

"Okay, okay, we'll have to wait for tomorrow." But she didn't sound like she was going to survive without losing it during the interim.

"Miranda, *mi hermosa*." He waited for her to acknowledge him.

When she didn't, seeming to be lost in a world of potential unplanned pregnancies, he got up from the bed. She still didn't act like she even realized he was still in the room, so he went into her bathroom, where there was thankfully a surprisingly large tub. The apartment complex was old and the porcelain tub looked original to the building, deeper and slightly wider than those he'd seen in more modern dwellings of the same caliber.

Basilio ran a bath, pouring some salts into the water from a stash he'd found under the sink. When he went back into the bedroom, Miranda was still sitting on the bed, her slightly out of focus expression filled with dismay.

"I ran you a bath."

"You think that will help?"

"I do."

"How? You think the hot water will somehow miraculously render your swimmers inert? Somehow, I don't see it."

"You need to relax," he clarified. "It will help with that."

She stared at him like she was trying to read something in his gaze. Finally, she nodded.

Miranda allowed him to lead her into the now-steamy bathroom, her hand limp in his. This lost and dispirited Miranda wasn't one he recognized, and frankly, it bothered him.

Sinking into the hot water, she sighed as if releasing tension, but her mouth remained flat, her eyes still unfocused.

Basilio bathed his beautiful lover, being careful not to let his touches grow sexual, no matter how the sight of her naked body incited his own flesh. Finally, after several minutes of him cupping the hot water and letting it pour down her skin, Miranda collapsed against the angled back of the tub, letting her body slide down so most of it was submerged.

Since there were no bubbles, the submersion did his libido no favors.

Still, he managed to control himself as he spoke to her about everything but sex, babies and her past.

At first, her responses were desultory or disjointed by turns, but eventually she began to share in the conversation, expressing the opinion that autumn wasn't really autumn without the leaves changing color. It was a throwaway conversation, but her willingness to engage made Basilio nearly weak with relief.

She'd really been thrown by them having unprotected sex and coming to the realization they'd shared nothing of their health status with each other.

Understandable, really. She knew almost nothing about him. He, on the other hand, had walked into this with plenty of information on Miranda Smith, née Weber. The report on her had included her recent sexual activity, or lack thereof, and her health status. The first time they had sex, he'd known he didn't need to see test results.

She'd let her desire override good sense.

He'd done exactly the same thing when he woke up beside her, his mind filled with the memory dreams he'd been having.

He wasn't sure why he wasn't as disturbed by the prospect of her being pregnant as she was, but Miranda was definitely not a woman who took this kind of situation in stride.

Her lack of practical knowledge about the morning-after pill only showed what he'd suspected. Miranda Smith simply did not take risks like the one they'd taken. A very primitive part of him liked knowing she was out of control when they had sex as he'd proved himself to be.

It made no sense in their situation. Their interlude

couldn't last. There was too much standing between them for him to even consider a long-distance relationship with this woman.

Yet he found more satisfaction in bathing her than he did in intercourse with many of his past lovers. Her silky skin. Her soft, modest curves. It was all perfect.

Miranda suddenly rose up from the hot water, leaving him scrambling to his feet.

"I'll take the morning-after pill, but if I've already ovulated, it's not going to work." Water glistened on her silky skin.

He had to focus on what she'd said rather than the body he found so perfect. Okay, they were back to unplanned baby prospect for conversation. "Think positive."

"I've learned to be a realist." She stepped out of the draining water and onto the bath mat.

"But you are naturally optimistic. I hear it in the way you talk about the children you're trying to help." He reached out to dry her off with the towel he'd grabbed from the rack.

She took the brightly colored terry cloth from him, stepping as far away as she could in the limited space. "I have hope for them."

"But not yourself?"

"I'm not unhappy." She finished drying off and wrapped the towel around her torso, hiding her nudity from him.

The action felt significant.

"No." He reached for her hand, holding it as he led the way back into the bedroom, inexplicably grateful when she let him. "But you think the worst will happen."

"Is a baby the worst thing? I guess you'd think so."

"That is not what I said." Damn. She was adept at reading meaning into the least word.

"But it's what you meant."

"No."

"So you're saying that if I'm pregnant, you'll be part of the baby's life."

He didn't suggest other more definitive answers to an unwanted pregnancy. He could read between the lines, too, and hopefully with more accuracy. Despite what it would surely mean for her life, Miranda wouldn't consider the baby unwanted.

"I would, yes." His own child would trump his brother's sensibilities. It would be a way to keep Miranda in Basilio's life.

He did his best to quash the foolish thought, but it would not go away.

She stopped beside the bed and faced him. "You're serious?"

"We may not know each other well, but you are already aware of how loyal I am to my family."

Tension drained out of her, her lovely face relaxing, her body losing its too-tense posture. "Okay, good. Not that I think I'm pregnant."

She could have fooled him.

"I mean, what are the chances one time would do it?" she asked like he hadn't brought up that very point before. "People try for years for children."

He'd mentioned that, too, but he wasn't going to remind her. She was finally coming down off the ledge.

"Are you ready to go back to bed?" They had at least a couple of hours before they needed to get up.

She resisted his tug that would have resulted in her sitting on the edge of the bed. "Um, do you have access to your health status on your phone?"

"Of course." What sexually active person in today's world didn't?

"Great. Um…can I see it?"

He nearly smacked his own forehead in a moment of realization. Of course she wanted that. He should have thought of it as soon as she mentioned not seeing them earlier. "*No problemo.* Let me pull it up."

"Um… I've got mine, too."

"And you will show me and then you will relax, hmm?"

"Maybe?" She got her phone from the charger beside the bed.

It only took a minute for them to look at one another's phones.

"So you haven't, um, had other unprotected sex…you know, since your last physical?"

"No." He would have told her that he'd never had unprotected sex before, because it was true, but that might make her think there was something more between them.

Something beyond sex unlike anything he'd ever known. Something possibly permanent when they could be anything but.

"You don't regularly engage in high-risk behavior?" She sounded like she was repeating something she'd read.

He answered her regardless. "No, I do not."

"Okay, good. That's good." She gave him a severely uncomfortable look. "You can ask me, too."

"You would not have freaked out so badly if this was something you were used to."

Her expression cleared, like she was relieved he wouldn't be asking her personal questions about her sex life. "That's true. I'm glad you realize that."

"You already told me you aren't easy."

"I could have been lying."

"I do not think lying is something you do often, or well." Which was why Basilio had believed her about the day five years ago and Tiffany's part in it, as well as Miranda's claims about his brother's abhorrent behavior.

"You're right." She bit her bottom lip, her manner vulnerable. "I hate dishonesty."

A frisson of unexpected concern went through him. She was not going to take well to learning that there had been an ulterior motive behind their meeting. *If* she ever learned it. He couldn't be naive to the possibility, though. She was too intelligent for him to dismiss the chance.

Danger of exposure or not, he had a job to do.

For her sake now as much as for Basilio's family.

He needed to convince Miranda to cancel that interview. Basilio could not allow himself to be sidetracked by her addictive reaction in bed, or even the possibility of pregnancy.

If she thought Carlos had ruined her life already, it would be nothing compared to opening herself up to the haters and the gossip hounds that would come out of the woodwork once she did an interview on national television.

Ask any celebrity, politician or person of interest who lived under the scrutiny of the paparazzi. People interested in scandal could be much more ruthless than Basilio in pursuing their own agendas. They were not interested in truth, only stories that increased their ratings, circulation or viral presence online.

Not that Carlos and his PR people wouldn't have to make concessions, too. Now that Basilio knew the truth of what happened five years before, he wasn't going to allow them to smear Miranda's name any longer. He, more than anyone, understood the power of reputation, and Miranda had worked as hard as he in her own way to rebuild hers.

But he'd warned her that ruthlessness was part of his makeup. What he hadn't said was that he could be downright brutal when pursuing a goal, as many had learned to their detriment in the years since he'd taken over his father's company.

Including his father's ex-wives, who were used to asking for money beyond what they were legally entitled to, whenever they wanted. He'd cut off any payments other than what was outlined in each divorce decree. It had infuriated his various stepmothers, but they'd settled down when he'd told them he had already put the entire company in his own name, making his father a pauper on paper, and then threatened to take them back to court to adjust alimony payments.

Even his own mother had learned to live within the bounds of the generous monthly allowance she received.

And Basilio had never once regretted the hard choices he had to make. Until now. While he would not allow it to change the outcome, he hated the thought of Miranda's passionate acceptance turning to distrust.

So he would just have to make sure that did not happen.

# CHAPTER SIX

ANTICIPATION RIDING HER like an experienced jockey, refusing to be dislodged no matter how much she tried, Randi shut down her computer.

She shouldn't be looking forward to seeing Baz so much. It was dangerous.

They had plans when she got off work. Just like they had every evening for the past week.

They'd had dinner a second time with Andreas and Kayla to celebrate the seller accepting Kayla's for Kids' offer for the new property. Baz had been right and the owner had donated the furnishings that had not been moved to their new school facility. They'd been to the Pompeii exhibit at the Oregon Museum of Science and Industry, attending a fascinating lecture afterward. And Baz had not made Randi feel provincial or geeky for being so awed by the display of Roman history.

They'd attended a piano performance at the Arlene Schnitzer Concert Hall that had moved Randi to tears. Baz had gently teased her while offering his handkerchief, but he'd enjoyed it, too, making not a single comparison to other great soloists he'd heard.

Today she was getting off early so they could go to the zoo. There was a baby elephant that she couldn't wait to see.

And she had her own good news in regard to the babies. She'd peed on the stick that morning and discovered she was not pregnant. While she'd felt a tiny sliver of disappointment, it was overridden by profound relief. Randi wasn't ready for parenthood.

And as much as she wished she could keep Baz in her life, she knew that wasn't realistic. Nor did she want the only reason they had to communicate to be a child they had together.

She had no fantasies—okay, none that she would admit to—that he'd want something more permanent with her if a child was in the mix. Baz was eminently practical. If he offered to help her raise the baby, he would do it, but that didn't mean he and she would have a relationship.

So baby elephants would be plenty of cuteness for them to share before he went back to Spain.

No matter what her heart might want.

She'd done her best to ignore its leanings, but had been no more successful than trying not to look forward to their time together with abject enthusiasm.

Randi was falling in love. The most terrifying thing about it was that her feelings were a hundred times stronger than they'd been for the almost fiancé. Which meant when Baz did go back to Spain and never called again, she'd be looking a tsunami of pain right in the face.

And there was nothing she could do to stop it.

Her heart was already engaged and it was a stubborn organ.

Interrupting her hopeless thoughts, Baz came through her open office door in the most casual outfit she'd seen to date. His slacks still looked tailored, but he was wearing an expensive-looking dark blue sweater over a black T-shirt, his coat a sleek leather jacket with an off-center zip. He looked hot and modern, when she knew in many ways he was anything but.

"You ready for the zoo?" she asked, trying to ignore the way her heart rate increased the second she saw him.

"You are sure you wouldn't rather go to the Portland Art Museum? I've read they have an impressive selection on exhibit."

She laughed, not in the least deterred. "Nope. Baby elephants. What could be cuter?"

"Baby people?"

"You don't sound too sure."

"I missed most of my nephew and niece's babyhoods." The chagrin in his expression and tone let her know he regretted that.

"Too busy bringing Perez Holdings back from the brink?" She stood up from her desk and grabbed her purse and jacket.

"*Sí.*"

"There will be other babies in the family," she comforted. Maybe even his own. Though not with her. Dismissing the depressing thought, she opined, "I'm pretty much of the opinion that if it's a baby, it's going to be adorable. People or animal."

"Even baby snakes?"

She shivered. He had to go there? "Okay, no. I'm not a reptile fan."

"You realize that's speciesism?"

"Is that even a word?"

"It is."

"Doesn't matter. I don't want to see baby reptiles, of any kind." Okay, maybe baby turtles. But that was it.

"Lizards can be quite fascinating." He looked like he was laughing at her.

She didn't care. "You can visit that area of the zoo on your own."

He gave her a pirate's grin. "Oh, I think not. If I'm visiting the zoo, you are coming to every habitat with me."

"Not a chance." It didn't matter how many people loved snakes and lizards. More power to them, but Randi was not in their group.

He stepped away from the door to help her into her jacket. "We'll see."

"Not if we don't get there soon, we won't," she said as he gently lifted her hair from beneath the coat's collar.

The baby elephant was every bit as darling as Randi thought it would be, but even more enchanting was how fascinated Baz behaved by every single animal they saw. The billionaire acted like he'd never seen an animal, any animal, up close. She couldn't wait until they got to the interactive exhibit.

"How long since the last time you were at the zoo?" she asked outside the elephant enclosure.

He waved at a zookeeper and the woman nodded. "I've never been."

Randi wondered what that was about.

"Not even when you were little?" she asked, too surprised by Baz's admission to focus on the odd interaction with the zookeeper. While she'd never been, she knew that Spain boasted a couple of phenomenal zoos and several aquariums of note. "What about aquariums?"

"No." Maybe he hadn't lived near any of them.

Though surely his father would have taken a trip to give the experience to the only son that lived with him. "But…" It just seemed so wrong. "What did you do as a child?"

"I learned to live without my mother, and how to live with the new women in my father's life."

Okay, that was not what she meant, but it was some major insight into how Baz saw his own childhood. "You said you and your father were close."

"I said he was a good father and a more hands-on parent than my mother, but he was running a multinational company. No time for trips to the park, the zoo or the like. No time for pets, either."

Appalled, but doing her best to hide it, Randi said, "If he was that dedicated to the company, I'm surprised it was doing so badly when you took over."

"He made some bad decisions. He was too emotionally invested in properties that lost income, too focused on the women in his life to always see when the business needed more attention."

That didn't sound like a father who had much attention left over for his son. Baz's loyalty to his family was even more laudable considering how he'd actually been raised.

"You don't suffer the same weaknesses."

"No, I do not."

"Seriously, though. What did you do for fun as a child?" Okay, he didn't visit a zoo, but he had to have played and spent time with his father in some way to have such a good opinion of his parenting.

"I had toys, playmates."

"What did your dad do with you?"

Baz paused for a moment. "He taught me history by taking me to the places history was made. He taught me to enjoy museums and art galleries."

"As a child?" she asked, a little disbelieving.

"He never treated me like I could not understand the value of what was on display. He told me stories that made the exhibits and the art I was looking at interesting. *Papá* took me to work with him from the time I was a small child, letting me play in his office, though I'm sure that wasn't conducive to doing business. And he taught me to sail." The warmth that memory brought out in Baz was obvious in his tone and the darkening of his espresso eyes.

"Um…sure, that sounds fun." She was not a huge fan of boats. It wasn't a rational fear, but after her mom tried to drown her in the bath when she was six, big bodies of water gave Randi nightmares.

It didn't have to make sense; it just was.

Baz laughed. "I enjoyed it."

"Do you still sail?"

"Not often, but when I need silence, to be away from the constant demands on my time."

She'd noticed how many texts and calls he got. He didn't answer them all, but Baz kept his finger on the pulse of his company. While he never picked up the phone during sex, she'd heard him on the phone in the middle of the night more than once, and he'd rolled over to text something in the dark.

Randi instinctively knew it was business, and when she let him know she was awake, Baz often told her whatever the issue, question or update had been. She liked that he didn't make her ask. The few words she overheard confirmed the business nature of his calls.

Besides, she'd done an internet searching on Baz and found out that he'd broken up with his latest girlfriend several months before. None of the gorgeous, sleek companions in between were seen on his arm more than once, so she believed when he said he wasn't with anyone else.

"Does your father still sail with you?"

He smiled, as if at a fond memory. "At least twice a year. We skipper a boat in the Christmas Regatta and at least one summer regatta each year."

"That sounds fun," she said a little wistfully.

If nothing else, she'd love to see the side of Basilio Perez that came out when he was skippering a boat on the open water. She was sure it was something few ever got to know.

"We both enjoy it," he confirmed. "How about you, *mi hermosa*? Do you sail?"

Randi shook her head, maybe a little too vehemently. "I'm not fond of boats." Or the bodies of water they floated on.

"Really?" His dark brows drew together in confusion, like he couldn't imagine such a thing.

"Oh, yes. Really." She was definite. As much as she'd like to see the relaxed Baz who got away from it all, she would never be able to climb on board the boat. She didn't even like walking on the docks that jutted out into the water. "I prefer my feet on dry ground."

"Boats are not wet." There was laughter in his voice as he informed her, "They float above the water, not under it."

"If you're lucky."

"Are you afraid of water?"

"Of course not. You've seen me in the bath." Not that she'd taken as many baths in the past two years as she had since meeting him. She preferred showers. Only she never got that sinking feeling when she was with him, and relaxing into the hot water had become something pleasurable.

Something it had not been since she was six.

"That's not what I'm talking about."

"I thought we were talking about baby elephants."

A zookeeper came up to them. "We're ready for you now."

Baz turned a brilliant smile on Randi. "Speaking of, would you like to meet her up close?"

"You're not serious." Randi looked between him and the zookeeper.

Both stared back expectantly.

"You are serious!" Randi exclaimed, still not quite believing Baz had set this up. "We can go into the enclosure?" With all the elephants?

"Not quite. We have the baby in the indoor area." The zookeeper led the way to a huge enclosure fit with numerous skylights. The baby elephant was playing with a large red ball near a tree with many branches.

"The rest of the elephants are outside." The zookeeper turned to Baz. "They told you we have to keep the visit short, right? She's still young enough that keeping her from her mom for very long is not a great idea."

"That is fine."

Randi looked up at Baz. "How did you manage this?"

"With the help of my very efficient executive assistant and a large donation to the pachyderm program here at the zoo."

They got to spend about fifteen minutes with the baby elephant, petting the bristly hair on its head and watching her play.

"She seems to like your hair," Baz teased as the baby elephant ruffled through Randi's shoulder-length brown hair for the second time. "She wants to pet you, too."

"Maybe it's the tea tree oil in my shampoo." Elephants ate leaves, so that made sense to Randi.

"It could be," the zookeeper agreed with a smile.

"Or maybe she just likes you," Baz offered.

Too quickly, they were exiting the inner enclosure after thanking the keeper for allowing them the visit.

Randi couldn't help asking how much Baz had donated to make their time with the baby elephant possible. When he told her, her knees went a little weak. "Wow, um…okay. I can't imagine spending that on a weekend date, much less fifteen minutes."

Baz shrugged as they walked toward the next animal habitat. "It made you happy. And she was as charming as you implied she would be."

"Well, I'm glad you are enjoying yourself. You certainly went out of your way to make sure this will be *the* zoo visit I always remember."

"I'm glad. And I am enjoying myself a lot more than I expected to." If he sounded a little shocked by the fact, she wasn't going to take offense.

They spent another hour at the zoo before driving downtown for dinner. Baz was solicitous and attentive at the tiny but exclusive restaurant that served Asian fusion food, encouraging Randi to try dishes she hadn't before, and comparing the American version of the food to that which he would have found in Madrid.

He wasn't critical, merely urbane in his observations.

"I'd love to visit Spain someday," she admitted.

His lips turned down for a second, his eyes revealing some kind of regret before his face went neutral again. "Perhaps you will."

"Maybe." But not with him. That was a given. And if not with him, would visiting his homeland cause too many painful memories? Probably.

After dinner he drove toward his own executive condo, rather than her apartment as they had agreed outside the restaurant. "So, the art museum tomorrow?"

"I can't," she said with genuine regret. "I'm going shopping with Kayla to find an outfit to wear for my television interview."

"Skip the interview and you can spend the evening with me," he offered beguilingly.

"You know I can't do that." But a giant part of Randi wished she could.

"No, I do not know that." He pulled the car to a stop at a red light and turned to look at her, his expression serious. "This interview is going to bring much more pain into your life than the good you imagine it will."

"You can't know that."

"I assure you, I can. Which of us has more experience with the media?"

"I have plenty experience." All of it awful. She was ready to have the truth about her out there. She needed it.

Only the idea of the interview? Terrified her. And what could happen afterward? He was right. It could turn her life into another circus where she was performing the high-wire act on a greased rope without a safety net. But like Kayla had said, Randi had to do *something*.

Both women had agreed they'd had their fill of being victims in their own lives.

"No. You have been attacked, hurt and victimized by the media." His tone was implacable as he pulled away from the light. "You believe that will change when you get your side of the story out."

"You don't, though?" Why didn't he?

It would help her if Andreas was all for the interview, but it was Kayla who understood Randi's need to act, to fight back, and had pushed for Randi to get her side of the story out in such a way. Andreas had warned them both doing the spot could boomerang back on Randi, bringing the crazies out of the woodwork as well as the critics that would never be swayed by the truth.

Both men, who had a clearly more cynical view of humanity than the sisters, had expressed caution about Randi telling her story in such a way.

"No." In profile, Baz's jaw looked hewn from granite. "I believe if you keep this story going, while you are bound to find supporters, you will end up on the receiving end of more hate and cruelty. It's unlikely anyone who has written about you in the past will reverse their stand."

"How can you be so sure of that?"

"Tell me this. Do you think the Madisons will sit back and accept your version of events?" Baz asked, rather than answered. Maybe his question was the answer.

"But I have proof." The same proof she'd refused to go public with five years ago out of compassion for what the family was already going through.

"And they have a PR machine. You said so yourself."

"This time I have someone on my side who will help me fight back." More than one someone. She had her sister. She had Andreas. And Randi's father and grandparents had always stood up with her.

They just hadn't had the power and influence to do it with any real effect.

"You cannot expect that of me." Baz sounded almost panicked, or as panicked as Mr. Cool-Shark-Businessman was likely to get. "I will not be in Portland indefinitely."

"I wasn't talking about you." But now she knew that he would not be one of the people in her corner. And that was fine.

She hadn't expected anything else. Not really. Hope? Well, that was a drug she knew better than to indulge in.

"Andreas?" Baz asked.

"Yes." Among others. "He's my brother by marriage and he told me I'm the family he chose. He's big on loyalty to family that deserves it, like his wife and me."

"He can't prevent the internet trolls from coming out of the woodwork, or the less scrupulous paparazzi from hunting you down."

"Maybe they'll attack the Madisons this time."

"Is that what you really want?"

No, but... "They deserve it! They destroyed my life."

"The parents, maybe. But the children?" Baz pressed on with that ruthlessness he'd warned her about. "Do you want little Jamie attacked at school because of something his mother did? Isn't it bad enough he has a mother who could neglect him so shamefully?"

"I... Look... It's not..." It was no good. Randi had been ignoring the impact her interview might have on the Madisons' children on purpose. Knowing if she thought about it, she'd never be able to go through with the interview. "I don't want to hurt Jamie, or his sister."

"Then you cannot do the interview."

"But what about me?" she asked painfully. "What about *my* life? *My* family? It's started all over again already. I'm getting awful things posted about me online, news articles full of lies written about the incident five years ago. I can't just move away and change my name again. There's too much interest in Andreas and Kayla. There will always be a reporter interested in the story if I don't tell my side."

"If you tell your side, you'll cause a furor of interest, and the story will live much longer with the truth of Tiffany's shameful neglect. There is another option, you know?"

"No, I don't know."

"We can change the story entirely. What if I could convince the Madisons to not only sign a gag order for future commentary on the incident, but also to issue a press release saying they have never blamed you for the tragic, *unavoidable* accident? If I could ensure their PR machine would not only leave you alone, but also turn their attention toward presenting you in a positive light? Would that work for you? Would it give you what you need?"

"You would do that?" She thought his comment about going back to Spain meant Baz had no interest in getting involved. In any way. "Why would you do that?"

His knuckles turned white from Baz's grip on the steering wheel. "Because I do not want you to end up more hurt than you already have been."

Hope blossomed, but then collapsed under reality. "It won't work. Andreas already tried to reason with Mr. Madison. It didn't go well."

Which was an understatement.

"Mr. Madison owes you an apology."

"That's what Andreas said."

"I will make sure you get it. Andreas is good at what he does, but he does not have my experience dealing with situations like this."

"You have experience with situations like this?" she asked with disbelief.

"Not exactly, but I have three stepmothers and another one about to marry my father. I have learned how to deal with unreasonable and entitled people, getting them to rein in their expectations."

"You really think you can convince that man to say he's sorry?" Much less the rest of it.

"I think I can do more than that. I can get a sizable donation for Kayla's for Kids, a press release from him and his wife deeply regretting the continued media interest in their old tragedy and the gag order I mentioned, naturally."

He was serious. He really meant it. Baz would use his considerable power and influence to right a wrong that had plagued Randi's life for five long years. Nothing could undo the trauma she'd endured hitting a child with her car. She hadn't been able to drive for two years afterward, but if he could stop the piranhas from circling, that would be amazing.

Relief poured through Randi and she realized in that moment how much she truly hadn't wanted to do the interview. "If you think it will work, I'll do it."

"You'll cancel the interview?" He sounded relieved all out of proportion.

Maybe he did care. At least a little.

"*After* I get an apology, the press release goes out and they sign the gag order." She wasn't a complete pushover, no matter how much she didn't want to see Jamie and his sister forced to deal with the aftermath of the interview.

"Give me twenty-four hours."

He thought he could get it accomplished that quickly? She only hoped Baz was right. "I can't believe you're doing this for me."

"Why wouldn't I?"

She didn't have an answer for him, other than the fact that they had sex, not a relationship. "Are you always this helpful to women you date casually?" she asked by way of an answer.

"What we have is—" He stopped abruptly, looking startled by what he was about to say. Baz cleared his throat. "Casual, yes, but that does not mean I cannot do this small thing for you."

"Trust me. Dealing with Carl Madison is not a small thing."

"For you, maybe. For me? *Sí, lo es.*"

*Yes, it is*, she internally translated and smiled. "For a corporate mega shark, you sure have a white-knight complex going on."

He grimaced. "I assure you, I am no white knight."

Her smile did not dim. It was kind of sweet how he didn't want her to think he was *that* guy when he so obviously was.

The executive condo he was staying in was in a multistory brick building on one of the pretty tree-lined streets near the downtown center. Baz pulled his luxury rental into the secure underground parking garage after the liveried attendant opened the gate for them.

Even the elevator up to his floor was swank, the walls paneled in light wood; no flyers for upcoming local events pasted to these walls.

Though there was a brass plaque informing residents that the concierge would be happy to help them find entertainment or dining options as well as anything else they might require.

A condo complex with a concierge? Now, that was upscale.

They took the elevator to the top floor. Of course. The doors swished open to an elegant but modern foyer, a square settee on one wall, a console table flanked by two chairs and topped with a vase of lilies on the opposite. Everything in shades of creams and browns, it had a peaceful vibe and she could imagine visitors for the residents waiting here comfortably. Four corridors led off from the space to what she assumed were entrances to each corner penthouse apartment.

"Finally!" A demanding and oddly familiar voice shattered the peace of the space. "Where the hell have you been? You haven't answered any of my calls, Baz. That is not acceptable."

Although she couldn't yet see the man, standing as she was on the other side of Baz, Randi now recognized the voice coming from the corridor on their right and it sent ice through her veins.

Carl Madison.

# CHAPTER SEVEN

WHAT IN THE world was Carl Madison doing here and why was he berating Baz? Had Randi's temporary lover already instigated talks on her behalf with the awful man?

And why did he think he could call Basilio by the more familiar nickname, Baz?

"Carl, what the hell are you doing here?" Baz asked with undisguised fury.

So, not friends, then, but they were on a first-name basis. How did that work? What was going on? Why would Mr. Madison have come to Baz's penthouse?

"If you answered your damn phone I would not have had to track you down," Mr. Madison said, sounding both annoyed and aggrieved. "That bitch is going to do that interview in two weeks. The station is already doing internet promotion for the spot, alluding to a brand-new revelation of *document-supported facts*. What are you doing about it?"

"Hell, Carlos. *Eres un idiota!*" Baz lunged away from Randi toward the man he'd just called Carlos. Not Carl. He grabbed Mr. Madison by the lapels of his jacket and jerked him forward. *"No usarás un lenguaje como ese sobre o alrededor de Miranda."*

Baz's explosion into motion had shocked her, but the fury in his tone as he demanded the other man not use that kind of language about or around her made her feel a little better in a situation she did not understand.

"Speak English." Mr. Madison was trying to break Baz's hold on his jacket to no avail. "You're in America, little brother."

"Little brother?" Randi asked, absolutely not wanting to believe the implication of what she was hearing, but unable to ignore the evidence of her eyes and ears.

Mr. Madison jerked at the sound of her voice, looking past his brother to meet Randi's bewildered gaze. Surprise and consternation crossed his face before it settled into lines of straight-out annoyance.

"Oh, hell. Why did you bring her here?" Mr. Madison demanded as Baz moved to block the older man's line of sight to her. "I guess it's out of the bag now. Not that you were making progress." Oh, the disgust just dripped from Carl Madison's voice.

But *progress*? What exactly was out of the bag? Randi gave herself a mental shake, reminding herself she was no doe-eyed optimist. If it walked like a duck, it was going to quack.

Basilio Perez was Carl...no, *Carlos* Madison's brother. All the clues had been there. The siblings whose mother had taken them to raise in another country, even giving them the last name of her second husband. Carl Madison had been born Carlos Perez.

And he was a member of the family Baz had been so clear he owed all his loyalty to, one of the people Baz had made it clear he was willing to be downright merciless on behalf of.

Never had Randi been so tempted to use a certain four-letter expletive. Not even when the toe-rag trying to peer around his brother to glare at her had hit and threatened her.

"All of this was about you convincing me not to do the interview," she accused Baz's back.

His big body stiffened. Then his brother dropped against the wall, stumbling to his knees, as Baz spun to face Randi. "I told you why I do not want you to do the interview."

She almost bought his distress, but she couldn't afford to spend that kind of emotional currency.

"You lied to me." She couldn't have hidden the pain that knowledge caused her, so she didn't try.

"I told you I was no white knight."

"You think that makes it okay?" she cried. This could not be real.

The first man in years she'd shared her body with had been using her just like the last one. Her heart felt like it was exploding in her chest, detonating from the pain expanding inside her.

"Nothing has changed from five minutes ago. Yes, I regret to say that sorry excuse for humanity is my older brother, but he was not in our bed with us."

"You had sex with her to get her to call off the interview? You do have a ruthless streak, don't you?" Mr. Madison sounded like he was impressed.

Randi just wanted to throw up.

Baz spun back to the older man and got right into his face, in a move more emotional than orchestrated. "Shut up. This has nothing to do with you."

"Like hell," Mr. Madison barked.

"Of course it does," Randi said painfully at the same time.

She understood why Baz was so upset. His brother's impatience had undone all of Basilio Perez's efforts in, and out of, the bedroom. He'd had her, too. She'd been on the verge of doing exactly what the brothers wanted.

Baz turned back, stepping toward her. "No, it really does not. Carlos has treated you shamefully. I still want to fix that."

"How is deceiving and using me going to fix anything?" For her anyway.

She could see what his agenda had been on behalf of his family easily enough, but no way did that translate into making things better for her.

He opened his mouth to speak, but seemed unsure what

to say. Randi doubted very much that the great Basilio Perez often found himself lost for words.

She put her hand up, forestalling whatever his facile brain was coming up with. "I can't believe anything you say." He'd been dishonest with her from the start. "You orchestrated our meeting, didn't you?"

His jaw clenched, but he nodded. "I did."

"You lied about everything!"

"Actually, I lied about very little." He stepped closer to her and she moved back, maintaining their distance. He frowned, but stopped. "The only thing I withheld from you was the name of my family here."

"You knew I would never suspect you of being related to the people who had destroyed my life. The times we talked about the accident, you deliberately pretended not to know anything about it." How was pretense not a lie?

"We destroyed your life?" Mr. Madison was apparently done being ignored. "You put our son in a coma for two weeks!"

"I never denied driving the car, but I *wasn't* speeding. I *wasn't* driving negligently. Jamie ran out from between parked cars, right in front of my bumper. I did my best to avoid him. If I hadn't, things would have been so much worse. I know the doctors told you that." Because they'd told her when she'd inquired about the little boy's state of health.

The entire situation had been beyond devastating. One of the reasons she hadn't fought back against all the criticism, despite the proof she had access to that showed so much of what was said about her was a total fabrication, was because she'd felt a horrific guilt. Deserved or not, Randi had never completely gotten over the moment of impact between her car and that tiny body. She probably never would.

Mr. Madison dismissed Randi's words with some ugly language, but no actual argument to the contrary.

Baz pointed at his brother, his expression bordering on

fury. "The accident was unavoidable once *your wife* let your four-year-old son wander off toward a busy street."

"Is that what that bitch told you?"

Baz moved so fast, Randi gasped. But he had his brother up by his collar again and spoke right into his face. "I told you not to call her that!"

Mr. Madison's face turned red, his nasty expression in no way diminished. "Remember who your family is here, Baz!"

"Right now I'm ashamed of the connection."

"How dare you say that?"

"How dare *you* hit a defenseless woman?"

Randi wasn't exactly defenseless, but she agreed the jerk should never have gotten physical with her. She wished he'd just forget she existed.

"That bitch is not defenseless!"

"I warned you!" Baz cocked his arm and then punched his brother, right in the face, before throwing him toward the wall. "How does that feel?"

Mr. Madison swiped at his now-bleeding nose. "I can't believe you hit me!"

"We are of a size." He indicated Randi with his hand. "She, however, is nowhere near your weight class. And. You. Hit. Her."

"I told you things got out of hand. I shouldn't have done that."

"That is not good enough." Baz seemed to pull his cool in around him, his voice turning more frigid than a Midwest winter. "You will keep a civil tongue in your head or I will knock out every one of your capped teeth."

Cautiously eyeing his younger brother, Mr. Madison pushed himself up the wall. "Okay, I get it. You're protective, though Heaven only knows why."

Protective? Right. Not so much from where Randi was standing.

Betrayal was flaying her with the sting of twenty lashes.

"Sex between us…it was all about you seducing me into doing what you wanted."

And man, but she did not want to discuss this in front of Carl Madison.

Baz held himself rigidly, but took several seconds to come back around to face her. He reached toward her again.

But she stepped back farther, hitting the wall, unable to bear the idea of even the most casual touch. "Just admit it. Don't keep lying."

"I told you. I didn't actually lie to you."

"You deceived me and that isn't going away on a technicality. Do you honestly think I would have spent five minutes, let alone five days, in your company if I knew who you were related to?" One thing was for sure—she wasn't compounding that mistake. "No wonder you stood up for people I thought were strangers to you. They were part of the family you are so willing to protect at all costs!"

"But I saw your side, as well. You know I did. Carlos knows I did. I am certain that is one of the reasons he so stupidly showed up here today. He knew I was not interested in protecting him and Tiffany if it meant more of the same intimidation tactics and lies."

Didn't that sound nice? But it didn't in any way mitigate the truth. "You had sex with me as a ploy!"

"I—"

"Don't you dare try to deceive me again. At least be honest about it now," she practically begged him.

His head dropped, his pride draining away if she believed it. "I did. But—"

"No, no *buts*, no excuses." Hearing the confirmation didn't make her feel any better. "At least you're being honest. Finally."

"I will not lie to you."

She laughed, the sound harsh and unnatural, coming from her. "Like I believe you."

"You have my word."

"Which is worth nothing. According to you, you never actually told me anything untrue in the first place. Only that doesn't make one second of your underhanded behavior any better. Why can't you see that?"

"My deception was not meant to harm you."

"You're so used to getting your way, you don't care what means you use to do it. Just like your brother." She glared at Carl Madison, who watched her and his brother like a spectator at a tennis match. "The final joke is on you. Your male Mata Hari had convinced me to cancel the interview on the way over."

"That's great!" Suddenly Mr. Madison was all smiles, despite his rumpled clothes and bloody face. "You'll be glad you did."

The threat was there in his tone and it firmed her resolve. "I said the joke was on you because you being here, showing me what Baz… Basilio's real game was, it changed my mind. I'm doing that interview, but I won't just be talking about what happened five years ago. I'm telling the world how you convinced your brother to prostitute himself for you. I'm showing pictures of my face after you hit me. I'm telling the network about the assault charges I leveled against you and how you've broken the restraining order. You think you've got all the cards? You think you can ruin my life again? Think again! I may not have a white knight in my corner, but I have a family, and they are as loyal to me as he is to you. Only they aren't underhanded and sneaky about it. You'll see the attack coming, but you still won't be able to defend yourselves!"

With that she spun and jabbed the elevator button. She was leaving. She couldn't stand another second in those two men's company.

She saw the elevator doors open through the blur of angry tears. Grateful it had still been on their floor, she stepped into it.

Baz slipped in with her. "Miranda, please look at me."

"Go to hell." She couldn't look at him. It hurt too much.

"I did not mean to hurt you."

She looked at him then, too shocked at his stupidity. "What did you think was going to happen?"

"I thought I would tell you the truth on my own terms."

"So you admit there was a truth to tell?" Saying he hadn't actually lied to her!

"A revelation to be made, definitely."

"You hid your connection to the Madisons from me."

"I did."

"So?"

"So I think we have something special."

"Are you kidding me? We don't have *anything* real."

"You don't mean that." His confidence was misplaced.

She lifted her gaze to his, not caring if he saw the devastation in hers. "How could I mean anything else? Don't you realize how deeply you've betrayed me?"

His dark eyes widened, like the idea shocked him. "That was not my intention."

"Really? You knew exactly what you were doing when you seduced me in hopes of using our sexual relationship to influence me into doing what you want."

"Surely the seduction was mutual."

"Don't be any more of an ass than you have to!"

"I know you are angry—"

"You think?"

He made an aborted movement with his hands, dropping them to his sides, like he remembered she didn't want him touching her. "But once you've had time to think, you will realize my intentions grew to include protecting you, as well."

"Don't count on it. I've had all the revelations about you I'm going to." She glared into his espresso gaze, so there could be no question she meant what she said. "I never want to see anyone from your blighted family again in my lifetime and that's the only reason I'm not filing a civil suit against all of you!"

"You don't mean that."

Could he really be that dense? "Oh, yes, I really do."

"What about the baby?"

She wanted to scream at him for even asking that question, but she instead gritted out, "There is no baby."

"We could work on that." His tone and expression didn't suggest he was kidding.

All the air whooshed from her lungs. "You… That's…"

"We're good together, better than good. We connect in a way I have never experienced with another woman."

The elevator reached the ground floor and she stepped out. "Connect with this!" For the first time in her life, Randi flipped someone off.

She stormed toward the doors to the street.

Ignoring her clear desire to be rid of him, Baz followed. "I'll drive you home."

"Not a chance."

"Let me call a taxi for you at least."

"I can call my own darn Uber if I want one." A ride on the MAX, lost in the crowd of Portlanders, sounded good right now, though.

She shoved open the lobby doors and stepped onto the street. Rain poured down, but she didn't care. Like Kayla said often enough, she might be sweet, but she wasn't made of sugar; she wasn't going to melt in a little Oregon liquid sunshine.

Baz followed her as she hiked it to the nearest MAX station. If she remembered correctly, it was about ten blocks down and over.

"Please, Miranda. You do not need to go off like this."

She spun to face him, rain running in rivulets down her face. "Can't you leave me alone? Your plan failed. Deal with it."

"You are going to catch your death in this rain." He stripped off his leather jacket and held it over her head, while he grew increasingly soaked.

"I'll be fine! It's not your problem."

"You should stand under an awning while you call and wait for your driver." He indicated an awning-covered doorway to their left with his head.

She shook hers. "I'm taking the train."

"Alone?" Shock at the idea infused that single word until it was a full statement.

"I don't need an escort." To prove it, she walked away from the shelter of his coat and off down the street. "I've been riding public transportation on my own for a very long time."

"That cannot be safe!" His words proved he followed her as she'd suspected he would.

Basilio Perez wasn't just pitiless about achieving his own objectives, but the man gave new definition to the word *stubborn*.

"Oh, get out of your gold-plated tower," she threw over her shoulder. "Those of us not in your tax bracket use public transportation all the time."

"You have your own car."

"That doesn't mean I don't know how to take a bus or a train."

"I think you would argue with me about anything right now."

Tears mixed with the rain on her cheeks. "Okay, maybe you're not completely stupid."

"I will walk you to the MAX station." He had managed to maneuver his coat over her head again, like a moving awning as he stayed in step with her.

"Can't you take a hint? I don't want to see you."

"Then do not look behind you." He allowed his body to move to her rear while still keeping the protection over her from the rain.

"Why are you so stubborn?"

"Being anything less would never serve me."

She shook her head. "Do you know how close to hating you I am?"

He said nothing, but there was an air about him, like her words surprised him. Did he really expect her to keep admiring him after what she'd learned?

Unwilling to ponder his feelings or thoughts any longer, she increased her pace toward the MAX station in the cold rain.

True to his word, Baz followed her but kept behind her, out of her line of sight. She did her best to ignore the sense of safety his presence gave her, or how wet and cold he must be getting while protecting her from the downpour.

When they reached the platform, she bought a ticket with her phone and then gasped in outrage when she noticed Baz doing the same thing.

"Seriously, Mr. Perez, you need to go away!"

"I'm not comfortable with you riding the train alone."

"Don't be such a control freak. I'm safer on the train than I was around your brother. Maybe even you."

"What is that supposed to mean? I would never physically harm you."

"You punched your own brother!"

"If you had not been there, I probably would have done more." And Baz didn't look in the least repentant about that fact. "He deserved a dose of his own temper."

"Just like your family to resort to violence when things don't go your way." Guilt assailed her as the words left her mouth.

She didn't believe them, and Baz had been defending her when he hit his brother. It wasn't lost on her that Baz had meted out exactly what had been done to her by Carl Madison and his bodyguard.

"When you get to know me better, you will realize how untrue that statement is."

"I'm not going to get to know you better."

Baz didn't reply, simply looked up as the train came into the station.

He took a seat behind her after giving the one beside her a considering look. Her glare must have told him what a bad idea sitting there would be.

She spent the ride trying to ignore his presence and swallow back the tears that just did not want to go away. She also called her sister to see if she or Andreas could pick Randi up from the MAX stop closest to her apartment. Otherwise, it would have been a couple-mile walk to her apartment from there, with no nearby buses that could shorten it.

Kayla said of course she'd be there and then asked what was wrong.

"I'll tell you when you pick me up," Randi promised, unwilling to get into it in front of Baz, much less all the strangers on the train.

Basilio watched Miranda climb into her sister's car with frustration. He did not understand his own actions. *Si*, he was still committed to protecting the young ones of his family, but following her onto the train?

He had used her safety as the excuse for doing so, but he'd known it was more. He could not stand to let Miranda walk away without another word, without trying to make her understand. Not that he'd gotten the chance to do that. And still, he'd been glad to sit behind her on the MAX, to simply stay near.

Cracks were forming in his formidable defenses around his innermost emotions. He did not like it, but if she called right that minute, he would have the driver turn the car around without hesitation to be with her.

If only Carlos had not screwed everything up so spectacularly.

His brother was truly the *idiota* Basilio had called him. Carlos's impatience had cost them any chance of Miranda backing out of the interview and so he told the older man when he found him *inside* his penthouse when Basilio returned.

He'd called for a car with no shame. He'd been soaked through and had no intention of waiting around for a train to take him back to the stop he'd gotten on, only to be followed by another walk in the rain.

"How was I supposed to know you'd bring the little tar—" Carlos broke off at Basilio's look. "That woman here?"

"Why would I not bring her here?" Basilio walked into his bedroom without waiting for an answer and stripped out of his wet clothes.

His brother yelled from the other room, "Because she's the enemy!"

Basilio donned fresh slacks and a black cashmere turtleneck before rejoining his brother. "Miranda is not my enemy. She was as much a victim five years ago as Jamie. If anyone was at fault for that tragedy, it was Tiffany." Basilio held up his hand to forestall his brother's denial. "And now because of your impatience and lack of trust in me, millions of morning show viewers will learn that truth."

Not to mention other facts that would stir up plenty of scandal for both the Madison and Perez names.

"You have to stop her!"

"How? She despises me now." But didn't quite hate him. That knowledge had shocked Basilio, but also given him some measure of hope.

"Threaten her, threaten her brother-in-law's company."

"You assume I have the power to do that?"

"You know you do."

"But I have no desire to. Now that I know the truth of the circumstances, all threats toward Miranda and her family are off the table."

"*We're* still your family."

"Only when it is convenient for you." And the connection was becoming less and less advantageous to Basilio.

"Don't whine."

"I'm hardly doing that, simply pointing out that you can't play the family card and expect me to ignore how often you forget I'm your brother."

"Our father would expect you to help me."

"Our father would be appalled to realize you remained married to a woman who put your son so firmly in harm's way."

"Just because the man doesn't understand marital fidelity and commitment doesn't mean I don't. Tiffany is my wife and I love her."

"While that sentiment is creditable, you know how little regard I have for that emotion as an excuse for inexcusable behavior." He gave Carlos a long, unfriendly look his brother would do well to take heed of. "Be very careful how you speak of a man who is truly *mi familia*."

"He divorced your mother, too."

Basilio just stared at his brother until the older man squirmed in his seat. "Remember that your company owes a lot of its success to the connection you have with Perez Holdings. Respect those connections *in every way*, or lose them. In. Every. Way."

He was done playing happy families with Carlos. The man might have done what he had in order to protect his own wife, but that did not change the fact that his behavior had been completely lacking in honor or integrity. It was one thing to do what needed to be done, another entirely to completely lose sight of one's moral compass while doing so.

It was Basilio's hope that once Miranda had calmed down, she would realize that while he might be ruthless, he was never without honor.

"You're threatening me?" Carlos demanded with a sneer. "Armand would never let you withdraw support from your brother's company."

"*Mi papá* no longer owns even a nominal interest in the company."

"But he's still a director."

"Because I will it to be so."

"You took the family company from our father."

"I took over the bankrupt company, yes, and I brought it forth new from the ashes of poor decisions and debt. Perez Holdings is *my* company and any decision I make stands as *Papá* and all of his ex-wives had learned."

"You think you're something so special, lording your billions over us."

Billions that had been nothing but negative numbers when Basilio took the company over ten years earlier. "I think that if you make the mistake of making me your enemy, you will deeply regret it sooner rather than later. And to be clear, if you allow your PR people to continue to attack and spread lies about Miranda Smith, you will in de facto be making me your enemy."

"You don't mean that!"

"When have I ever said something I do not mean?" Basilio had not garnered his reputation bluffing.

Everyone who had done business with him, including his older brother, knew that Basilio never made empty threats. He followed through. Sometimes with overkill. Better to let people see one meant what one said than have them believing you harbored a weakness in one's character.

"Listen closely, Carlos, for what I'm about to say, I will not repeat, nor will I give you a second time to screw up."

"What the hell? Who do you think you are?"

"A man who could burn your company down to the ground if I so desire."

Carlos paled, his belligerent expression suddenly morphing into something Basilio could work with. Fear. "You wouldn't do that. It's my stepfather's company anyway."

# CHAPTER EIGHT

"EVEN LESS REASON for me to care if it is destroyed." And if Carlos did not comprehend that, he was an even bigger fool than Basilio already thought him.

Carlos blustered, "Our father would never do something so underhanded."

"Our father would never have done what you have to Miranda, either. I think we can agree that we are both different from the man who sired us in some very important ways."

"Say what you're going to say."

"You will call your PR dogs off Miranda. In fact, you will give them a new directive. It is your job to repair her reputation as much as it is possible to do."

"That interview she's going to do will take care of that."

Basilio ignored his brother's interruption. "You will craft a formal apology for your assault on her."

"I pushed her. That's not an assault."

"I read the police report and the trial transcript. Both of which are public record. *You* hit her and your bodyguard pushed her down. If you don't want that splashed across the news media with more furor than anything you could ever devise, you will listen."

"More threats?"

"Common decency should be enough to convince you to better behavior, but it is not. Threats will have to suffice, but please remember. I never bluff."

"I know you don't."

"Good." Basilio took a firmer grip on his temper. Never before had he been moved to violence outside his time in the gym, where it was part of training his body. "You will sign a gag order, promising never to comment on the incident of five years ago again, other than to support the story that the Madison family in no way blames, or has ever blamed, Miranda Smith, née Weber, for the tragic but unavoidable accident. You will release a press announcement to that effect, as well."

"No way. If I do that, people are going to start asking why. Someone is going to figure out that Tiffany lost track of Jamie."

"Lost track of would imply she was watching him at all, and evidence is not in her favor."

"I can't let this destroy my family."

"You were happy to destroy Miranda's family."

"We never attacked her father or grandparents."

"Her father had to change schools from the place he'd worked most of his adult life. Her grandparents faced the jackal reporters you set on Miranda. None of this is negotiable, Carlos."

"You know I prefer Carl."

"That matters less than nothing in this moment, but let us be clear. I do not approve of the way you've divorced yourself from our father by taking the name of your stepfather and Americanizing your name. I find your attitude to family and honor contemptible."

Carlos flinched as if struck. "I'm your *older* brother. It is not your job to correct me."

"Someone needs to. Had you and Gracia been allowed to spend time regularly with our father, instead of being raised in America by your mother and stepfather exclusively, perhaps you would not be so entitled and lacking in character."

"You don't need to be so offensive. Our father was the one who had an affair and married his bit on the side."

"That bit on the side was my mother and she suffered the same indignity and yet did not turn that into an excuse for me to live without a conscience."

"I'm sure your business rivals would not say the same."

"Integrity is part and parcel of every deal I've made, no matter how brutal I've had to be in the business arena. You cannot even begin to say the same thing."

"All of this stuff you want me to do for Miranda is going to destroy my family and cause serious issues for the Madison Realty Group."

"You should have considered the fact that there are consequences to every action, good or bad."

"It's your job to help your family."

"And if you hadn't shown up acting like a loudmouthed buffoon, Miranda would have agreed to cancel the interview. Now she's set to let us all crash and burn."

"And you're going to let that happen? The Perez name is going to be dragged through the mud, too, and we both know how important that is to you."

"I am aware." He had to hope that once her temper had cooled some, Miranda might consider her actions and the impact they would have on Jamie and Grace. "She won't back down on my behalf, or even yours, but Miranda has more compassion in her tiny finger than you and the entire Madison family has in its collective body."

Carlos looked at him wonderingly. "You've fallen for the little gold digger."

"Excuse me?" He didn't care about the accusation that he'd fallen for Miranda, but no way in hell was he tolerating more name-calling on her behalf.

An *aha* expression crossed Carlos's features. "I mean Miranda."

"She is no gold digger. She never had any expectation of a lasting relationship with me." Only now did he realize, after she'd walked away from him with such finality, that perhaps he wished she did.

"She's a saint," Carlos said, his voice laced with sarcasm.

"*Es verdad*, she is something very special."

"You *have* fallen for her!"

"I never denied it."

"Never mind what she's set to do to our family, which apparently you no longer care about, but you can't have a relationship with a woman like that! You could do so much better."

"There is no better."

"You cannot be serious."

"You think not? When have you known me to joke?"

"She's a nobody!"

"She's a woman who dedicates her life to the welfare of children. What could be more laudable?"

"That right there should tell you that she feels guilty about what happened to Jamie. That she *is* guilty."

"Don't be more stupid than you can help." Miranda had said something else had sparked her desire to go into social work.

Basilio hoped that there was still a chance she would tell him what that was. Though that hope was slim. Basilio was no quitter, though. And that was something the little spitfire would learn.

"So, even without the promise of her canceling the interview, you want me to basically throw my family under the bus."

"*Sí.* If you do, there is a chance, slim as it might be, that she will agree to back out of the morning news show."

"I can't do that, Baz. If you think with your brain and not your dick, you'd realize that."

"I don't care which brain you use. Just use it to consider what I will do to you and your company if you don't follow through on what I've asked."

"Gracia brought you over to help us, not make things worse."

"Gracia asked for my help on the basis of a series of lies. You are lucky I'm even giving you the choice to take a less damaging path than full disclosure."

"Thank you so much," Carlos said with bitter sarcasm. "When your girlfriend plans to reveal everything anyway."

"That was her hurt and anger talking."

"You think you can seduce her into backing down?" Carlos asked with clear hope.

"I believe her own sense of compassion and concern for others will be enough."

"Now who's being stupid?"

"Still you." Basilio shrugged at his brother's huff of offense. "You asked."

"Tell me at least you're going to try to seduce her again. It worked once. It could work again."

"Oh, I'm going to get her into bed again, but I won't be trying to convince her of anything but accepting me back into her life."

"You're lovestruck! I never would have thought the great Basilio Perez could be brought down by a mere woman."

"I am in no way brought down." He was the same man he'd always been. The problem here was that his brother had never actually known that man. "If you knew me at all, you would be aware that I do not believe in the concept of romantic love."

Growing up with a father who fell in and out of love so easily and quickly, how could Basilio believe that emotion was anything but a temporary burst of endorphins responsible for some of history's worst decisions, especially the most immediate history of his family?

"And yet you are willing to devastate the family you have never shown anything but loyalty to for the sake of this woman. How is that not love?"

"The fact I will not support the destruction of an innocent life—for the second time, no less—is hardly some kind of proof I believe in fairy tales."

"Whatever you say."

"I hope for your sake that you mean that."

Shaking his head, Carlos stood. "I need to talk to Tiffany."

"I expect to hear from you or a media rep within forty-eight hours."

"You really are a cold bastard, aren't you?"

"So it has been said." Basilio thought of something else he realized needed to be put in place. "You and Tiffany will sign a contract for a visitation schedule for your children with *Papá* and myself in Spain."

"What? What are you talking about?"

"Your children deserve to have adults in their lives who will teach them the meaning of integrity and true family loyalty."

"You can say that after what you are making me do?"

"Without a single doubt, *sí.*"

"You can't force me to give you visitation with my children."

"Can't I?"

Once again, Carlos's naturally olive complexion paled. "Forced visitation isn't going to endear you to them."

"You assume they will not enjoy their time in Spain with a doting grandfather."

"And you? They'll be terrified of you."

"They are not afraid of me now. You will do and say nothing to change that, either. Not if you want continued business connections with the Perez group."

"You're big on the threats."

"They should not be necessary." Basilio allowed every bit of disgust he felt for his brother show in his voice.

The older man winced like he'd gotten the message. "I should have made a bigger effort to be a brother to you. You wouldn't be doing this if I had."

"It's doubtful, but maybe. However, the past is the past and cannot be changed."

"Maybe we could work on being brothers now."

Basilio didn't laugh at his brother's obvious attempt to use the family card again. "Go home and speak to your wife and whoever else you need to. Just remember my deadline."

Carlos frowned when Basilio ignored his overture, but for once he showed some intelligence and left the condo without another word.

Basilio was in no way shocked when he got a phone call from his oldest stepmother. He told her in no uncertain terms what he thought of what had been done to Miranda in the name of protecting Tiffany, as well as the fact Basilio had no intention of backing down from what he had told Carlos. Mrs. Madison tried crying and then shouting at him. When none of her cajoling or threatening worked, she hung up on him.

Thirty minutes later he received a call from his father. This one took more out of Basilio, but he'd learned long ago how to stand up to his father. He could never have saved the company otherwise, much less stop the financial hemorrhaging that was his father's ex-wives.

"So this woman is important enough to you for you to abandon your family."

"She is innocent and does not deserve what was done to her. Had they told me the truth in the beginning, this is the outcome I would have been looking for."

"You think so? You are a ruthless man, Basilio, my son. I do not believe you would have cared nearly so much about the impact your brother's actions had on Miranda's life if you had not come to care for her."

"You know I do not believe in that nonsense."

"Your cynicism toward love is my fault." His father sounded sad about that fact.

"You also taught me what I know about honor and integrity. Do not tell me you approve of the lies Carlos has spread about Miranda, or the way his wife was so grossly neglectful she did not know Jamie had left the park until she heard the sirens and looked up from her phone. How long does it take a four-year-old to wander two city blocks?"

"They have taken measures to make sure such a thing does not happen again."

"Yes, I noticed the way she's never left alone with the children. You don't think she might want simply to change her behavior?"

"Do not judge so harshly. You have never been a parent."

"But you have, and no matter what else you had going on in your life, I was always safe with you."

"Thank you for saying that."

"I'm not going to back off. Carlos knows what he needs to do. I don't suppose he told you that part of my demands was for his children to visit us in Spain regularly."

"No. He did not. You're going to make sure I get to see my grandchildren more than once every couple of years when Carlos allows me to visit?"

"That is the plan, yes. The way Carlos and Gracia grew up without your influence is not something we want repeated in the next generation."

"They are not bad people."

"Just supremely spoiled, self-indulgent and too comfortable with dishonesty as a means to protect them from facing the consequences of their own actions."

"Were you honest with this young woman when you met her?"

"No, but I never lied outright to her, and I never would have lied about her, causing her hurt."

"You *do* care about her."

Basilio wasn't answering that claim again. He changed the subject and managed to end the call without discussing Miranda any further.

Randi sat next to Kayla on her sofa, each of them eating out of the pint containers of their favorite ice cream flavors. She'd already done the crying bit when Randi told her sister about the whole sorry mess. Now it was time for mindless comfort, or so Kayla claimed.

"You're sure it was all an act?" Kayla asked as Meg Ryan finally admitted her feelings to Billy Crystal in one of Randi's favorite throwback movies. "Baz sure acted like a guy hung up on a woman."

"He's Carl Madison's brother." Shouldn't that say it all?

"You can't hold him accountable for having such a lousy person as a brother. Our mom is no reflection of who we are."

"He seduced me to get me to cancel the interview."

"Did he say that?"

"Yes!" Well, he hadn't denied it. That was as good as.

"And you didn't knee him in the family jewels?"

"There was enough violence going around."

Kayla nodded, her curly black hair bouncing a little. "That's kind of what I mean, though. I think his feelings changed. He stood up for you, in a white-knight sort of way."

"If you say so."

"Didn't you say that he was going to convince his brother to do a press release absolving you of guilt in the accident?" Kayla asked.

"He was probably lying!"

"He doesn't seem like a man who lies a lot."

"How can you say that? He hid his connection to the Madisons from me."

"But he wasn't lying outright to you. He told you all about having a brother and sister that didn't live in Spain, even a niece and nephew."

"How was I supposed to leap from that to the truth?"

"Well, I don't think he meant you to, but I also think he told you as much truth as he could."

"Only so he could hurt me."

"No, his plan would have helped you more than it would the Madisons."

"You're assuming he was sincere about it."

"I guess I am."

"I'm not."

Her sister didn't keep pushing it. Just gave her a one-armed hug before putting in another romantic comedy.

* * *

It was close to midnight a day later when Miranda reached for her phone. She'd ignored several texts and messages from Baz. But she couldn't sleep. The night before had been bad enough, but now she was nearly drunk with exhaustion, only her brain would not shut down. She could not get Baz's deal out of her head, or the prospect of hurting two innocent, defenseless children with her actions.

She dialed his number, almost hoping she woke him from a sound sleep. The only thing better would be for him to be lying awake just like she was. Fat chance of that, though.

The man had no conscience to bother.

He answered on the first ring. "Miranda?"

"Yes, it's me. Didn't your phone tell you who was calling?"

"*Sí*, but I had a hard time believing it. You have not replied to my texts or messages."

"I deleted them without reading or listening to any."

"I see."

"I doubt it." He'd have to have feelings to understand hers.

"But you have called me now."

"That deal you offered me in the car…"

"It was not a deal. I simply outlined what I was willing to do for you."

"In exchange for me not doing the interview. That makes it a deal."

"If I told you I planned to keep my side regardless?"

Her heart stuttered, but she refused to be taken in so easily. "I would not believe you, and if I did, I'd wonder what your angle was."

"All right."

"All right what?"

"I accept you do not trust me at all."

"How could I?" she demanded, her voice low with pain. "You lied to me from the moment we met."

"I tried very hard *not* to lie to you."

"So you say." That his words were what Kayla said might be true didn't matter. Randi couldn't let it matter. Trusting him would only bring her more pain. "Look, I called because the arguments you made for me not doing the interview are still valid, even if they were made by a lying bastard."

Besides, no matter what she'd threatened, Randi had no desire to go onto national television and humiliate herself by telling the world that she'd got taken in once again by a smooth operator who wanted to use sex as a way to get to her.

"I'm deeply relieved you think so, but not surprised."

"You aren't?" she couldn't stop herself asking.

"No. You are a very compassionate, caring woman, and highly intelligent."

Why did he have to say things like that? "So complimentary to the enemy."

"I do not consider you the enemy."

"Well, I can't say the same about you." Her heart and head might not be in the same place, but he never had to know that.

"I am sorry to hear that."

"So, the deal still stands?"

"I will keep my side of things, yes."

"Okay, I'll need to see the press announcement released and some proof the rest of it is happening before I call the news station and cancel the interview. But don't bother with the apology from Mr. Madison. No way would it be sincere, so really, what's the point?"

"Oh, there is definitely a point." Residual anger laced Baz's voice, and she had to accept that no matter what he'd done to her, Baz was genuinely disgusted by his older brother's behavior.

But that didn't mean he was right. "I don't agree."

"I will make sure everything you want is done. Immediately."

"I want to go back five years and not get behind the wheel, but no one can make that happen," she admitted with more candor than she probably should have.

He made a sound, like her words had hurt him, but that couldn't be right, could it? He'd have to care to hurt on her behalf.

"I wish I could make that happen for you," he said, his voice rich with sincerity she could not trust. "But Jamie is fine now and your life will not implode again. I give you my word."

"For whatever that is worth." She sighed, not wanting to keep sniping. "Hopefully, for both my sake and that of your family, you'll follow through."

"I will." It sounded like a vow.

Randi had a hard time not instinctively trusting that tone. "Okay. I guess we'll see."

He was silent for a few seconds and then he made a sound like he'd made a decision. "There is one stipulation."

No. No way. "Carl Madison doesn't get to insist on anything."

"It is not so onerous, for either of us."

"What are you talking about?"

"I will stay by your side until the day of the interview has passed."

"To make sure I don't go back on my word?" she asked, offended. The fact her heart had leaped at the suggestion wasn't something she wanted to think about. "That's not necessary and you know it."

"*Mi cariña*, admit it—you do not hate my company. And I find yours very enjoyable."

"I'm not your darling."

"Are you so sure about that?"

"You can't want to do this. You have a multibillion-dollar company to run. In Spain!"

"We may both have to make concessions to spend the

next days together, but I assure you, I do not find the idea
of those weeks in your company onerous in the least."

"Maybe because I didn't spend the last one lying to *you*."

"He wants to do what?"

Miranda pulled the phone away from her ear at Kayla's
loud shriek. "You heard me. He wants to spend the next two
weeks following me around like a private eye or something."

"Or a puppy dog." Kayla's laughter came across the line.

"Yeah, no. Basilio Perez is no lost puppy."

"You can say that after the way he followed you on the
MAX?" Kayla kept teasing.

"So he's a control freak and I wasn't doing what he
wanted."

"Or you know, he was having an Andreas in New York
moment."

Kayla had told Randi about how she and Andreas got together, but this was not like that and she told her sister so.

"So, are you going along with it?"

"I want the stuff he promised. I want my life back. I think
his plan has a better chance than the interview of defusing
the situation long-term."

"As much as I want the world to know the truth about
you, because you're my sister and I think everyone should
think you're as great as I do, I agree. Darn it."

Randi smiled. "You're a good sister, but I think this is
the right thing to do."

And that was why she found herself packing a bag to
join Baz at his executive condo that day after work. He'd offered to stay in her apartment, but she didn't want any more
memories she had to forget haunting her in her own home.

Besides, his condo had two bedrooms. Her apartment
only had one.

# CHAPTER NINE

RANDI LIFTED HER hand to knock on the door of Baz's penthouse, but somehow she couldn't make the final connection between her knuckle and the wood.

Was she really going to do this?

Could she spend two weeks in the company of a man who had used sex to convince her to do what he wanted? More important, a man who had managed to break down the protective walls she'd built around her heart only to decimate it.

Her internal debate was interrupted by the door swinging open.

Baz stood there, his expression hard to read. "You made it."

"Yes."

He stepped back and waved her inside, grabbing her bag as she went by. "I'll just put this in the bedroom."

"You'd better mean *my* bedroom."

He inclined his head in acknowledgment as he walked away.

Rather than follow him down the hall to the bedrooms, she went into the main living area, but stopped short at what she found there. The table had been set with linens, crystal and candlesticks. Soft jazz played over the condo's built-in sound system, a fire was lit in the gas fireplace and the lights set to a soft glow.

Baz came up beside her. "Are you hungry? The food is from that steak house you told me about."

Her mouth watered, but she gazed at him stonily. "It

looks awfully romantic for a dinner between two adversaries."

"We are not adversaries."

"Just because you say something doesn't make it true."

He didn't reply, but took her arm gently and led her to the table. Once he'd helped her into her seat, Baz lit the candles.

"That's really not necessary."

"I think it is."

"We aren't on a date." She shook out her napkin with brisk movements before sliding it over her lap. "I'm here because I have to be."

"I am aware, *mi hermosa*."

"Stop with the Spanish endearments."

"You prefer English ones?"

"That's not what I meant and you know it."

"I know that our steaks will be cold before we eat them at this rate."

The meat was delicious, as were the garlic mashed potatoes and lightly sauced sautéed vegetables that came with it. The good food, soft music and warm ambience helped Randi to relax, when she thought there was no way she could ever be at peace in Baz's company again.

Baz kept the conversation light and away from topics that might blow up between them, which wasn't to say he didn't talk about anything personal. He seemed intent on her getting to know him and his history. The Spaniard regaled her with stories of his various stepmothers and their attempts to tame or bring out the refined in Armand Perez by turns.

"*Madre*, she always wanted *Papá* to play the big businessman about town, but her successor was more interested in starting yet another family. *Papá*, not so much."

Randi made a noncommittal sound.

Baz showed no frustration with her lack of response, just as he had chosen to ignore her desultory forays into conversation throughout the meal. "No, Armand Perez had three children, and that was enough for him. But she would not give up, hosting dinners *en famille*, dropping baby name books around the house, redecorating the nursery."

"*En famille* is French, not Spanish."

"I may not have gone to university, but I am not ignorant." He flashed her his all-too-sexy smile. "I am fluent in five languages. French is one of them."

"Ignorance isn't always about formal education."

"So I believe."

"For instance, having a bevy of degrees wouldn't have stopped you from being anything but ignorant when it comes to the feelings of others." Needing to get away from him, she stood up and carried her dishes into the kitchen.

The man had used her own body's response against her, and if he'd realized it, her *heart*. But he thought that somehow the whys of them going to bed together the first time didn't matter. Because why? Because the sex was great? Great sex wasn't going to stop her heart from being broken.

They'd had it. More than once and her heart was a shattered organ in her chest.

"You can leave them. A maid comes in the morning and again in the afternoon."

"Then she can deal with what is in the sink. I'm not leaving a dirty table overnight."

"Naturally not." He placed his dishes and cutlery with hers. "I wasn't trying to ignore your feelings, Miranda."

"I don't know how you can say that." All the relaxation that dinner had managed drained out of her, leaving Randi's body tense and her heart beating just a little fast. She stepped away from the sink, and Baz, before she turned to look up at him.

"Five years ago, when everything happened, I was only nineteen. Despite my past, I was still a very naive nineteen-year-old. I believed the best of people. When Davy came along, I thought he was really interested in me. My heart was bruised from my almost fiancé's desertion and I soaked up his attention like a sponge. Do you want to know what I discovered on the one and only night we had sex?"

"What? What did you find out?" Baz asked, his voice husky, his accent just that little bit thicker.

"That he was only dating me, that *he'd had sex with me*, to get the dirt on the girl who had hit Carl and Tiffany Madison's son with her car."

"That bastard. What is this Davy's last name?"

"Seriously? If he's a bastard, what are you?"

Baz winced, but he caught her gaze with his deep brown one, sending some kind of message she could not interpret. "I wasn't looking for dirt."

"No, you were just looking for malleability. I don't know how you can claim to have had no intention of hurting me. You'd have to be an emotionless monster not to know that doing the same thing to me as Davy, the enterprising reporter, would more than hurt. It would devastate."

"I didn't know about him."

"But you did know that you engineered our meeting with the express purpose of convincing me not to do the interview. Then you…" Randi had to take several deep breaths before she could collect her thoughts and emotions. "You decided to use sex as a weapon against me just like he did."

"Not like him. I wasn't trying to get a juicy story."

"No, just manipulate me with my body's reaction to you." With her heart, not that she believed he would understand how deep it had gone for her so quickly.

She wasn't even sure Baz believed in romantic love. The way he talked about his father's marriages indicated a real cynicism toward the concept.

"I did plan to use sex to get you to trust me," he admitted, like it pained him to do so. "I needed you to listen with an open mind when I told you why doing the interview would be a mistake."

"Don't pretend you had a single concern about me and how the interview would impact me when you settled on your plan to seduce me."

He frowned, his dark brows drawing together. "But how it would impact you matters to me *now*, very much."

"And I'm supposed to believe you?"

"I would like it very much if you did."

"I don't know if I can." She wasn't being stubborn. Her heart hurt, every second of every day since she'd discovered his deceit. "When I realized who and what Davy was, I was humiliated. And hurt. But nothing in even the same universe to what I felt the moment I realized you were Carl Madison's brother, that everything between us had been part of an agenda."

"I cannot change why we met, but I will prove to you that we are too good together to walk away from each other over it. That your feelings do indeed matter to me."

"I don't know how."

"Leave that to me. I am an excellent problem-solver."

"I'm a problem you have to solve?"

"The situation between us is the problem. You are the most passionate, engaging, beautiful woman I have ever met."

"Now I know you are lying. I am no supermodel."

"Good. I would not be nearly as attracted to you if you were, no matter how charming your personality."

Oh, goodness. She was going to fall right back into this man's bed if she didn't watch herself. "Do you have any romantic comedies for that expensive media system in the living room?"

"That *expensive* media system has access to several movie-streaming services. I am sure you can find whatever movie you would prefer."

"Okay, then."

"*Bien*, I am glad to please."

He surprised her by sitting with her to watch *French Kiss*.

"I can't believe you've never seen this one. It's a classic."

"I admit I watch movies rarely and never romantic ones."

"I love them. I want to believe in happy beginnings."

"I thought the term was happy ending?"

"An ending implies that's all there is, but the couple getting together is only the beginning of the adventure."

"Perhaps if my father understood that, he would not have married so many times."

"Some people think relationships shouldn't take any work."

"You do not agree?"

"Of course not. Every relationship requires effort, whether it's with a friend, a sister, a parent, a coworker. Why would maintaining emotional connection with your partner be any different?"

Basilio cut his connection to the conference call. He needed to get back to Spain. The big question was, could he convince Miranda to accompany him?

For a woman whose only committed relationship had crashed and burned five years earlier, she had insights that put his father's attitudes to shame. Basilio respected and loved his father, but Miranda's words had resonated with him. He knew that when things got tough or even mildly challenging in his marriages, his father started looking elsewhere.

The idea that the wedding was just the beginning of the journey, not the end, was the antithesis of how Basilio had grown up. But he liked it.

If he was to marry, it would be to a woman who felt as Miranda did.

For that to even be a possibility, he had to convince her that he would not hurt her again.

And to do that, he needed to take her to Spain, to introduce her to his world and show her that she fit in it.

* * *

"I can't leave right now. You know we're in the middle of opening a second Kayla's for Kids facility." Randi had returned to Baz's condo again that evening to a similar setting to the night before.

The table was once again set beautifully, this time a gorgeous oversize bouquet of richly colored fall blooms in the center of the table.

Who had he asked to discover that while Randi did not have a favorite flower, she preferred those of the season?

"My executive assistant has found someone eminently qualified to fill in for you."

"What? You can't just bring in a temp to do something like this."

"She is not a temp. She is, in fact, a woman with a great deal of experience with facilities of this kind. She will work on not only bringing in new funding, but also getting the second facility up and running."

"You're trying to make me obsolete with my sister's charity?"

"No." He looked genuinely offended. "What kind of man do you think I am? No, do not answer that, *cariña*. I want you with me in Spain."

"You make it sound like we're in a relationship and you're trying to keep me with you."

"Doesn't it?"

"We are not in a relationship." They weren't. Whatever they had ended when she found out he was just using her.

The memory of him saying they could make a baby when she told him she wasn't pregnant assailed her. With another guy, that would have been a throwaway comment. Or sarcasm at the very least.

Not Basilio Perez, though.

But then what did she know about him? She'd thought he was a random billionaire she'd run into on the sidewalk, that there was no way he could have an agenda. That he was a safe lover, if temporary.

None of that had turned out to be true.

"Will you come to Spain?"

"Do I really have a choice?"

"We always have a choice."

"This whole staying together for the next two weeks is ridiculous."

"But you agreed to it."

"I'm not going anywhere unless Kayla agrees to this replacement you found for me. And I'm not going to spend my time there on vacation. You'll need to make sure I can stay available via phone, video calls and my email."

"Despite what you clearly think of me, I am not a man of the Dark Ages. We have all the modern technologies in our home."

"We? Our?"

"My father lives in my hacienda when he is in Madrid."

"Is he there now?" she asked suspiciously.

"No, in fact. He is visiting his latest fiancée's family in Monaco."

"She's not Spanish?"

"Why should this surprise you? Certainly you've worked out by now that Carlos and Gracia's mother is American."

"And your mother?"

"From Catalonia."

"That makes sense. You are *very* Spanish."

"What does that mean?"

"No one would mistake you for an Englishman, despite that being the accent you speak with using this language."

"I would imagine not."

She shook her head. She wasn't even sure what *she* meant. It was just a feeling, but it wasn't like she had a lot of experience with the nuances between European cultures.

* * *

Surprisingly, Kayla had no trouble with Randi taking off for Spain in the middle of the new facility setup. "This woman Baz's executive assistant found for us has experience neither one of us has. She'll be a great resource."

Randi couldn't deny it. The new shelter liaison had started her job running, preempting several potential problems in the first few hours she'd been there.

"She would be a better manager for the shelters," Randi admitted.

"No, but she will be a great resource and she's making it possible for you to visit Spain."

"It's not a vacation. Baz is forcing me to go so he can ensure I don't do the interview after promising not to."

"Are you sure about that?"

"What else?"

"The man fell for you and he's looking for the time and opportunity to prove to you that he's not the monster you've decided he is."

"Kayla," Randi groaned. "I know you found happiness with your longtime best friend, but not every guy is as trustworthy as Andreas."

Randi wasn't sure *any* man was. Her trust factor was at zero right now.

"Andreas is not exactly perfect."

"Don't be telling falsehood to your sister." Andreas's voice came over the phone from somewhere near Kayla.

Kayla and Randi both laughed.

"Well, he's not lacking self-confidence anyway," Randi said with a smile, surprised at the feeling of lightness in her chest.

"Trust me, he's hurt me. More than once. Loving someone means you figure out how to forgive the stuff that can't be changed."

"And if you can't?"

"Then that relationship isn't good for you."

"You make it sound so simple."

"Life is anything but."

"You know I've always wanted to travel to Europe."

"And you know that Andreas and I would have happily taken you. This isn't about seeing the bullfighters of Madrid."

Randi shivered. "No, it's not about that, for sure."

"You want to find out if you can learn to trust the man again."

"Isn't that just opening myself up for more pain?"

"Life isn't just complicated, it's risky, but if you don't take the risks, you can't have the rewards."

Randi didn't reply. Her thoughts were too jumbled.

"Randi?" Andreas asked.

"I'm here. Kayla gave you her phone."

"I may have confiscated it."

"What's going on?"

"It is just that I see a lot of similarity between myself and Baz."

"You do?"

"I had him investigated."

"You knew he was related to Carl Madison?"

"I found out the same day you did. The final report came in about an hour before your phone call to Kayla. I hadn't even told my wife yet."

"You were looking out for me."

"Always. You are *my* sister now, too."

"Thank you."

"No thanks necessary. Just give the man a chance. He's ruthless in business, but he is not underhanded. He has integrity."

"He deceived me."

"He did, but do you really think he only took you to bed to get your agreement to cancel the interview?"

"He admitted it."

"He may have been deceiving himself."

"Or not."

"Or not. But if your sister hadn't known me better than I knew myself, if she hadn't stuck by my side that first time I ended our romantic relationship, remained my friend, I would have been lost. I would not be the man I am today."

"Kayla is pretty special."

"So are you, Miranda Smith."

Just not special enough for Baz to want her for herself and not what she could do for him.

Basilio bit back a sigh as Miranda accepted a fizzy mineral water from the flight attendant, her usual warmth and enthusiasm glaringly absent. She wasn't rude. She did not pout. But the bright inner light he'd grown enamored of was not shining from her.

There was no pleasure in knowing that his deception was the most likely culprit.

He did not understand how his actions could have such a profound effect on her after such a short time together, but then his own reaction to Miranda confused Basilio. The day she'd found out Basilio's connection to Carlos's family, her pain, her clear sense of betrayal, both had made Basilio feel like a monster. He'd been unable to allow her to just walk away, and the interview had been the last thing on his mind when he chased after her.

He had made efforts to prevent her from ejecting him completely from her life that he would not have made for any other woman.

Again, his desire to bring her to Spain had nothing to do with protecting his family and everything to do with protecting something precious.

It smacked loudly of an emotional decision. Basilio did not do overly emotional. It was too dangerous a barometer for rational choices.

And yet here he was, on the Perez jet, sitting in his favorite leather chair facing the table he usually used to work, Miranda right beside him, her inner fire banked.

He could not leave it like that.

He needed a conversational gambit, something to spark the natural curiosity she'd shown so far. Even after she'd become angry with him, she hadn't been able to hide her interest in his life back in Spain. That was why he'd taken the risk of trying to convince her to come with him to his home in Madrid. "You will like the hacienda."

She looked up from her e-reader, a tiny spark of interest flaring before she blanked her face. "Will I?"

"It is over two hundred years old."

"Inside Madrid?"

"On the outskirts of the city, but there are many historic buildings in the city center."

Triumph rang through him when curiosity flared in her pretty gray eyes. "When I lived in Southern California, one of my favorite things to do was visiting Old Town San Diego. The buildings were so beautiful, the museums that showed an old way of life, fascinating."

"The Mission Style architecture there has a great deal of Spanish influence."

"Yes, it does."

"Hopefully you will find the original to the inspiration as interesting."

She set her e-reader down on the table. "You really want me to see this trip as some kind of vacation, don't you?"

"I would prefer you were looking forward to the benefits, yes." He wanted to show her his home, had a completely irrational desire for her to fall in love with it.

She gave him a skeptical look, her posture stiff. "As opposed to the detriments?"

"And what are those, do you think?"

"I don't know," she said with heavy sarcasm. "What about having to leave the job I love, the shelter's clients that are so important to me, at the last minute?"

"But you've left them in good hands and you will stay connected, *si*?"

"That is the hope. Regardless, I wasn't planning on an international trip right now. Or any trip of any kind, and I know you know that." She adjusted her fitted suit jacket, so unlike her usual clothing, but no less alluring.

The blue-gray fabric brought out the color of her eyes, the cut highlighting her elegant curves. Basilio wanted nothing more than to peel away the layers, revealing the entrancing body beneath.

"Life is full of surprises." Like meeting a woman who played such havoc with his self-restraint.

"Not all of them are pleasant."

"But surely a trip to Spain is."

"Just because you love your home doesn't mean everyone will."

"But you are not just everyone."

She frowned at him, her gaze filled with wariness. "Whatever that means."

"I find it better to accept and seek to gain from life's little vagaries, rather than get mired in the plan that might have been."

"You? Mr. Control Freak?"

He would have denied the moniker, but thought now was not the time. "Indeed."

"I have a hard time seeing it."

"You think I was anticipating a trip to America a week ago?" He'd had to cancel important meetings and work at inconvenient hours to stay as long as he had.

"I suppose not." She chewed on her bottom lip, thinking. "I didn't make you come, though, did I?"

"No, but meeting you was the benefit of doing so." She looked like she was going to protest that, so he continued. "Business rarely goes exactly as one might expect. I've purchased properties I didn't expect to, let go of ones I thought

I would initially keep. And all those things have worked out for the best."

She sighed, her eyes warm with unexpected compassion. "I suppose all those new stepmoms taught you to roll with the punches early on."

"Perhaps you are right." Really, there was no maybe about it.

Basilio had figured out early on that he could rail against the constant changes his father's love life imposed on him, or he could seek to thrive in each new circumstance. Basilio chose to thrive.

"I think my experiences did the opposite for me." She looked away to the window in silence for long seconds before turning her head to meet his gaze again. Hers filled with unexpected vulnerability. "I don't like surprises. They make me nervous. Change is always hard for me."

"I imagine with a mother as unstable as yours, you learned your own lessons early. Like not all surprises are good ones."

Her hands fisted in her lap, her gray eyes widening in surprise. "You know about my mom?"

He nodded. "I wanted to wait for you to tell me, but you have probably already figured out that patience is not one of my virtues."

"Considering how fast you got me into bed, I'd say not."

And he wanted her there again. "You did not complain."

"No, but then I was convinced you couldn't have any agenda but wanting sex. Even if you weren't offering anything more than a night of pleasure, that felt safe to me."

"Despite your lack of experience, you accepted the lack of commitment with equanimity." Not to mention their instant focus on the physical. "It surprised me." And delighted him by turn.

"Believing there could be no way you were lying about your motives for getting me into bed gave me a false sense of security. I wasn't looking for a long-term relationship. I was looking for honesty."

"Considering your past, I can now understand why that would have been so important to you." He hated that Miranda no longer trusted him, or felt safe being physically intimate with him.

He'd been unable to convince her that he no longer had ulterior motives where she was concerned, and he knew that was his own fault.

She fidgeted with the buttons on her jacket, picked up her e-reader and then put it back down again. Finally, she took a deep breath, let it out and asked, "So, you had me investigated?"

"I had done that early on." Surely she would have realized that by now? "I ordered a deeper look. I got the report last night."

"I wondered what you were reading while I watched my movies. I thought it was work."

"It was, for part of the night. Being away from my office has been a challenge."

"Was looking at a Portland property a lie, too?" she asked, her eyes narrowed.

Her irritation should not have been a turn-on, but he found her feistiness exciting. Doing his best to ignore his body's response to her, he answered, "No. There is an old hotel I was interested in, but ultimately it would require millions in remodeling to bring it up to present codes and update the facility to the standards of other similar Perez Holdings. It's a beautiful property, though."

"That's too bad."

He hoped that was disappointment he heard in her voice, and that a little of it at least was because without a property he'd have little reason—that she would accept at present anyway—to return to Portland.

Deciding to test that theory, he offered, "My broker found me another potential property."

Her gaze locked onto his. "He did?"

"Yes."

"What did you think of it?" she asked with poorly disguised eagerness.

Relief that she still wanted a reason for him to return to Portland, even if she didn't want to admit it, made him speak with warm enthusiasm. "It has a lot of potential."

"So you'll come back to Portland."

*"Sí."* He smiled. "For more than the hotel." And what she did with that knowledge was up to her.

# CHAPTER TEN

THE WARINESS CAME back into Randi's expression before she turned her head to look out the window again. "Anyway, you know about my mom."

Surprised by the return to a subject he could tell was difficult for her, he answered honestly. "I know what the investigator was able to find out in a twenty-four-hour window. She lost custody of you to your father, with no option for visitation, when you were six. Your parents divorced and your mother spent a couple of years in a psychiatric facility."

"Pretending to be crazy." Miranda looked back at him, her gray eyes haunted. "So she wouldn't go to jail for trying to drown me in my bath."

All the air left Basilio's lungs. Miranda's mother had tried to kill her? No. His mind could not accept that; he could not accept the risk that she might have died before they'd ever met. "Pretending?" Didn't the woman have to be insane to have tried to kill her daughter? Wasn't that the very definition of an imbalance?

"She was high on her drug of choice at the time and furious with my father for refusing to give her money to buy more. So she decided to take away something he loved more than her. At least that's how she saw it."

"By trying to drown you?"

"My dad caught her."

"*Gracias a Dios!* What if he had not been there?"

Miranda's vulnerable gaze said she'd considered that possibility, many times, maybe even had nightmares about it.

"He kept a close eye on me with her, but he couldn't always be there. He was that time, though, and it saved my life."

"And instead of going to prison, she went into a mental facility?"

"You get it." There was a lessening of the haunting in Miranda's stormy gray eyes. "You really do. So many people, they kept telling me I needed to forgive her, have a relationship with her, but she just hurts people. She uses them. Only my dad and then Kayla got that, but she'd hurt them, too."

Something about his acceptance gave Miranda peace, and Basilio could feel nothing but gratitude for that. She deserved a lessening of her burden, and if he could give it to her, he would. "Not everyone who looks sympathetic on paper really is."

"Exactly." Miranda managed a small smile. "She's always been good at playing the crazy card when she's caught out. But since she has always refused any kind of therapy or medical treatment outside of her time in the hospital, I've never really bought into the sincerity of it. I've worked with many people truly challenged by mental illness in my job. Some who wanted to learn ways to better cope, some who didn't, but none who could turn it on and off like a tap the way my mother has always done."

"She tormented your life, didn't she?"

"Very much until I was six, more than my dad realized. Not so much after, but because of my grandparents, she's remained in the periphery of my life."

"They believe she's not responsible for her actions," he guessed.

Miranda's grimace told him he'd guessed right. "They're wonderful people who always see the best in anyone."

"I do not like thinking of that woman having access to you, even a step removed." He wanted to pull Miranda into his arms.

She wrapped her arms around herself, making him want to comfort her even more. "Honestly? I don't, either. I've managed to avoid seeing her since I was fifteen, and that only happened because Grandma got the time of a visit wrong and my mother was still at her house when Dad and I showed up."

His mouth twisted with cynicism. "Some mistake."

She laughed, the sound dry and harsh, but humor all the same. "Right? My dad arranged all future visits at our house so it couldn't happen again. I think I'll always fear her because she has no conscience. If she thinks hurting me, or them, or anyone else, will get her what she wants in the moment, she'll do it. No compunction, no regret."

"I am very sorry." A plethora of stepmothers seemed like a very normal childhood in comparison. "Is that why you don't like boats?"

"I know it doesn't make any sense, but yes. I mean, seas and rivers aren't the same at all. Only in my head, water is water."

Basilio flipped up the two armrests between their seats and then put his arm around her, laying his other hand over hers fisted together in her lap. "Your head is the only one that counts in this matter."

"Talking about her with you, I realize I've made her into a bogeyman, but I don't need to."

"You love your grandparents, so you worry for them."

She nodded. "Family, yeah? But still, you've helped me let go of a sense of doom that has been shadowing my life for too long, even after I moved away from everyone in my family. I have to thank you for that."

"No thanks necessary." She deserved full-on happiness.

She looked away for a second, but then met his gaze again, hers open in a way he wasn't sure he'd ever see again. "Until I met you, I hadn't had a bath to relax or for the sake of enjoyment in almost two decades," she admitted as her body melted into his.

"If I had known—"

"No, that was a good thing, the way I felt safe in water

with you." She sat up, pulling away from him, gently pushing his hand away, too. "Whatever came after, you helped me to overcome a lifelong fear."

"But you are still uncertain about boats." And him.

"I think so." But she sounded more speculative than certain.

It made him wonder if he could help her feel safe in his presence and overcome a phobia at the same time. "Perhaps I can help you change that."

The look she gave him was blatantly considering, but tinged with hope he wasn't sure she wanted him to see. "Maybe."

"You're very noncommittal."

"Wary."

"Ouch."

"Are you surprised?"

"No, but I wish it was not that way."

"Why? Why do you care?"

"Do I have to have a reason? Is it not enough that I do? Very much." Her honesty deserved his own. No matter how uncomfortable the admission made him.

"Thank you."

"For?" Caring? He could not stop himself.

"Being honest."

A strange expression came over Baz's face. "When I told you about spending the next two weeks together…" He paused, looking uncharacteristically uncertain.

"Yes? What about it?"

"You assumed it was a requirement Carlos had insisted on."

"To make sure I didn't go back on my word." Like she was the one people had to worry about lying.

"There was never any doubt that you would keep your word."

"Thanks for that, but it's a bit late, don't you think?"

"It was never a consideration." His tone brooked no argument.

But that didn't make any sense. "Then why say I had to be chaperoned like a recalcitrant teenager on a bad date?"

Basilio loosened his tie, his movement jerky. "It was not a requirement at all." He made the fantastic admission and then waited for her reaction, his expression stoic, only a slight tic in his jaw giving away that just maybe he was a little nervous.

"What? That makes no sense." On the verge of yelling like a harpy, Randi made a concerted effort to modulate her tone. "I'm here on this ridiculously luxurious plane with you, flying to Spain, during a crucial time for Kayla's for Kids because I didn't have a choice."

He winced. "I hope that is not true."

"Of course it is." But was it?

Had she really agreed to this crazy trip because she felt cornered? Her conscience pricked because she knew that deep inside, where she hid feelings that she knew could hurt her, Randi had to acknowledge the truth.

She was on her way to Spain because the thought of never seeing Baz again had been ten times more terrible than the idea of spending time in his company, whatever the reason.

"I never lied to you," he said quickly.

"You let me believe I didn't have a choice."

"Say rather, I did not work very hard at dissuading you."

Had he tried at all? Her muddled brain couldn't be sure in that moment what was real and what was not. "Why? Why mislead me again?"

"I have told you, I believe we have something special, something worth figuring out a way back to."

He couldn't be implying what it sounded like, but she had to be sure. "Are you saying you love me?" she asked, hearing the disbelief in her own voice.

"Romantic love is something I always promised myself

I would never fall prey to." The words sounded sure, but his tone? It sounded hollow.

"Because of how easily your dad falls in and out of love."

Baz inclined his head in agreement. "His has been a life lesson on the subject, certainly."

Her heart died a little at hearing those words, but love was not the main issue here. Was it? "You deceived me. Again."

"If you consider it, you will realize I was very careful *not* to lie to you."

She tried very hard to remember the conversations they'd had about the trip verbatim. "You never actually agreed with me when I assumed it was a requirement of Carl Madison's, or when I said I had no choice about coming to Spain."

"No, I did not."

"But you still let *me* believe it."

"When I disagreed, you disregarded my words."

Randi should have been more angry, but she wasn't. This time felt different. Was it because she had ignored him when he said he wasn't her enemy? Maybe it was opening up to Basilio and having him take her part immediately. Maybe it was the fact that he had managed to convince his brother to do exactly as Basilio had promised he would. Maybe it was even the fact that he'd risked her ire to make a way for them to reconnect.

Or maybe it was just the fact that while they'd been having casual sex and friendship on the side, her heart had gotten involved.

Whatever the reason, Randi wanted Baz to make this right, to convince her she hadn't been duped again.

"Baz…" She let her voice trail off, not sure what she wanted to say.

He took her hand again, holding it tightly in his own. "You told me very firmly you would not believe the truth."

"What truth?"

"That regardless of whether you canceled the interview,

I would make sure Carlos followed through on the things I had promised."

She hadn't canceled the interview until after she'd seen proof of that, but Basilio had even gotten his own PR people involved in planning and executing the best strategy for clearing Randi's name without her having to bare her soul in front of millions of strangers. They'd video-conferenced after she'd agreed to make the trip to Spain, the very savvy PR reps asking questions that helped shape a brilliant campaign to protect her. The head of the team had mentioned that Baz had called them in the very night she'd discovered his connection to the Madisons, before Randi had agreed to give up the interview.

She wasn't sure what to do with that information.

Unwilling to pull away from his touch again, and even more unwilling to examine why, she licked her lips nervously then admitted, "Andreas and Kayla appreciated his letters of apology more than I did."

"You did not believe in Carlos's sincerity."

"No, I didn't."

"He is sincere, though, if not for the reason I wish it were so." And Baz's espresso gaze said he was, too. Sincere, that was.

"Oh, really?"

"His actions have caused me to curtail my support of his company and threaten to cut it off all together." Baz's implacable tone said he wasn't kidding or exaggerating.

"But he's your family."

"And he acted abysmally. Would you stand up for your mother in similar circumstances?"

"I wouldn't stand up for her at all, under *any* circumstances." Randi laid her free hand on Basilio's thigh. "But your brother has not given you reason to withdraw your support. He hasn't hurt you or turned on you."

At least to Randi's knowledge. Baz was the one who had punched his brother in the face. For insulting Randi.

She didn't know what she could or should believe right then.

"His actions against you, a compassionate, caring, *honest* woman, were enough to precipitate my own."

Was he speaking the truth? And if he was, what did that mean for them?

She couldn't trust him, her mind insisted. Only her heart wanted to believe. "And now Carl Madison is genuinely sorry because his actions had consequences he wasn't expecting."

"*Sí.*"

"That is more believable than he had a sudden change of heart."

"One can only hope he will eventually see the error of his ways, but if he does not…" Baz paused, his expression taking on a ruthlessness she'd never actually seen directed toward herself. "He is aware the order of protection you took out against him is the least of his worries if he comes anywhere near you or attempts to contact you in any way."

"Wow." Randi hadn't been expecting that. "Okay."

"I have arranged for regular visits from his children. I believe they need the influence of their Spanish family."

"That's pretty arrogant, but I can't disagree. If for nothing else, his children deserve to be raised with a taste of their heritage. Just because he decided to reject it doesn't mean they're going to want to." And after her experience with Kayla, Randi was particularly sensitive about the idea of withholding children from loving, decent grandparents.

Her sister's childhood would have been so different if she'd had the support of their grandparents, like Randi had.

"I agree." The words showed Baz was listening to her, but his focus was fixed on her lips. Again.

There was no doubt the man wanted her. Her desire for him was simmering under the surface, hard to control, even harder to hide.

Heat suffused Randi's body and she couldn't do a thing

about it. He wanted to kiss her and she wanted that kiss. So much.

The muscles of his thigh bunched under her hand and she realized only then how dangerous that connection was. She yanked her hand away.

"Don't." He reached for her wrist.

"Don't what?"

He placed her hand back on his thigh, pressing it down with his. "I like when you touch me."

"But—"

He placed his finger against her open mouth, but instead of pressing to quiet her, he traced first her upper lip and then her lower one. "Such a pretty mouth."

Desire shivered through her, her vaginal walls spasming with need. Oh, man. She was in trouble if such a small caress had this effect on her.

He leaned down and she didn't do a single thing to stop him, didn't tell him no, just sat there waiting for what she knew was coming. Her brain warned her she was on a slippery, dangerous path, but her body was not listening.

Neither was her heart.

The kiss, when it came, was soft, a caress of lips against lips, no tongue, no urgency. And it went all the way to her soul. One hand remained over hers; the other came up to cup her nape, under her hair, and hers came up of its own volition to rest against his chest.

The tender, almost chaste kiss went on for long moments, bridging a gap she didn't know something so simple could do.

It was terrifying how much the press of his mouth against hers impacted her.

It was that fear that made her break the kiss and pull away from him. "You shouldn't have done that."

"I disagree. Kissing you is never a mistake."

"I'm sure your family would not agree."

"Meet my father before you decide to speak for him. He will adore you."

"I thought you said he wasn't going to be in Madrid when we arrived."

"He will not, but you will meet him."

"You're talking like we have a future together."

"It does sound like that, doesn't it?"

"How am I supposed to take that? You don't even believe in love."

"Erotic love, no, but I love my family. Even my disreputable brother, who has much to do to earn my respect again, if that can be done."

She shook her head, trying to clear it. The man was too persuasive and confusing. "No more kissing."

"I cannot promise that. You are very kissable."

"You're being ridiculous."

"The truth is foolish to you?"

"No. That's not what I… Listen, you can't just go around kissing me. We aren't dating anymore."

"I would like to fix that."

"You deceived me a second time. How could I *ever* trust you again?"

"Perhaps you could examine my intentions in both cases?"

"I'd rather know you were never going to lie to me again, by omission or commission," she clarified when he opened his mouth to deny actually lying again.

"This is important to you?"

"Would you like knowing I was happy to deceive you?"

"No."

"Then?"

He was silent for almost a full minute, considering. "I can make that promise."

"Now I just have to believe it." But the fact he'd really thought about it went a long way toward her doing so.

A brief flare of pain flashed over his handsome features. "That is the hope, *cariña*."

"You're not going to stop using endearments on me, are you?"

"Does it truly offend you?"

"No, it's just…" Too pleasant. Too seductive. Too intimate. But to admit any of that would be to admit she still had feelings for him when he didn't even believe in those feelings. "It irritates me."

"Are we not both committed to honesty between us?"

She sighed. "Yes."

"So?"

"It did irritate me." Right after she found out about his reason for engineering their meeting, but now the endearments were part of that slippery slope that both enamored and scared her.

"Now?" he pressed.

"I like it too much," she admitted, not entirely sure this full honesty between them was a good thing.

"That is good to hear."

"You are a very annoying man."

"And you are the one woman I want."

"Right now."

"Do you want promises for the future?"

"No, of course not. I don't want anything from you."

"Are you lying to me again, or only to yourself now?"

"I'm tired. I think I'll get some shut-eye." Not waiting for him to respond, she reclined her seat and closed her eyes, trying to shut him out.

But nothing could make her any less aware of the gorgeous, tantalizingly sexual man sitting beside her on the private jet.

No wonder Baz didn't mind having his father living with him.

His home was a darn palace. A very private palace.

Hidden away at the end of a long drive with access via a wrought iron gate that slid back when Baz had pressed something on his phone, the exterior stucco of the giant three-story abode was painted a traditional pastel with white trim. The enormous house was surrounded completely by a second-story balcony, with decorative railing. It served as shade for the oversize slate porch on the ground floor that also wrapped around the stately building.

The grounds looked like something out of a *How to Garden for Rich People* book, laid out in perfect geometric patterns, each bush trimmed into submission, every blade of grass cut just so and a pristine green. Deep-red carnations filled the flower beds on either side of the double-size, eight-foot-high front doors.

Baz pulled his sleek Jaguar to a stop on the circular drive laid with white pebble just as a butler in a smart black suit opened the door on the left. Seriously? He had a butler? With a home this size, he probably had a whole army of servants.

Randi stared out the window, making no move to open her car door. She craned her head, trying to see as much as she could without actually getting out. "Good grief!"

"What?" Baz asked, his own door already open and his seat belt off.

Randi just shook her head, startling when the door beside her opened without her touching it.

The butler stepped back from the car. "Welcome to Casa Clavel, Miss Smith."

Feeling like she'd stepped into some kind of fantasy, Randi made herself climb out of the luxury sports car. "Um…*gracias*. I'm happy to be here," she lied in Spanish.

What she was, was overwhelmed.

The butler nodded and then turned to Baz, who had gotten out and come around the car. "Welcome home, sir," he said in Spanish.

"It is very good to be home, Emilio." Baz replied in the

same language, his body relaxed in a way she hadn't seen since meeting him.

"You call this place home?" she asked with disbelief.

"What else would you have me call the place where I live?" Humor laced his voice as he offered her his hand.

Feeling out of place and in need of a connection to reality, she took it. "Royalty would be comfortable living here."

"And have stayed behind its walls throughout the years. It was built in the mid-eighteenth century."

"Though it has remained in the same family for more than two centuries, Casa Clavel has been completely remodeled and refurbished as recently as five years ago," the butler offered with obvious pride.

"I wouldn't expect anything less."

Neither man seemed to detect the sarcasm lacing her words.

The inside was every bit as imposing as the outside, and yet somehow felt like a home. Like a place she could stay without feeling like she didn't belong. Which was totally weird, considering the fact that no way could Randi *belong* in a place like this.

She didn't even try to hide her gawking as she took in the soaring ceilings, giant foyer and grand staircase. The floors were marble, a huge gold drape pulled back between the foyer and what looked to be a living room the size of a gymnasium, but way more elegant with its cream, black and gold accented decor.

Baz squeezed her hand, giving her a reassuring smile. "There is a conservatory in the back of the house, where we have citrus trees that bear fruit year-round, and we grow more of the carnations the house is named for. It is my favorite place to have breakfast and to relax."

"Of course it has a conservatory." She looked around at the massive rooms, halls leading to more living space and the giant chandelier hanging in the center of the foyer. "My entire apartment complex would fit in this place."

"It is only about eighteen thousand square feet."

"Only?" she asked faintly as another man, not the butler, walked by, carrying her luggage.

"Most modern-built mansions of this caliber are twice as large."

"That's insane. Who needs that much room?" Okay, maybe billionaires did, for entertaining or something.

Baz shrugged. "I would say I do. The staff inhabits the top floor. They have their own recreation room, in addition to sitting rooms in each of their suites."

And the rest of this massive hacienda was for Baz and his family. It *was* an apartment complex. "How many bedrooms in a place like this?"

"There are quarters for eight live-in staff members, though not all are occupied, six suites in the family hall and ten guest rooms on the other side of the house."

Ginormous could be good. Her room would be on the other side of the house from his. Distance would make it easier for Randi to stay away from temptation.

"Would you like to refresh yourself from the journey?" the butler asked.

"Yes, sure. That would be great." If she didn't get away from Baz soon, it was going to be her doing the kissing.

And that way lay nothing but pain.

"I'll take her up," Baz told the black-clad man.

"Very good, sir."

"Would you like a tray brought up?" an older woman, who Randi assumed was the housekeeper, asked.

"*Sí*. Something light," Baz replied before Randi could tell the woman not to go to any trouble.

Randi frowned at Baz. "If I want something, I could go down to the kitchen."

"But since you have not had a tour of the house yet, it would be a chore to find it."

"I'd probably end up falling in the indoor pool," Randi joked.

"Oh, that's unlikely. The pool has a very wide apron," Emilio offered. "But if you would like to go swimming this afternoon, it is heated and ready for use."

"You have an indoor pool?"

"It is half indoor, half outdoor on the back of the house." Baz's eyes warmed with emotion. "My grandfather installed it for my grandmother. She was a keen swimmer year-round."

"Your grandparents live here?"

"They did until their deaths over a decade ago."

"About the same time you were forced to take over the company."

Baz led her up the wide marble staircase. "Two years before. My grandfather would have been very disappointed I didn't go to university."

"I'm sure he was proud of you, regardless." Randi wasn't going to think about why she felt the need to comfort Baz.

The portraits displayed in gilded frames hanging on the wall of the hall they walked along looked old. "Are those your ancestors?"

"They are. The Perez family has been in Madrid since before the Inquisition."

He pushed open a heavy oak door, leading her into a huge bedroom suite, complete with her own sitting room and balcony off the bedroom. One of the doors led to a spa-like bathroom, naturally, and the other into a walk-in closet that could have been used as another small bedroom. She said as much.

Baz nodded. "What are now the walk-in closets used to be sleeping quarters for maids and valets for my ancestors."

"This is pretty impressive for guest accommodations."

"While the guest rooms are perfectly elegant, only two have their own sitting rooms."

"And I got one? I'm honored." She ran her hand over the carving on the canopied four-poster bed. "I can see where

Casa Clavel has been updated, but you retained the historic tone to the place. It's wonderful."

"I am glad you like it, but this is the family hall."

"What?" she asked, spinning around to face him. "I'm not family."

"I wanted you close. There was no reason to put you in the guest hall as we are the only people in the hacienda at present."

"But…" There went her plan to keep her distance from him.

"If you do not like this room, we can move you."

"You know it's not the room."

"I am glad to hear that."

"You're really used to getting your own way, aren't you?"

"Is that a bad thing?"

"For me, maybe it is."

"Because I want something you do not?" He removed his suit coat and laid it over a chair that looked like it was original to the house. "You must know I would never push you into anything you found objectionable."

"Like you didn't push me into coming to Spain?" Trick, more like.

Only, if she was honest with herself, she'd admit she wanted a way across the chasm separating them, too. She just didn't know if that desire was going to cause her more pleasure or pain.

## CHAPTER ELEVEN

BAZ TUGGED ON his tie, loosening it and then pulling it off. It landed in a neat line over his jacket. "I would not have forced you. You have to know that."

Did she? Honesty compelled her to admit, "I do." She sighed. "I did. As contrary as it may sound, if I'd thought you really were forcing me, I would have refused to come and let the chips fall where they may."

More important, why was he taking off his clothes?

"So you, too, are used to doing as you like." He toed off his shoes, pushing them under the chair with his foot.

"Maybe, but with a lot more limits than you." Should she say something about the slow, casual striptease?

His socks were next, but so far he was keeping the important garments on. "Trust me. A man in my position has many constraints on his life and actions."

She scoffed, "You live like a king." Literally.

"And like any royalty, I have responsibilities to the people who rely on me, to my company, to my family. I am not responsible for the well-being of a nation, but nothing I choose for my life is without consequences for others, sometimes many others. I always remember that."

"You're saying you're not a despot."

"I am a man with a great many responsibilities." He unbuckled his belt and dropped it with the jacket and tie.

"Why are you undressing?" she asked, her voice a little high-pitched.

He shrugged. "I am merely getting comfortable. That is one of the benefits of being home, is it not?"

"Sure, but it wasn't just the desire to be back in your own home that prompted your return to Spain, right? Those responsibilities you were talking about are calling to you, aren't they?"

Her hint seemed to fall on deaf ears as he unbuttoned the top two buttons on his shirt. *"Sí."*

"Do you need to get to work, then?" she asked hopefully.

"Are you trying to get rid of me?" He smiled at her and then took her hand before she had a chance to answer, pulling her toward the French doors leading to the balcony. "I worked on the plane while you napped. I can enjoy some uninterrupted time with you now."

She'd closed her eyes to avoid more deep discussions and had ended up falling asleep, not waking until a few minutes before they landed.

"I haven't been sleeping well," she excused herself.

He nodded like he understood. Maybe he did.

She stepped toward the rail, turning her face up to the sun. "I love fall in a warm climate."

"Oregon's more definitive seasons are not to your liking?"

"The rain is okay, but I don't like being cold. It doesn't get extreme in Portland, like the Midwest. Or so Kayla tells me, but we've had some pretty chilly days already this fall and I know last winter they got snow several days in Portland."

"And there are places covered in snow for six months out of the year."

"I know, but I wouldn't want to live there. I'm a warm baby."

"You were raised in Southern California. That is understandable. I have never wanted to move to a colder climate, either. A vacation to the snowy mountains is sufficient exposure for me."

"I was starting to miss the sunshine," she admitted. "It

was worth it to be close to Kayla, though. It's been great getting to know my sister."

"Why were you raised apart?"

"My mom abandoned her at a truck stop when she was three, before I was born. We didn't even know the other existed until Andreas hired an investigator to find Kayla's family."

Baz's mouth twisted with distaste. "Your mother is a piece of work."

"She is that. I'm nothing like her."

"No, of course not."

"But I could pass her genes on if I have children. Most days I don't think it's worth the risk." Just sometimes, Randi wondered what it would be like to carry a baby inside her.

He brushed the hair away the gentle wind had blown into her face. "You could also pass along your kindness, compassion, intelligence, beauty and strength of character."

"Don't say stuff like that."

"I will not refrain from the truth."

"You're so certain of yourself."

"I know what I want."

"What is that?" she asked, needing him to spell out just what he expected here.

"I want another chance with you."

He'd gone to a lot of trouble for more uncommitted sex from the same partner and she told him so.

"Maybe I desire more than uncommitted sex."

"No. Don't. Don't imply you want something more than that. We both know it would never work."

"You are so certain?"

"Your life is here in Spain. I just started working for my sister's charity. I'm still getting to know her."

"Then let us start with the sex."

"Wha—?"

His lips cut off her words, his hands warm on her hips.

And just that fast, Randi's worries and decision to stay away from him physically melted into nothingness.

She'd never responded to another man the way she did him and probably never would again. No matter what he felt for her, she was pretty sure she'd fallen in love with Basilio Perez.

It was too fast. It was unreasonable. It made no kind of sense. Emotions didn't just sprout up and take over a person's heart, but hers was locked down with an emotional craving no one else was ever going to quench.

It didn't have to be logical. She'd fallen. Her feelings were real. So real she knew she was in for a world of pain when she went back to the States and left him to his glittery world of billionaires and beauties.

But right now she could have this. Sex. A connection. And she was going to take it.

Randi was going to wring every ounce of pleasure out of the next two weeks that she could get. The one thing she wasn't going to do, though, was ever admit her feelings to a man who had declared with conviction that he didn't buy into the romantic love concept.

Besides, you had to trust someone to admit your love for them, to let it spill over and infect every area of your life. And Randi still didn't trust Baz.

Baz's kiss turned heated, the exploratory nature disappearing almost immediately when she responded with unfettered passion.

He lifted her up, helping her to wrap her legs around him, and carried her, still kissing back, into the bedroom.

Randi laughed, reveling in the pleasure of his touch as he dropped her onto the bed. "You've got a real caveman streak."

"I have been called primitive more than once."

"By other lovers?" she wondered, not really wanting an answer.

"No. I have never had trouble with control with another

woman. Not like I do with you. My past liaisons have always been very civilized."

"I wouldn't call you civilized in bed." Far from it. Her voice caught as he began stripping the smart suit she'd worn for travel off her body.

It was not her usual look, not nearly casual enough, but she'd wanted armor when she saw him early this morning, and the suit had been necessary. Now she just wanted the tailored jacket and pencil skirt off. Her fingers fumbled with the tiny buttons on the blouse until Baz took hold of both sides and jerked it open, buttons popping, fabric tearing.

His urgency turned her on even more, making her ache for his touch in her most intimate places. He stopped and just stared down at her lingerie. "Did you wear this for me?"

"You know I like to wear pretty underwear."

His espresso gaze heated, singeing her with its intensity. "*Sí*, but you had to know I would get you out of that prim and proper suit."

"No, that wasn't the plan." At least in her conscious mind.

She was honest enough to admit, to herself at least, that her subconscious may well have had different ideas.

"Oh, it was always the plan. I would have had you on the plane if you hadn't looked so peaceful sleeping."

"You're arrogant."

"And?"

"On the verge of losing out on a good thing if you get too cocky." So, that? Was a total lie.

She wasn't stopping what they were doing for anything. Her body craved his. Her heart craved whatever connection she could have before walking away.

If there was emotional pain mixed with her incandescent pleasure, Randi was a big girl. She could handle it.

She had plenty experience in that regard.

"We would not want that."

"No…" She gasped as his hot mouth landed on her curve above the line of her aqua satin demi bra.

His tongue ran along the edge of her bra, branding her with the oral caress.

Oh, man. She had no resistance to his touch. Even the slightest connection between their bodies had her ready for the deepest of intimacy. Had he pressed, they would have joined the Mile-High Club on the way over from Portland.

His short breaths, the way his hands were so urgent on her body, said he was just as susceptible to her.

Baz pushed the demi bra down and suddenly hot, wet suction engulfed her nipple, sending pleasure down her body, right into the core of her.

"Yes, Baz, please…"

His hands worked at getting rid of the rest of their clothes while he continued to pleasure her with his mouth. Her body bowed upward, electric impulses making her muscles contract with the overwhelming bliss.

When they were both completely naked, her last bits of clothing peeled away with passion-imbued reverence, he stopped and just stared at her, the waning fall sun casting his olive skin in a golden glow. "You are so perfect."

She shook her head. "Hardly."

*"Sí. Perfección."*

"Saying it in Spanish doesn't make it any more true."

"I want you, *cariña*. I have never been in bed with a woman I found so enthralling. No other woman has ever drawn me like you do."

"How can that be true?"

"I don't know." His tone and expression said he really didn't. "But it is."

"What we have in bed is special."

"So I've been telling you."

"Show me."

"It will be my pleasure."

Only the minute he started kissing her body again, his hands busy caressing spots he'd taught her were unexpected erogenous zones, she realized she didn't want to just lie there and accept the delight he brought to her body. She wanted to do some touching of her own.

Lots and lots of touching.

Randi pushed against Baz's shoulder until he lifted his head and torso so she could press him onto his back. Then it was her turn to taste his body, to map his rock-hard muscles with her fingertips.

"What are you doing to me, *mi hermosa*?"

"Whatever I want." It was nothing less than the truth.

Regardless of what had happened between them, she felt more freedom to explore with this man than she ever had with her two previous lovers.

Baz didn't try to give directions. He didn't subtly encourage her to move one way or another with his own body. No, he let her kiss him, first on the lips then on every sexy hollow and dip on his gorgeous, masculine body.

When she wrapped her fingers around his hot and oh, so hard erection, his groan was all the encouragement she needed to keep doing what she wanted. She caressed him with inexpert but enthusiastic movements before sliding down his body so she could take him into her mouth.

The sound he made then was primitive and full of male need.

She would have smiled in triumph, but her mouth was full. She did her best to take as much as she could between her lips, breathing through her nose when he bumped the back of her throat. She kept an up and down motion with her hand on his rigid column of flesh.

Suddenly, he was pulling her head away from his sex, his breathing harsh. "I don't want to come in your mouth."

She didn't ask why not because she wanted the same thing he did. Him inside her.

He pulled her up until she straddled him. "Are you ready for me?"

"Yes."

"Put this on me." He handed her a condom.

She didn't ask where it came from. Right then, Randi didn't care.

She tore open the packet with her teeth and then pulled out the thin latex circle. Concentrating so her hands did not shake too badly, passion riding her hard, she rolled the protection down over his straining erection.

He moaned as her hand slid down with the latex. "Yes, Miranda, *cariña*, that is so good."

She loved the way even this act was part of the pleasure.

Baz grabbed her hips, and in an arousing feat of strength, he lifted her up until her labia kissed the head of his latex-covered erection. Then he guided her down, centimeter by slow centimeter as he rocked upward with slow, steady movements, until he was seated completely inside her.

They both froze for several seconds. For her part, Randi was simply overwhelmed by sensation. Baz had an expression on his handsome features she was afraid to trust, but his dark gaze bored into hers with profound emotion.

"This between us, this is too good, too special, too important, to simply dismiss."

She nodded, unable to deny the truth of his words.

His hips canted once, then twice, both of them gasping at the increased sensation until desire for him took over even the soul-deep emotion and she had to move.

Baz's eyes closed for a second, the rictus of pleasure on his face telling her better than words could how much he was enjoying her riding him.

Then his eyelids opened, revealing a gaze almost black with pleasure, and his hands came up her body to cup her breasts. He kneaded the modest curves, expertly playing with nipples already engorged with blood and sensitized by his earlier touch.

Randi shifted her angle and suddenly his big sex was caressing that spot inside her that sent jolts of ecstasy throughout her body. Bliss coiled tight inside her, waves of pleasure emanating from her womb until she knew her climax was imminent.

"That's right, *mi amor*." He thrust up against her, increasing Randi's pleasure. "Move just like that."

She wasn't about to stop but didn't have the breath to tell him so. She found her breath a moment later, though, in order to let loose a scream of ecstasy when one of his hands slid down her body until his thumb could brush against her swollen clitoris. Just like that, the pleasure inside her detonated, explosions of bliss making her muscles contract. Her heart beat so fast she could barely breathe, and her cry of completion choked off by more of the same.

He kept moving under her, even as she fell forward against him, his thumb prolonging her moment of annihilating pleasure.

Still hard inside her, Baz stilled, his hands locked onto her thighs so she couldn't move, either. "So good, *mi cariña*."

"You didn't come."

His smile was all sexy, confident male. "I am not finished with you yet."

"What?" She felt finished.

But then he moved under her, sending jolts of electric bliss sparking along her nerve endings, and she thought, maybe not.

The expression on his handsome Spanish features was nothing short of devilish as he rolled them, his shifting body inside her sending more aftershocks through Randi.

He kissed her for long minutes, but then he withdrew from her body completely.

She protested until he moved down her body to bury his mouth between her legs. As his tongue flicked out to barely touch her clitoris, she found herself panting with renewed pleasure. He kept the touches featherlight for several minutes until she found her body moving to meet the tantalizing caresses. Then he increased the pressure, his finger pressing up inside her even as he nibbled against her swollen bundle of nerves.

Baz showed her that when it came to giving pleasure with his mouth he was a master, drawing forth a second, even stronger, climax from her before he surged up her body to push inside her again.

Tears ran hotly down her temples as the pleasure and the emotional intensity of their physical connection overwhelmed Randi.

He brushed at the wetness with his fingertips. "You are mine, *hermosa*. Made especially for my body to connect to yours."

She couldn't think of anything to say; she was too raw from what was happening between them, but she wouldn't have denied his claim if she *could* make her brain-to-mouth function work.

He plunged in and out of her, finally losing his vaunted control, driving them both higher and higher, words of praise in his native tongue dripping from his lips.

Her throat raw from screaming, Randi climaxed for a third time, this time taking him over the precipice of pleasure with her, his hoarse shout triumphant.

He kissed her possessively, intense passion coming through the way his lips moved so adamantly over hers. After long moments of him telling her a story with his lips against hers, the kiss gentled until finally, he broke the connection, pulling carefully from her body.

"I must take care of this." He waved his hand toward the condom now covering his semierect sex.

She couldn't even work up the energy to move a single finger, much less shift her body. "Okay."

He came back to the bed and lifted her into his arms.

"Where are we going?" she asked, her postcoital lethargy making her not really care what his answer was. She found a secret part of herself that thoroughly enjoyed his caveman tendencies and not a single bit of energy to protest it.

"My bed, where you belong, *mi amor*."

That was the second time he'd called her that. His love. She knew he didn't mean it the way she wanted him to, but his use of it now... It meant something. Didn't it?

True to his word, he carried her naked body out of the room and down the hall to the room next door. She should have guessed he would be so close by. If anything, his private suite was even more decadent than the one she'd been assigned.

She took in her surroundings with sleepy eyes as he carried her through to the bedroom and then maneuvered into his bed, climbing in with her and wrapping her in his arms.

"I shouldn't be tired," she slurred. "Slept on the plane."

"I've worn you out." Pride infused his voice.

She couldn't take him to task for it. He was right. Randi let her eyes slide shut and snuggled into Baz's body. She would work on shoring her defenses against him later.

# CHAPTER TWELVE

The following days settled into a pattern.

Randi and Baz shared breakfast each morning before he left for his office. Then she spent a few hours answering emails and going over things for Kayla's for Kids that weren't impacted by the time difference.

Somehow Mr. Billionaire Business Mogul had managed to work short days for the entire two weeks Randi had been there. He came back to the hacienda for a late lunch, which Randi waited to eat with him. Afterward, he took her sightseeing, introducing her to his favorite places in and around Madrid as well as full-on tourist traps.

She was totally entranced by the Royal Palace. No wonder he considered his hacienda just a home. Spain's palace in Madrid was the biggest royal palace in Europe, its Sabatini and Campo del Moro Gardens beyond beautiful. She wanted to go back before she left Madrid, but then she would really enjoy revisiting Almudena Cathedral, the Prado Museum and the Alcalá Gate again, too.

In the evenings they each spent another couple of hours working, when their contacts in North America would be awake and at their own desks. Afterward, they had a late dinner, sometimes in the glamorous hacienda dining room, sometimes at Michelin Star restaurants, and a couple of times they had amazing food at hole-in-the-wall eateries she would never expect Baz to frequent. But always, always, they ended up back in Baz's bed, making love into the wee hours of the morning, their passion never waning.

Every day the life she was living in Spain became more

and more the life she *wanted* to live. And that was a very dangerous mind-set.

Two days before she was supposed to fly home, Randi went looking for Baz in his office. He'd set her up at a beautiful desk in the Casa Clavel library. Filled with books and populated with furniture his family had collected over the centuries, the room was rich with history. And she loved it. Baz's study was through a connecting door, and Randi liked how close he was while they worked together in the evenings, too.

He was on the phone, so she sat down to wait until he was done, more than a little confused by the two phone calls she'd just had.

Baz's dark gaze flared with pleasure at the sight of her and he smiled when she sat down, putting a finger up to tell her he would only be a minute.

She nodded, smiling back, for once doing nothing to hide or suppress how pleased she was to be near him.

His eyes widened in surprise, his mouth dropping open in shock. He had to visibly collect himself before he ended his call with an abruptness that surprised *her*.

"To what do I owe this pleasure?" He stood up and came around the big, ornate desk that he'd told her had been a gift to one of his ancestors from King Carlos III.

Baz moved close to Randi like he was irresistibly drawn to her.

She knew the feeling. It was all Randi could do to stay in her chair. "I've just had a couple of very interesting calls."

He cocked his head to the side like he had no idea what she was talking about.

"I was going over the final purchase details for the new facility with the broker."

*"Si?"* Still, Baz looked like he had no idea where this was going.

"He was confused about the *gift* of the furnishings to the

shelter. In fact, he said *we* were paying for them, which I knew we weren't doing. Or at least I thought I did."

"Oh."

"Yes, oh. Apparently, there is a special account that has been set aside to pay for the furnishings as well as any renovations that need to be made on the facility."

Baz shrugged. "Kayla's for Kids is a more than worthy endeavor."

"So, you did donate the two million dollars sitting in that account?"

"I did."

"Why didn't you tell me?"

"I didn't want you to refuse the gift because you were angry with me."

"It was for the shelter, not for me. You must have realized I would appreciate your generosity."

"I didn't want you to appreciate my money."

No. Baz wanted Randi to appreciate *him*. And the way she'd smiled at him when she came into the study had so shocked him, he'd cut off a business call to find out why she'd done it.

She gave in to the need to stand up and walked over to him, initiating contact like she never did, stepping into his personal space, placing her hands on his chest. "You're a really amazing guy, Basilio Perez."

"Because I gave the shelter some money?" he asked, not sounding particularly happy by that thought.

She leaned up and kissed the underside of his chiseled jaw. "Because you kept it a secret, because you didn't use it to try to get on my good side."

His arms came around her and he dipped his head and kissed her full on the mouth, his tongue playing with the seam of her lips before he lifted his head to say, "I'm very glad I finally did something right."

"You did more than one thing. You're paying for the new

shelter liaison. Kayla said she's not coming out of the shelter's budget, but that she has a two-year contract."

"I would like to accept your appreciation, but hiring Mrs. Patel was purely selfish on my part. I wanted you to be free to travel with me when necessary. To perhaps even relocate here."

Her heart nearly exploded in her chest. "You want me to move to Spain?"

*"Sí."*

"But why?"

"Because I cannot make Portland my permanent place of residence. While Perez Holdings is an international company, my support staff, my best acquisition groups, they are all here in Spain."

"You want something long-term with me," she realized, bemused.

He stared at her like she'd lost her mind. "Do you think I went to such efforts for a few more nights of sex, even incredible sex?"

"But…you said…no commitment." Her thoughts came out in disjointed little bursts.

"No, *mi amor. You* said no commitment and refused to believe anything else. Has this past week felt like no commitment?" His hands pressed into her lower back, bringing their bodies together.

"I…" How could she answer that? It *had* felt casual, but she was beginning to realize that was because she hadn't allowed herself to consider anything else. Because it had also felt like the beginning of a life together. "So to be clear, you're saying you want a relationship with me?"

"With a view to marriage, *sí.*"

"Marriage?" she squeaked.

"What else? I will never be content to see you with another man. I hope you would be bothered by the idea of me being with another woman."

"Um…yes." It would gut her. Which was one of the reasons she was glad he lived in Spain.

"But what about my sister? The shelter."

"I currently travel to the States every couple of months. I could up that schedule to once a month, or at least every six weeks."

"You would do that?"

"I'm already looking at properties to open a Loving Sisters Shelter here in Madrid."

"I've never heard of that organization."

"That's because it is a new name for a multinational non-profit run by you and your sister, focused on the welfare of children and youth."

"What? No…we didn't… You're looking at facilities?"

"I have found three prospects, two in the city center, and one on the outskirts of Madrid I was hoping you'd look at next week."

"Next week? But I was supposed to fly home the day after tomorrow."

"I was hoping to convince you to stay longer. Things have been working out, haven't they? You like living here."

"You're serious about this, aren't you?"

"I am serious about you."

"Baz, I think you might love me." She couldn't believe she'd blurted it out like that.

His face closed up, pain flaring briefly in his eyes. "If I don't?"

"Whatever you feel for me is enough." She didn't need perfection. She didn't need him to give voice to feelings that he was clearly not ready to deal with yet.

And might never be.

The *perfect* relationship was a fantasy anyway. She knew that. Even Andreas and Kayla had their issues. All couples did. But they fit. They loved each other and that wouldn't be any less valid without the words.

"You are sure? You'll stay?" His smile was incandescent. "You have forgiven me for deceiving you in the beginning?"

"Yes." To all of it.

He began moving toward the settee against the wall. "I believe we need to celebrate."

"Champagne?"

"How about champagne sex, fizzy and delicious?"

"You're quite the romantic."

"If you say so."

"I do."

The kissing and touching that followed had a vulnerable quality to it that neither had shown the other to this point. She straddled his thighs as he sat naked on the brocade-covered sofa. "Do you have a condom?"

"In my desk drawer."

She gave him a look.

"I put them there the day after I brought you here."

"So you don't have sex with women in your office."

"I have never had sex with any other women anywhere in my home. This hacienda is my refuge."

She kissed him for such a good answer and then climbed off him to retrieve the condom. He groaned and tried to hold on to her, making them both laugh.

They made love, her body encasing his, her hips moving in a rhythm that maximized both their pleasure. He kissed her, over and over again, his hands kneading her backside, his hips thrusting up to meet hers. They came together, her cry and his groan muffled by their kiss.

Armand Perez returned to Casa Clavel the following week, exhibiting nothing but delight at the news that his son and Randi were now an official couple.

"Will you be moving to Spain permanently, or will you try to make this work long distance?" Armand asked over dinner the first night of his return.

Randi swallowed, not sure how she wanted to answer

that. She'd told Baz she would stay with her *yes*, but knew he hadn't been clear she was answering all his questions with the single word. She'd realized that later by something he said.

Now Baz looked at her, waiting for her answer to his father's question, as interested as Armand. Only Baz's gaze held vulnerability as well as cautious expectation. It was the vulnerability and caution that helped her give her answer, to make it official.

She smiled at Armand. "We are going to look at spots for a possible shelter tomorrow."

"That is good. Our Madrid children can always use another advocate."

"You *are* moving here?" Baz asked, looking for confirmation she was happy to give him.

"I'll call Kayla after dinner and let her know. Last week I just told her I was staying longer." Maybe Randi hadn't been all that sure of her decision, but she was now. "I think she'll like the idea of expanding Kayla's for Kids to Loving Sisters Shelter."

Randi was right. Her sister loved the idea of going international with the services for displaced and at-risk children. She wasn't as keen on Randi living in Spain.

"I'm going to miss you."

"Baz said we'll come to America once a month, at least every six weeks. You and Andreas can visit us in Spain, as well."

"Once a month? You promise?"

"Some visits you'll have to meet me in California, so I can see Dad and the grandparents."

"Of course I will. Oh, Randi. I'm so happy it's working out between you, but don't you think maybe you're moving fast?"

"Yes. It is fast. Yes, it is scary, but it feels right. More than right, it feels necessary. I trust him."

"Really? Even after?"

"Partly because of what he did. Baz is the kind of guy who will do whatever it takes to keep his family safe. That will include me."

"You're already talking marriage?" Kayla shrieked.

"Not every corporate shark takes six years to figure out that the best woman in the world for him is already taking up space in his life."

Kayla laughed. "Yeah, Andreas was pretty blind. He's not anymore, though."

"Yeah, I've noticed."

When the phone rang an hour later, as Randi and Baz were preparing for bed, Kayla's name flashed on the screen along with the picture of her gorgeous smile. Randi grabbed the phone. "Hey, sis, what's up?"

"Have you been keeping up on the Google alert for your name?"

"What? No, actually. Baz took care of stuff before I left. I've enjoyed not having to track my name and wonder if today would be the day I'd get vilified in the press again." Her heart tightened, her stomach cramping. "Are you saying Carl Madison went back on the agreement?"

That fast Baz was there, putting his hand out for the phone. She gave it to him without a second thought.

"Kayla, it is Basilio. What is going on?"

He grimaced, listening to whatever Kayla was saying, his expression turning more and more grim as her sister's agitated tones came through the phone.

Finally, he said, "Do not worry about it, Kayla. I will take care of it."

Kayla said something.

"No, of course not."

She said something else.

His lips tilted in a partial smile. "Thank you. We will see you soon."

They ended the call.

"Didn't she want to talk to me again?" Randi asked.

"She understood I needed to tell you the latest development."

"What latest development?"

Baz pulled her over to their bed and helped her climb inside before joining her, his arm a solid presence around her waist as they faced each other.

He traced her jawbone and then tucked her hair behind Randi's ear. "I do not want you to worry."

"Just tell me."

"The researchers at the television station you were going to do the interview on are much better at their job than any media outlet so far. They got ahold of the police reports, both from five years ago and recently when Carlos assaulted you."

"What? How?" Agitated and worried, she plucked at the bedding. "I didn't say anything. I didn't even hint. I promise, Baz. Andreas's contact set up the interview and no one knew exactly what I planned to say, just that I was going to give my side of the story."

"Of course you didn't. You have too much integrity to go back on your word."

"That's what you told Kayla. That of course I hadn't done it," Randi said wonderingly.

"Naturally."

She threw herself at Baz. "I love you so much. I know you don't believe in it, but I'm not keeping the words inside."

His arms automatically wrapped around her, pulling her tight against his near-naked body. "Because I believe in your integrity?"

"Because everything. You're ruthless, but you weren't lying when you said it was both with and on behalf of your family. You're kind. You're generous even if you'd like to hide that fact. You're incredibly loyal. And, well, you're sexier than any other man alive."

"I believe you are profoundly biased."

"That's the way it's supposed to be. In love."

He got a strange look on his face. "Love. I promised myself that I would never fall for that construct."

"I'm allowed to love you, whatever promises you've made to yourself. You'd better accept that now. We won't be talking marriage if you don't." That was a deal-breaker for her. It was one thing to accept a man who never said the words, but exhibited the emotion; another thing entirely to expect her never to speak of her love for him.

He smiled wryly. "I broke the promise."

"What? What are you saying?" She cuddled closer to him, looking up into his espresso gaze, tendrils of hope curling around her heart and seeping into her soul.

"I'm saying that the only thing that explains what we have between us, my need not only to have you in my bed, but also in my life, and not just for now, but for the rest of that life…" He stopped speaking, just looking down at her, his dark eyes filled with wonder, warmth and a lot of heat. "I love you, Miranda. You have broken through every chain locking my heart tight."

Tears filled her eyes. "I didn't think you'd ever admit it to yourself, much less me."

"How can I show less courage than you?"

"I'm not brave."

"Despite all you have experienced, you believe in the goodness in people. You believe you can make a difference in the lives of children. You trust me. That is a gift of the highest magnitude."

"I love when you start talking all formal."

"It is easier when my emotions are trying to take over my brain, especially when I'm not communicating in the language of my birth."

"I thought you didn't do powerful emotion."

"I find that I do."

The tears spilled over. "Oh, Baz."
"I love you, now and forever." He rolled her under him.
She smiled up into his handsome face. "Into eternity."

# EPILOGUE

CARLOS THREW A fit when Basilio called him about the truth coming out, but ultimately agreed to do what his younger brother instructed.

He didn't want to lose the support of Perez Holdings. Between his PR team and the one dedicated to Perez Holdings, they mitigated as much damage as possible. But this time around the truth was out there for everyone to judge.

Tiffany ended up taking an extended holiday in Australia; the children came to Spain to stay with Basilio, Miranda and Armand. Miranda was glad to be out of the US while the story got a chance to blow over. She refused all requests for interviews, photo ops or anything else that might put her into the public eye.

She was ridiculously content in Basilio's home and his life, her days busy with the children, her duties with Kayla's for Kids and the new Loving Sisters Shelter. Miranda found peace unlike she'd known in five years as she grew closer to Grace and Jamie, the little boy who had not only survived the accident, but now flourished with keen intelligence and typical little-boy enthusiasm for life.

When they returned the children to the States two weeks later, it was to learn that Kayla was pregnant.

She and her beautiful son attended Miranda and Baz's wedding the following year. The infant, too small to take part in the ceremony, sat on his proud *papá*'s lap. The little girl they had adopted out of foster care, however, was just the right age to act as a flower girl. She stood beside her mother and Miranda as she and Baz spoke vows of love and lifelong commitment. It was only afterward she learned that Baz had hired security to keep her mother away from her special day.

He took protecting Miranda very seriously and spoke of his love for her every day. She was always eager to return the words, truly content, knowing she was genuinely and always safe for the first time in her life.

* * * * *

# MILLS & BOON

## Coming next month

### THE ITALIAN'S CHRISTMAS HOUSEKEEPER
#### Sharon Kendrick

'The only thing which will stop me, is you,' he continued, his voice a deep silken purr. 'So stop me, Molly. Turn away and walk out right now and do us both a favour, because something tells me this is a bad idea.'

He was giving her the opportunity to leave but Molly knew she wasn't going to take it – because when did things like this ever happen to people like her? She wasn't like most women her age. She'd never had sex. Never come even close, despite her few forays onto a dating website which had all ended in disaster. Yet now a man she barely knew was proposing seduction and suddenly she was up for it, and she didn't care if it was *bad*. Hadn't she spent her whole life trying to be good? And where had it got her?

Her heart was crashing against her rib-cage as she stared up into his rugged features and greedily drank them in. 'I don't care if it's a bad idea,' she whispered. 'Maybe I want it as much as you do.'

Continue reading
THE ITALIAN'S CHRISTMAS HOUSEKEEPER
Sharon Kendrick

*Available next month*
www.millsandboon.co.uk

# COMING SOON!

We really hope you enjoyed reading this book. If you're looking for more romance, be sure to head to the shops when new books are available on

## Thursday
## 18th October

To see which titles are coming soon, please visit
**millsandboon.co.uk**

# LET'S TALK
## *Romance*

For exclusive extracts, competitions
and special offers, find us online:

**f** facebook.com/millsandboon

**⊙** @millsandboonuk

**🐦** @millsandboon

Or get in touch on 0844 844 1351*

For all the latest titles coming soon, visit
millsandboon.co.uk/nextmonth